Deucalion Academy: Pawn of the Gods

The Dominions

Ruby Vincent

Published by Ruby Vincent, 2022.

Prologue

Shouts invaded the small space, ripping through the log walls. Our home was so tiny, whispers traveled from end to end without trouble—the reason my dolls and I had to stop sharing secrets.

A thud sounded from outside, rattling the cabin. Mama tucked the blankets tighter around me. I reached for Daria, but Mother was already there—picking her off the rickety bedside table and tucking my doll under my arm.

"Do you remember the story of Olympia, my darling?" Mama perched on the end of my bed, smiling softly. No matter how much gray snuck in her golden-brown curls or how much bigger the dark circles under her eyes grew, she would always be the prettiest, most beautiful mommy in all five dominions. She would smile when I told her that too.

"No," I replied, though I did.

Mom tsked under her breath. "Well, we can't have that. Should I tell you the story?"

I nodded, relaxing onto my pillow as swords clanged beyond my window.

Mother waved her hand and swirling light painted my ceiling—spinning, moving, darkening, brightening, and coming together. I gasped at the starry, celestial sky.

Mama said her power was useless. It provided us with neither food, medicine, shelter, nor income. But I loved it. In a world full of ugly, scary things, my mother made it pretty with just a wave of her hand.

"Long ago," she began, "the gods of Olympia ruled the heavens, hades, and everything above, below, and in between. But they were not like other gods, and do you know why?"

My answer spilled off the tip of my lips. "They liked humans."

"They were fascinated by humans," Mom whispered. She tickled my nose with hers until I giggled. "The way they lived, worked, and died. How they loved, toiled, and strove for more. Instead of staying high above them on Mount Olympus, the gods couldn't resist interacting with the mortals who shared their shape, but not their power."

My eyes widened at the changing figures. Glowing, beautiful beings threw lightning, raced chariots across the heavens, and rose from sea-foam.

"The gods bestowed great gifts on the mortals they favored—from wealth and riches to children born of god and man. Entire cities flourished under their patron god's indulgence, while the enemies of those people suffered under their god's wrath.

"The Grecian people believed in the Olympians so fiercely and with such devotion, their faith became an unstoppable force that fed the gods and made them unstoppable in turn. With the gods on their side, the Greek empire stretched wide—conquering many civilizations. Then—"

"—away! Lead it away!" a voice shouted, tightening Mama's brow. "Back toward the fields!"

"Then the Roman empire claimed Greece and all in its path," Mama said, a touch louder. "But the Romans were wise, my love. They may have changed their names, but still, they too worshiped the gods of Olympus. They hoped the gods would favor them too, and grant them a vast kingdom and the power to defend it. Everything was perfect until... it wasn't."

I clutched Daria tighter. This was the best part of the story. "What happened, Mama?"

"Oh, my dear. Zeus, Hera, Athena, and the gods granted the mortals much, but they asked for much more in return. Women bore Zeus's children only to suffer terrible curses and messy ends at Hera's hands. The townspeople gave poor offerings in Poseidon's temple one day, and the next, their home was washed off the map. Maybe all of that could've been endured if not for—"

"—the monsters," I whispered.

Lips pursed, she nodded. "With the gods' great capacity for blessings, came their great capacity for evil. They birthed humans, fire, the seasons, and drove the sun across the sky. They also birthed sirens, cerberi, harpies, and hydras," she said. "Monsters hated the gods. Some used to be mortals. Some were gods or the children of gods that were banished from Mount Olympus. They weren't worthy enough to sit on a throne beside Zeus and Hera."

"That made them angry."

"Very angry," Mama agreed. "But, of course, they couldn't take their anger out on the mighty, immortal gods of Olympus, so instead, they went after the next best thing—their favorite pets: the humans.

"Endless attacks. Constant battles. Legions lost. Families wiped out. Villages burned down. The people were fighting a war from within and without. They were at the end of their rope when whispers spread of the Christian god." Mama gestured again and my small room filled with huddled people in sandals and tunics—whispering and sharing texts. "At first, those in power did their duty to drive out this new god and all talk of him, but it was all too late.

"Here was a god that asked nothing of them but their faith. He wouldn't strike them down for having no temple offerings. He wouldn't seduce and then abandon them to the punishment of his jealous wife. He wouldn't turn a blind eye while monsters of his own creation destroyed everything they built.

"Before the gods of Olympus knew it, their temples were torn down and churches were built in their place. Down came their statues and up went the cross. The humans were turning their back on them and soon they had no choice"—she waved and swords clanged in the air—"but war."

I kissed Daria's forehead. "They went to war with the Christian god."

"Yes, they did, my love. And they lost."

I sighed long and deep as I always did at this part. It was so obvious to a ten-year-old like me that all the Olympian gods had to do was be nicer to the humans, but like Markos Adamos who kept throwing dirt at me when I walked home from lessons, some people just can't help being a stupid turnip head.

"The Greek gods or the Roman gods, the mortals stopped worshiping them under any name, all throughout the world. And without their faith to sustain them, the gods grew weaker and weaker until they were nothing but pale copies of their former selves. I ask you, sweet Aella, what is a god who has no one to believe in him?"

Shaking my head, I said sadly, "He is nothing."

"That is what they were becoming. Nothing." The battle, the gods, and the stars winked out, leaving my room in darkness. "The gods faded from existence as they did from the hearts and minds of man, so in one last effort to save themselves and live to see the day Mount Olympus was restored, they reduced their forms down to their very essence and scattered into pieces."

The space lit at the very end of her sentence, filling with dozens upon dozens of tiny, glowing orbs.

"Those pieces spread through the earth, finding the strong and worthy, and burrowed into their souls. Today we call them..."

"Demigods."

Grinning, she nuzzled my nose again. "There's my smart girl. I knew you were fibbing about forgetting the story. Will you tell me the rest?"

"The demigods had great power, but they weren't safe on their own. Monsters could feel the es—es—"

"Essence," Mama said.

"They felt the es-sence of the gods in the people and attacked them. So, from all over the world, demigods came together and created Olympia," I cried, throwing my arms out. "Where we can live together and protect each other."

"That's exactly right, my love."

"Surround it! Get on the other side!"

Mama threw another tight-lipped frown at my window. "That is what Olympia is all about. Demigods coming together to live, protect, and fight for one another. The legend says the gods bound to our souls so that they'd live on in our belief. One day, we'd grow strong enough to put the gods back on their throne and reclaim this world in the name of Olympus. But you know what I think?"

I shook my head, even though I did.

"It doesn't matter if the legends are true, or how we demigods came to be. What matters is the life we've built together: one where people of all colors, creeds, and power are bound—living and fighting side by side.

"There are wars in Olympia, but they are not between neighboring villages. There is theft, but not by five-fingered hands. There is murder but..." Her gaze drifted away. "It is not us harming one another.

"That cannot be said in another town, village, or city beyond the border of Olympia. Here, we take care of each other. That is why you never need be afraid, Aella. You will always have defenders. You will always have shelter. And you will always have family." She stroked my dimpled cheek. "No matter what happens to me."

My smile faded. Mama ended her tale in the usual way, until that final sentence. "What do you mean? Nothing's going to happen to you. Right?"

But she wasn't looking at me. Standing up, she edged toward the window. "I need you to remember that, Aella. You'll never be alone. Here in Olympia, we're all sons and daughters of the gods. We're all fam—"

A piercing crash rocked our home on the foundations. I screamed, losing hold of Daria as I leaped across the bed, reaching for Mama. My fingertips brushed hers as the door blew out of the frame and bowled my mother over.

A fearsome, terrifying face filled my vision. Bulging red eyes reflected me—casting my own small, pale-faced terror back in mocking. Its jaw unhinged, singeing my nose with the hideous smell of sulfur and blood wafting on its breath.

I screamed as her claws came down on that small, pale face.

Aella

I jerked awake, gasping. Panic gripped me as darkness hit my eyes, transporting me to another time and place.

"...we take care of each other. That is why you never need be afraid, Aella. You will always have defenders. You will always have shelter. And you will always have family. No matter what happens to me..."

Sitting up, I scoffed. "What a load of crock."

The words faded, and the memory along with it. *Good riddance.*

The reason for the cave's darkness became clear immediately. As did the reason I was torn out of sleep.

I grimaced, peeling myself out of my soaked bedroll. Then I swore a foul curse that the storm swallowed when I got a look at the soggy remains of my bread.

My shelter options were limited, giving me no choice but to choose a cave downstream of the river. A raging storm blew in and spilled most of it in the cave to cuddle up with me and my fire.

I inched toward the cave mouth. Shrieking winds blew me back, spitting icy rain in my face as my prize. Sticking my head out, my hair was soaked in an instant, but my suspicions were confirmed.

"Typhons."

The storm whipped, raged, and thundered, but there was no lightning—that only meant one thing. This wasn't a natural storm, it was a harbinger. A warning. A smack and laugh in the face that it was already too late, typhons were here.

I scanned the whipping, dancing trees, calculating my chances. I was too close to the border to stop now. A day's journey would bring me to the edge of Calliope's Forest and the gorge—my only chance.

Maybe I should wait until the typhons pass.

I discarded that idea almost immediately. I was a day away from the border, but the watchers were half a day behind me. Daughters of Artemis made up the border watchers. They rarely lost their prey.

My grip tightened on my wet pack. *Until now. I have to get out of Olympia for everyone's sake. This is one catch they won't regret letting slip through their fingers.* I gazed at the dark, swirling clouds. *The typhons might be a good thing. With them in the area and us so close to the town of Leda, the watchers would have to go after the more dangerous threat. What's one deserter against the most fearsome monster in our land?*

Pulling my hood low over my eyes, I stepped out into the storm.

I ran light on my feet, darting from tree cover to tree cover. Why I bothered, I didn't know. Freezing cold seeped into my bones, draining the energy a night of wasted sleep didn't give me. Under the beaming sun, Calliope's Forest was beauty and peace itself. Grass a brilliant, verdant green, tickled your ankles. Flowers of all types and colors nuzzled against mighty tree roots, where they ought not to be, but the forest nymphs liked to build their homes beneath the trees.

If you looked closely, you'd see the tiny deities riding the backs of squirrels and you'd wonder why anyone would live in a place that wasn't Olympia. That is until you witnessed endless, unforgiving rain drown that verdant grass in a soppy mud puddle that tried to rip the boots off your frozen feet. A flood growing higher and higher to wash away the nymphs' home and scatter them who knew where.

There were no butterflies or sun-drenched meadows smelling of Hecate flowers in the Calliope's Forest of today. Monsters ruined it as they ruined everything good about my home. Everything good about what we once were.

A break in the trees appeared ahead, giving way to a clearing. I paused at the tree line and squinted through the dark. I couldn't see movement out there, but that meant little. For all their hulking, oversized bodies, typhons were quick and stealthy. You didn't know one had you in their sights until their shadow fell over you.

I tramped all through the night into day. It poured without end the entire time. I had no doubt the cave I slept in was now a cenote. Unlucky for me, I couldn't keep the water out of my pack, so my food was nothing but a sopping mess. My spare clothes were too wet and cold to make a difference to my wet and cold body. My canteen was running low even though water surrounded me. Typhon-made rain wasn't natural water. In a few days, it would turn the forest brown and sickly, and do even worse to me if I swallowed it.

But there was good news. With typhons nearby, all the manner of monsters or mischievous nymphs that would've attacked me or slowed me down, found somewhere else to be. I was making excellent time to the border. By my internal map, I should be there before nightfall.

I rounded a massive eucalyptus tree, and screamed.

A figure appeared over the tangled, stretching roots. Gold-dipped eyes beheld me, unwavering as her limbs, hair, even her features shifted and morphed to her heart's content.

I tripped scrambling to get away. The mud finally claimed its prize, holding tight to my boot and dumping me against a tree trunk. I huddled against the wood—screaming, crying, ripping hanks of my hair and throwing it at her as if my strands were weapons.

I was nothing in her divine presence. A worthless speck and growing smaller. I should rip out my bones, drain my blood, tear out my eyes rather than see what my unworthy being was never meant to see.

"*I don't think so, little one.*" Her voice slithered from the pit of my soul, whispering clear in my ear over the raging storm, and my screams. "*Surely you don't think I'll let you go that easily.*"

Just like that, she was gone, and I was free.

I snatched up my boot and ran without bothering to put it on. *I'm so close. I have to get out. I have to get out now!*

Branches whipped and snapped at my face, opening cuts on my cheek as if under orders from the bitch goddess herself.

Tears mingled with the poisoned water. Why me? Of all the unlucky, cursed-by-fate demigods in this wasteland, why did the goddess have to choose me?

I tossed my head, roaring as visions of that night assaulted my mind. Before she found me, I foolishly thought my life couldn't get any worse. If all those legends and stories my mother told me were true, I suddenly understood the humans I never met better than any being in Olympia. They forced the gods out of their lives with sheer force of will. An aggressive disbelief in them that almost brought about the end of everything—but would've been worth it.

The gods were monsters.

They cursed, tortured, and ruined people to reflect the soulless emptiness they carried inside. An eternal life gets boring. Tormenting one lonely little girl barely on the cusp of her eighteenth year had to bring some entertainment.

A low, hissing chuckle sounded all around me. Seemed I was closer to the truth than I thought.

For hours I ran. My lungs burned. My bare foot collected bruises and cuts from unseen rocks and broken branches buried beneath the mud. I needed a break miles back, but still, I ran.

You're so close. Don't give up, Aella. Olympia has done me no favors, but I won't subject it to the fate she has in store. Get out. Get across!

The words spurred me on—keeping me going when strength, energy, and endurance failed.

I'd be no use to her in the human territory. Once you left Olympia, there was no going back. The ancient spells created by the daughters of Hecate—the fearsome enchantress—ensured that any pathways closed themselves behind you. It was another deterrent to stop us from leaving.

Go, and leave behind everything you know and everyone you love for a world that knows nothing of gods or power, nor are they interested in finding out. A deterrent that worked on most demigods, but for me, it was the best thing that would happen to me since I was ten and a monster tore into my home and destroyed my life.

Barred from entering Olympia, I'd be no use to the goddess and her horrifying plans. I would hurt no one, and the demigods wouldn't have reason to do to me what I knew they must.

I burst through the trees, and there it was.

Slowing to a stop, I gasped and immediately sucked in rain. Hurriedly I spat it out before it got comfortable on my tongue. It wouldn't do to die... when I finally reached the border.

I gazed out at the wide, barren expanse. The whispers I heard throughout the villages described the other side of the border as a gorge. That was too small a word for the sharp drop-off and red rock basin bed stretching farther than my sight could follow.

I approached the edge, looking for—what?

A bridge? A ladder? A pegasus to drop out of the sky and fly me away?

If that's what I was looking for, none of those things appeared.

"Okay, okay," I breathed. "Crossing the border without permission from the council is forbidden. They were never going to make this easy, but there is a way to do it. The question is how?"

I peered over the one-hundred-foot drop. *Get inside the mind of twelve stuffy, imperious, saggy-jowled men and women who were losing too many soldiers to desertion. They couldn't bring down the border without the spell to put it back up, and daughters of Hecate were known for taking their spells to the grave. So what could the old council do to encourage anyone who got this far to turn around?*

"Make me believe trying to cross meant my death."

No sooner were the words out of my mouth than I lifted my foot and stepped off the edge.

Falling. Spinning. Screaming through the stomach lodged in my throat.

I accepted my foolish mistake as the ground rose to meet me, then I accepted my end. If I couldn't leave Olympia, then I had to die. This was always my only way—

The red rock basin winked out. Darkness flooded in around me, cradling me as my descent slowed to a near stop.

I floated through an expanse of nothingness—darkness above, below, and all around me. Was this supposed to happen, or did I end up in the bottomless void where all the deserters go?

Blinking, a pinprick of light pierced the gloom. I had half a thought to go toward it, and suddenly I was.

The light grew, revealing that it wasn't just a light. It was the sun. My sun. Whole, round, ever-burning, and casting its warmth on a home that wasn't mine.

I knew instantly that the scene I was looking upon wasn't a place in Olympia. The people looked the same with their arms, legs, and frontways eyes, but their identical bodies were covered in strange clothing. Some type of blue fabric where their pants would be, and overcoats that hung open instead of shielding them from the cold as overcoats were supposed to do.

Human after human strolled a forest that would've mirrored Calliope's if not for black rivers cutting hideous paths through the green. Trash littered among the tree roots where nymph flower homes should be, and they walked past the garbage like they couldn't see it. The closer I floated, the stranger the scene became. Everywhere I looked, people held rectangular objects to their faces while they talked to themselves.

Are they mad... or am I?

Gazing over the trees, I fell on an impossible sight. Structures rose higher than the tallest oak in the Neander Meadow. Taller than the Elysian Imperial Palace. As tall as the heavens herself.

Such things could not be possib—

I jerked as if an invisible force hooked me around the middle. I flew back—farther, farther, farther away from that impossible world... and fell.

Thud!

Gasping, I gazed up at the sky as it emptied on my face. I didn't need to look around to know I was back in Olympia.

What happened? I was there. I was right there and then it was gone.

Was that window in another world a trick? Was it another deterrent to get me to turn back? Showing me a mad town with impossible buildings and people who chose to talk to themselves instead of the humans around them?

Can't be, I thought. *Neither Hypnos, the god of dreams, nor his children could imagine something as bizarre as that. It had to be my destination, so why didn't I get to it?*

Picking myself up, I ran off the edge, welcoming the void between worlds. I got so close before I was pulled back. Maybe what I needed to do was propel myself forward quicker—cross the barrier before Olympia had a chance to snatch back her prey.

I got within inches of the window—close enough to count the teeth on a smiling pair of parents, holding up another rectangle to their toddling child, then I whipped back.

The ground punched the air out of my lungs, and left a bruise for the trouble. I pushed up off the sodden earth, rubbing my shoulder. Was I imagining it or did that hurt more the second time?

Shaking it off, I stripped off my pack and wet overcoat. I was almost there. A little more and I'd make it.

I leaped off the cliff, pedaling through the air before I hit the void.

The third time I got closer still. My fingertips disappeared through the window, and I swore they touched warm air and a gentle breeze.

The barrier snatched me back, and my stomach shot in my throat.

"Ahhh!"

I tumbled to the ground, landing hard on my hurt shoulder. Pain ricocheted through my body, jarring my jaw snap shut on my tongue. I hissed as blood filled my mouth.

There was no question. The border was spitting me out higher and higher off the ground each time. A few more times of this and I'd be breaking bones, one of them my spine.

It took three tries just to get my fingers through the barrier. How many times will it take me to get my entire battered body through?

"The answer is simpler than you think, young one."

I snapped up, whipping around.

"Genius lies in its simplicity."

My mind retreated to a small, quiet place. A creature as tall as the eucalyptuses crushed the brush beneath its serpent's body. Half a dozen tentacles sprouted from his torso, each tipped with three razor-sharp claws. Free of the trees, he spread his batlike wings—their span longer than ten of me lined head to feet.

I looked into his boarish face; yellow, slitted eyes; rows of brown fangs, and spider legs sprouting from his head like hair, then pitched forward and vomited. I couldn't help it.

Everything from their hideous patchwork bodies to the raging storms that followed them like puppies nipping at their masters' heels, was meant to instill fear in all who saw them.

Typhons were not merely monsters, they were gods. All of them sons of the first Typhon—offspring of the goddess Gaia and god Tartarus. From Typhon, all monsters were born, granting him the title: Father of Monsters. But only the sons grown from pieces of his own body became beings as fierce and terrifying as him. Of all the monsters of Olympia, typhons were the most dangerous. Villagers that woke to find a lightning-less storm overhead, were instructed to pack up their things and evacuate. Leave them to the Deucalion Army.

That's no longer an option for me.

One— Three— Five more typhons emerged from the forest. Beside the vomit disappearing in the water before me, I did nothing. Made no move.

My options narrowed to one. Despite his taunting that the way through was simple, the answer was not making itself clear to me. If I stepped off that cliff again, the barrier would spit me out hard enough to break my bruised shoulder for good. Then I'd have to face six of the most fearsome creatures in our land with one useless arm.

I could run, but that would only provide them a little entertainment before their meal. They looked slow and hulking, but those wings weren't for show. They'd take to the sky and surround me before I made it three feet.

Though none of that is what scared me. My grand plan was to shake the border watchers loose as they went after the greater threat—the typhons. If the best hunters and trackers in the land were following the massive, obvious paths their slithering bottom ends cut through the forest, they were heading right this way.

To me.

They can't take me back. They can't force me into the academy. They just can't. I rose up on shaking knees, and ordered them to stop. This is my only choice. I would face it with my head high.

I walked up to the circling beasts—stomach churning at forms each more hideous than the last—and held my arms up in surrender.

Strange snickering hisses rose up around me.

"What's this?" my new friend asked. "Begging for mercy? Praying that we'll spare you if we see you're unarmed?"

The clear intelligence in his voice surprised me, though there was no reason it should. Olympian monsters were hunting and killing us to near extinction. A feat that wouldn't be so easy if demigods were top of the predator chain like we wanted to believe.

"No begging. No praying," I said clearly. "Go ahead and kill me. Just do it quick."

That strange, unsettling laugh spread through the gorge as the typhons traded looks.

"So young and lovely to be suicidal." The one doing all the talking was clearly the one in charge. He moved in on me while the others hung back. "Your escape to the mundane world fails, so you offer yourself up as a lamb to the slaughter? You won't even fight back, little demigod? Why is that?"

I coiled like a spring the closer he came. My pants picked up, eyeing the lethal claws tipping each one of those tentacles. I pushed against it, trying to fight it, but it wasn't working. Fear leaked through my calm façade, and something else came with it.

No. Please no! If I must die, let me die as Aella.

My fingertips tingled in defiance, calling the same feeling in my lower legs.

"What? Now you don't speak?" His claw tipped my chin, pinpricking the tiniest spot of blood. I bit my lips hard to stop them trembling.

Ever face your worst fear? A tarantula in your home? A snake that slithers in your path on the road? And you tell yourself not to be afraid because you're bigger, faster, and smarter. Did that internal pep talk ever work?

Now imagine trying to force your fear away when you're not bigger. You're not faster. And you're not smarter.

"P-please," I hissed. "If you're to kill me, just do it! Before— Before—"

"Before what, young one?" He cocked his horrifying head. "Before the border watchers come? Are you more afraid of them than you are of us? You wouldn't happen to be the masked assassin that murdered the Apollo councilman and then fled the Imperial Palace while the guards were still fumbling for their spears?"

Surprise broke through my panic. Someone killed the Apollo councilman? I no longer knew Olympia as I once did. Circumstances saw to it that I lived a dark, ignorant life, but even in the deepest hole, everyone knew of the council.

Every demigod had power, but none matched the Twelve. The strongest of each child of Olympus was granted a seat on the council. That particular seat went to a son of Apollo who could shoot beams of light that burned hotter than the sun. Years ago, when he fought in battle, he reduced whole hordes of bronze bulls to scorched smears on the earth. Marcus Sideris was so powerful that he didn't ride with guards or other soldiers. He just roamed the countryside solo, taking down monsters wherever they dared to raise their heads.

How could anyone kill a man like that?

Maybe they took my silence as an answer, because something that could only be described as a smile stretched each of their grotesque faces. A shudder rippled through me, and I looked down—whimpering at the black spreading down my fingers like a spilled inkwell. Pain followed as my fingernails elongated to claws that would be as deadly as theirs.

No! I will die as myself, not a monster!

"—impressive," the typhon crooned. "Out of respect for killing that gods' scum, I will grant your wish." He raised his tentacles high, leaving his serpent's end to wrap around my torso and lift me up. "A quick death."

As I said, I didn't fight, or plead, or pray. I closed my eyes as growing claws shredded my boots. My change would come too late. I would die on my own terms. The first choice I ever made in what turned out to be a short, miserable life.

Maybe it'll be better in hades. Sacrificing myself for a world that's done me no favors has to get me into Elysium. An afterlife in paradise sounds pretty nice to—

"Arrrgggh!"

His body constricted, choking a gasp out of me. My eyes popped open and I beheld a sight worse than the deadliest monsters of legend.

"Aim for their eyes!"

They seemed to come from everywhere. Horses burst from the trees, carrying hooded women in oiled cloth and quivers. They rained arrows on the typhons without a moment's hesitation.

The five spectators abandoned me. They roared their rage, taking to the sky to descend on their enemy. They all did—except for the one who held me.

"Ahh," he belted, his head thrashing and all those tentacles writhing.

Grimacing, I strained to breathe as he gripped me tighter and tighter. What was wrong with him? Why wasn't he fighting with his brothers?

The typhon's wings bent and crumpled unnaturally. I screamed even before it happened.

He exploded. Blood, guts, and claws showered me like poisoned rain. I collapsed in the gore, screeching my head off. "Oh my gods! What—?"

I cut off so abruptly, I choked on the words I tried to say. A figure stood a few feet from me—still as the battle raged around us. The hood of his oiled cloak pulled over his face, obscuring all but his chin in shadows. He was dressed differently than the other watchers. No quiver hung off his back, and the gold-tipped boots on his feet were not standard issue to any watcher I came across.

Slowly, he lowered his hand.

Stinging black ichor covered every inch of me. I stared through the typhon's remains covering my eyes. *Did he do this?*

As if he plucked the question from my mind, the man spun on the battle and held his palm toward a vulture-headed typhon with half a dozen eyes more than two. Arrows were in a few of them, but those left gave him plenty to engage. Before my eyes, his body seized and he let out a scream that curdled my insides.

I had never seen a power like this, and I never would again.

Whipping around, I scrambled to the edge of the gorge. The typhon said the answer for getting through was simple. I had an idea. Let it work, or let the next fall snap my neck.

The goddess's laughter rang in my ears as my talons pierced the mud, pulling me forward. My vision sharpened on my salvation—eyes changing to gift me hawklike sight. I snarled, lips peeling back over razor-sharp teeth.

"*Where are you going, pet?*" Amusement teased her question. "*Don't run off now that the fun has started. Stay. Kill those worthless demigod bugs.*"

I willed myself on, gritting through pain as my legs bent at unnatural, inhuman angles. I had never gotten this far into the transformation before. But then, I also had never been this terrified.

The answer was simple. Designed by people who wanted fear to turn deserters around. In the end, there could only be one answer.

"*Kill them!*"

I reached the edge and tipped—

"Ahhh!" Screams ripped from my soul.

I was burning, burning, everything burning! My blood heated beneath my skin—scorching my veins, cooking my organs, igniting my bones—and I felt it all.

"Secure the traitor!"

Iron hands secured my ankles, yanking me back from the edge. I was helpless as bodies pinned me in the mud, binding my legs and wrists. How could I fight back? Pain was not fear, and pain was all I'd ever feel again... as a mere human.

The last thing I saw before black crowded my vision were those gold-tipped boots.

Alexander

Medora and Larisa hauled the unconscious girl to her feet—No, wait.

I squinted from beneath my hood, getting a proper look as the last of the rain washed the mud and blood off her face. Not a girl, a woman.

Good. Now no one could bleat and whine about me boiling the insides of some child. Not that it would matter to me if they did. Traitors young and old deserved what I had coming for them.

"What should we do with her?" asked Larisa. She wasn't asking me.

The goddess Artemis had only daughters, no sons. Those daughters made up the border watchers and they've never taken orders from a man. They weren't about to start now.

"She forced us to track her through typhon rain," Medora, leader of the watchers, replied. "Most of our food is now inedible and we're running low on water since we were forced to share with the horses. We don't have the supplies to feed another mouth on the long journey back to the palace and her trial." Medora turned a reptilian smile on me. She was actually a handsome woman with high cheekbones, full lips, and a head of wavy hair that glinted bronze in the sun. Anyone would call her attractive, except when she smiled. "Thankfully, we needn't trek her all the way back to the council when we have a representative right here."

Medora threw her at me. I made no attempt to catch the traitor, looking on with a raised brow as she crumpled at my feet.

"Alexander and his men will take her into custody. You four have ridden with us long enough."

My guards fell in around me. I joined the watchers solo and somehow picked up three hangers-on along the way. Father said I wasn't to travel Olympia without guards. He was used to his orders being obeyed.

"Say goodbye, ladies," Medora gruffed. "You had your fun using these boys as stress relief, but now it's back to the real work."

"Stress relief? Is that what you call what me, Larisa, Katherine, and Hali got up to last night?" I mockingly bowed. "If that's the case, ladies, you may use me shamelessly whenever the mood strikes you."

Larisa laughed—far from embarrassed. Joining the watchers was no easy decision, seeing as it came with a vow to never marry, never have children, and never leave. They patrolled for eleven months out of the year with only women for company. There was a reason I preferred to spend my summers with the watchers. Uncomplicated sex was all they served, and my table was fit for a buffet.

"We'll keep that in mind," Larisa teased. "Have fun with that." The *that* in question being my new charge. "Tell the council we recommend execution. She dove right into the typhons' storm for a reason. She was hoping the beasts would kill us so she could make her escape." Larisa spat on her cheek. The woman had excellent aim. "Filthy traitor."

The watchers cleared out, leaving us with the new unwelcome member of our team.

Castor stepped forward. "Alex, we're low on food and water too. Why should we bother carting her back to the palace when we know the sentence? She'll be executed for even making it this far." A hard, scarred face peered at me from under his hood. "I say we kill her now and be done with it."

I didn't spare a glance at the woman at my feet. Turning my back, I said, "Fine with me."

Heat warmed my neck as the son of Hephaestus summoned his flames. I wondered if she would wake in time to burn to death.

"Stop," Jason barked. "It is not our place to hand down sentences. Besides, are we pretending we didn't hear what that creature insinuated? If she is Marcus's assassin, his family deserves to look in her eyes when the jury orders her death."

I didn't slow my stride. "Bring her or don't. What difference does it make to me?"

I hopped on my horse, clicking my tongue to spur her on. The cloudless, clear sky bared no trace of the tragedy. No, the evidence of it remained in the exploded entrails marring the clearing, and the once-prosperous forest that would be yellowing grass and rotted fruit in a few days' time.

But wasn't that always the way? The gods ripped the heavens open and spewed their messes for us to clean up. What did a man care about stepping on an anthill? The ruin of their home was just another stroll through town for him.

I sneered at my maudlin thoughts. My father was right. Bringing mind-healers into the Deucalion Army to "discuss our mental wounds" was a soppy, feeble waste of time. How would whining and wailing help? There would always be another monster, another battle, another death, another wound. Better to get the fuck up and rebuild that anthill. The next boot that comes won't stop to hear your feelings.

Rolling my neck, I glanced back at what remained of the typhons. What was worth discussing was how quickly I took down five beasts of their size. All of the usual lectures waiting for me at home would falter. My time with the watchers—tracking down traitors and killing every monster we came across—improved my abilities in every way. No one could say my summer would've been better spent behind the gilded gates of Trono City, practicing dull drills in the training room.

Maybe we'll cut close to the Asphodel Mountain villages and check out the flock of griffins that moved in close by. With focus I'll shave minutes off my time. Bring down the beasts faster. I flicked to Jason as he hitched the girl over his horse's back like a saddlebag. *Or maybe she'll give me an excuse—talk back, disobey, or snore in her sleep—and I'll finish what I should've at that cliff.*

Smirking, I tapped my heel in her side, pushing Sofi on.

Whichever was fine with me. Practice was practice.

Aella

One hundred and fifteen. One hundred and sixteen. Ooh, a whole bunch, I thought, attention lighting on the patch. Seventeen, eighteen, nineteen, twenty, and one hundred and twenty-one.

I craned my neck, looking for more dandelions. Counting weeds along the path wasn't the most exciting way to pass the time, but what else was I supposed to do other than that... and dodge their suspicious looks.

Again, the scarred one they called Castor glared at me out of the corner of my eye. I understood his suspicion. I'd been nothing but a model prisoner since I woke from my fever dreams to find the nightmare wasn't yet over.

But it soon would be.

They were taking me to Trono City where I'd be executed. Death was the only choice left since I didn't make it through the border. It'd be their only choice if I tried to escape again, so why try?

My greatest fear was that they'd force me to enter the academy, but Castor took great pleasure in telling me that my making them follow me through a pack of typhons was tantamount to attempted murder. Deucalion Academy was off the table.

I accepted that and all their threats of what would happen to me if I ran, in blank-faced silence.

In Trono I'd be given a quick death. If I tried to run from them, the gold-booted soldier would explode me like a ripe grape in the Olympia summer heat. They would get no trouble from me.

"What's wrong with you?" Castor snapped. "Did you trade your tongue for cowardice? Speak!"

I granted him a cool look. "And say what?"

"Ooh, so she does speak. Well, don't stop now," he said when silence befell me again. "Aren't you going to tell us your side? Explain why you abandoned your people? You look to be about eighteen years old. Which means you're due to enter the academy next week, and yet you were going the wrong way." His lips twisted. "Why did you run? Did you really think a better life awaited you in the mundane dominion? Those selfish bastards brought the gods to their knees. What did you think they'd do with a gutless demigod speck like you?"

I gave him the back of my head and returned to my dandelion counting. "I give no excuses, nor will I defend my actions. I accept the punishment for my crimes."

Castor scoffed. "If only all captured traitors were as agreeable as you." He said that, though I picked up a trace of dissatisfaction in his tone. Was it because I didn't satisfy his curiosity, or because he wanted more of a fight?

I didn't spare the question another thought either way.

Our party fell quiet through the final trek through Calliope's Forest. I remembered this path. A few hours on it would take us through the village where I spent the last of my money on bread and cheese. Bread and cheese that were ruined in the storm.

My stomach growled a loud, embarrassing echo. I was starving.

The closer we got to the village, the more I wondered at my chances of them spending good money to feed the *gutless demigod speck*.

They'd sooner let me fall off this horse in hunger.

"We're coming up on Scythia Village," said the mysterious soldier with his hood still pulled low. "We'll book in an inn for the night, stock up on supplies, and sleep in real beds. It's a seven days' ride to Trono City. Enjoy the rest. You won't get another until we get there."

"What about the prisoner?" Jason asked.

"They have a jail. Book her in for the night."

"Is that wise?" Jason was tall, stocky, middle-aged, and weathered from the lines on his face to the set of his dimpled jaw. The mysterious soldier sounded young, but the men around me deferred to him.

Wouldn't you, when faced with a power like his?

Of course. Power trumps all in this dominion. I suspect that held true in the others as well.

"If she's guilty of *all* she's accused of, she's already proven she can achieve impossible escapes. I suggest we don't let her out of our sight."

"Children of Hecate spell the jails against escape. But if it will allay your fears, you three are welcome to take shifts guarding her. You wanted to waste the people's time with a trial. You can waste your own getting her back in one piece. She's your problem."

I bristled at his tone. So much dislike in one small speech. You would've thought we were a married couple and my attempt to flee was to get to my lover in another land.

Rolling fields stretched out around us, enticing us to dance with the tall undulating grass. I turned my face to the sun, secretly glad my last days would be under its shine, instead of mud, floods, and poisoned rain.

Voices soon assaulted my peaceful daydream. I kept my eyes closed, staying in it just a while longer.

The hustle and bustle of village life pressed in on my ears, dragging memories to the surface. I remembered my little town on the sea. Boats would cling to the harbor, baring the battle scars of siren and scylla attacks. Men bellowed across the decks, waking those of us with homes nearby for a dawn rise.

I didn't mind. If I was lucky, Mama was already up with a basket of honey cakes and figs. We'd take them down to the docks where my grizzled new friends would tell me of the amazing world on the other side of the sea. The Calypso Meadows. The Eternal Maze. The shining capital of Trono City.

I told them one day I'd get on their boat and sail away to the world beyond. Did stowing away in a crate of salted pork and hauling ass when we docked at a random border town count as keeping my vow?

Maybe not, but it seems in the end I didn't lie about making it to Trono City. A grim smile twisted my lips.

"What are you smirking about?" Rough hands hauled me off the horse. I opened my eyes to Castor's piercing green orbs. "Don't move. We'll be booking you in for your cozy night soon enough."

I flicked over his shoulder, landing on the Golden Fleece Inn. My brows pricked at the sight.

The Golden Fleece wasn't a rough, copper-coin tavern whose claim to fame was the number of passed-out drunks stacked up outside. This was a nice establishment.

The stone courtyard was swept clean and laid with tables for the guests carousing. Well-dressed patrons drank, laughed, and played cards. Two floors of white stone, painted wood, and clinging vines gave a hint to how much more there was to offer inside.

This was not the kind of place that had patrons with a soldier's salary. Just who were these men?

The fourth member of their party climbed off his horse and handed the reins to a stable boy. I don't know why I called the other man a mystery when the true mystery was this silent figure who said even less than me on the journey. I heard them call him Nico, but except to grunt his agreement or disagreement with something they said, he didn't speak a word.

Nico and Castor headed inside to begin an evening that would be more fun than mine. That left the three of us.

"Alexander," Jason called.

Ah, Alexander. We finally have a name.

"I'll get the supplies after I complete the first shift. Send Castor with the list when he relieves me."

Alexander swung his leg off the horse, jumping down. Wind tickled my ears, gusting past me to fill his hood and blow it off his head.

My breath stopped.

For all that I pictured of the young soldier with the terrifying power, my imaginings fell laughably short.

Thick raven locks swept back from his temple, leaving the world to sink inside and drown in swirling flinty green eyes. A cute round tip topped the end of his nose, but no one would mistakenly think this softened him. Or, I dare say, mistakenly call his nose cute.

Hard lines molded his square jaw and a ruthlessly trim beard dusted it in shadows. He ran a hand through his hair and, just for a moment, I glimpsed where it curled around his ears. I blushed like he let me in on a secret—just between him and me.

Alexander was without a doubt the most gorgeous man I would ever meet in this lifetime or the next. As his full, dusky-pink lips grinned, I knew he plucked that thought right out of my head.

I snapped my head around, cheeks flaming. To be fair to myself, during the years other girls were building up a defense against a handsome face, I was off dealing with more pressing concerns.

"Whatever, Jason," Alexander replied. "Now get that rat in a cage before she passes out from the blood rushing to her cheeks."

Tensing, I bit back a retort as he strode away. By the gods, he was unpleasant. He must have a special hatred in his heart for deserters. What else did someone so handsome and powerful have to be angry about?

Jason walked me bound across town, collecting stares as we went. I put the onlookers out of my mind, walking the cobblestone path as though this was just another day, and I was just another normal girl giggling with friends over handsome boys.

I bet that would've been my life if I found my way to this village before the goddess came along. I would've made friends with the other young men and women prepping to leave for the academy. Our days we'd spend basking in the melting heat out in the dancing fields. At night, we'd gather in the courtyards drinking and toasting our last days as children.

"Whatever you are up to, you won't get away with it."

The happy scene shattered.

"I do not buy into this meek, compliant prisoner routine," Jason said. He didn't sound angry. On the contrary, I put his tone down as matter of fact. "There's a reason you're so content to be brought back to Trono City. Is it to finish what you started?"

Yes. "I'm sure I don't know what you mean."

"I've brought in a dozen traitors over the past few years. None of them went to their deaths as calmly as you." Jason stopped abruptly. I was surprised to see we were at the jail. "Fighting for our lives is ingrained in us. It's a basic human instinct that not even the god of death can steal." He faced me head-on, trapping me in his gaze. "That can only mean you're fighting for something you feel is more important. I will find out what it is."

Jason's words hung over me long after the key turned in the lock and I settled on the pile of damp hay that was to be my bed.

I am fighting for something more important. I laid my head down, eyes fluttering shut. *I'm fighting for those friends laughing in the courtyard. They deserved one more night as children before they marched to war.*

CLANG! CLANG!

"Wake up, traitor."

Snapping up, I tipped over and smacked my head against my stone prison. Pain sang in my skull.

"Huh. Jason's assassin theory is looking more and more unlikely. People in that profession tend to not sleep so soundly."

My vision cleared on Alexander. He changed out of his travel-worn clothes for soft black pants, a tunic that clung too tightly to his hard chest, and silver-tipped boots. The effect of him freshly showered, relaxed, and catching stray droplets of apple juice as he bit into the fruit—served to make the impossible possible. He was even more gorgeous.

"Wipe your face. You've got hay sticking to your drool-covered cheek."

I swiped the offending things off, body heating up. He was more handsome, and even more of a jackass's dung hole. The last fact was doing a good job combating the effects of the first.

"Here." Alexander held a bundled cloth through the bars. Opening it I found bread, olives, cheese, and—

"Honey cake," I whispered. The memories of Mama hurt, so I pushed them away. "Why would you give me food?"

"Did you think we were going to starve you for the next week?"

"No. I meant why are *you* giving me food? You made it clear I wasn't your problem."

He shrugged, still biting into that too-juicy apple. "I lost a card game. Jason is brutal about prompt debt repayments."

I grimaced at the insinuation that sharing my company was a step above worse than reneging on a bet.

"Are you going to eat that?" he demanded. "If not, give it back. We don't waste food."

"I'll eat it," I said, voice quiet. I may have even said thank you, but it was too low for him to prove it. It seemed weird to thank him, but even though he was a dung hole, deep down I knew these four could treat me a lot worse.

Deserters were as reviled as murderers. Sounds extreme, but we lived an extreme life in Olympia. For every monster we put down, twenty more sprung in their place. They bred so quickly and easily, we were overrun before the Deucalion Army formed hundreds of years ago.

There were no delusions. We were only slowing the tide, not pushing it back. The day would never come that Olympia was free of monsters, but if anyone was to have a chance at old age. If children were ever to laugh and play in the streets. If lovers were to marry. If young women were to giggle over handsome men, we needed the army fighting day in and day out to keep the typhons, lamias, gorgons, harpies, and giants away from peaceful towns like this.

Today, every able-bodied adult that wasn't raising children or providing services that were vital to the community, was in the army. It wasn't a choice or a question.

At eighteen, we were legally required to report to the academy for training. If we didn't show up, we were tracked down and dragged to the academy in irons. If we ran, we finally did get a choice—enroll in the academy or swing from the traitor's noose. In the old days, they hung those traitors in their hometowns, so their mothers' screams were the last thing they heard.

Oh, yes. There was a deep-rooted hatred for the men and women who dared to live the carefree life the army gave them, and then turned around and spat in their face when it was time to do their turn.

These four could treat me much worse. They could deliver me to Trono City battered and bruised, and the officials would merely scoff at the traitor and deal me another blow.

I smiled mirthlessly around a mouthful of honey cake. The funny thing is if they did try to beat or bruise me, that would undoubtedly unlock the beast inside. I would change, do something horrible, and then the goddess would force me to flee and continue carrying out her plans.

Trying to teach the traitor a lesson would result in my escape. I wondered if my unpleasant escort would find that amusing.

I chanced a peek. He blinked lazily at me like I was no more interesting than the beetle that crawled out of my hay pile. *No. I get the feeling he finds very little amusing.*

"What do you think?"

It took me a minute to realize he was asking about the food. "It's very good," I admitted. "The cakes are almost as good as my mother used to make."

"Excellent. The daughter of Hecate I paid to put a truth serum in those cakes, swore it was too sweet for you to notice the taste."

"What!" I gagged, forcing it back up. Horrified, I flung the food—feeling no satisfaction when the bread bounced off his unlined forehead. "What have you done?!"

"If you don't mind, I'll ask the questions. The serum only lasts for a short time," he drawled. "I'm going to find out exactly what it is you're hiding. Including why you ran away from the academy, but march so happily to your death."

Fear gripped me, strangling my tongue. Dull pain throbbed my nail beds as the talons began to grow.

"No!" I screamed at him and me. "You can't ask me anything! Please! You have no idea what's at stake."

"What are you talking about? What's at stake?"

I pierced my cheeks clamping my hands over my mouth. How could I have been so stupid? There was no such thing as soldiers being kind to traitors.

Shrewd eyes raked me up and down, then in a blink, Alexander's face smoothed out. "Calm down, hay rat. A properly brewed truth potion is forty gold coins. You can trust I'd never waste that amount of money on the likes of you.

"There was nothing in that but dough, honey, and walnuts." He smirked as my horror morphed into a different type. "Jason wants to divert our course and take you to Kuna City. The very fact that you seem to want to go to the capital is why we shouldn't take you there.

"Kuna is a two weeks' ride, so I said hades no. Then I lost the game." Alexander blew out a sigh. "He said if I proved you weren't hiding something, then we'd go to Trono as planned." Straightening off the bars, he tossed his apple core at the pile of food I wouldn't get to eat. "Better get some sleep. Thanks to you, we're spending two weeks sleeping on the ground and a horse's back."

I had nothing to say as he walked out. Alexander tricked me so easily, my head was still spinning. Of course it didn't matter where they executed me. Jason was wrong to believe I had some special reason for wanting to go to Trono, but how far he would go to prove it was the true problem.

What if the next batch of honey cakes did have truth potion in them? I couldn't refuse to eat for two weeks. Better yet, what if they skipped the cakes and playing nice, and tortured me to get the truth. If they did it in the name of protecting Olympians, they wouldn't face consequences, and they knew it.

I was at the mercy of men who could do whatever they wanted to me... and now they knew I had a secret.

CLINKING METAL JANGLED in my ears, gently pulling me from sleep.

The underground prison cell was darkness absolute. At night, the guard extinguished the lone torch on his way upstairs to his cushioned chair and desk. When you put a person in hell, why not make it worse for them?

"Give that to me," an unfamiliar voice hissed. "Do not go down there—whatever you hear. This prisoner must be questioned in connection to the death of the councilman Marcus Sideris. I won't have any softhearted *traitors* stand in the way of justice being carried out."

"I'm no traitor, sir." The sycophantic quivering voice wasn't familiar to me either. "You'll have no interruptions. This door stays locked until you leave."

Questioned about the death of the councilman? I was the only prisoner in the jail, so obviously they were talking about me, but what could make them think a random typhon's guess had any weight? Whoever did it took down the most powerful son of Apollo in all of Olympia and apparently lived to tell about it.

Was it when I fainted in the mud, or when I threw bread at Alexander's head that convinced them this impossible assassin was me?

Light broke the gloom, leading his way downstairs. I rose to my feet when Nico stopped in front of my cell. Holding my gaze, he placed the torch in its holder. I stiffened as he stuck the key in the lock and turned.

"You don't need to come in here to question me."

"I disagree." His voice was surprisingly light and musical for such a portly, grizzled man. Nico appeared to be about Jason's age—putting him at least twenty years older than me. He wasn't as round as the elderly men who used to sit outside the tavern in my old village, balancing mugs on their guts. But there was a soft, doughy laxness about him that said wherever he was stationed, he didn't see much action, or training.

His bulbous, crooked nose cast a long shadow across his slash of a mouth. *He did see enough action that someone broke his nose.*

"Turn around."

"Excuse me? Why?"

Nico raised a hand. A force like a cannon blast knocked me off my feet, slamming me against the wall. Another blast of wind rocked the windowless cell.

I spun around, coming face to stone with the wall. There wasn't a chance to breathe before Nico was on me. Cuffs circled my wrists.

"What are you doing!?"

"Shut up!" Nico hauled me around and threw me to the floor. I landed hard—wind knocked out of me.

I lay still, my mind slowing as I took stock. Something was very wrong. Wrong in the way he stopped and towered over me, staring in the stretched-out silence like he was making up his mind.

Like he's about to make a serious mistake.

Swallowing hard, I willed saliva in my dry mouth. "Whatever it is you came in here to do," I said slowly. "Don't. Bad things happen when I'm upset."

A hard kick caved my stomach. "How dare you threaten me, traitor bitch. You're just like those smug, stuck-up Artemis tramps. Jason, Castor, and that *Alexander* ran through their pussies like Drakones burning through a village. I touch the ass of one whore who wanted it, and she spreads word through the watchers to ice me out. Those bitches would turn their backs and walk away whenever they saw me!"

"H-huh," I rasped. "You deserved worse."

I expected the next kick. Gritting my teeth, I refused to scream under the resounding pain. I wasn't afraid of this shitty excuse for a man. The lack of growing talons and ink-dipped limbs proved it.

No, what he was doing was making me really, really mad... which could be so much worse.

If he didn't stop. If he took this to the place he was gearing up for, I would start to change, and this time, I wouldn't fight it. I wouldn't fight her.

That can't happen, my mind screamed, though it didn't need to. No one knew better than me what was at stake.

"This... is a very bad idea." My voice was barely higher than a croak, but it was even. "I'm telling you to turn around, lock that cell, and get out of here while you still can."

Nico threw his head back laughing.

"I don't want to hurt you," I cried, raising my voice over the noise. "I don't want to hurt anyone."

"Ahh. You're not going to hurt me." My gut churned at his smirk. "And if you're a good girl, don't scream, and don't struggle, I won't hurt you too much either."

Flickering torchlight cast moving shadows over me—mocking and mimicking the slow removal of his belt. A heavy, quieting emotion sludged my bones when it hit the dirty stone floor.

"Mmh," he moaned, tangling in my hair. Still I refused to whimper as he yanked me up, bending my head back. "You are pretty for a traitor. I will take no pleasure in watching such a beautiful face turn blue and bloated in the noose." His dirty fingers brushed my lips. "It is only right I use you before you go to waste."

Bile burned my throat. He spoke to me like I was a half-eaten leg of lamb about to be thrown to the dogs.

"*Vile creature.*" She spoke from everywhere and nowhere, but all who heard her was me. "*I expected little else from a son of Zephyrus. All of those wind gods were nothing but hot air. The only thing mighty about them was their Olympus-sized insecure streak.*"

I fought to block her out with everything I had. "You still have a chance." Nico ripped my tunic, pulling it over my breast band. Panic welled in my chest. "There is no humanity to appeal to in you. But there is self-preservation. If you walk out of here now, you live—"

He slapped me across the face, snapping my head around. "I told you to shut up."

"Do you see? Do you see now?" she whispered. *"He behaves exactly how Zephyrus did when he was whole. The parasitic seed Zephyrus implanted in this human's soul has corrupted him. Do not tell me you march to your death to save the likes of him?"*

I trembled, trying so hard not to listen. Not to agree. Not to—

"No," I whispered. "Not him."

Nico twisted my knee, forcing me to straighten my legs. Those dirty, filthy fingers fumbled with my pants button.

My foot flashed, burying my talons so deep in his gut they scraped bone.

Eyes bugging, he choked, showering my ripped tunic in blood.

That was the first time I thought of the horrid appendages as mine. It was the first that as she appeared before me—terrifying and wonderful and burning and shredding my soul apart—that I didn't scream.

Darkness swallowed my humanity, leaving Nico alone with the goddess and her pet.

Alexander

"I told you. I warned you! We should've killed her in the forest and left her body to be eaten by nymphs!"

"Futile," I breezed. "Forest nymphs aren't carnivorous."

Castor bristled. "Is this funny? Is it a joke to you, Xander? Nico is dead!"

Sidestepping him, I headed out of the courtyard, taking the dawn-lighted path to the jail. Castor had been yelling and bitching me out since he burst into my room, shouting that the traitor murdered Nico. What I had to do with this, I hadn't the faintest idea. I told him to kill the girl. Wasn't my fault the man still took orders from Jason even though they were the same rank.

"What do you expect me to do about it?" I tossed over my shoulder. "You want someone to bring Nico back from the dead, call a child of Asclepius."

Flame-broiled fingers clamped my shoulder, searing a print in the leather that reached for my skin. "Damn, you're a cold bastard," he hissed, hauling me around. "Nico's served your father for ten years. Show some—"

My power spilled from my hand like a river rushing off a cliff—surging, unstoppable, unforgiving.

Castor seized, mouth open in a silent scream as I burned five, ten, twenty years off his heart's lifespan.

"That's right. Nico did serve my father for a decade and I could give a pile of minotaur shit about him. I've dealt with you following me and secretly reporting my movements for months. Imagine how little I'll care for your death."

I released him. Castor fell, shaking and twitching on the ground. Pure hatred shone in his eyes.

"Only a medusa's glare kills. Want to do something about that look in your eye?" I held out my arms. "Now's your chance."

Castor clenched his teeth, face purpling a concerning hue. Then he looked away. "No, sir. Forgive me for stepping out of line. It won't happen again."

Scorching rage surged behind my calm mask. For a second, my fingers twitched to finish the job. Explode yet another sycophantic bootlicker on the pavement.

I strode off, hanging on to the urge. Why kill him when Castor ended up doing me a favor? Offering up someone I could take my rage out on.

Rounding the final corner, their voices hit me before they saw me.

"—what he said. He ordered me to stay at my post and not enter no matter what I heard. I had no idea that those screams—those screams were..." The jailor trailed off, his words and his pallor deserting him.

Jason was the composed soldier turning to face me—if not for the pronounced wrinkle between his brows.

Jason showing an emotion? Just what exactly did this girl do?

"You'd better see for yourself," he said, answering my unasked question. He pushed open the door and gestured for me to go ahead.

I eyed him, wondering briefly if this was a trap. Castor, and now Jason, were being oddly tight lipped about how exactly Nico was killed. What was waiting down there that they wanted me unprepared for?

The warning came and went. Can't know it's a trap until you spring it.

I pushed in, clomping too-heavy steps that echoed eerily among the stone. Stepping off the staircase, I found Nico waiting for me... or at least, one piece of him.

My steps slowed, but didn't stop as I walked past the fingers. No, what ground me to a halt was the heart that lay in the middle of the pathway like a lover's gift. A distasteful way of putting it, but I couldn't think of another. There were mangled parts of him absolutely everywhere, so why was his heart whole and intact like she plucked it gently from his chest and offered it up like a present?

I stepped over his ear, coming to a stop in front of the cell. Seafoam eyes stuck me through the shadows, pinning me where I stood. There was no denying she was lovely. From the first glimpse I caught of her, outrunning the Artemis watchers through the open-air market. She bumped into a stall owner and actually stopped to apologize.

When she turned around, I laughed. Us humans truly were the gods' joke. Say one good thing about monsters, they looked as vile and deadly as they were. But not us. The blackest hearts were always wrapped in the prettiest paper. There was no fun in it for them—

I gazed at the gore that was once Nico.

—if we saw this coming.

"He was in the cell with her," Jason spoke up, appearing at my side. "Nico went in and cuffed her. The key was in the lock."

That peaked my brow. "Keys in the lock? Why didn't you escape?"

Jason answered since her lips remained sealed. "She couldn't get past the door and jailor upstairs."

I was shaking my head before he finished. "Now we know that's not true. If she could do this to one of the most powerful sons of Zephyrus, a little door and one overweight guard weren't going to stop her. If she can do this," I said slowly. "Why aren't you, me, and Castor rotting bits on a forest trail?"

"Whys and what-ifs don't matter now, the facts do. And the fact is she and Nico were alone in this cell with no other way in or out. Look around you, Xander. She eviscerated him!"

Yelling? Oh, yes. Jason was rattled.

"She is now a threat to us and anyone who tries to transport her." He nodded grimly. "The jailor is waking up the magistrate. He will oversee her execution right here in this cell. No one will say we didn't take appropriate measures within the bounds of the law."

I was listening to him, though I wasn't looking at him. My eyes scanned every inch of the scene, and the small figure sitting quietly in the corner. They noticed something, and narrowed.

"Give me the keys."

"Excuse me?"

"Keys, Jason. Now."

"You can't go in there."

"What I can't do is repeat myself nicely." I flexed my fists in clear warning. "Give me the keys."

Jason did not fear me. He was an old soldier who fought giants and dragons while I was mewling in the nursery. No, he handed me the keys for the simple reason that he didn't report to my father. He'd still keep his job if I up and got myself killed by a hundred-pound girl with too-green eyes.

Is that what you plan to do? I wondered, stepping over the biggest pile of Nico. *Do you want to kill me, little traitor? To take your chance when you didn't at so many opportunities.*

So why did you now?

"When was Nico's watch?" I asked Jason.

"Midnight till we found him an hour ago."

"Meaning you and Castor got through your shifts without a scratch, but it's Nico she decides to kill?"

"The mind of a murderer is a labyrinth. You'll lose yourself trying to understand their motives."

I fixed on the reddish-blue bruise that caught my attention. Those looked like fingerprints on her jaw, and a handprint on her cheek. My study continued down, noting her ripped tunic, seeing the unbuttoned pants, and taking in the belt that lay untouched on the hay pile.

Nico and his clothes were ripped to shreds. The only way the belt could've escaped the massacre… is if it was taken off before it started.

The girl studied me as intently as I studied her. Her gaze was a drill in my head, bringing my attention up to those porcelain cheeks now uneven in color. Those full, Cupid's bow lips now puffy and swollen. Those long, harp-string lashes now painted in blood. And those flowing waves of golden hair now mangled from rough handling.

"I'm in the business of killing monsters," I murmured, drifting to the remains of Nico Xenakis. "Looks like you are too."

Our eyes met, and passed the only understanding there would ever be between us.

I made up my mind.

"Jason, tell the jailor he can send the magistrate back to bed. Then, scrape Castor off the sidewalk and have him put in his next daily report to my father that we're not bringing this one back to Trono City or Kuna." I got to my feet. "He can send the missive to Headmaster Drakos instead. He's got a new novice reporting to Deucalion Academy this year."

"What? No!" the pretty paper screeched, speaking for the first time since I discovered the true beast inside. "You can't— I won't go!"

"Don't mistake this for mercy." The growl blew her back. "It is now painfully clear that you were humoring us. Pretending you were our prisoner when we were actually your escorts to the afterlife. You chose either to escape from Olympia or die in it as if either is your decision to make."

I smiled at her falling expression as I shut and locked the cell. "There'll never come a day when I won't see a traitor punished.

You'll go to Deucalion Academy because that's exactly where you don't want to be. Who knows, maybe you'll learn something of duty, honor, and sacrifice while you're there." I laughed. "Though, I admit I don't care if you do. Just promise me you'll hate every minute of it."

"Fuck you! You steamy pile of griffin shit! The only thing I'll promise is to wipe that smirk off your face!"

I headed out, guffawing to split my sides.

"Come back here! Come back, you—"

An impressive string of obscenities followed me up the stairs. Who knew the meek little thing had it in her? This summer turned out to be much more fun than I thought.

Sirena

My reflection twirled for me, blowing kisses whenever our eyes met. Dresses woven by the imperial seamstress Zelenia herself, and I was to leave them behind in my closet in favor of boyish pants and restrictive cuirasses.

"It's completely ridiculous that the academy is mandatory for members of the Imperial Palace too."

"You're so right, Sirena."

"Ridiculous."

"As if you need the training."

I barely heard the fawning agreement of my attendants. Frowning, I surveyed my cleavage. Didn't I ask these to be cut lower? The woman dropped my neckline a fraction of an inch—if that.

"Ugh. Why do I have to do everything myself?" I tore the rag off and tossed it at my maid, Annis. "Have the necklines lowered two inches on all of those dresses immediately."

"Yes, Sirena," she replied, scurrying out.

Naked, I padded across the expanse of my palace room. Jade columns held the canopy over my silk-topped bed. The pattern painted on my headboard matched the design on my cool tile floor. A fact that would be confirmed when it wasn't covered in discarded clothes. The list of packing requirements for the academy was as offensive as it was short.

No dresses. No more than seven tunics. No more than seven pairs of pants and they must be brown or black.

The audacity of telling me what I can and cannot wear. I, a daughter of Hera, the queen of the heavens herself. It was my dearest wish that one of those mousy instructors would try to make me wear brown pants.

I carried my foul mood onto the patio, searching the skies for Tawny. Where had that blasted creature gotten to? Was everyone and everything out to irritate me today?

Sighing, I leaned against the balustrade—looking out over the palace gardens and, all around us, Trono City. Why anyone would live somewhere else was beyond me. This was the home of intelligence, beauty, and refinement. This was the crowning jewel on the map of Olympia, from the Weeping Mountains of Arachne to the Isles of Paradise.

This was the only place worth defending. The Deucalion Army should be stationed in and around Trono City, and the city alone. Let the ignorant, peasant demigods of the towns and villages defend the land their mothers hunched over and spat them out on. Let them handle their own schooling. Let them do their own training. Half the money in the palace coffers went to the academy because it had to be free to everyone.

Such a fucking waste it curled my lip to think about it. So much would change when I finally took my rightful spot on the council. The days of handouts and wasting money on the worthless were coming to a quick end.

"He's not here."

I turned as Mother entered my room.

"If you were hoping Alexander would catch a glimpse of the naked maiden on the balcony and fall hopelessly in love, I must dash your dreams. He sent word this morning that he's escorting a novice to the academy and won't be back before it's time for you to leave."

I slipped my robe off the bed and covered myself. "I was looking for Tawny, not Xander."

"Oh?" Mother said with a delicate lilt that betrayed her true feelings. "Because that pigeon will grant you the most powerful match since Hera and Zeus themselves wed on Mount Olympus? Naturally, she's your first priority."

Was this a natural trait of all daughters of Aphrodite? To shatter their opponent's confidence with a few well-aimed sarcastic quips. I'd certainly witnessed her do it dozens of times during my mother's reign as the Aphrodite councilwoman—one of the twelve most powerful demigods in the land.

Of course it was. My mother didn't earn her place by being a weakling. She raised me to be no different—especially in the face of her.

"Relax, Mother. Xander and I belong together. Our marriage is inevitable. So why would I stress about it and give myself early frown lines?" I reached for the dresses Annis left behind. "Should I bring the green or the red one to the academy?"

"The red obviously. How many times must I tell you green makes you look sickly?" she snapped, flinging the twenty-gold-piece green dress over her shoulder and off the balcony with uncanny aim. "I simply do not understand you, Sirena. You say you're committed to making this match happen. More importantly, you say Alexander is committed to this match, but the reports his father received all summer claimed he was happily hopping from bedroll to bedroll of the Artemis watchers."

"That was nothing!" I cried, temper flaring. "None of those mud-splattered sluts are interested in marriage, or could claim Xander if they were. He was blowing off steam. Getting all of that out of his system before *I* become the only woman in his life they'll report on."

"Is that so?" Mother ate the distance between us, making me lower myself on the bed without word or touch. Intimidation was not her power. No, that was the natural result of her true power: reducing her enemies to sea-foam. I wish I could say she would never use that power on me, but I'm certain my father once thought the same… before she reduced him to bursting bubbles on the lawn. He swore he would never cheat on her again.

Mother made sure of it.

"Well, if that's the case, I expect to send out the announcement of your engagement by the end of your novice year. We'll hold the wedding in the summer. We can't have Alexander spending another one *blowing off steam.*"

I raised my chin, meeting her gaze coolly. "A summer wedding sounds perfect. We'll invite the rulers of the far cities and isles. The celebration will be heard throughout the land."

"Excellent, darling." Mother placed two barely there kisses on my brow. "Now, about that little problem of yours…" I stiffened. "You have a plan to take care of that this year, don't you? I can't have you embarrassing me, my shining jewel."

"It won't be an issue," I said firmly. "I've got it taken care of."

"Good." Mother grasped my chin between two fingers, bringing me close to the face so much like mine. "What is it men have always denied us?"

"Respect," I said like so many times before.

"So what will we have at all costs?"

I smirked, mimicking her own.

"Power."

Aella

“This is unwise.”

Jason made an effort to lower his voice, but everything carried through these thin walls. Including Alexander's late-night rendezvous with the tavern maid who served us our tough meat and overcooked cabbage. You'd think my own room at the inn would be an upgrade to the cell. You'd think it until you were forced to listen to the high-pitched moaning of an overenthusiastic woman, and her creative use of dirty talk.

“Do you dispute my right to change her sentence?” I heard Alexander say. “Captured deserters have been sent to the academy for decades before her, and they will decades after.”

“Those deserters didn't cut a soldier into pieces. I have questioned her for days. She refuses to name her power or the god she got it from. She refuses to say why she ran, or why she'd rather die than attend the academy.” Rare emotion leeched into his stern tone. “Considering we've gotten an intimate look at what she can do, is it wise to force her into a place she clearly does not want to be? How many people will she kill when she makes her escape?”

“There hasn't been a successful escape from the academy in decades. The gates are more than strong enough to contain her...” His voice faded down the hall. “...going nowhere...”

“*I would like that one,*” the goddess purred. “*If only he wasn't host to the parasite of Zeus.*”

Huddled between the bed and wall, I covered my eyes, ducking my head in the corner, and it did nothing to lessen the effect of her presence. Many times she'd proven she could communicate with me anytime and anywhere with a whisper in my ear. The goddess chose to expose her divinity to a mortal for a simple reason: she liked that it hurt.

"I don't... understand," I forced out. "Why am I here? Why didn't you break me out of the prison when you had control?"

"*You know very well why!*" The shout boomed in my chest, making me cry out. "*The ceremony wasn't completed. Your* outburst *at the end saw to it that I was granted control over your body, but not your mind. You're just another mindless beast when you change into my perfect, beautiful pet. Once we complete the ceremony, you'll be a mindless beast who follows orders.*"

That was news to me. Not that I ruined the ceremony on the night I wouldn't let myself remember. It was a surprise that she didn't control me as completely as she hoped.

"And you never will," I rasped. "I won't complete the ceremony. Every day that passes is an opportunity to get my body back. You'll never win. I promise you that."

"*Oh, my sweet child, how little you understand. I knew the weavers of fate themselves. I watched them spin this tale in the unbreakable thread of the universe. I have already won,*" she sang. "*This world was mine from the moment that dagger pierced your flesh. You'd notice if you were polite enough to meet my eyes... that I haven't stopped smiling.*"

The goddess's laughter lingered after she faded. She took the conviction of my speech with her.

Did it really matter that she didn't have control over me when the monster took over? The chilling fact remained that whenever fear gave her an opening, she could turn me into a beast that killed indiscriminately. Seeing as she wanted to decimate all the demigods, it didn't really matter that she couldn't aim me at one in particular. Turn me enough times, I'd get to them all eventually.

I dropped my head on the wall, stomach heaving. This would be so much easier if I wasn't stumbling around alone in a world I was largely ignorant of. Normal life ended for me at ten years old. I didn't know if there was someone or something that could save me from her. I didn't even know who *her* was.

The goddess refused to name herself, and what use were the fuzzy recollections of Mama's illusions? None of them depicted the writhing, shifting form that burned my eyes for staring too long. I couldn't even learn of who I needed saving from, nor could I ask someone to tell me. For all of Jason's relentless questioning, the goddess made it plain what would happen to anyone who discovered our secret. I tested her on that, and she proved she was a woman of her word.

Pushing myself up, I paced as far back and forth as the leg manacle would allow me. *You can't give up, Aella. The goddess wouldn't be so determined to complete the ceremony if complete control over me didn't matter.*

Maybe that's because there's a way to undo what she's done to me. I seized on the wild thought. *She said this story was already written in the fabric of the universe, but that was anger in her voice over the abrupt end of the ceremony. That was not supposed to happen, so while I still have my mind, I need to use it. Find a way to stop her.*

I nodded to myself—determination creeping in. This was the only plan I had left. I tried to escape Olympia. I tried offering my life to a typhon. I tried execution.

I even tried killing myself. I had the blade in my hand and everything. But the natural fear of death crept in, and that was all she needed to turn me, and then the monster threw the dagger into the sea. Now it was time to do something I never thought of.

Save myself.

"Those irons make a gods-awful racket clanging up and down with your pacing." Alexander leaned in my doorway, tearing bites off another apple. "Is this the first time you've slept indoors? We civilized folk like to be considerate to our neighbors beside and below."

"Like you and your bedmate were last night?" I barked. Gods, what was with this guy? He just riled me up the wrong way. "If they're so loud, take them off."

He grinned. "Just the mere fact that you want something, makes me disinclined to give it to you."

"Oh, yes? Then I really like your mouth. Please don't cut it off and shove it up your ass."

Alexander's laugh was deep and rich like the amber honey that sweetened my favorite treat.

It made him even more loathsome.

"Wow. You did an excellent job hiding that fighting spirit." Amusement looked good on his smooth lips and thick brows. Although I had yet to see an emotion that looked bad on him. "I do like that she's come out to play now. You'll need this side of you to survive the academy."

I dismissed him. "If you're not here with food or keys to these manacles, go away."

Alexander didn't seem to have heard. "So, what are you? Daughter of Ares? Daughter of Keres?" he mused. "I met a daughter of Keres on the Satyr Plains. She could make a beast's limbs come apart with a look. They'd just unknit themselves like the threads holding them together came apart. I'm making it sound less painful than it is."

No, that sounded plenty painful.

"Doesn't matter what I am."

"Does your name not matter too?" he asked, moving into my line of sight. "Or do you prefer the many nicknames I've chosen for you?"

"My name doesn't matter because of your many nicknames," I returned. "Even if I told you, you'd still call me traitor."

He gave me a long look. "Fair enough. How about this? If you tell me your name and where you're from, the nicknames stop."

"Really? No more traitor, rat, or *pretty paper*?" The last one was new and confusing. Why did he call me pretty with so much disdain?

Alexander laid a hand over his heart. "You have my word."

Weighing my options, I couldn't find a downside. My name wasn't a secret. I just didn't want my interrogator, Jason, to believe he could get me to open up. Too much knowledge of what was going on in my head would get him killed. He hadn't been kind to me, but neither had he been cruel. I didn't want him dead.

"My name is Aella Galanis. I'm from a small village trapped between the sea and stone. Port Delphin."

He bobbed his head, then flicked past me. "Did you get that, Jason? Aella Galanis. Port Delphin." I whipped around, eyes bugging at our shadow listener. "Now you can dispatch a few Hermes sons to find out everything there is to know about her."

Alexander shook his head, walking out. "Gods, I should take over questioning her. It's much easier than you're making it look."

"I— You said—"

"Pack your bags, Aella," he broke in. "Tomorrow begins your new life in Deucalion Academy."

I told him what I thought of that through the slammed door and all through the night while he tried to get off with his tavern maid. His guest finally gave up around midnight, but I didn't—shouting and swearing that he'd never get me through the gates of the academy.

I needed to find my way out of another pair of chains. All the time I had left would be devoted to searching spell and magic shops for a way to dispel an actual parasite in my soul. I'd visit every library. I'd learn everything there was to know about every deity there was. I would not go to Deucalion Academy.

"Are you listening to me?" I headbutted his liver, yanking a grunt out of him. I had a good angle from my position in the back of the cart. "I'm not going!"

"Rhea and Cronus, woman!" Alexander burst out. "What will it take to shut you up?"

I told him I would if he did something filthy and illegal with a donkey.

"Gag her," he told Castor. "And tie her up at the back of the cart!"

I got in one last headbutt before Castor dragged me over the bags and secured my chains far enough from Alexander Jackass. That was his surname and legacy, no matter what anyone told me.

"Why do you think she hasn't tried to escape?" Castor asked the guys. "We've witnessed her power. Why doesn't she use it?"

"My guess is she's a daughter of Ares," Alexander replied. I fumed at the way they spoke about me like I wasn't sitting right there. "You know they can only use their powers under specific circumstances. Like if that hand you have on her hip goes any lower."

Castor flung away like I burned. "An accident. I'd never try anything on with a traitor."

It was an accident. His hand ended up there when he was wrestling me to the wood. He didn't notice in the midst of his conversation. What did surprise me was that Alexander both noticed and bothered to warn him off touching me inappropriately. Maybe I didn't imagine that moment between us when our gazes locked in that dirty cell.

He did know what Nico tried to do to me, and not only did he approve. He was impressed.

So impressed he's sentencing me to another kind of prison to uphold a law that should be abolished. Yeah, he can still go fuck a donkey.

I appreciated what the army did to protect us all and our way of life. But now that I knew what it was—what it *felt* like to kill against my will, I never understood the deserters more. A life where you don't get to choose... isn't any kind of life at all.

"It's also likely," Jason put in, "that she's counted up the odds against her and made the wise choice."

Pushing myself up, I glowered at the source of his comment. Jason said it wasn't safe for them to transport me three against one wild card, and the man wasn't one for idle remarks. That morning when Alexander checked me out of the inn, we walked outside to the twenty-man escort waiting to take little old me to Deucalion Academy.

How badly I wanted to shout that I wasn't dangerous. But of course that was the furthest thing from the truth.

I kicked the bag filled with *my* required items. Alexander took great pleasure in describing my course schedule too. Lots of training, fighting, and learning to kill in the most brutal institution of all the dominions. One flash of fear and an opponent would see talons where my fingernails should be. One well-timed "boo!" and huge beast eyes would glare at my scarer.

They would see something they weren't supposed to. They would ask questions they shouldn't. And the goddess would make me kill them.

"You don't know what you're doing," I shouted through my gag. "Please, let me go!"

"What was that?" Alexander cupped his ear. "Speak up, Aella. Can't quite hear you."

I kicked the bag, imagining it was his head. Was there a worse man alive than Alexander Jackass?

"Just relax," he called back. "Enjoy the view."

I flipped on my back to make sure my obscene gesture pointed where it was meant. I got a chuckle for my troubles.

Screaming in frustration, I threw myself against the cart and gave in to my surroundings. Let one thing be said about my home, there was no part of Olympia that wasn't beautiful. According to long-ago tales from my mother, the reason there were so few children of Demeter was because the goddess chose to scatter herself among the dancing trees, fields of grain, and each petal of sweet-smelling flowers. She'd make roses, daisies, and chrysanthemums rain in my tiny, cramped room as she told me that's why every blade of grass was vibrant with life. They were touched by a goddess.

I could believe it as we rumbled down the dirt path. The leaves swirling in the wind were greener than green. One look evoked lily pads floating on a clear stream; the first cut into a juicy, ripe avocado sailed from the island where they grew; the shore lapping at your toes; snow dripping off stems.

Alexander's eyes.

I jerked at the sudden intrusive thought, a frown marring my lips. Where had that come from?

"...is the way..." Voices floated on the air. "...say no..."

I raised my head, and there it was, shining on the horizon. My prison: Deucalion Academy.

Though, I don't think anyone who wasn't forced through the gates would see it that way. I wasn't gazing at a schoolhouse the likes of which I remembered—a little stone hut with no windows, creaky desks, and a teacher who didn't care to stop scratching his butt in our eyeline when he turned to write on the board.

The place I spoke of knew nothing of the palace before me. Pristine white stone glinted in the early morning sun, blinding me so I couldn't stare too long at the towering statues lining the stone steps beyond the gates. I counted three—four—five floors stacked on Corinthian columns and each one topped with a piedmont depicting a different historical battle scene.

I could tell this from that far away because every part of the academy was larger than life. Even from a distance, I couldn't see all of it in one look.

"Peace is the way." I sat up on my knees as we approached the gates, peering over the guards' heads. "Say no to violence. No to war." The chant popped the wall of silence, letting a flood of noise in.

It was as though we emerged from our own private path to rejoin the world once again. Carts and horses lined alongside the gates, letting out demigods from all over the land. Winter coats and boots worn by the northern mountain demigods. The sleeveless tunics and short-style pants of demigods from the isles. The glitters and jewels of the demigods of the cities, though I assumed those particular city folk were of the noble variety.

Gathered near the entrance were a group of people dressed in all white, from their woven boots to the flowers in their hair. They chanted to people who walked past like they didn't see them.

"Peace is the way," said an older woman with a scar on her cheek that curved her mouth unevenly on one side. "You can say no to violence. Say no to war."

"Children of Eirene," Jason said to my unasked question. "They protest conscription, the army, the academy, and campaigns to hunt down monsters. None of them actually have the power of the goddess though. She doesn't choose humans as her host."

"Because whatever these simpletons think, there is no such thing as peace without war in a human society," Castor said, glaring at the poor woman. "There comes a time in everyone's life where they must choose violence, or surrender their life, liberty, or loved ones to an enemy that will." He turned that glare at me. "Is that it? Are you one of these Eirene fools? Is that why you refuse to use your power on us?"

I gave him a flat look. To my surprise, he removed my gag to let me answer.

"No," I said clearly. "I've never heard of them, but I already know your explanation doesn't give them credit. I doubt they believe we should all lie down and expose our bellies if furies blow into town."

"They don't." Our cart slowed to a stop behind a gathering line. "They believe the only students who join the academy should be those who choose to enroll," Jason said. "They'll be taught self-defense, and then sent home to their villages to form local protection forces. If a monster attacks, they'll defend their homes. Otherwise, they live their lives."

I inclined my head. "Doesn't sound unreasonable to me."

"It's ridiculous," Alexander said flatly. "Fifty more typhons were bred during the course of this conversation. Campaigns to hunt down and slaughter them are the only way to keep their numbers down, and that's just to keep them down. We'll never win this war because we'll never kill them all, but the same can't be said about us. One year without the army, and they'll outnumber us fifty beasts to one demigod. It won't be a war then. It'll be a slaughter." He locked on to me over his shoulder. "That's why all of us—every single one—must fight. You don't get to say no."

I didn't fool myself. That last sentence was just for me.

"There is more than one argument to every debate," I said in a tone that sounded fair to me. Alexander peeled his lips back like I headbutted him again.

"An argument more valid than preventing our extinction?"

"It's not about more or less. When you choose a stand like *preventing our extinction*, you twist every action you take into a moral one, and dismiss anyone who disagrees with you as a traitor. That kind of black-and-white thinking is why they're shouting outside the gates instead of sitting down with someone who is at least willing to listen.

"None of those people down there want the demigod race wiped from existence, and I'm pretty sure you know that. So what's the harm in trying to listen and understand where they're coming from? Even if you disagree in the end, you'd probably be a lot less angry if you accepted that just because a mother wants her son to come back from war, it doesn't mean she devalues the sacrifices of your mother's son.

"We're not fighting a war just to survive. It was never about that," I said. "We're fighting for children sleeping safe in their beds. Couples falling in love. Families laughing and eating around the table. We fight for everything that makes a war worth fighting. And the Children of Eirene are too. They're just doing it in a different way. Jackass." No, I couldn't have left that last insult out, but I didn't think that's why I was getting the looks I was.

Not only were Alexander, Castor, and Jason staring at me, but my twenty-odd-man guard escort all gave me assessing looks.

"Jason," Alexander said, eyes narrowing. "How long did you say it would take to get information back on Aella Galanis?"

"No more than a week."

"Send that on as soon as you get it."

Jason nodded at him, but looked at me. I didn't understand what I said that turned all of their expressions suspicious, but I had a feeling the main point did not get through.

"What?" I finally snapped. "Why are you looking at me like that?"

"You dress—and curse—like a peasant, but you speak like a noble," Alexander said. "How does a girl from a small village trapped between the sea and stone string together such an articulate response?"

Heat burned the back of my neck. "My people aren't stupid. Neither is any *peasant* I've met."

"Not stupid, no," Jason said in that deep, unhurried baritone. "But schooling is only free in Olympia up to the age of thirteen. To take additional classes you must pay. To attend university, you must pay more. The average family from Port Delphin can't afford it."

I turned away. "The line's moving. We can go."

"Just another one of your secrets, eh, Aella?" Gods, that smirk always came bounding back like a dog who caught a stick.

"Sir," one of the guards said. "What do we do if she is a runaway noble?"

Alexander spurred the horses on. "We tell her family they can have her back in four years."

It seemed to take an eternity for our time to come. I didn't want inside that academy, but I definitely wanted out of this cart. My butt, hands, and legs went numb ages ago.

It was Alexander who unchained me, shoved my bag in my hands, and grasped my elbow in a firm grip.

"You're done after we walk through the gates," he told them. "Jason, I'm the first one you contact after that information on her comes through. Castor, you're dismissed from imperial service."

"What!" He nearly fell climbing out of the cart. "Why?!"

"I don't like spies. If we cross paths again, you'll discover the boundless depths of that hatred." He hauled me around, leaving Castor's gaping shock in our wake. "Pick up your feet, Aella. Wouldn't want to be late on your first day."

I couldn't stop a glance back. "You didn't have to do that," I said softly.

"No? Are you saying you would be kinder to the woman who told the watchers she saw you heading into Calliope's Forest that morning?"

"Depends. Was she following orders she had no choice but to obey?" I bore a hole in his head. "Shouldn't such a strong supporter of the army understand the chain of command? Or do you believe every now and then, there's room for rebellion?"

He blew out a sigh. "Gods, I miss the days you sat mute on a horse's ass, counting dandelions."

I blinked. He knew that's what I was doing? Just how often did he peek at me while pretending I didn't exist?

"All I'm saying is give that man his job back, or admit you're a hypocrite."

"All I'm saying is there's a hole in your pants. Everyone can see your milky-pale ass."

My eyes bugged. "What!" I snapped around, craning my head to see. My feet tangled and down I went. "Ahh!"

Hands grabbed and put me back on my feet. They didn't belong to Alexander. He was too busy smirking his ass off.

"There isn't a hole in my pants," I gritted.

He shrugged. "No, but don't you wish you could do a lot worse than dismiss me for lying to your face? See, no one likes a deceiving piece of shit. Admit it or you're a hypocrite."

"Oh, I'm going to admit a few things to you, Jackass. Clear your schedule for the week."

If anything, his smirk widened. "I'll take a rain check on that. Now stop stalling." He grabbed hold of my arm. "Get through the gates."

That's rich accusing me of stalling while he's spinning tales about my milky-pale ass. All the same, I did appreciate the extra minutes outside the gates. They gave me a few precious moments to think of a way out.

There are guards on either side of me. If I run, I won't make it two feet. If by some miracle I did slip through their net, the only place to go would be miles and miles of woods with no food, water, or map. The nymphs would be taunting my starving corpse in a week's time. There was no stopping this.

Alexander and I stepped off the dirt path onto the stone steps.

All I could do now was find a way to escape the inescapable fortress.

"You did it." I tugged free of him and was mildly surprised that he actually let me go. "You can run off now. But before you go." I stepped in his path. "I just want to say... that I despise you and it's my deepest wish that you eat a plate of tainted meat and shit for so long and hard, that you blow a hole through your pants."

Alexander laughed so hard, he wheezed. It was an adorable sound that made me want to slap him.

"Goodbye, Alexander." I took his hand and shook it. "I hope we never meet again."

"Oh, sweet Aella," he crooned. "What is it I told you? The fact that you want it makes me disinclined to give it to you. I'm not going anywhere." His voice reached me over a dull ringing in my ears. "We're spending the next four years together."

"Xander? Hey, Xander, over here."

"You would do that?" I croaked. "Post yourself outside my room for four years just to make sure I don't run? Does everyone in the army have your dedication to stopping deserters!"

"I'm not in the army. Not yet anyway. I'm a novice just like you." My sluggish brain recounted his age, placing it smack next to mine. "But it's cute you think I care about you that much."

I tossed my head. "Wait. No. If you're only eighteen, why were you riding with the watchers? Why were Jason and Castor obeying your orders, and how do you have the authority to dismiss him? More than that, what gives you the right to change my sentence and bring me here?"

"Goodness, did you reign as queen of the cave people? I have every right and all the authority. My father is the Zeus councilman,

Maximos Damien. He's leader of the Twelve, the most powerful demigod alive, and heads the only high-governing body in Olympia."

My sluggish mind did more recounting, more adjustments, and did not like what it concluded. I did know of Maximos, but I never heard of his son. The man standing before me.

"Xander!"

"As the one set to take his seat one day, tell me who would dare disobey me?" A slow grin curled those lips. "Or call me a jackass?"

"Xander, did you hear me calling you?"

I looked up as a cloud of rose scent hit my nose, heralding the arrival of the most glamorous woman I'd ever seen. Her flowy, bloodred dress billowed behind her—marking a path through the people stopping and staring. Hair the color of roasting chestnuts fell around her shoulders, framing big brown eyes, an upturned nose, and a small mouth twisted in distaste.

"What's this?" She raked me up and down. "Go away."

"Wow. Nice to meet you too."

She rolled her eyes. "Of course it's nice to meet me, but I couldn't give a shit who you are. I said go away." She shoved my forehead, nearly popping me off my feet. "Come on, Xander. Everyone's here already."

She led him off, leaving me the one standing there in shock and confusion. What the hell was that!

I fumed for a full minute. The length of time it took me to peel my eyes off her, and glance toward the gates. The *open* gates.

My anger faded. Was it that simple? Did I just have to walk back out?

I took a step. Then two. No one called out or stopped me.

Three steps.

Five.

Four—

Grinding to a halt, I spun on my heels as those twenty guards snapped to attention and converged on the gates. The answer was no. It was not that simple.

My gaze drifted to Alexander on its own power. He was standing within a group of three guys and that horrible girl, and he was staring right at me. He saw exactly what I tried to do.

"That was brutal."

I jumped. "What? I wasn't doing anything."

A curly-haired, smiling guy moved between me and Alexander. "You don't have to be to draw Sirena's ire. Here's a heads-up you got the hard way. She's pretty territorial over Xander. They're engaged to be engaged to be engaged."

"I could not care less about Alexander Damien."

"Then you're my kind of people." He threw an arm around my shoulders, giving me my second shock of the morning. "My name's Theron Zervas. From Trono City. You?"

"I'm..." My brain stalled at the oddness of this random stranger touching and being kind to me after weeks on the run.

"Pausing to make something up?"

I laughed and was shocked I did. It had also been weeks since I made that sound. "No. My name is Aella Galanis. I'm from Port Delphin."

"Nice. Named after an Amazon warrior. Mother had high hopes for you."

My smile melted away as quickly as it appeared. Of course it couldn't last long.

Theron guided me through the crowd of people idling on the lawn and steps. Part of me was curious to ask what we were all waiting for. The rest of me told that part to worry about something important. Who cared about the customs of a school I wouldn't be attending for long?

"Over here. Let me introduce you to my friends."

We found ourselves before a small group gathered under the cypress trees. A slim, pretty girl with short brown hair he introduced as Nitsa. The shaggy-haired guy who kept flipping his curls out of his eyes was called Tycho. And leaning against the tree between them was a long-haired girl with a stocky build named Ionna, gazing blankly at the sky. She could've been listening to our conversation, or she was in her own world.

"Nice to meet you guys. Are you all from Trono City?"

"Yep," Nitsa replied. "We all went to the same school. Glad we can keep it up for another four years."

"Cool." I looked around. "So, do you know what everyone's waiting for?"

Tycho jerked his chin at the entrance. "We can't do anything until we're placed in our class. Can't unpack in our dorms. Can't get our class schedules. So, they don't even let us inside until it's done. We're to wait here until they get us for placement."

"What's placement?"

Ionna dropped her head to squint at me. Her friends all did the same.

"How do you not know?" Nitsa asked.

"I don't know anything about this place," I said, sweeping out over the colonnades. "Where I lived was isolated from the world. A jackass would call me queen of the cave people."

"Ah, okay," Theron said. "Then all this is going to seem strange if you're hearing it for the first time. Maybe even cruel. Some could say barbaric."

"Cool it," Tycho hissed. "It's one thing bitching this place out over a game of dice in our rooms. It's another doing it here. If they hear you, you'll get punished for insubordination."

"He'll what?" I said. "Who told you that?"

Tycho pulled a book from his bag. "It's all here in the information they sent us." He gestured at mine. "You know. With the pack list and stuff."

"Everything happened really fast," I admitted. "This was packed for me. I never got the information."

"Flying totally blind, then," Nitsa said. "Don't worry. Just stick with us and you'll be fine."

I thanked her while casting a glance back at Alexander. He knew I was flying blind, but happily walked off with his soon-to-be fiancée and left me clueless. I wasn't looking for his good side, and he damn sure wasn't showing it.

"Can I ask you guys something? Why do they say this place is inescapable? That's a scary, prison-type word."

Theron chuckled. "It's not a prison. We can leave for the summer. It's just that some of the training and tests can get... intense. Years ago, there was a rash of midnight runs."

"Midnight runs?"

"Yep. A student says good night to his friends, heads up to bed, then the next morning his sheets are empty and the window is ajar. Taking off in the middle of the night."

"Got it." I sighed. "So to stop it, they did what?"

They all shrugged. "Just some spells and enchantments," Nitsa said. "They take them down two days a year. At the start of the training year and at the end."

Spells and enchantments. I got up close and personal with a spell to keep us caged at the border. But even that spell had a way through it in case the Olympians ever lost all hope and had to evacuate. Maybe these spells have a loophole too.

Gotta find out what those spells are first, another voice said. *Better not to spring one that sets alarms off through the academy. Alexander would love to put me in chains again.*

"Hey, guys, look," Nitsa hissed. "The doors are opening."

Two soaring white stone doors echoed through the valley, scraping across the marble. Three people stepped out. They were too high up and far away for me to make out what they looked like or if they were men or women. Were we supposed to go up there to them? Were they coming—?

"Ladies and gentlemen." The greeting boomed over the crowd, knocking me and a dozen other people off their feet. "Welcome to Deucalion Academy."

I clapped a hand over my ringing ears, gaping at the assembled culprits. How on earth was he doing that?

"I am your headmaster, Drakos. It is my pleasure to see so many fine young men and women taking their place in the service of Olympia. Some of you will not make it. I dare say, most of you won't."

I started. What did he just say?

"But those that do, will go on to carry the legacy of the gods and the hopes of the people on their shoulders. There is no finer sacrifice. No greater duty. And no higher honor.

"Good luck to you, novices."

With that, one of the figures—Headmaster Drakos—turned and went inside.

"Did he really just come out here to tell us most of us are going to die, but congratulations to the rest?"

"I've heard a lot about Headmaster Drakos," Theron said. "That he's warm and encouraging was never mentioned."

"Well said, Headmaster." Again I covered my ears. "Let me extend my own welcome to you all. I am your combat instructor, Commander Vasili. You may address me as commander or sir.

"Over the year, I will get to know you, your strengths, and your weaknesses. By the end of these four years, I will only know strengths. Is that understood?"

"Yes, sir," the crowd chorused.

"For many, it's been long days and nights of travel. I believe a rested fighter is a focused one. Let us get through the day's requirements, so you can retire to your chambers. Classes begin bright and early at sunrise tomorrow morning. Late arrivals will be punished."

That was the second time someone used that word and didn't follow it with clarification. What did punishment look like in Deucalion Academy? A place where the headmaster spoke of the low survival rate without irony or concern.

"Leave your bags where they are and follow the path leading around the left side of the building. Your placement starts now."

We did as we were told—stacked our things in a pile under the trees, then followed the shuffling crowd around the building.

The gates didn't come in this close to the academy. They extended into the forest, claiming a piece of it for the grounds. I started looking for how far the gates went in, and then I was just looking.

Sunbeams broke through the leaves, leaving shifting spotlights on giggling, flitting dryads—the nymphs of the forest. Ancient male artists drew them as gorgeous green deities of flowing moss hair and shining eyes because that's how they appeared to them. To my very female vision, they looked like a bunch of thin, gnarled tree stumps waddling around. But that didn't make them any less beautiful.

"Creepy, aren't they?" Nitsa drew my attention. "Hard to imagine the gods mating with them."

"Gods do what they want with whoever they want." My voice chilled even me. "You're not held to the rules when you're the one making them."

"Very true," she said softly.

Something rose out of the corner of my eye. The closer we got, I picked it out as a—

"Stadium?"

"That's right," Theron called back. "Placement begins."

Another word people kept saying without explanation. I would stop asking though. I was giving myself away as clueless and too many questions about my past were dangerous. If we were all novices, we were all starting at zero. I'd pick things up along with everyone else.

Our group broke apart, heading for different entrances into the stadium. I stuck with Theron and his friends, the five of us going straight instead of up to the higher seats. We filed into the second row as the seats filled up. Gazing around the novices, I noted that these were all the eighteen-year-olds from every corner of Olympia. Knowing that... it struck me that there were not very many of us.

Hundreds of people pushing and shoving on a lawn seemed like a lot. Hundreds of people in a stadium built for thousands... Were our numbers really this low? Or were the missing just better at hiding than me?

I was pulled out of my musings by a man stepping out in the middle of the arena. I pegged him as Commander Vasili with a single look. His blond hair cut close to the scalp, the opposite of the thick, full beard trying and failing to cover his square jaw. Though we would be battling no monsters today that I knew of, he wore a cuirass, short sword on his hip, and greaves to protect his shins. Not a flicker of emotion rode his sculpted face, but my impressions about him were already forming.

Vasili unstrapped a horn from his belt and held it to his throat. "Let's begin," he boomed. "Your instructions are simple. When your name is called, you'll step up here, name your power, the god or goddess who gifted it to you, then demonstrate that power. If you need materials for the demonstration, make that known. Understood?"

Everyone chorused agreement except me. I knew this was going to happen. I couldn't be in a school that trained demigods to use their power without answering the question of mine. I simply hoped they might have saved that question for after I escaped.

"Alexis Andino."

The commander stepped off and a tall, ungainly guy took his place. He swept his murmuring audience with a look like he wished he was somewhere else, throwing up.

"This isn't right," I whispered. "Why does he have to do this in front of everyone? We could easily wait outside while they call us into the stadium one by one."

Theron shook his head. "One thing they'll never do at Deucalion is make things easier for us."

My lips pressed together. There was nothing to say in response.

"Speak up, boy," the commander barked. He sat at a table at the end of the arena with a list and two silent companions on either side of him—a woman in a white coat and an elderly man in old-timey Greek robes.

"Er-Erebus, sir," Alexis got out. "Son of Erebus. The god of darkness and shadows. I can m-make it dark."

"Demonstrate."

No sooner was the order out of his mouth than the sun winked out of existence. Total and complete darkness dipped my vision in black. Screams and cries went up all around me, telling Alexis to stop. I couldn't see who was freaking out. I couldn't even see Theron and Ionna sitting next to me.

In a blink, the light returned—shining on a guy whose only fear was public speaking, not performance anxiety.

"Excellent," Vasili said. "Titan class."

"What's the Titan class?" I broke my promise not to ask questions almost immediately.

"The top class," Theron said. "It's for trainees whose powers will make a difference in the war effort."

I nodded. Stealing the light from our enemies would come in handy. The border watchers would've caught me a lot faster if I were stumbling around in the dark.

"Kosma Ariti."

The next demigod stepped up, appearing no more comfortable than the first. "Daughter of Poseidon. I can speak to horses," she said. "If one is brought from the stables, I can—"

"No need," Vasili broke in. "Sisyphean class."

My mouth dropped open. "Did he just say—?"

"Yes," Nitsa replied.

"Doesn't that mean—?"

"Yes, it does."

I dropped my head in disbelief. Sisyphean. That was the word for a task that was hard and thankless, but in the end, futile. It was a battle that couldn't be won. It was a labor that would never be completed.

It was another word for useless.

One after the other, novices stepped up and revealed their powers. One after the other, those powers were deemed vital, or pointless.

"Sebastian Barba."

A hush fell over the stadium—so sudden, I looked this way and that for the source. Did something happen?

"Oh my gods," Nitsa whispered. "*The* Sebastian Barba? Is he really here?"

"Look." Theron pointed to the right of us. "That must be him. He's here."

"He had to come, didn't he?" Tycho said. "Either that or be hunted as a deserter."

I stuck my head in the huddle. "What are you guys talking about? Who is he?"

They shushed me.

The Sebastian Barba walked onto the platform and faced me. I swallowed through a suddenly parched, aching throat.

"Son of Adonis," I whispered.

"You'd think so, wouldn't you," Nitsa said, eyes glazing over as fast as mine. "How could anyone who looks like him not be?"

No one could ever say the gods' choice of host was random. There had to be a method to their madness, and you knew when you saw that every child of Adonis was as unnaturally gorgeous as the god of beauty himself.

As the person standing before me.

Long flaxen hair swept down his back, constrained with a single band. The sun drenched his gypsum skin as though he denied her touch for years, and now she would bronze every inch of him with abandon. He rolled his neck—flexing wide, muscled shoulders—and I watched his bottom-heavy lips pucker as he blew out a bored breath.

Yes, he was bored. It was obvious in the dull sheen in his azure eyes and the displeasure wrinkling his broad, Roman nose. A short time ago, I would've said he was the most handsome man I'd ever seen, but that damn blasted Alexander put paid to that. Just as he ruined that moment by invading my thoughts.

Scowling, I shoved that silly, lust-addled nonsense out of my head. Like Alexander taught me all too well, pretty paper merely disguised the rotting pile on the inside. Sebastian Barba would drop my jaw and collect my swoons when he proved he only had the looks of Adonis—not the personality.

"He's even more rare than a child of Adonis," Theron said. "He's a son of Hades."

"Okay?" I drew out. "Cool?"

"That's all you have to say?" Tycho goggled at me. "When he says they're rare, he's not kidding. There's only like three in all of

Olympia, and they don't live in Trono. This is the first I've ever seen one in person."

"Very cool?"

"It is," Nitsa said. "Hades is generous with his children by far. Every one of his children throughout Olympian history has been granted powers that could topple kings. Like Midas with the gold touch. And Phedora who could douse her enemies with a deadly venom just by brushing their skin."

"I heard he's more powerful than both of them," Tycho added. "My father said he can summon an army of the dead."

Theron put in, "My mother said he can travel in and out of hades itself. That's how he evades the spies the council sends after him."

"Imagine," Nitsa breathed. "There are treasures, and horrors, in the depths of hades that only he can get to. No wonder they keep sending spies to watch him."

"I am Sebastian Barba." The three of them snapped their mouths shut so fast, there was an audible sound. He had their full attention. "Son of Hades."

They leaned in, hanging off their seats, and damned if I wasn't too. I couldn't help it. They got me curious.

"I can..." Sebastian paused as though he knew he had us all hanging on with bated breath. "...make creatures out of smoke."

His hand flashed and a cloud of black smoke appeared. Shifting, whispering, and reforming, it came together in the shape of a magnificent screech owl. The living vapors flew to the sky, and dissipated.

"That's it?" someone shouted.

Tycho, Nitsa, and Theron slumped, spines giving out with disappointment.

"I'm afraid so," Sebastian lofted. "I take it this ridiculous exhibition is now over."

"It is," Vasili replied, "and valiant attempt, but it was not going to be that easy. Titan class."

Sebastian left without argument.

"Titan?" I repeated. "Did he do that because he knows Barba can do more than summon puffs of smoke, or because he hopes he can?"

"He can." Theron's tone was firm. "A child of Hades has never gotten a power so pathetic. They've also never been the friendly, team-player type. He stays under the radar so he can't be used. Unfortunately, no one gets that option in Olympia."

I was starting to figure that out.

"Nitsa Castellanos."

She flashed us a tight smile. "That's me. Get ready to be shocked and amazed."

Her friends chuckled and patted her back on the way down. I didn't know what to say or do. They knew what her power was, and if she was being serious or sarcastic.

Nitsa stepped into the stadium. Skin the color of autumn flushed sickly under the burning sun. "I'm Nitsa," she called. "Daughter of Hera. I can shape-shift."

"Demonstrate."

Closing her eyes, Nitsa doubled over—tucking her head between her legs.

Is she sick? I stood up to help when Nitsa winked out of existence, and a moon-faced cow blinked at me from her place.

The audience burst out laughing.

"ENOUGH!"

I rocked back, falling hard on my ass. Laughs abruptly ended in favor of groans and moans. I would've been happy that Vasili shut them up, if it wasn't his fault she had to do this in front of everyone. I wasn't surprised to hear his decision.

"Sisyphean."

The pattern was clear. Any power that could kill or help others kill was worthy of the Titan class. Anything else was useless. Vasili turned down demigods that could sweeten dreams, grow wheat, talk to animals of all kinds, grant good fortune, and fly.

Nitsa shuffled out of the stadium, still in her cow form. A second passed before I realized her clothes were in a pile on the floor.

"I'll help her," Ionna said, standing up.

Vasili didn't comment on her running out, grabbing the clothes, and chasing after Nitsa. "Sirena Cirillo."

Alexander's *fiancée* peeled herself off his arm. I knew where he was sitting across and two rows up from me. I just did my best not to look at him. Now that I had, I hopped on my chance to study his friends too.

Sirena's absence let one of the guys claim her seat and continue telling a story that was apparently hilarious. The four of them cracked up—Alexander laughing loudest and freest of all. I could almost mistake him for human, just sitting there laughing it up with his boys. But then I'd remember his face in that cell when he claimed the final choice I had left without shame or remorse. What made him different than the goddess? With the way he ordered people about, destroyed livelihoods, and bragged about his powerful father, he certainly thought himself a god.

"Sirena Cirillo. Daughter of Hera." She actually paused like she was waiting for applause. Even more shocking, she got it. Sirena smiled and waved to her fans—blowing kisses here and there. "I can also shape-shift, but not to worry, sir. The goddess knew what she was doing when she left the cows for the peasants, and the power for the worthy."

No wonder Alexander liked her. She was the cruel donkey I told him to fuck.

"Demonstrate."

Taking a deep breath, Sirena straightened her neck and raised her arms above her head—posing like a dancer. I blinked and I missed it. Sirena vanished and a beautiful snowy owl flew— No, a bat flapped its wings— Not a bat. An eagle. A falcon. A phoenix. A pegasus.

Gasping, I lurched back, grabbing Theron's hand automatically.

A fifty-foot dragon filled the stadium. Sunshine glinted off silver-painted scales, widening my eyes with wonder. Wings so pale they were translucent stretched above her head, adopting nearly the same pose as she tipped her head and roared.

"She can change into monsters?"

"Sirena can change into any and everything that can fly. She can even change into creatures that don't live in Olympia. She isn't limited to what she knows."

"Amazing," I blurted.

He blew out a sigh. "That's what everyone's been saying her entire life."

"Ever wonder how and why certain people get the powers they do? Both Nitsa and Sirena were chosen by Hera, but one can turn into a dragon while the other turns into a cow. There's no making sense of it."

"I wonder if they asked why too," Tycho spoke up. "Do you think Hades wanted to be trapped in hell while his brothers ruled the skies and the seas? It's a random, unfair world for all of us—gods and demigods alike."

The dragon disappeared and down floated Sirena—naked as the nymphs scurrying through the trees. Lewd whoops and cheers sounded around me, earning another ear-ringing reprimand from Vasili.

"Titan class."

Sirena walked off unfazed—head high and looking plenty pleased that again, all eyes were on her. She left her clothes behind, which confused me until a girl ran out and scooped them up for her.

"Daciana. High priestess of the Volana clan."

A name and title? Vasili didn't read all that out for anyone else. "Volana clan? I've never heard of it."

"You're about to find out why," Tycho said.

I got a good look at the high priestess of the Volana clan, scanning over her wavy brown and bronze hair, wide nose, elven eyes, and pleasant smile.

She cleared her throat. "My goddess is Luame. She sings to the wind and runs with the moon." Understanding hit me like a brick.

"I am a werewolf."

"Demonstrate."

Calm as could be, Daciana removed her clothes and set them in a neat pile beside her. Watching her transform was nothing like the blink-of-an-eye changes of Nitsa and Sirena. Her fur sprouted first, layering her face and body in black, downy strands. So fascinated was I by the slow elongation of her nose, I didn't see the tail sprout from her back until it flicked the air—long and powerful.

Her bones popped. Legs bent. Arms lengthened. Torso widened and stretched. She didn't make a sound, though I wondered if she was in pain. Every bit of her broke apart and reformed in front of my eyes.

She wasn't a fifty-foot dragon, but if you told me this wolf could take on one, I wouldn't doubt it. There was power in her lethal-sharp seven-inch teeth and even longer fangs. She moved and pure muscle rippled throughout her body.

"She's beautiful."

The wolf swung to me, gazing straight into my eyes. Did she hear me? Her ears were as big as my face, so it was possible she did.

"Sisyphean."

"What!" I burst out. "Are you kidding?"

"Silence."

"But—"

"Don't," Theron hissed. "He's not slighting her. The high priestess is part of the interdominion program. She leaves Olympia at the end of training. She didn't leave her home to fight our war."

"Interdominion program?" I had questions—lots of them. So much for not showing my ignorance. The first chance I got, I had to speak to her.

She got to leave this place without a death sentence for the trouble. How did she get into Olympia? More importantly, how would she get out?

"Alexander Damien."

"He must have a lot of trouble with that," I murmured. "People getting his name wrong."

Theron's brows furrowed. "What do you mean? That is his name."

"No. It's Alexander Jackass."

Theron laughed so sharp and sudden, it echoed through the arena. He clapped a hand over his mouth, but it was too late. Dozens of eyes fell on him, including Alexander's.

The son of Zeus slid off my new friend and fell on me, his green pools sending out tendrils that stripped me bare, leaving me more exposed than Sirena and Daciana ever could be. He didn't let me go as he moved to the middle of the platform. Those secret over-ear curls and that little wheezy sound he made when he laughed too hard to stop. Alexander was going to share something else—just for me.

I wasn't allowed to look away.

"Son of Zeus," he said, the truth dripping from his lips in that deep, rolling way he spoke. "All living beings have electricity in their bodies. In his wisdom, Zeus granted me the power to tap into that electricity and increase it tenfold." Alexander said it to Vasili but spoke to me. "I'd be happy to demonstrate, but as I said, it only works on living beings."

I knew it was coming before he finished. "I'll need help from you." His finger leveled between my eyes.

I burned, and not with the heat of his power. Obscenities rose to the tip of my tongue.

"Theron." His finger moved off me. "Old friend, step up here. Give me a hand."

"I—I— No," he cried.

Alexander cocked his head. "No? Why not? You know I can control it. Surely you're not worried I'll kill you."

"No, but—"

"Then what's the problem?" he sliced in, tone hard. "Stand up."

"Go on, boy," ordered the commander. "We don't have all day."

I gasped at Vasili in disbelief. Or I would've if my eyes could leave Alexander. I'd felt those cursed powers in action. Heard the most feared monster in our dominion scream all the way to its death. He wanted to do that to an *old friend* of his... just because he laughed?

"No!" Theron burst out. "No, I'm not doing it. Get someone else. Or better yet, just put him in the fucking Titan class already. All of Olympia already knows what he can do."

"And now we know what you do, Theron Zervas, son of the Dionysus councilwoman. You back down at the slightest chance of pain. You going to back down from a battle next? Throw down your shield and run away crying 'cause the mean echidna scratched you?"

"Boo!"

"Coward!"

"Weakling!"

Theron flushed as the entire stadium turned on him. Boos and insults pelted him—a few of them included traitor.

This is ridiculous! They call him a traitor for refusing to play Alexander's sick games? What is wrong with these people?

"Stop it," I shrieked. "If you all are so happy to be burned alive from the inside, one of you volunteer!"

"Oh ho." Alexander laughed. "He needs a woman to defend him too."

"Shut up, you—!"

"Aella," Theron bellowed, blowing me back. "Enough."

Me? He was yelling at me?

Muscles jumping in his jaw, Theron pushed past me and stormed out to the platform. The fury on his face when he glared at me on the way stunned me into stillness. Theron Zervas did not want my help.

Theron was ten feet away and still walking to him when Alexander dropped him.

"Ahh!" Agony ripped from his throat, curdling my insides like I was contorting on the ground with him.

I bit my lip hard as the screaming went on... and on... and on.

"Stop it!" I screamed, blood dripping down my chin. "Damn you, stop!"

The cries cut off just like that. Expressionless, Alexander turned his back on the crumpled heap he called friend, and strode off without a backward glance.

Alexander had wanted to share another secret with me: his bottomless cruelty.

It was a while before Theron staggered to his feet—chest heaving. No one said a word or went to help him.

Theron didn't return to his seat. He left the stadium and didn't come back.

A hand rested over mine. "Don't sit there with that guilt on your face," Tycho whispered. "You were trying to help him. Where you're from, that makes you a good person—as it should. But in

Trono, you can't show weakness. Once Alexander challenged him, it was either step up or be labeled a coward for the rest of his life."

"Trono City sounds like an outhouse."

He snorted. "There's a reason the name Paradise was given to another part of Olympia."

I sat through the next names in a blur. What kind of place have I come to? What kind of world did I live in? Demigods from every village, town, isle, and city of Olympia, and the only one who wasn't shouting Theron down with insults was me. The only one to speak up and end his torture... was me.

Are these stone-hearted warriors my people? Did all compassion and kindness leave them at the age of eighteen?

But maybe I wasn't the one with a right to say anything. I didn't know what hardened them. I was taken out of Olympia long before I tried to escape it. The goddess saw to that.

"Aella Galanis."

I didn't fight it. Didn't fuss or argue or hesitate. This was coming whether I wanted it to or not. I might as well get it over with.

I took my place on the platform, facing Vasili and his silent companions, and no one else. "I am Aella Galanis," I said clearly. "I don't have a power to show you. I don't have power at all."

"I'm not a demigod."

"What?"

"What did she just say?"

"Not a demigod?"

Muttering broke out around me while Commander Vasili slowly raised his head. "Excuse me?"

"I'm not a demigod."

A frown marred his handsome features, shifting them into the unkind, hardened appearance that better suited him. "You mistake me for a man who likes his time wasted. Show us your power now, girl. I will not ask again."

Raising my chin, I met his gaze steadily. "I'm not lying. It's rare, but it happens. I was never chosen by a god or goddess. Not a drop of the divine lives in my blood. I am, for lack of a better word, a mundane."

There it was, the only possible truth. I cursed, and raged, and cried about why the goddess chose me, but enough of her rants about parasites and filthy demigods cleared dust off the image. She chose me... because I wasn't one.

A judge rose from the table. It wasn't the commander. Smoothing down her white coat, the woman who had yet to introduce herself studied me up and down as she ate the distance. "My dear, what you're speaking about is more than rare. In two thousand years, there have been four reported instances of this happening. An Olympian rejected by every known god. We're to believe you're the fifth when the most likely explanation is you're lying because you want to be sent home."

I absolutely wanted to be sent away from here, and if a simple lie could make it happen, this wouldn't be the school with a reputation so fearsome, it reached me in the dark place that had shielded me from knowledge of almost everything else.

"I'm not stupid to think you wouldn't expect that," I replied. "It's been eighteen years and no ability has shown itself. Even if it was something I couldn't see—like the power to give good fortune or peaceful dreams—wouldn't I *feel* it? Wouldn't I know?"

Silently, she nodded.

"Then, there it is. We're all witnessing a historic moment. The fifth non-demigod in Olympian record."

The mutterings were growing louder. No one knew what to make of me, but a few of them had ideas on what to *do* with me.

"Execute her! This isn't the mundane world."

"Get rid of the worthless bitch."

"Let's not be drastic," the woman said lightly. "We haven't yet reached the point that we must accept you're making history."

I frowned. "What do you mean?"

"Just because your power hasn't manifested, doesn't mean it never will. There's every chance you're a daughter of Ares. They can only summon their power when they feel intense hatred."

"That was my mother's explanation when I was the age of nine and giggling with my dolls. I am a woman now and I assure you"—the goddess flashed in my mind, and even the memory of her true form burned—"I've felt hatred."

"Hmm." The woman went back to her seat. It was then I noticed Alexander was not in the stands where he should be. He was standing behind Commander Vasili.

No. No, no, no! He cannot tell him of what happened in the prison, believing that will prove me a liar. A god's curse is not a god's power. The first Medusa would attest to that.

"I say no," the woman said, dragging me off Alexander. "You do have power, my dear, you simply haven't discovered it yet. I once knew a man who was also convinced he had no power, then at the age of twenty-eight years, he set foot on his first boat and the seas calmed beneath his feet. He didn't know he could control the tides, because he'd never seen the ocean.

"You are exactly where you need to be now, young one. Here at Deucalion, we will help you discover who you really are."

"But I—"

"Or," the commander said, "you will be sentenced to twelve years hard labor. As was the lying traitor of two years hence who spun the same story, and then refused to participate in training. In the end, he was made useful to his people."

Alexander bent and whispered in Vasili's ear. I surged forward. *What the hades are you telling him!*

"I see," Vasili said. "Aella Galanis. Sisyphean class."

I looked from Alexander to the commander, then back to that blasted grin. My protest stalled on my tongue.

Arguing with him would only move me from one prison to another. I've seen men on hard labor. They're cursed to do the worst and most dangerous jobs, but the manacles never leave their wrists. I can't break free of the goddess if I can't break free of my jailors.

Accept it for now. The plan remains the same. I will leave the academy on my own terms.

I left the stadium. Making my way out of the shadows, someone called my name.

"Aella, over here." Ionna waved me under the awning. She, Nitsa, and Daciana sat on the steps of a side entrance into the academy. "Are you finished? How did it go?"

"Sisyphean," I replied, leaving out the details.

"Nice," Nitsa said, giving me a smile that trembled. "We'll be together."

"Are you okay?" I put my arm around her. "Were you hoping for something different?"

She shook her head. "I knew I would be in Sisyphean, but that doesn't make it any easier to tell my parents. They and my three older brothers were Titans. Having a *useless* daughter doesn't go down easy."

"You're not useless. The way they think about these things is ridiculous. You have one of the most incredible powers out of the bunch."

She snorted. "I'm a *cow*, Aella. There are thousands of them grazing the fields. What exactly is so incredible about turning into a lowly, common animal?"

"Do you retain your mind when you change? Do you see and understand everything that's going on?"

"Yeah. So?"

"Then you're not a lowly common animal. You're a spy, Nitsa. You're the best sentry in the land," I said. "Demigods can't get close to a herd of minotaurs because they can smell them coming from miles away. They're the hardest monsters to track, but you. They'll just dismiss you as a lowly cow, and it'll be the last mistake they make. Sounds pretty fucking useful to me."

"I... I never thought of it that way. A spy," she whispered, rolling it around on her tongue. "A tracker. No one would see me coming." Nitsa bumped my shoulder. "Thank you."

"I've got to go back," Ionna announced. "If he's hit the *G*s, he'll be calling my name soon. You guys are done. Get us a good dorm room before they're all snatched up."

"She's right," Nitsa said. "No point sitting around here when we could be scoping out the place. Three brothers and I've never been inside. Can't wait to see what's real and what's one of their silly tricks."

Her good mood was back in full force. Nitsa took off, hurrying to grab her bags and begin her first day in the academy that labeled her useless. I followed at a slower pace. Daciana fell in step with me.

"Thank you for that. We'd been trying to cheer her up for half an hour. You did it instantly."

"I meant everything I said. I can think of a great way to utilize every person who was shoved in the Sisyphean class. For one thing, the guy who can grow wheat from stone is a marvel. He can keep an entire battalion fed, and they wouldn't need to rely on the locals—taking food out of the mouths of poor villagers."

"Wise thinking."

"What do you think?"

She shrugged lightly—pretty face serene. "It's not for me to have an opinion. It wouldn't hold any weight if I did. I am a stranger to this land. One that was plotting her escape home until you."

I looked around. "What? Me?"

"Yes, you," Daciana said with a laugh. "Demigods don't know much about werewolves. Or they do and they don't care that my heightened hearing heard everything they said about me when I shifted. From the graphically lewd remarks to the comments that I was a disgusting beast, should be put down like the other monsters, or be captured like a wild animal and forced to serve the army."

"They said what? They're the fucking beasts!"

She didn't lose her amused smile. "My father did the interdominion program when he was young. He told me what to expect. He also told me that when someone shows you who they are, believe them.

"Out of everything said about me, you were the only one to appreciate my form for the beautiful gift from the goddess that it is. Also, you defended me when you believed I was being treated unfairly. You've shown me you're kind and without prejudice, so I'll believe it. You and I will be friends."

I shared her smile. "And you just spent half an hour trying to cheer up a girl you didn't even know. I believe that's who you are too." I held up my arm. "Friends."

Head cocking, Daciana looked at the appendage in confusion. I giggled as she grabbed my wrist and gave it a little shake.

"No, like this." I tipped her elbow and bumped our forearms. "It's an army thing. Can't shake hands when you're holding swords, shields, and lances. So we bump arms."

"Fascinating. I'm learning from you already."

Sebastian

I watched *Aella Galanis* and her werewolf friend from the shadow of the stadium. They walked off in the other direction, saying goodbye to the farce behind me to find a better time with their new friends in their new dorm.

"Such a sweet idea," I mocked. "An even better cover. No one will suspect she's anything but a pretty novice training with her friends."

"Something isn't right with her," Linus said in my ear. "There's a sickness. A sickness in her very soul."

My head bobbed, fixed on her as she continued on the path. "I sensed it too. The moment she stepped through those gates. She is not what she should be."

"What will you do?"

"What I always do. Kill her if she's a threat. Collect her if she's an asset." The reply dropped cold and emotionless from my lips. "But for now, we'll just watch her."

"But what could she be?" Linus pressed.

A smile stretched my lips. "Something Olympia hasn't seen for two thousand years.

"She's something new."

Aella

There's no reason I should've formed ideas about what existed behind the white doors, and those expectations were blown all the same.

I spun on the atrium's polished floors, and the mammoth statues of the twelve Olympian gods spun with me. With one hand, they palmed the ceiling. In the other, Zeus threw lightning, Hera held a babe, Artemis drew her bow, Poseidon raised his trident.

"Come on," Nitsa called. She and Daciana waited in front of another, albeit smaller, pair of doors. "The map says the Sisyphean dorms are this way."

"Do we have to call it that?" I jogged to catch up. "Just because they named us Sisyphean, doesn't mean we have to as well."

"I've decided I won't let it bother me either way." She raised her chin. "No one is going to tell me that I'm useless to my home. If I'm fighting for it, I can never be useless."

Daciana pushed open the door, spilling us into a long marble hallway. The two of them consulted the way while I looked around, memorizing my escape route.

I hadn't seen guards outside, and so far, none inside. That was one point in my favor.

"Nitsa, does it say anything in the book about a curfew?"

"Course not. We're not children. But we also train from sunup to sundown, so whatever midnight fun you're planning will have consequences in the morning."

I hid a smile. She wasn't far off about the midnight plans.

"This door." We stopped in front of the third one at the end of the hallway. "This leads to the dormitory wings. That leads to the food hall and the classrooms. That one leads to the training rooms. We'll explore after we dump our bags."

We entered another hallway, the near opposite of the one we left. Stone packed us in, drawing us shoulder to shoulder. Doors lined the left side going down and twisting around the corner. They were labeled simply "Sisyphean Dorm One." "Sisyphean Dorm Two." Etc.

I drew ahead to the end of the hall and craned my neck around the corner. One side had more Sisyphean dorms. The other side had a single staircase entrance with a golden sign above that read "Titan Wing."

"This one looks nice. Aella, check it out."

Their calls drew me to Sisyphean Dorm Eleven. A low whistle cut through my lips.

"Not bad at all."

One grand circle lay before me with ten alcoves starting and ending where I stood. Each alcove boasted a stone, curved archway that granted us a glimpse of the bed, desk, bookshelf, and dressing table on the other side. In the middle of it all was a sunken common area of squashy couches and cushions.

Nitsa flung herself on one. "If our rooms are this nice, imagine how incredible the Titan dorms are. My brother said that each one came with a beautiful personal attendant who caters to you and rubs your feet." She flashed me a flat look. "As you guessed, they're idiots and I've learned to ignore everything they say."

I laughed. "Let's go find out for ourselves, then. The entrance is right down the hall."

"Better we don't get in trouble on the first day." Daciana tossed me her welcome book. "Sisypheans aren't allowed in the Titan wing except by personal invitation."

"It doesn't really say that, does it?" I flipped through and there it was—word for word. "Never mind. I need to unpack and find the showers. I feel like I've been traveling for years."

"But I'll bet you haven't traveled as far as me," Daciana teased. "So... I'll be taking that shower first!" She snatched up her stuff and raced out. Shrieking, I ran after her and was popped off my feet and tossed on the couch.

Nitsa saluted me in the doorway. "Too slow, Port Delphin. Looks like you're third."

Okay. Now it was on.

I chased after them—our laughter echoing through the hall-way.

Alexander

"**S**he's tricky. Did you hear her trying to pull that 'I'm not a demigod' bullshit? She hasn't stopped trying to desert since she tipped that apple cart in the market square and sent Larisa flying over a table of silks."

I paced the length of my bedroom, getting toasted on all sides by the roaring fire.

As dormitories went, this place didn't hold a candle to the rooms in the Imperial Palace. One had to wonder, then, why the headmasters of old spent so much Imperial Palace money to make the outside grander than the shining city of Mount Olympus.

For our troubles, the Titans were granted a bed that would barely fit two people comfortably, a dressing table and vanity, fireplace, desk, shelving, and an attached bathroom. The only true perk to this wing was not having to share. Although that perk was doing fuck all for me.

Calix made himself comfortable on my bed, his erection at full tilt as he flipped through a collection of erotic drawings by a man, or woman, who went by the pseudonym Eros. Galen and Ajax reclined in my armchairs, warming their rank-ass feet by the fire.

"What the fuck are you three even doing in here?"

"Listening to you moan nonstop about some girl," Ajax returned. "What's the deal with her? And why should we care?"

"Care about whatever the hell you want." I flung his boot at his head. "And put those back on before the smell sets in and I have to change rooms."

The asshole and his twin brother smirked in my face as they rubbed their sweaty feet on my carpet. If they weren't my brothers in every way that mattered, I'd have popped their empty heads.

"But who is she?" Calix spoke up. "Did she turn you down for a fuck? Bet it's the first time that happened."

"No, she didn't. But she would," I admitted. "She has told me loudly and often that she despises me, and will laugh herself sick when I'm struck down by the many ailments she's wishing upon me."

"Damn. She said that to your face?" He forced his attention off the book to flash me raised brows. "The girl's fearless."

"She's mouthy," I corrected, irritation blazing hotter than the fire. "And crude. Like she got a high-priced education just to learn filthier words. She has the nerve to judge me close-minded."

"Ah, so she knows you well."

I lifted the mattress and dumped Calix off. The fool howled on the carpet. Life was nothing but a joke to him and that would never change.

"Something about her doesn't make sense, though. She pretends to know nothing of our world. She claimed not to know who I was until I told her."

"That is strange," Galen said. "Does there exist a place in Olympia that is beyond the council's reach? Even the mountain people have to pay their taxes."

"No such place exists. She's lying but I can't say why or for what purpose."

"To get close to you," Ajax offered.

I tossed that idea aside easily. "She would've been happier to have never met me. I don't doubt that."

"You don't doubt it," Calix said, making himself at home on my bed again. "But it damn sure makes you mad. This one's gotten under your skin."

"Don't be ridiculous."

Ajax sighed. "All I know is if you spend another second talking about this girl, Sirena will sense it and burst in here to take all our heads off. Cool your obsession around her."

"I'm not obsessed. Aella Galanis is nothing. She is less than nothing. But I was forced to take responsibility for her since I commuted her sentence. If she runs off like she's clearly still planning to do, it's on me. Her sentence will be my sentence."

I wished I could say I was exaggerating, but such was the law in Olympia. One time—just one—a tale of woe convinced a border watcher to free her charge and help her across the border. The council immediately passed a law stating that whoever was in charge of bringing a traitor in, would meet the same fate if that traitor got away.

In any other circumstances, this law, like the rest, wouldn't apply to me. But my father sent word that morning that I shouldn't look his way for any hope of leniency. He was less than pleased with me for reducing the sentence of a traitor who murdered a guard—on top of publicly firing one of his favorite spies. I wasn't supposed to leave Trono City at all, let alone spend the summer causing trouble for him.

I asked myself what Aella would do if she knew she held my life in her hands. *Redouble her efforts to escape.*

Suddenly, the rest of what Ajax said penetrated. "Hold on, why would Sirena care about me and Aella?"

I gritted my teeth. *Me and Aella. Why did I say it like that?*

"Are you kidding? If anyone's obsessed with anybody, she is with you. That woman will be the one who marries you and has your babies if she's got to kill every female on the planet to make it happen."

"Nonsense." I promptly dismissed every fool word out of his mouth. "Sirena and I have known each other since we were in swaddling. You just can't conceive of a man and woman being friends without that relationship eventually leading to sex. It's one of your many failings as a man."

It was my turn to take a boot to the head.

"Xander?" *Knock. Knock.* "Are you in there?"

Sirena pushed in without waiting for a reply. "There you are." Running over, she popped a kiss on my cheek. "I was looking for you guys. A bunch of us are heading out to the river for a moonlit swim. You coming?"

"Can't," I said. "I've been on the road for weeks. Tonight, I'm finding a training room and getting in a proper workout."

"Come on, Xander. Don't be boring." She squeezed my arm. "You're really going to pass up skinny-dipping with me to play with a plastic sword in a stinky old training room?"

"Bet he would if Aella Galanis was there," Ajax muttered.

Galen winked exaggeratedly. "Just to make sure she wasn't up to something, of course."

Idiots.

"Who?" Sirena demanded. "Who's this Aella?"

"No one important." I slipped out of her hold. "I'm getting some training in, but I'll see if I can meet up with you guys after."

I left, and was in search of a training room. That I would also search out Aella's dorm room on the way was out of necessity. I had to know where she was at all times.

I would vouch for her power. I would get her off a murder charge for a corrupt soldier's death. I would even save the silly clod from herself and refuse to grant her death wish.

But one thing I would not do for a traitor... is die for her.

Aella

"This isn't so bad." Theron tossed his stuff on a bed and then himself after it. "If I can't have my own room, at least I'm sharing with you guys."

If his wish was to share a dorm with his friends, fate smiled on him like it never did for me. Ionna, Tycho, and Theron were all placed in Sisyphean.

"Might just be the six of us too," Ionna spoke up. "This year's novice class is a bit… thin. I bet there are more beds than bodies."

"Fine with me." Nitsa was already set to work making her alcove cozy. Drawings of her family filled her shelves where the books were supposed to go. Drawing out a knit blanket, she set the starry night sky over our plain white sheets.

Daciana stretched on the couch, looking wholly relaxed and at home with this close-knit group. "Is it rude to ask people what their powers are?"

"No," Tycho said. "Not rude at all. It's the first thing strangers ask after 'what's your name?'"

"Then, what are your powers?"

My ears quirked up. I stopped fussing with the clothes Jason packed me and stuck my head out of my alcove.

"I'm a son of Persephone," Tycho said. "Children of Hades are rare. Children of Persephone aren't. She was the queen of the underworld and had real authority—unlike Hera who had to give in to Zeus's whims." He sucked in a breath. "Basically, I can speak words of power. Whatever I say must be obeyed."

"Are you serious?" I gave up on hiding my eavesdropping. "Don't take this the wrong way, but what are you doing here?"

He shared a look with his friends. "Everyone's impressed when I tell them, until I remind that Persephone was queen of hades. My words of power only work... on the dead."

"Ahh," I drew out. "I see."

"Thought you might. It's not a fun power. Seven years old and making my dead dog sit, stay, and follow me scared my parents. They banned me from using it for years." He lifted his shoulders. "I continued the ban on my own. I have no use for a power like that. The dead should be allowed to rest."

"Goodness. Now I do feel it was rude to ask," Daciana said.

He chuckled. "Honestly, it's cool. There is shame in misusing a power, not in having it. I didn't choose it, but I'll choose what I'll do with it. Thankfully, Commander Vasili agrees that I won't do anything with it."

Ionna squeezed his shoulder. "I'll say it so you don't have to ask. I'm a daughter of Apollo. He granted me the gift of prophetic visions." She raised a hand, stopping me as I opened my mouth. "Don't be impressed with me either. My visions are confusing, dipped in double meanings, and often downright wrong. I can't trust a single thing I see."

"I'm sorry," Daciana said. "That must be really hard."

Ionna looked away, jaw stiffening. "Yes, it is," she whispered. With that, she ducked into her alcove. We left her in peace.

"Guess that leaves me," Theron said. "I won't be coy about it. I'm a son of Ares."

And now I was fully out of the alcove, erasing the distance between us.

"Ares?" Daciana repeated. "But I heard it said children of Ares can only use their power when they feel intense hatred."

He nodded, expression blank. "That's correct. Which means every other day of the week, I'm as mundane as our counterparts in the neighboring dominion."

"I can't believe a power could be so specific."

"Ares was the god of violence and brutality. He represents no more than the horror of war. A piece of that god's essence wasn't going to result in bunny shape-shifters or flower conjurers."

"Do you know what your power actually is?" I asked. "When… you can summon it."

"I'd know even if I couldn't. All of his children have the same power," he replied. "We can summon the destructive force of an explosion. The intensity of the explosion matches the intensity of the hatred." Theron gave me a funny look. "Why don't you know this?"

"Where I lived was isolated. Remember?"

"Right. Sorry. You remind me the world doesn't revolve around Trono and its shallow problems."

"Hey, we've all got stuff."

"Yeah, I heard that…" He shuffled on his feet. "Are you sure that you're not a child of Ares too? I got my ass kicked for years for being a 'powerless dog.' One day, Eryx Mallas decided he wasn't content with me and went after my little sister too." Theron's eyes glazed. "That was the first I felt it. I wanted to hurt him, Aella. I wanted him to feel pain like he never had before… and then he did."

A deep, pressing silence spread through the room.

Shaking himself, Theron cleared his throat. "All I'm saying is, I thought I knew hatred, but it's not despising olives or wishing your mother's new husband would leave out the door he came in. It's tapping into a dark, brutal side of you that not only hates a thing, but wants it to suffer like no one ever has. If you haven't tapped into that side yet, there's still a chance you're a demigod. Even if you're the child of the most reviled one."

I plopped on the couch with Daciana. "I wish I could say I haven't but… yes, I've felt that hatred," I whispered. "No power followed." I swept over my new friends. "How bad will it be for me if my story doesn't end the same as the man on his first boat? Those four other non-demigods, what happened to them?"

"They lived short, difficult lives as little more than exiles," Theron said. "People saw them as thieves that couldn't give back to the home they were living off of. That's why they passed a law sentencing them to hard labor—though they did nothing wrong."

"It also stops people from pretending they don't have power to get out of the army," Tycho added. "The main point is it'll get bad for you."

"Tycho! Theron!" Nitsa hissed.

"What? I'm not going to lie to her." Tycho leaned in, taking my hand. "Life will be hell for you, Aella, and you don't deserve it. My advice is to pick a minor god and claim a power too nebulous to prove. Like the god of dedication or the god of opportunities. Say your power lets good opportunities find people, and the next time something good happens, they'll think of you."

"Basically, I'm to live as a fraud." The sentence dropped dully from my lips.

"It's better than living as a hard laborer and then an outcast until some prejudiced beast decides you shouldn't live at all."

"Tycho!" Nitsa shoved him out of the way. "Stop scaring her. You're *not* going to live that way—as an outcast or a fraud. There is power in you, Aella. I know it. Give yourself a chance to find it."

Getting to my feet, I gifted her a soft smile. "I will, Nitsa, thank you. I think I'm going to take a walk and clear my head."

"Of course," Daciana said. "We'll explore when you get back."

Ducking into my three-walled room, I pulled on my boots and overcoat. Nitsa was a sweet, kind soul. But she was also wrong.

I've been on land and sea. I've struggled to breathe on the thin mountain air and swam with the sea nymphs. I've loved, hated, danced, cried, and held in fascination with every new creature I met. If an animal was meant to speak to me, or if the tides were meant to calm beneath my feet, they would've done so by now.

I was not a demigod. Neither was my future to fake my way through the academy until the goddess sank her claws in me for good and brought the destruction of our world. *Or* I spent years toiling under hard labor. I would get out of here and find a way to stop what was done to me.

My soft-heeled boots padded across the marble. Just as when we came in, there wasn't a single guard or sentry loitering about the halls. I passed through the atrium of the gods and out into the star-lit night.

Tall grass tickled my shins down a trodden forest path. Seemed like students regularly came this way, so this part couldn't be subject to the various spells and enchantments fashioned to keep us in. That's all the welcome book had to say, "various spells and enchantments."

I'll let this path take me to the gates, then I'll see what defenses there are to keep me on the right side of it.

I'd known true darkness earlier that day at the power of Alexis Andino. It made this torchless, moonlit path radiant in comparison.

Giggles sounded from the trees. The rustle of leaves followed me, getting closer as the nymphs trailed new prey. Any second now they—

A twig bounced off the back of my skull. *Giggle. Giggle.* An empty bird's nest scratched my ear and landed at my feet. I stepped over it and kept going.

Young nymphs were more mischievous than their older counterparts. The forest was their territory and they reserved the right to harass anyone who crossed their path. In about a hundred years, they'd accept humans in their forest as a fact of life, and even grow fond of more than a few demigod men.

I wasn't walking for long when I reached the gates. If I expected more fanfare, I was disappointed. Half a mile down the path it ended in a brush of overgrown bush, and then a few feet beyond, there sat the wrought iron tool of my imprisonment.

"Well," I sighed. "I won't get through by staring at it."

Grasping the bars, I climbed the iron curlicues and immortal laurel leaves like rungs, and flung myself over. I hit the ground, disappearing into brush that tried to keep me—branches snagging my hair and clothes.

"Oh my gods, that's it? I did it? I can't believe…" Trailing off, I turned my head toward the giggling… and the path littered with twigs, stones, and nests they threw at me. I was right back where I started.

"Wow," I said to my audience. "The children of Hecate have a real love affair with this spell, don't they. I don't get anywhere, but I do get to fall on my ass for the trouble."

"Hee hee. Silly human."

"Stupid girl."

I swallowed their mocking. I deserved it for thinking it'd be that easy. Should I try again? Maybe persistence would be rewarded, and after enough tries, the magic would take pity on me.

I snorted. No, I didn't think so either. "Any chance you'll tell me how to get over?"

I couldn't tell where her voice came from. "Why would we do that?"

"Because I'll"—I cast about for an idea—"bring you an offering, goddesses of the forest."

"What could you possibly offer us?" Her voice rasped like tree branches scraping together.

"Name it. Everyone wants something."

"Hmm."

"What say you?"

"Does she lie?"

Their whispers went back and forth over, beside, and all around me.

"Okay, human. We will tell you how to get over the fence. What you do from there will be amusing to watch."

Meaning another barrier awaited me on the other side.

That wasn't a surprise. But, if this worked, I could find another section of forest and bribe those nymphs to help me past the next obstacle. This might not be so impossible after all.

"You will bring us blankets and swaddling for our young one. The nights are too cold for the babe."

I stilled. "Young one. What do you mean?"

"Just what we said." The leaves rustled, and little gnarled faces glared through. "Blankets and swaddling now. Before we change our minds."

"But you said babe," I rasped, throat drying. "There are no baby nymphs. You grow from adolescence to adulthood like a sapling becomes a tree, but you are never babies." I pushed up on shaky knees. "And you never get cold."

"Why does this girl presume to tell us about ourselves?" a voice hissed. "Where is our offering? We demand our offering."

"Tell me where the baby is."

"Now she makes another request without fulfilling her promise of the first. Faithless human."

"Trickster child."

"Lying human."

Their voices began to fade—the rustling sounding farther and farther away.

"No, wait! I— I have the swaddling here." I tore off my coat and held it up, spinning to show the trees the soft, woolen lining. "This will keep your babe warm through the harshest winter. Take me to them, so I can show you how to wrap the child. The buttons are tricky."

"Buttons on swaddling?" She sounded close. I tipped my head back and there she was, dangling off the highest branch. "Is this a new kind?"

"Oh yes. Humans have started using them recently, but they're so much better. This way the baby can't kick them off."

"Oooh, wise."

"Smart girl."

"Good girl," said a pleased voice on my left. "We will accept this better swaddling. You will show us how to do the buttons. Follow Mahaila. She will show you the way."

Mahaila? Where—?

A hard object landed on my shoulder, pulling a cry from me. The dryad tugged on my ear. "You will go that way." She turned my head to the left. "You will walk until I say stop. You will go now." Nymphs were goddesses in their own right, and they ordered humans around like one.

Taking a deep breath, I stepped off the path. The rustling overhead increased tenfold as though the whole forest was rocked by whipping gusts of wind. They were all coming to see the girl wrap their babe in a woolen gift and lay them to rest. But how could this be? Had the nymphs truly found and adopted a human child? Was this babe abandoned by a desperate student? Were they out here all night while we were decorating our dorm rooms and chatting up new friends?

"Stop." I halted just short of an ankle-high tree root. "You will turn right. You will step between the twin oaks. You will not disturb them."

I followed her orders, squeezing carefully between the narrow opening between two oak trees. The world only the dryads knew unfolded before me.

A soft, mossy bed of green blanketed the tiny oasis between the trees. Overhead, the branches twisted and tangled, forming a natural roof from which the vines and flowers dangled. Amidst it all, in a bed of leaves, moss, and grass, lay a sleeping babe.

He didn't look new to this world. A plumpness to his cheeks and thickness in his curls put him at a few months old. He looked peaceful and sweet, sucking on his fist while he dreamed. He also didn't look to be harmed—though if he was, I wouldn't have blamed the nymphs. The nymphs of legend would raise and protect gods that were in danger from their divine parents. They weren't strangers to adopting babes that needed a family.

But this will not be yours, little one. I cannot walk away from an abandoned child, even if the nymphs are willing to care for him.

"You will swaddle him," Mahaila said. "You will teach us the buttons."

They were right that he needed blankets. The poor thing was put out in only some thin wrappings to catch waste and nothing else.

"Okay." I laid my coat out and placed the child within the warmth. "Now tell me how to get over the gate enchantment."

"Simple, child. The power is in the link. The link must be broken."

I paused. "The link must be broken? I don't know what that means."

"Break the link. Break the circle, then anyone can leave."

"Break the circle," I whispered. "You mean... break the gate. The spell is activated when the gate closes whole and intact. And if I can't break the gate?"

"All spells can be undone by the person who cast them."

"By the person who— That person died hundreds of years ago," I cried.

"That person cast her spell and went inside the human dwelling when the sun touched the horizon. Find her and make her undo her human trickery."

The second option wasn't an option at all. No way I was forcing a child of Hecate and likely instructor to do anything. They'd have me trussed up and on my way to hard labor so fast, I wouldn't know which way was up before I hit the dirt in chains.

So, I'll find a way to destroy the fence, but that's a problem for another night. First, I have to get through this one.

I finished wrapping the baby in my coat and held him to my chest. "Thank you for all your help. I'm going now, and I'm taking the child."

"What does she say?"

"He is ours."

"Put him down!"

Rocking back on my heels, I got ready. "I can't leave him here. There are people nearby who can help. Find his mother or a family who'll care for him." A thick, pungent smell hit my nose. Goodness, the poor thing needed changing too. "He comes with me."

"He's not yours to take, girl."

"He's not yours to keep," I flung. "And this isn't a debate."

I shot through the trees, tearing through the brush for the path. Inhuman screeches echoed in the forest—the trees were crying.

"Bring him back!"

"Our babe! She's stolen our babe!"

"Give us the child!"

Pain exploded in the back of my head, popping black spots in my vision. I heard a *thud* on the ground behind me. Whatever she threw at me was much bigger and heavier than a twig. An object struck my back. My shin. My elbow. I stumbled, pitching forward when a rock cracked my shoulder. I felt the bruise forming beneath my tunic.

Head pointed down, I saw them come. Dozens upon dozens of dryads raced over tree roots, shot out of the bush, scrambled up the trunks with their natural weapons. I held the child close, the poor thing waking to screams—mine.

Stone and wood rained down on me, biting agony in my flesh wherever they struck. "Stop! You'll hurt the baby!"

"Agh!" My pants slipped down my hip bone, suddenly carrying new weight. The dryad scrambled up my body like I was the oak tree that birthed her. Launching at my face, the hit from her tiny fist snapped my neck nearly all the way around. "Evil girl. Human thief! Give us our child."

I would say something for the terrible day this abandoned child was having. At least in the midst of it all, he found the fiercest protectors in Olympia. Too bad they would not have him.

I picked up the pace and burst out of the bush onto the path. Tiny brown and green adversaries dropped from the trees everywhere I looked. The path was clear no more.

"Help! Someone help!" Dull pain didn't pound my nail bed. No tingling sprouted up my arms and legs, and my eyes remained as ordinary as the rest. I was drunk on adrenaline and pain, but I wasn't scared.

The goddess's *pet* would not intervene, and I had not a single shred of power, weapons, or fighting ability to save us. But hundreds of people in that damn blasted academy did. Someone had to come.

They leaped on me from above and below. "You will water the forest with your blood—" I swatted blindly and sent her shrieking. Nymphs yanked my hair, crawled under my tunic, rained blows on my back, and—

I screamed as teeth pierced my skin. "Help!" The academy steps appeared through a break in the trees. "We're over here!"

The dryads yanked, pulled, and piled on me—trying to bring me down with sheer numbers. I was a bucking steer being roped and lashed into submission. After this night, I wouldn't need the ability to talk to them to know how it felt.

"We're almost there," I gasped. "Almost—"

A flash moved out of the corner of my eye. I barely got out a cry before she smashed the rock over my head, exploding agony in my temple. I staggered and crashed into a tree, nearly dropping the baby. My skull split a seam, pouring blood down my face.

The child started crying in earnest.

"Give him to us."

"He needs us."

"He is ours."

"Cruel girl."

I heard the fear in their pain—the tears and suffering. I was taking a child from his mothers, and in their eyes that's all they knew.

Dryads rushed over my body to the babe, tugging on the coat to get him out of my loosening grip.

Come on, Aella, go. Go! Pushing off the tree, I bolted—surprising half a dozen dryads into falling off. *Five feet. Four. Three feet. Two—*

A cry bellowed overhead, heralding a sharp snap. A brown streak fell into my path, and I was flying. My legs soared over my head—upending me and the child, and both of us screaming the whole way.

I crashed flat on my back, wind evacuating my lungs. The mental shout to keep running came too late.

Nymphs swarmed me. Pinning down my legs, wrenching my arms off the babe, holding my head and shoulders down. They crowed their victory as they finally claimed their charge.

"Kill the thieving bitch!" That was a word they stole off the wind. "She will never harm our child again."

A waddling little tree stump stomped down my chest... hefting a stone.

"No," I croaked. The baby's cries faded as they carried him back into the woods. "Don't..."

Stepping on my neck, she cracked the stone on my face. Blood spurted from my ruined nose. She thought nothing of the blood, or stepping on the broken appendage. Screams ripped from my throat.

She hefted the stone again, bringing it down on my skull.

"Enough!"

I waited for the blow to come. And waited. And waited.

Peeling my eyes open, I jerked at the hate-filled, murderous glare filling my vision. The dryad glared at me, but she didn't move. She didn't drop her stone.

"Are you okay?" Gentle hands grasped me, helping me to my feet. My captors just rolled off me, making no move to stop me as they hit the ground and stayed there. "Gods, what did you do to provoke a dryad attack? I've never seen them do that before."

"I..." I glanced up, and the words died on my tongue.

Hazel orbs blinked at me, squinting in true concern as he brushed my forehead and came away tacky with blood. He hadn't stunned me because he was handsome—though he was that. Thick brown, almost black eyebrows crowned his hooded eyes, drawing your attention there, though what you wanted to stare at was his high, sculpted cheekbones and pronounced cleft chin. That water droplets were dripping down said cheekbones and chin only heightened their seductive power.

But no, what shocked me into silence was that I already knew this face. He was one of the guys laughing and joking with Alexander in the stadium.

"Are you okay?"

"I'm fine," I replied, shaking myself. "What did you do to them? Why aren't they moving?"

"I froze them in time. Son of Kronos." He dropped this like one said they would mend a tear in their pant leg. It was no big production. "You're lucky I was on my way back and heard you. Another second and I would've frozen the moment your skull cracked open."

"I can't believe it, but luck did smile on me." I peeled away from him and poked my head in the brush. A horde of frozen nymphs held the child, his mouth open in a silent cry. "And you."

I faced our rescuer.

"Fuck! Where did that come from?"

"Someone must've abandoned him in the woods. The dryads adopted him and didn't take too well to me carrying him away."

With a snap of his fingers, he unfroze the baby and only the baby. I'd never seen such power, let alone witnessed it wielded with such control.

The babe resumed his crying immediately.

"That explains what set them off." He tossed his wet hair, flicking droplets on the murderous dryads. "I'm Galen, by the way."

"I'm—"

"Aella Galanis." An odd smile twisted his lips. "I've heard of you."

"I—"

"Thieves! Murderers!" A rock struck the ground beside me.

"There are more coming," I cried.

"We need to go!"

We raced toward the steps, staying ahead of that *rustle, rustle, rustling*.

"You first," Galen ordered, propelling me up the stairs. I chanced a peek back, my awe a living thing as he froze wave after wave of dryads pouring through the forest. They just kept coming.

"Shit!" Galen gave up and bounded after me. They couldn't get to us from behind those doors.

I was first to reach them. Falling on the entrance, I strained to move the marble inch by agonizing inch.

"Hurry! Get through!"

Dryads bit at his heels, pelting him as they did me. Galen hit on the last step and collapsed through the gap. He kicked the door, swinging it shut. Dozens of screeching deities wailed on the other side.

Chest heaving, Galen dropped his head on the marble. "Is it always like this with you, Aella Galanis?"

I bounced the baby, settling him. The helpless thing needed a bath and changing right away. He smelled terrible.

"I can promise this is the first time I rescued a child from a vengeful forest. If luck continues to shine on me, it'll be my last."

"Come on." Galen peeled himself off the floor. "We'll find the headmaster. He'll take over from here." Galen put an arm around me, then frowned. "What's that smell?"

"It's the baby. They asked me for fresh swaddling for a reason."

"But... that smells like..." Galen peeled back my jacket, releasing the ripe scent. "Sulfur! Aella, put it down! That's not a—"

The child sprang out of my arms, screeching an ear-piercing, keening wail.

"Get down!"

Galen sprang between us and threw me to the floor. I bounced on the tile—flat-backed and in perfect view to see the child that wasn't a child split its face open and roar through a maw of sharp, rotted teeth.

Galen's hand snapped up and it seized his wrist, twisting it away and jumping off his arm. The creature grabbed his neck.

"Noooo!"

His teeth sank in and tore, ripping out his throat. My scream echoed through the parliament of gods.

The monster sprang off his chest, knocking Galen off his feet. He collapsed in my arms for I was there in an instant. "Galen, no! No, please."

His jaw worked and breaths gasped. I pressed a hand to his ruined throat as if I could hold the blood in.

"L-look... out..."

A screech sounded behind me. I twisted as it leaped—its blood-stained mouth gaping and aimed at my neck. My hand flashed, cleaving the beast in three.

Its parts splattered in a mess of black-tainted blood and the now overpowering reek of sulfur. Head rolling, my knee stopped its escape—letting my shifting face be the last thing imprinted on its bulging red eyes.

I smashed my black scaled fist on his face, cracking open his skull better than any stone.

The world blurred in my rage, pain, and fear. I saw nothing—knew nothing—under my relentless tearing, smashing, and pounding.

"*Yes, my pet. Give in to the grief. Surrender to fear and despair,*" she whispered. "*Demigods are coming. Kill them. Let them know our pain.*"

I jolted to, ripped out of my fog. My claws and scales retracted fast—only blood and gore remained to prove they were there.

A sharp hiss of displeasure was her only acknowledgment of me. I was on my own, cradling Galen's body, when a bunch of dripping wet demigods entered the atrium through another door.

"I'm sorry," I cried, holding him closer. "I'm so sorry."

"Hey. What's going on?"

"Who is that?"

"Isn't he—?"

"Galen!" Thunderous footsteps, then I was shoved out of the way—into grasping hands. "Galen, no! Not like this, brother. Speak to me. Please."

Those hands spun me around. Alexander's pale face and oh-so-green eyes filled my vision. "Aella, what happened? My gods, Galen. What did you see? Who did this?"

The noise and screams and cries around me faded. I saw only Alexander as he came apart before me. His soul unknitting itself as if the threads holding it together unraveled.

It hurt me infinitely more than I could ever say.

"LET ME REPEAT EVENTS as you have stated them. You went out for a walk to clear your head, when you heard a child's cries carrying on the wind. You went to investigate and found an abandoned baby being cared for by the dryads. You then stole the child back, which incited the dryads to attack and chase you out of the woods.

"Galen Teresi heard your shouts for help and came to your rescue. The three of you escaped inside the academy where Galen finally noticed the smell coming from the child wasn't that of a soiled diaper, but that of a shape-shifting tenebrae demon. Discovered, the demon murdered Mr. Teresi and then... died."

I swallowed hard.

"Are those the events as they happened, Miss Galanis?"

My voice was a thin rasp. "Yes, Headmaster."

I didn't think I could end up in the headmaster's chambers so soon—in the middle of the night before my first day could officially become my second. Another time, the room's opulence would leave a lasting impression on me. As it was, the stretching stone walls, hanging tapestries of divine battles past, stacks beside stacks of bookshelves, and the long, grim shadows stretching over them all under a single lit candle's losing fight against the gloom— All of it would leave me as soon as I walked out of this room. If I ever did.

I cast a look at Commander Vasili standing tall and imposing behind the headmaster. On his left was the woman in the white coat, finally named Stavra Remis—the academy historian.

"How could it have gotten in?" I heard myself say. "Aren't there spells and enchantments to keep monsters out?"

"Of course," Drakos said. "Many layers of protection had to be lowered to allow the trainees and novices in. It's not the first time demons that can don a human shape have used that opportunity. They're able to because of another adjustment in the protections that allow non-demigods to reside in the forest.

"Dryads must be with their trees, so there is no choice in this other than ripping them out by their roots. The demon got as far as it was ever going to get... until you."

I winced. "If the spells wouldn't let it past the trees, why did I make a difference?"

"Because your life was in danger. You were holding the beast. Barring it from entering meant barring you as well. You would've been killed and barriers are meant to react to a demigod in danger, and hold your well-being above all."

A single brow climbed his forehead, the only window into his thoughts. "You see how the tenebrae arranged the perfect scenario. Either he turned on the dryads and slaughtered them, or a soft-hearted little girl stole and brought him into the academy where he'd slaughter everyone inside. Quite a clever beast."

A long silence stretched between us. He may have been leaving an opening for me to speak and explain how I fucked up so badly, but I had nothing to say. I already agreed with him.

I fucked up.

"I have a few questions, if I may." Headmaster Drakos steepled his fingers, then laid them down, pointing his fingers like arrows at my heart. "Why did you not recognize the smell and therefore the child for what it was? Sulfur is quite distinctive."

"I..." My gaze drifted down to my bloody fingers. I flinched. "I just thought the child smelled bad from soiling itself. I've never come across a tenebrae demon. I didn't know the smell of sulfur revealed them."

Three stony faces stared back at me. "I dare say, very few people have come across a tenebrae demon, Miss Galanis." Drakos's rich tenor flowed soft and slow like the river along a stone bed. "Even fewer have lived to tell about it. The demon spirits are so dangerous, learning how to identify and avoid them is a part of the standard curriculum in every schoolhouse, in every town, village, and city in Olympia. Did you not attend school?"

The question was asked in an even tone, but the way the three of them towered so dominating and judging gave me pause.

"I... I did," I got out. "Up to the age of ten. Then I... couldn't continue."

"Why is that?"

I said nothing.

Drakos dipped his head and a band of silver-and-black locks fell over his brow. That silver sprinkled heavily through his hair, beard, and mustache, but it did not age him. No, it somehow only served to add distinction to a young man's handsome face—telling the world as his other features couldn't that he was a man of experience and authority.

"Alright, let us put that aside for the moment," Drakos continued. "When you were in the forest clearing your head, and you heard this child's cry, why didn't you question the odd circumstances you found yourself in? Did you truly think that on the first day of training—after the school had been closed to all but instructors for months—that a heavily pregnant novice walked in, gave birth in the woods, and then ran off to join her class as if nothing happened?"

My cheeks burned. "The child looked a few months old. I thought— A girl could've—"

"—brought a child through the gates and then abandoned them without anyone noticing?" he finished. "Or did you think one of my instructors decided to do away with a child?"

I couldn't answer. Stupidity burned hot and flush beneath my skin. He was right. If I had stopped and thought for a single moment, I would've realized something wasn't right. And Galen would be alive.

"No response? Very well, let's continue to my last, and most pressing, question. What reduced that demon to pieces and smears on my atrium, Aella Galanis—captured traitor and confessed non-demigod?"

"*Oh, do, please, tell them.*" She giggled. "*Let me have my fun tonight. Gift me the tainted, parasitic hearts.*"

"I don't know." I balled my fists to stop them shaking. "It attacked Galen. I went to help him and turned my back on the horrid thing. The next thing I knew it was bits and blood. I didn't see who did it. I'm just glad they did."

His gaze hardened. Rising from his seat, Drakos leaned over and snatched my hand. The moonlight cast its unforgiving truth on the black-and-red stains. "Turned your back, you say. You are lying to me, Aella Galanis—"

"No—"

"You will be silent." He didn't shout or raise his voice, and still, he quieted me better than if he had. "You are a liar. Whether you are lying to conceal the truth of your power, the truth of what you did to Galen Teresi, or lying to hide both remains to be seen. I have no patience for liars, Miss Galanis. We are in a war for our very survival, and if we cannot trust the soldier standing beside us, we've already lost."

His midnight-black eyes bore holes through mine. "I will give you one last chance to share why you did not finish your education, how you could enter my school so ignorant of the monsters around you and the tricks they play, and who really killed that demon." My palm slipped through his grasp. "I'm listening."

Holding his gaze, not a word passed through my lips.

Drakos gave nothing away as the silence pressed. He simply watched me from across the divide—all but his eyes cloaked in shadows.

I jumped when he spoke. "Stavra, it seems Miss Galanis isn't in the mood to be forthcoming. Kindly escort her to the reflection room where she'll have the clarity to think on what we've discussed, and hopefully make a different choice."

"Yes, Headmaster." Rounding the desk, she held out an arm. "Come, Aella."

I leaned away from her. "Go where? What's the reflection room?"

"It's exactly what it sounds like. A place where you can think without distractions. The commander can come with us, if you like."

"Oh... Okay," I said, resting my palm on her wrist.

We were a quiet trio leaving the headmaster's office and walking down another oppressively white hallway. The clash was even more glaring after sitting in the dim, black-and-gray hole known as the headmaster's office.

Madame Remis led us out into the main hall, then through the doors hiding the classrooms. This corridor was much like the dorm hall. It narrowed to push us closer together.

"This way."

Battle Strategy. History. Self-Mastery. Combat. Field Medicine.

I read what my missing course schedule had yet to tell me—the lessons I'd be taking at the academy. In a few hours, I'd pass through these doors again with my classmates, and we'd be one short.

Tears prickled behind my eyes. I was completely human. Completely Aella. And I still got a man killed. Apparently I didn't need to be a monster to hurt my people.

I was a danger to them all by myself.

"Why did you not recognize the smell and therefore the child for what it was?"

I didn't know. I swear I didn't know, Galen. I'm so sorry.

We came to a stop in front of a small, wooden door wholly out of place among all the stone, marble, and white. Madame Remis gestured for me to go ahead of her. "Careful on the steps."

Her warning was understood with a single look down, down, down. A spiral staircase twisted through the bowels of the school, leading to what—I couldn't see.

"What's down there?" I asked, backing away.

She smiled at me. "The reflection room, Aella. As we said. No one is trying to trick or scare you." Remis gently pressed on my back, moving me on. "After you."

I thought about arguing, but in the end, I picked up my feet and continued down. A place to sit and think didn't sound so bad right now. It'd give me time to think of a better explanation for Drakos when he asked how that demon died. It would also give me a chance to craft an apology that would never be good enough for the guy who cradled Galen's body, yelling for his brother.

Another small wooden door awaited us at the bottom of the stairs. I was the one who opened it, setting foot inside a dim, windowless room—

—with nothing inside.

Well, not nothing exactly. There was a lone chair pushed against the wall beside a three-legged table. On it sat a covered plate and a goblet of water. Turning in place, I landed on the metal statue leaning on the opposite wall and kept going. There was nothing else to see.

"This is the reflection room?" My voice echoed strangely. "I'm meant to stay down here. For how long?"

Madame Remis's smile held. "Aella, please sit."

I did so, feeling more and more disturbed in the prison-cell space. Was this a trick? Was this where they were holding me until Jason returned with his twenty-man guard to take me to Kuna City? My stupidity got a Titan novice killed. If there was any reason Headmaster Drakos wouldn't want a traitor around, I just gave him one.

Commander Vasili enclosed us in, heightening my anxiety. What was this? Why was he so quiet and Remis so pleasant?

"Here. You must be hungry." Remis removed the top off the plate. "Novices often forget to eat in the bustle of the first day."

"No, thank you," I said as my stomach growled, betraying me instantly. A plate of seeded rolls taunted me—appearing as warm and fresh as if they were made and placed there minutes ago.

"If you won't have one, I will." Remis and Vasili claimed a roll. They ate them more happily than I was, sitting there with my vocal stomach. Hesitantly, I claimed one for myself.

"Now, then," Remis began. "You know why you're here. Questions have been called into your past. As well as the true circumstances behind Galen Teresi's death and the end of that demon. By the end of your reflection time, Headmaster Drakos expects full and honest answers to these questions, or there will be consequences. Is this understood?"

"Understood."

Drakos could have all the expectations he wanted. I would not tell him my past or what was done to me. Let me save one man's life that day.

"Do you like it?" Remis asked, gesturing to the roll. "It's Tantalean bread. It arrests your body's normal functions, and makes it so you don't need to eat or drink for a certain period of time."

My jaw froze.

"It also stops the need to expel waste."

"Excuse me?" I spat it on the ground. "Why would you give this to me!"

"Because," she said—still smiling, still pleasant. "You'll be down here for a while. Leaving you in need of food, water, and a bathroom is cruelty the likes of which only a monster would inflict. The bread allows you to reflect without endangering your well-being."

The *bread* spoiled on my tongue. "So it's true. You are trapping me in this room. Why call it a reflection room when there's already a name for it: prison cell."

"We are not trapping you in this room, girl," the commander said. He moved to the iron statue and flipped a latch I hadn't noticed before. The calm, immortal woman split from her body. "We're putting you in here. This is the reflection room."

Cold leeched into my bones.

"It's nothing like a prison cell."

Because it was even worse. Lethal sharp spikes lined her dark, hopeless insides.

The reflection room was an iron maiden.

"N-no," I whispered. "No! You can't put me in there. I won't go!"

I raced to the door, hand closing on—

"Sleep."

Black crowded my vision. The world went dark.

Alexander

"One day."

"Out of the question."

"One fucking day!"

I punched the desk. A candle wobbled, then tipped over, instantly catching the carpet alight. Drakos dumped a goblet of reddish liquid on the flames and extinguished them without a change in expression.

"Now that you've raised your voice and thrown a tantrum like a child, you've convinced me," he droned. "I'll saddle your pegasus myself."

"You piece of—" My hand snapped up—aimed and willing at his head. Now there was a reaction.

A deep, raspy laugh echoed through the too-dark room. "By all means, kill me, Mr. Damien. My replacement will only tell you the same thing. Novices may be granted leave from the academy in the event of an immediate family member's death. 'Like a brother to me' is not the same as a brother. You will not attend Mr. Teresi's funeral," he dropped. "If you attempt to flout this order by using your father's position or try to leave the academy without permission, you will be deemed a deserter. Do you understand?"

"Fuck you!" Rage swelled in my chest. Boiling, burning, biting worse than anything I'd ever done to man or monster. "I'm not deserting. It's one day. One day to lay my brother to rest."

Drakos lightly lifted his shoulders. "Do not think me unsympathetic. I lost many a brother-in-arms. Men and women I'd have given my life for, torn into pieces before my eyes. And do you want to know what I did? I stepped over their parts and kept fighting," he hissed. "The war doesn't stop while you weep by a gravesite. On the battlefield, you will not be given 'one day.' You should expect no such thing within these walls."

Control snapped. My power spilled through my body—sizzling and humming beneath my skin as living electricity rushed out to meet its own. To invite it to play. To invite it to burn.

To entice it to kill.

What kind of officious, heartless bastard denied someone the right to say a last goodbye to a man they've known since our time in the nursery wing? A man who saved my life.

These rules are stupid. They're idiotic and much too rigid! We're more than soldiers. We're people and we have the right to—

"Shouldn't such a strong supporter of the army understand the chain of command? Or do you believe every now and then, there's room for rebellion?"

The words pierced my mind—so sudden and unwanted, I jerked and dropped my hand. My power fled back to the depths where it lived—fading like the feel of the sun when you step inside.

What the hades was wrong with me? Drakos was worthless slime and his death wouldn't steal a minute of my sleep, but in that moment, it wasn't him that enraged me. It was the rules he vowed to uphold. The rules *I* vowed to uphold.

Since when do I rationalize like a traitor? I dropped hard in a chair. *What had a week in that woman's presence done to me?*

"It seems my execution has been scheduled for another day."

I ground my teeth. Killing him would not make me a traitor. It'd make me a hero. "Seems so," I returned. "My training is too important. Everyone must stay and carry out their duty." The words burned my lips.

"So, this is what we'll do. We'll hold a memorial here at the academy. A day of remembrance for Galen." I nodded to myself, easing as the plan to honor my brother came together. "A statue and a plaque will be erected in his honor. I'll send for the commission tonight. A decent child of Hephaestus will have it done in a week. That's when we'll hold it," I said. "Next week."

I pinned him with a look. "If you think of denying me this simple and reasonable request, I will hunt down everyone you love, know, pass by on the street, and boil their blood till Olympia is stained red. You can spend the rest of your days stepping over their parts."

His eyes glinted through the shadows. The only part of him I could clearly see... besides his smirk. "Do you think it wise to threaten me?" Hand moving slowly across the desk, he tapped a soft beat that sounded eerily familiar.

It occurred to me that I didn't know this man's power. At least it occurred to me for half a second. There was nothing he could do to me in the minuscule time he had before I exploded him all over the desk.

"I think it the wisest thing I've ever done."

If anything, Drakos's smirk widened. "I like you, boy. Like your spirit. Most walk through these doors and I know with a single look, they won't survive their novice year, let alone live to walk on a battlefield. But you..." He pointed through the dark. "There's a warrior's heart in your chest. And a killer's glint in your eye."

Said eyes hardened. I trusted he was seeing that glint then.

"You'll go far one day. Possibly further than your father *if*," he stressed ever so slightly, "you learn when it's time for strength, and when it's time for diplomacy. There's a reason the council allots me more money, leeway, and deference than suits them. Even they know not to push a man who's left no trace of the numerous assassins they've sent to kill me."

Our eyes locked across the divide. Neither speaking nor moving as the silence stretched. The guy didn't get this far by being pushed around by men twenty years his junior. I'd be impressed, if their heads didn't all pop the same way.

Drakos waved a hand, making me tense. "You may go."

I didn't move. "You haven't agreed to the memorial yet."

"Agreed?" His brow climbed so high it disappeared into the shadows. "I thought you were making demands, Damien, not pleading for agreement." He tsked. "How quickly you've fallen in my estimation. Seems you're not the warrior just yet."

My lips peeled back from my teeth. Drakos shifted the balance of power so swiftly, I asked myself if I ever had it.

"Permission is granted," he continued. "Galen Teresi was the first son of Kronos to come through these doors in fifty years. His was a rare and marvelous power that would've turned the tide in this war. Instead, he's lost to ignorance, carelessness, and a lack of training. A day of remembrance will be held if only so the students know and remember one thing: Olympia needs the academy. Without it, we're silly little waifs laying our heads between the maws of demons."

Silly little waifs. Finally, he brought her up so I didn't have to. "Where is Aella Galanis? I've looked for her. Burst into her dorm half a dozen times. Those Sisypheans all claim she never came back from talking with you."

"She was less than forthcoming answering my questions, so I gave her time to reconsider before we talked again."

"Where is she?" I hissed, eyes narrowing to slits. "I want to speak to her. Now."

"While she may be your responsibility, Galen Teresi was mine. No one speaks to her until I have the truth."

"What is she saying is the truth?" I growled when he didn't reply. "Tell me. I spent a week with her. At the very least I can confirm if your suspicions match mine."

Drakos leaned back, considering me. "What are your suspicions?"

Smart man. Won't let me see his cards until I reveal mine.

"There's more to her than she'll say," I forced out. "She's smart. Quick. She can hold her own in a conversation, but she could be from another dominion for the ignorance she displays of Olympia. I say things and she looks at me with true cluelessness. She led us on a desperate chase to the border, but when captured, she didn't put up a fight." I dipped my head. "That is until I sentenced her to come to the academy. The traitor's noose or the mundane dominion, she's not bothered about which she ends up in. But here... Aella does not want to be here."

He hummed. "Then, our suspicions do match. She claimed her lack of knowledge was the result of leaving school at the age of ten."

"Impossible. Ten-year-olds barely know their letters. If she didn't attend village schooling, then she was privately taught."

"A private tutor that left her woefully unprepared to survive in our world?" He shook his head. "Though, ignorance is not stupidity. Nor is it weakness. What was done to that demon after it killed Mr. Teresi..." Drakos let out a long, low whistle.

I mimicked him—leaning back in my seat and steepling my fingers. "Is there a question in there?"

"What is her power and why does she deny it? The report said she killed one of the guards transporting her in self-defense. Actually, self-defense was emphasized multiple times, but where it got vague were the details of the attack. How did she kill him?"

"He was torn to pieces," I dropped easily. "No part of him was left intact besides his heart."

If I expected a gasp, popped brows, or another whistle, I didn't get one. "Interesting."

"I thought so. It's a power we need in this battle whether she wants to be in it or not."

"I agree, but she goes so far as to risk hard labor by denying that power. She does not want to be here, with that I must agree. But how far would she go?"

I frowned. "What does that mean?"

"For a brief moment, I considered that last night wasn't an accident. It was an attempt to get her what she wanted. Either death or expulsion from the academy—"

"Hold on. An attempt to get what she wanted? How?"

He went on like I hadn't spoken. "But that would be a stretch. The girl carted around a tenebrae demon, carrying it dangerously close to her throat. There are less painful ways to commit suicide. She obviously didn't know what it was—"

I shot forward. "Wait. Did you say she carted around the demon?"

"That is exactly what I said. Miss Galanis was fooled by the shape-shifter into carrying it past the warding spells into the academy."

Pressure built against my eardrums, drowning my ears in a muffled world like the one I found at the bottom of Marsyas Lake.

"She was under attack by the dryads, and Mr. Teresi believed he was helping a student in need. When he got close enough to realize what she truly held—"

"It killed him." I couldn't tell if that was said by me. The pressure was building, and I was sinking.

Slowly, I straightened. "Thank you, sir. I understand the situation."

"Do you? Wonderful," he replied. "I intend to have the same clarity when next I speak to Miss Galanis."

"No need to wait. I'll tell you now." No, I couldn't mistake it. That growl was definitely me. "That traitorous liar got Galen killed. She will spend the rest of a long and miserable life wishing I exploded her in the poisoned mud. Do you have objections?" I was already across the room and strangling the doorknob. "I don't give a shit."

Aella

S weat trickled down my nose—slow, tickling, and unseen in the dark. To wipe it away was to line my prison with more shredded skin.

I shuddered, biting my lip hard. Pain sent a jolt to my brain and I peeled my eyes open. It made no difference to the dark, but falling asleep made a difference to my life.

That bread stopped me from feeling hunger, thirst, and the burning urge to pee. It did nothing to stop me from needing to sleep.

And that's by design. They want me to wobble on shaking legs, desperately fighting to stay awake while pointed sentries haunted the dark. After one night, anyone trapped in here is begging to give Headmaster Drakos everything he wants.

Don't let him break you. Stay awake, Aella.

Stay awake.

THE MAIDEN REVEALED her prize, and my blood graced the stone before me. I followed, collapsing in a heap on the ground.

"Get up, girl."

Commander Vasili grabbed my forearms. My blood slicked his hold, dropping me right back on the floor.

"Ahh!" Pain ravaged my entire front and the half of my face unfortunate enough to meet the spikes. "P-please... help..."

"I said get up."

I tried. Pushing up, my ruined hands dumped me flat. The world spun as two pairs of boots paused by either side of my head.

The commander and a man my double vision didn't recognize hooked me under the arms. I knew nothing other than I was moving. Leaving. My leather-wrapped toes knocked against each step as they carried me up.

I lifted my head and it lolled, tipping my chin to the ceiling. "How... long?"

I wasn't asking them. I was speaking to the shifting, morphing horror of the goddess. She was with me as the hours bled. Always with me, always laughing, but this time she didn't hurt me. I was in too much pain to feel more.

"Three days."

Cool air hit my face. A welcome gift before the wall of sound.

Voices. Stomping. Chairs scraping. Instructions shouted. It bowled me over, then under, making me squeeze my eyes shut at the sudden assault on my senses.

"—battle strategy."

"I have to study for this history test first. How about we...? Gods."

The voices, the stomping, the scraping, the shouting—all stopped.

"Who is that?"

"Where did she come from?"

"Reflection room." "Reflection room." "Reflection room."

The name bounced off the walls in every direction and stuck to me. It lingered on me long after they faded.

Along the marble floor, my toes dragged, trailing the way to Headmaster Drakos's office. My eyes adjusted over the threshold. The sun must've been high outside, but it was near pitch black in here.

Drakos stood behind his desk, Madame Remis by his side.

"Welcome, Miss Galanis. Please, join us."

Vasili and his friend dropped me on my ass before them. I screamed myself hoarse.

My back was no less mangled than my front. That's what happened when panic turns to fear... and I change. The beast—so much bigger than I could be—grew in our cage and impaled herself on a hundred spikes, thrashing in rage. At least that's what I had to assume when my mind returned and I was bleeding from everywhere. It's only because of what the goddess made me that I was still alive.

Barely.

"H-h-help."

"Help is here," said the blurred outline of Madame Remis. "I am a child of Asclepius, Aella. I can make those wounds vanish as though they were never there, taking the pain with it."

"If," Drakos said slowly, "you tell me everything. Who are you, Aella Galanis? What is your power and why do you deny it?"

I swallowed through a dry, scorched throat. "Help," I pled to the goddess. She twirled and skipped around the room, her face changing each time our eyes met. If she didn't want anyone to know her secrets, why didn't she act? Why didn't she free me? Why didn't she stop this?!

"Miss Galanis." A voice reached me from a faraway place. "Aella, are you listening?"

"Help me," I screamed at her. "Please!"

"Aella, help is here." Murmuring sounded in my ear. "Madame Remis, help her focus."

A cool hand rested on my forehead. The effect was instant.

Foggy thoughts cleared away, taking with it an aching pressure headache. I could see and think, and I knew one thing without looking for her.

The goddess wasn't there. She never was. I was screaming at a delusion.

Dear gods. I lurched away from Remis, head swinging as I gaped at them in horror. *What had they done to me?*

"Monsters."

"Not quite." Drakos had all the inflection of someone talking about the weather. "Tantalean bread lets you go days without food because it suspends your ability to die. True monsters wouldn't grant such courtesy. I'm not your enemy, Miss Galanis. The issue now is... are you mine?"

"I've done nothing." My cry was a thin rasp. "Nothing to deserve this."

"You're a traitor and a deserter."

"Not anymore," I forced through clenched teeth. "I'm here. I'm serving my *sentence*. What more do you want from me?"

He interlocked his hands and placed them on a text covered in ancient writing. It was older than Greek, and unrecognizable to me. "Is that how you see your place here? As a sentence? A punishment?"

I scoffed. "He asks this while I bleed on his rug!"

"Watch your tongue, girl."

Drakos raised a hand, staying Vasili. "The reflection room certainly hasn't dampened your fire. Good. Truly, it is," he said to my narrowed brows. "It is a weak and useless soldier that breaks so easily. People think my goal as leader is to extract unwavering obedience, and they are correct. But that obedience is not to me. It is to Olympia. Your faithfulness to her must be unwavering.

"You have that strength, but it is misplaced," he said softly. "It is to your secrets and your misguided notions of personal rights. Once we channel that strength where it belongs, you'll be magnificent, Aella.

"But that takes time. For now, I will ask you questions that I expect you to deny or evade. You will not be beaten on the third day. No," he said, smiling the first true smile I witnessed on his face. "Not you."

My head spun, and it wasn't due to the sleep deprivation. Drakos was complimenting me—in the most frightening way possible. I heard the subtext in his words clear as day. His job was to break me, and he had every intention of doing so.

"I... I..."

"Why did you stop attending school after the age of ten?"

My lips parted but nothing came out. I knew what I had to say, and I had a feeling so did Drakos. Why did it feel like a test I was meant to fail?

Doesn't matter if it is. Cracking that door would let the flood through. Explaining why my life ended at ten would lead to more questions. Answering would entice even more than those. He'll keep asking, I'll keep lying, and the vicious circle would never end. There's only one thing I can do.

I picked up my screaming body and leaned over the desk. "None of your business."

Drakos practically beamed. "Commander. Proficient Antole. Please escort Miss Galanis back to the reflection room."

I was screaming before he finished the sentence.

FOUR DAYS LATER, I told him everything he wanted to hear.

"Why did you stop attending school after the age of ten?"

Madame Remis's power stole the fog, the delusions, and the headache, but it didn't touch the pain. That was mine to keep until I answered all of their questions.

"When... When..." I licked cracked lips and tried again. Drakos, Vasili, and Remis made no move to rush me. It was just the four of us once again. "When I was ten, my town was attacked..."

"Attacked by what?" Drakos pressed.

Tears cut tracks down my blood-caked cheeks. So much for my strength and fire. In the end, it only took one week.

"A lamia."

Drakos and Remis shared a look. Vasili visibly stiffened. I knew the question on their minds before Drakos voiced it. "How did you survive?"

"I didn't," I croaked. "When the child devourer came to Port Delphin, snatching children from their beds, she spared one child. Took that child away with her and disappeared." I met their eyes. "Me."

"Impossible."

"Unheard of."

"More lies," Vasili barked. "A week in the room has taught her nothing. Enough with these games, turn her over to me. She will learn the consequences of insubordination."

I shuddered and pain racked my body. Was he claiming the last week was not a consequence? What more could they do to me?

"I'm not lying! I remember that night like it happened moments ago. Mama was telling me the story of Olympia while the battle raged outside. That's what they ordered mothers to do. Stay inside and protect your children while the rest fought." My eyes glazed—memories transporting me to that night. "I was just lying there like a little fool, clutching my doll when she burst in and about threw Mama through the wall.

"She took me just like that. Didn't pause. Didn't threaten. One moment I was in bed, the next I was screaming through her claws while she tore out of town, escaping to the mount—"

Vasili seized my chair arms, wrangling me around to face him. My eyes widened in his bulging, red-faced reflection. "Lamias do not leave a single child alive! They are descendants of the very first lamia. A queen who caught the eye of Zeus. Hera discovered their affair and killed the children of their union. Not satisfied with that terrible punishment, she turned the queen into a beast and cursed her to never sleep, so she'd spend every tortured waking moment mourning her loss.

"This drove her insane and she became the most loathsome, abhorrent monster to ever spawn!" Spittle dotted my cheek. "Never in the history of Olympia has a lamia spared a child. I will hear no more of your lies, girl. Tell us the truth, and do not dare to make me ask again."

I was proud of myself. I held his gaze for a full beat before turning away. "You can yell and threaten me all you like, but my answer will not change. You wanted my story, here it is. Will you listen or not?"

A firm hand grasped Vasili's shoulder. Remis moved him to the side and stood between us for good measure. "Explain. We're listening."

I took a deep breath, piecing together the remains of my resolve. I couldn't hide anymore... because I couldn't go back in that room. "Olympians don't know as much about lamias as they think. We see one, we kill it immediately to protect the children. There's no stopping to chat.

"Lamias aren't just descendants of that first mad queen. All of them, each and every one, were human. They were mothers." Drakos's face changed, but he didn't interrupt. "Like typhons sire more sons from pieces of their own body. Lamias use their devastation to birth their daughters—born from the loss of their children."

"Why is this relevant?" Drakos asked.

"Because they remember," I cried. "They remember their kids and how they came to be. They know they once lived a normal life and were then turned into a beast compelled to make all mothers suffer the way they suffer. Lamias *don't* kill every child they see. Do not misunderstand me. They kill most of them, but once in a while, they come across a babe that looks so much like the one they lost. They take them believing they've been given a second chance."

Remis shook her head. "If lamias were kidnapping children, we would know. Their parents would stop at nothing to get them back."

"Of course," I rasped, voice dull. "That's why they slaughter everyone in the house. I told you the first thing she did was put my mother through a wall. And since lamias... eat... their victims, no one was looking for my body. No one was coming after us."

Remis leveled me with a long, assessing look. "Can this be true, Headmaster?"

"Of course it's not true," Vasili burst out. "It's a clever tale she knows we can't prove or disprove. Where are all these children that have supposedly been taken? Why is this the first we're hearing of it in two thousand years?"

"I will explain if you'll let me." I swung between the three of them. "All of this is so simple. That's the worst part. How easy it was for her to destroy my life."

Drakos gave a sharp, short nod. *Continue.*

"Lamias make their nests at the peaks of the highest, most treacherous mountains. They scuttle over those sharp rocks and fatal drops like it's nothing. Might as well be lizards climbing a wall." That day came in sharp clarity. I was so terrified my throat seized. I couldn't even scream as she carried me higher and higher. "Only flying demigods could make it up there, and the one time someone did, he didn't survive to tell anyone of the trip."

"That's where you've been the last eight years?" Remis asked. "In a lamia's mountain nest."

I nodded and received a derisive scoff from Vasili. "It was awful. The air was so thin, for three days I whimpered on the cave floor just trying to breathe."

"Forgive me," Remis broke in. "I don't wish to call you a liar, but you give no sign of someone who's spent almost a decade trapped in a mountain cave alone with a monster. You're bright, confident, well-spoken, and not easily intimidated. I'd have an easier time believing you spent the last eight years on the Isles of Paradise, inhaling nectar."

"I didn't say she mistreated me." The low rasp spread through the room. "And I never said I was alone."

Drakos leaned back in his chair, hiding his face in shadows. "Explain."

"There were other girls in the cave. Three," I admitted. "She doted on us. Believed we were her children returned, so anything we wanted, she went out and got for us. Books, toys, food, treats, clothes. Anything except our freedom."

"Who were these girls?" Remis asked.

"The lamia—" I would not call her Mother. Even though she made me for eight long years, she would not get that title now that I was finally free of her. "The lamia called us Penelope, Lyra, Agnes, and me, Cora. But when she was gone, we talked about who we truly were and where we came from. Iris of Solona, Evangeline of the Isle Amara, and Chloe of Port Melpo.

"In that dark, lonely cave, we kept each other's spirits up. Iris taught us from the books. Evangeline played dolls with me. Chloe told us of the home we'd have together after we were free. That's all we did was plan for our freedom." My gaze sharpened. "For the day the army would finally come and rescue us. The others refused to believe that day wasn't coming."

"It did not come," Drakos said, "and yet here you sit. How did you escape? Did she let you go?"

"She let us all go," I whispered, eyes welling. "On Iris's, Evangeline's, and Chloe's eighteenth birthday, she let them go... right over a cliff."

A thick, suffocating silence filled the room.

"She killed them," Remis said. "The children you said she doted on. The ones that brought her dears back to her. Why on earth would she do such a thing?"

My lips trembled. Echoing through my mind were the screams of my only friends. My sisters. "They weren't her little girls anymore. What use is a child when they become an adult?"

Remis flicked off me, gazing at the commander.

I continued. "As my eighteenth year approached, I prepared to die too, but when the day came—"

"Careful, little one. Loose tongues become forked ones all too easily. You quite rudely fear my true, divinely beautiful form. All I need ever do is appear before you, and you are my pet once again."

I breathed slow through my nose. I didn't need the warning, but I would tread carefully all the same. I remember well what she made me do to the first and last person I told my story.

"Yes?" Drakos pressed.

Quickly, I cast about for something. *Anything.* "When the day came, I made a bargain with her. If she spared my life, I would go out and find her new daughters. Her Penelope, Lyra, Agnes, and Cora. I swore to her it would only take me thirty days. When I returned with the girls, she would have her family and I'd have my life. She agreed, but swore to me that if I betrayed her, she'd hunt me to the ends of Olympia and devour me slowly—one appendage a day."

Understanding dawned in Remis's eyes. "That's why you ran."

Thank gods she said it so I didn't have to. "Yes," I replied without hesitation. "I was never going through with that bargain. I spent my thirty days gathering supplies, then hitching a ride on any mode of transport that'd get me to the border. Don't you see? I can't stay here anymore.

"I'm a stranger in this land now. I don't know how to live or fight in Olympia. I'm marked by one of the most dangerous creatures in the land, so any village, town, or city I hide in becomes the target of a beast that kills and eats *children*. Tell me what choice I have?" I looked in each of their eyes. "Demigods don't know much about lamias, but I can tell you this. They never, *ever* forgive."

Drakos hummed low in his throat. "It is a strange predicament you are in. It is certainly the first time a deserter has brought me a reason that is—dare I say—noble."

"All I want to do is protect my people. I know what it's like when a monster takes everything from you."

"If what you say is true, and you spent the last eight years in a cave with books and another child as a teacher, that would explain your ignorance and why you didn't grasp the seriousness of your actions. Desertion is unacceptable even under the noblest of intentions. What you should have done is report straight to the army the second you secured your freedom."

Remis came alive, flicking from the commander to Drakos. "I doubt her monstrous foster mother taught her the army were the people she could trust. She was alone and scared and possessed a story even I'm still struggling to believe. In every true sense, life ended for her eight years ago. She is still that ten-year-old child, Matthias. She did what any child would do—run away."

"You say you're still struggling to believe her, but sounds to me that you do." Drakos was still hidden in the shadows.

"You read the report on her only last night." She dropped a sheaf of papers in front of him. "Aella Galanis: Deceased. She was presumed dead along with thirty-two other children murdered the night a lamia attacked Port Delphin."

I shot up in my seat and pain stabbed me from everywhere. "Wait. You already knew about the lamia? Then why do you say you don't believe me?!"

"I believe a lamia attacked your home," Drakos returned, pushing the papers aside. "I'd also believe your mother fled into the night with you and escaped on a dinghy that carried you both to a far-off isle. Where belief fails me is that there are survivors of lamia attacks stashed away on the highest mountain peaks, and no one discovered this for over a thousand years."

"I—"

"That's what makes her story believable," Remis cut in. "She could've told us a hundred tales we would've swallowed without question. She and her mother escaped. Trauma made them reclusive. The list goes on. Instead she tells us about a doting lamia and a cave of orphaned girls. All things we have no reason to believe, so it must be true."

"So, you have no more questions," the commander growled, making me jump. "The first thing she does is run away? It didn't occur to you to report your tale. Give hope to other grieving parents that their children may be alive out there and waiting to be rescued? Did you not think of that at all? Answer me, girl!"

He clamped my shoulder, ripping a scream from my lips.

"Commander, I must insist you calm down," Drakos said as Remis pushed him away from me. "Miss Galanis will answer every question put to her. There is no need for impatience."

There was a brief pause, that he expected me to fill. I clutched my shoulder—chest heaving through the blinding pain. "I did report it! The first town I stumbled into, I met a kind couple who took me in. They fed me, nursed my cut feet, and told me of the world today.

"I was in a bad way, but I kept trying to leave. Finally, I told them a lamia kept me captive for years and I was eager to get back to my family. Mr. Raptis and his wife waved me off, promising to send a letter to the nearest battalion that there were lamias holding captive children. I had no reason to think they wouldn't."

"If such a letter was sent, it would've reached as high as the council," Drakos said.

"Maybe. If the person who received it bothered to pass it on. It could've been tossed out and ignored. After all, it's been thousands of years. You would *know* if lamias were kidnapping children."

"Watch your lip," Vasili snapped. "It's easy enough to find out if such a letter ever existed. Where was it sent?"

I told him the battalion, the couple, and the village they lived in. There was no harm in doing so. They would question Mr. and Mrs. Raptis and receive the same story. I told them about my years with the lamia and no more—too afraid was I of the goddess to break her confidence. It was the next kind soul that I told the whole truth. No one would be asking him any questions.

"Okay, Miss Galanis. You were trapped in a cave with a lamia for almost a decade. When you escaped, you ran away to spare your life and the lives of those around you," Drakos said. "Let's say for now that's the truth. Am I also to believe Iris, Evangeline, and Chloe had no power? Surely at least three of you had means to escape."

I didn't miss the slight emphasis on three, or the disbelief throughout the entire question.

Didn't take us long to get to what he truly wants to know.

"It took every able-bodied man and woman in my village to fight one lamia, and they still failed. What were daughters of Athena, Hestia, and Apollo supposed to do? If we fought her, she would've thrown us out the cave mouth. Rebellion wasn't worth it. Not when we still believed one day she'd free us."

"But why wait for such an unlikely show of mercy?" Drakos's words slid out of the dark. "Why not render her into pieces as you did the guard that dared mistreat you?"

I tensed. *There it is. He finally asks.*

"*Now what will you say?*" she teased for my ears alone.

"Even if I had such a power, killing her while we were trapped on top of that mountain was suicide. She was the only access to food and water. She was the only one who could get us down."

"Fair enough. Your power had to be stifled for your own safety. Possibly the first time you used it deliberately was in that cell."

"I don't—"

Drakos shot forward. "Think carefully before you utter another syllable. There are worse things within these walls than the reflection room."

My weakened body shook. I feared him, but not as much as I feared *her*.

Eyes widening, I shot to my fingers gripping the chair arm. Beneath the blood, they were turning black.

No, no! My fear of the consequences of lying to him was combating my fear of telling him the truth. Oh the fucking irony.

"I don't have power," I blurted. "Your threats and torture chambers cannot change that. Call a child of Hecate. Call a child of the goddess of truth. I'm not a demigod."

"Then how did a soldier die in your locked cell? How did the demon?"

I said the truest thing I ever would. "They were killed by a monster. That monster wasn't me." Laughter rang in my ears. "Give me any amount of truth serum you desire. My answer will not change."

"Hmm. I can see we're hitting a wall, Miss Galanis. One you've dug yourself under quite nicely," Drakos clipped. "You've made your bluff. Now it's up to me to call it or give proof you're still lying."

"Of course she's lying." Purplish veins shone stark on Vasili's forehead. "If this was happening, we would know. If he was taken or killed, I would know!"

Remis cupped his cheek. My brows popped at such an intimate gesture. "Maybe not, Leonidas. The lamia attacked your home while you were miles away across the sea. If it took Philo, you weren't there to see—"

"Stavra!"

"—and doesn't that give us hope," she continued, raising her voice. "Hope when we had none at all. There's a chance he's out there somewhere. If it takes rooting out every lamia nest in Olympia, we won't stop until we've found Philo, or destroyed the monster who took him."

He shook off her grasp, lines hardening around his weary, grizzled jaw. "She has not given me hope. I can swear to you that of all the things this girl did here today, giving hope to those grieving families was not one of them."

Vasili slammed out the door. The force rattled books off Drakos's shelves.

"I know I haven't given hope," I said softly. "When the truth comes out, parents will drive themselves mad wondering if their children were spared. They'll risk life and limb to bring them home. That's if it's not already too late. Anyone who remains of Iris's, Chloe's, and Evangeline's families can now suffer the guilt of knowing they were waiting for them to save us... and they never came."

Remis made for the door. "I need to speak to him."

"One moment, Stavra." Drakos halted her in her tracks. "Miss Galanis has missed a week of training. I'm certain she's eager to return to her classmates—whole and ready to do her duty."

Hold on. Was he saying that I could...?

I didn't have to voice the question. Madame Remis laid her hand across my forehead again. A cool trickle spread through my body, taking the pain with it. I blinked and the endless stab wounds were gone.

"I don't understand," I said as Stavra shut the door behind her. "That's it? You're done questioning me?"

"I am."

I remained seated. "What about Galen? What about training? I'm not lying," I repeated. "I don't have powers and I won't live as a fraud, pretending I do. What am I to do for the next four years?"

"Galen Teresi was a tragic death that could've been avoided. One of the most powerful demigods to step through these doors—snuffed out for no reason at all."

"Not no reason," I said, dropping my gaze. "He didn't know it was a trick when he risked his life for me. Galen died a hero."

"Galen died for a know-nothing coward and traitor."

I blinked. What did he say?

"There was a question I didn't ask you, Miss Galanis, because now I know." Drakos rose to his full, imposing height. "You were out there alone in the forest because you were looking for a way over the fence. Don't deny it," he hissed, snapping my opening mouth closed. "You are a child, Aella Galanis. Running from the devastation in your wake instead of standing your ground.

"I was wrong about your strength, but not about your character. A promising future soldier was snuffed out for nothing... because he died protecting you."

I sank lower and lower in my chair. As low as my sinking heart.

"I do not want you in my academy. If I had my way, I'd execute you on the spot and save Trono the trial. You're not worthy to walk these hallowed halls among true warriors—each of them ready to fight to the end."

I shot out of my seat. "I am willing to fight. All I've been doing is fighting! What don't you understand? If I don't get out of here, I'll be the death of you all!"

The goddess chuckled. "*And I'll have you start with this interesting fellow. Such a nasty power he has. That'll make it so much more fun when it fails him against my pet. The best soldiers of the Olympian gods all falling at the feet of my little beastie.*

"*So much fun.*"

"Nonsense." Drakos waved a hand as if swatting my fears from the air. "We are not a school full of children. No lamia could make it past the barrier spells, and if it did, it'd be killed before it reached the steps. You'd have known that if you'd spared a second from your *noble* flight to trust the comrades you claim you're protecting."

Frustration exploded from my chest. "You have no idea," I shrieked. "No idea what I've gone through to protect Olympia. No idea of the sacrifices I'm still willing to make. I won't be judged by a pompous, soft-bottomed schoolteacher who speaks of battle while he sits safe behind his barrier spells!"

I knew it was the wrong thing to say the second it was out of my mouth. I'd seen very few emotions on the headmaster's face in the short time I knew the awful man, but as long as I lived, I prayed to the gods that I'd never again see that look.

"This pompous, soft-bottomed schoolteacher knows more of battle than you learned while sucking at your mama's teat, then whining for more as you cowered at the back of the cave." Drakos moved around the desk—a slow, deliberate movement that sent me running to the door—scrabbling at the knob. My talons dug deep grooves in the wood.

"Go ahead and run, little Aella. There are worse things within these walls."

I threw it open, tearing out.

"One way or another, my judgment is delivered."

Sebastian

I stopped dead on the staircase. "She said what?"

"Called him a pompous, soft-bottomed schoolteacher."

My brows shot up my forehead and disappeared into my hairline—as fast as I hoped Aella Galanis ran.

A low whistle cut through my lips. "She truly doesn't know what that man can do. Does that make her brave or stupid?"

"It's never wise to insult someone with that much power over your life." Linus absentmindedly rubbed his side. "Although, I must say, I admire her all the same. Seven days in the reflection room. They dragged her out of there on the edge of death, and still she told that bastard exactly what she thought."

"Yes, but did she tell him the truth?" I resumed my climb, enduring the stone walls brushing my shoulders as the staircase narrowed. "Do we believe this story of living as a lamia's captive pet for eight years?"

"It's so absurd it must be true."

"Find out for certain."

He snapped to his full six feet, seven inches. "Yes, my lord."

"And the guard in the cell," I mused. "I want every detail of what happened there."

"Surely we know, my lord. She killed him with a power she doesn't want revealed."

"Not a power," I said with surety. "Demigods glow with divinity. One drop of essence on their souls transforms them from the tips of their hair to their toenail clippings. It doesn't hide itself, unlike whatever's inside her. It's a flicker out of the corner of your eye. It's the black spots in your vision—there and not there. The wrongness of it almost forces me to look away."

I paused near the top. "She is hiding it for a very good reason, but her secrets won't be kept from me."

"You may not want to know her secrets, my lord. When your instincts say to turn away, it's because there's a battle ahead you're not prepared to fight. It might not be stupidity that gives the girl the confidence to face down a man like Drakos. One thing we do know is that people around her tend to die."

Humming, I continued up to the top of the tower. A gust of air swept my hair back and whipped it against the wall. The slight sound made him jump.

"Easy," I said. "Not a great place to get jumpy."

"You're telling me." He laughed—a strange one where his teeth didn't part. The chuckle simply hissed through them. "Didn't know anyone came up here. I'm always alone."

The guy sat atop the parapet, reclined within the gaps of the battlement. He was a year older than me and in his competent year, but youth clung to his round cheeks and floppy brown hair blowing in the wind.

"Is this the guy?" I asked.

"It's him," replied a younger, softer voice.

Nodding, I stepped into the light.

"This is a nice spot to think." My gaze swept the wide expanse of soaring towers and swaying trees. "Quiet. Secluded. You could scream and the wind would steal it away before it reached anyone on the ground."

"Uh, I guess." He laughed that odd laugh again. "Never thought of it like that, but I do agree with the quiet and secluded part, so if you don't mind..."

I smiled. "Not at all, Giles."

"How do you—?"

I shoved him off.

Leaning against the merlon, I followed his screams and his fall all the way down until both came to a sharp and sudden end.

"People die around her, do they?" I winked at Linus. "They say the same about me."

Aella

"Just stay close to us, okay? Strength in numbers."

"Strength in numbers?" I chuckled. "Are we under attack?"

Tycho, Nitsa, Theron, Ionna, and Daciana did not laugh with me. Nitsa moved around the couch, stepping in my bolt hole. "Aella, you missed a lot this week, including what people are saying about you. The whole school blames you for Galen's death."

My lips pressed in a thin line. "They should," I croaked. "It was my fault."

"I would not repeat that to anyone outside of this dorm," Theron said. "Don't give them any more ammunition."

"I own my mistakes, Theron."

"But not your accidents. Not this one, Aella." Grasping my shoulders, he made me face him. "Galen was the son of a former councilman. There were rumors that he would become the first child of a Titan to take a seat on the council. His powers were that rare. That powerful. You have no idea the hope he brought to the army.

"Imagine a battle where you can just freeze the typhon, lop off its head, and then everyone heads to the tavern for drinks and cards. Galen was going to turn the tide—spare the soldiers countless casualties... and now he's dead."

"Dead because he tried to help a girl who..." Nitsa trailed off. "Well, they're saying a lot of things about you, Aella."

"Like what?"

"Things that can't be true," she said firmly. "I knew you were a good person from the first day I met you. The Titans are spreading a bunch of lies to whip up the hate against you—"

"—so don't make it easy for them," Theron finished. "Stick close to us. Sisypheans look out for each other."

"Thanks, guys." I finished packing away my last notebook and hitched my bag on my shoulder. According to our schedule, we had battle strategy, history, self-mastery, field medicine, and combat training that day, the day after, and the day after that. From sunup to sundown five days a week, there was no letting up in our training.

"Why is this window blocked out?" I asked as we piled out of the dorm. "After lunch, there's an hour and a half before we report to field medicine. Do we have a break?"

Tycho snorted. "No. It's a special class for the Titans. Children of the same god get together and form battle strategies that play off one another's strengths. You know, if one child of Poseidon can create water out of the air, but the other can only draw from a source. Put them together and they're unstoppable.

"The Sisypheans don't participate," he said. "But we still have to watch. So no, not a break."

"Got it." I filled it in on my calendar. The majority of these classes I'd have to just sit through and endure, but two could be useful to me: field medicine and history.

The lamia brought books of all kinds, but none that praised gods or denounced monsters. If there were books on spells, potions, enchantments, or medicines that tamed a beast, I did not see one in the last eight years. As for knowledge of all the gods and goddesses that once ruled the heavens, earth, and underground—cursing humans to turn into monsters or shunning monster gods. The lamia wasn't handing that over to us either.

My first step was finding out who the goddess is. Was she another monster goddess like Echidna, the mother of monsters? That would explain why she had such a hatred of the gods.

But then I never heard of Echidna's descendants doing the things she could do. They don't change form. They don't prey on minds or infect souls. If I was dealing with the original Echidna herself, why did she need me? She had hundreds of thousands of children ready and willing to kill demigods. They've been doing it for centuries.

Sighing, I scribbled notes, questions, and things to research on the back of my schedule. The only thing I knew for sure was that I didn't know enough. My knowledge of the gods was limited to the tales my mother told me, and the nice, sanitized history they told small children. I didn't know Medusa was cursed by Athena because Poseidon raped her. Not until the lamia told Iris why she should feel no pride at being a child of Athena.

No one could argue what the two of them did to that innocent woman was hideous. After being violated in the worst way, Athena comes along, turns her hair into snakes, steals her beauty, and gives her eyes that turn a man to stone. There were more than a few figures in history that had good reason to hate the gods, but which one of them was so wronged, they wanted every trace of them wiped from existence even if it meant slaughtering the innocents who housed a piece of their essence.

That's the bitch I needed to find and stop.

Together we entered the lecture wing, me bringing up the rear of the group.

"Did you finish Georgiou's paper? Man, he's going to have your ass."

Boots shuffled in and out of my peripheral vision. The hall was stuffed with students heading in every direction. We may have the same schedule, but there were many instructors teaching them. According to my schedule, I had battle strategy with Captain Hondros. Luckily for us, they handed out schedules by going down the dorm hall and giving out one set until they ran out and moved on to another set of instructors. Everyone in my dorm had the same classes.

"I will not wear those hideous colors. Tan pants won't stop a scylla from coming for my throat."

"But what if... Psst, Sirena, look."

"What the fuck? You've got to be kidding me?"

I can't narrow it down by gods who wield curses. Looks like they can all do that. The way her form shifts, changes, and burns. That has to be unique to her. I'll focus—

"I can't believe they're letting you walk the halls after what you did to Galen."

Boots shot into my path, pulling me up short. I lifted my head and met the curled lips of Sirena Cirillo, the girl who couldn't resist taking a parting shot at Nitsa when she showed her up in the stadium. But it wasn't her I landed on.

Riding her shoulder was the cutest little brown-and-white pygmy owl. The little puffball preened his or her feathers, looking as adorable as it knew it was.

"Cute bird," I said mildly. "Excuse me."

I tried sidestepping her and found her directly in my path. "You got a good man killed, worthless class. Xander, Calix, and Ajax are destroyed because of you."

"Sirena, leave it," Nitsa said, shoving between us. "It was an accident. Aella's destroyed over it too."

Sirena grabbed her face and tossed her aside. She was a fan of that move. "Don't speak to me, cow."

Nitsa stumbled, and came charging back. It happened so fast. I blinked and Siren's right hand was the taloned end of a dragon's arm. Nitsa froze, bulging orbs an eyelash's breath from those points.

"Hey," I cried. "What the fuck are you doing? Trying to kill someone! Put that away."

Sirena smirked. "I'm defending myself from an opponent who tried to charge me. Everyone saw it."

"Yep."

"That's what I saw."

"Insecure Sisypheans starting fights they can't finish."

I goggled at the pushing crowd... and the hostility on their faces. Nitsa started the fight? She wasn't the one who got in my face and started throwing people around. Were these guys serious?

"Look," I said slowly. "I made a mistake and a life was lost. You can't imagine the guilt I feel, and I can't imagine the pain of the people closest to him." I tugged Nitsa behind me and away from those claws. One after another, my friends moved to our side. "I make no excuses for what I did. I ask for no favors, but this... Threatening my friends. We're not doing this. If you've got a problem with me, deal with me."

Sirena laughed out loud. "Aww. Isn't she cute, Tawny?" she cooed at the bird, popping a kiss on her feathers. "Coming in here, doling out orders as if anyone gives a shit what she says."

The entire hall howled, including novices in the Sisyphean class. I was starting to think the only friends I had in this castle were standing next to me.

I matched her smile. "No one has to give a shit what I say. I don't need their attention nearly as much as you." Surprise cracked her mask of superiority for the barest second. She wasn't used to people speaking to her like that. "Now if it's okay with you, *o* great and beautiful Sirena. Will you move aside so we can get to class?"

The smirk melted off her face, winking out like the light behind her eyes. Snickers floated above our heads. Not just from my friends, but from a few of hers.

Sirena turned to go, and I picked up my notes to get back to my train of thought. A green flash swiped across my vision.

"Ahh!" Pain split my cheek—hungry and spreading through my face. I cupped my ravaged skin, feeling blood coat my palm like ink.

"Hey!"

"What the hell?!"

"Are you insane, Sirena!"

My friends rushed me, pushing me back and away from her. Through the gape in their bodies, I saw that smirk return.

"The great and beautiful Sirena grants your request." She mockingly curtsied. "You may go to class."

Giving us her back, she strode off to guffawing, pats on the back, and more than a few cheers. So this is what my friends were trying to say, but were too nice to come right out with it.

The whole school hates me.

"Aella, are you all right?" Daciana moved in my line of sight, sparing me one last look of Sirena disappearing into her class. "You should go to the infirmary."

"There's no need. The cuts are shallow. Besides, I've missed enough classes. I can't afford to miss any more."

"Take this." Tycho offered me a handkerchief. I accepted it with thanks, if only to wipe the blood off my hands. Sudden and unwanted changes made me cut myself with my talons more than once. This was an injury I was getting used to.

You'll have to do better than that to cow me. Maybe when the very sight of you makes me want to rip my eyes out and die, your little intimidation tactics will work.

Straightening my back, I brushed the incident off and returned to my notes. Until I found a way out of the academy, my focus was on breaking the chains around my soul before the goddess tightened them further.

Our group made for the classroom at the end of the hall, two doors away from the reflection room. Phantom pain ripped under my skin.

I didn't have to ask why the room was located here in the lecture wing for us all to see and pass by. Headmaster Drakos wanted to make sure we never forgot what awaited us if we defied him.

I followed my friends inside a dim, gas-lantern-lit room and confirmed beyond all doubt—the goddesses of fate hated me more than any being in all five dominions.

Sirena sat front row before the instructor. By her side, was Alexander Damien. I avoided her delighted grin and slid past the back of Alexander's head. Moving on, I landed on another familiar face. Sebastian Barba, son of Hades, was in this class too.

Wonder if he revealed these supposed magnificent powers in the last week?

Sebastian glanced up and locked eyes with me as the question floated out of my head. Icy-blue pools trapped me, holding me still in the middle of the aisle. No, it wasn't him that held me still. It was me. I didn't want to look away.

It wasn't that he was beautiful—because, gods above, was he. It was the swirling mystery behind those eyes. Sebastian gazed at me like he knew more about me than I did, and wouldn't I give anything to know how?

Fixed on me, Sebastian's hand moved across the desk—slow and soft like he was caressing it. Gripping the chair, he guided it back, then tipped his head.

Wait. He wants me... to sit with him?

My feet moved on their own power.

"Over here, Aella." Daciana hooked my arm. "Another of your customs. The two classes have to sit on opposite sides of the room."

She drew me farther and farther away from Sebastian. He watched me the whole time.

"Everyone, in your seats."

I claimed one between Theron and Daciana. Looking around, I noted all the things different from the little schoolhouse in Port Delphin, and came away with absolutely everything.

That classroom had rickety oak desks scribbled with profanity. Those bookshelves were empty from children forgetting to return their borrows. Ceilings were low and flat. Walls were wooden and shaken by even the slightest breeze. The wonders of the cooling system created by a daughter of Hephaestus and son of Boreas hadn't made it that far across the sea and away from the cities.

This room was made to be its opposite. High, sloped ceilings depicted a famed battle scene between its rafters. The round tables were ornate, sturdy creations that easily seated four people. Gray stone walls would not be flattened by a raging storm sent in from the sea—like ours was destroyed twice. And as for the cooling system, I drew my coat a little tighter—amazed just to see one in person.

Boreas was the god of the winter wind. With his power and a daughter of Hephaestus's ingenuity, they found a way to trap the winter wind in a contraption that would disperse and recycle it through the air. It was one hundred and fifty gold coins just to be in a room with one. Seriously, inns with cooling units in their rooms charged that much and more. Only the wealthy could afford them, and here I was in a school that had them in almost every room.

Outfit the place nicely so everyone forgets they're in a prison that intends to keep them for four years, then turn them out to serve the army for life.

"Quiet. We have much to review this morning." Captain Hondros moved out from behind his podium. It was the first proper look I got of him, and his missing arm.

He stood high, but not as high as Commander Vasili. A head shorter than him and stockier too. Muscles piled on top of his shoulders, arms, and stretched the calves of his pants. Hondros opted for the long ponytail like Sebastian, though his was a wave of curls like the ones hidden around Alexander's pointed ears.

Thinking of Alexander made me look at him. Looking at him pissed me off, so I flicked back to Hondros. There wasn't a scar or sign of violence on the parts of him not concealed by clothes. The sign that he may have seen hard times in battle was the limb cut off below the elbow. But I couldn't say for certain. He could've also been born without it.

Loam-brown eyes swept us as I did him. "I won't ask if you did the reading, because you wouldn't dare set foot in my classroom unprepared. We will review. You will answer every question correctly. If you do not, the entire class will be assigned a two-scroll paper on the correct answer due tomorrow. Am I clear?"

"Yes, Captain," everyone chorused.

"After review, you begin work on this week's assignment: a battle strategy against a group of Stymphalian birds using your group's unique powers. Shall we begin?"

"Yes, Captain."

Hondros plucked a clipboard off his desk. His workspace was no less impressive than ours. A podium, a desk, a worktable, bookshelves lined along one wall, and the other a collection of tapestries featuring more famous battles.

"Beginning here." Hondros pointed at Alexander. "What is a sphinx's weakness?"

"Knowledge. She will kill herself if you answer all of her riddles correctly."

A curt nod was his only praise for a job well done. "Cirillo, how would you identify the true form of an empousa?"

"By looking at it. Empousas are demons that take the form of beautiful women to lure foolish men to their deaths. They don't adopt these forms for women." Sirena tossed him a wink. "That's why you army boys can't ride without us. You need the girls to protect you."

That got a laugh out of the class and nothing from Hondros. He continued on, asking each student a question from the reading.

Hondros paused after Theron. Looking from the clipboard to me, the clipboard, then back to me. It was ridiculous to think my absence from his class would go unnoticed. The answer of if he knew why I was gone for a week was revealed in his growing frown.

"Galanis."

"Yes, sir."

"Captain," he barked.

"Yes, Captain."

"How do you kill a kampe?"

I scanned the depths of my knowledge, searching for one mention of a kampe from the many nights Iris read to us to take our minds off the dreary monotony of every day.

It turned up its answer. "I don't know what a kampe is, Captain."

A muscle ticced in his jaw. "Then, it's fortunate you'll learn what they are in the process of writing me a two-scroll essay. Same goes for the rest of you."

Groans tensed me in my seat. "Useless fuck! You can't read either?"

"Enough," Captain sliced in. "Next question, Galanis."

What? Me again?

"How do the offspring of the Calydonian boar differ from their forefather? Why does this trait make them harder to kill?"

I felt it coming before I opened my mouth. "I know of the monster boars, but I didn't know they were different from the first."

"Idiot!"

"Everyone knows this!"

"Captain, give the useless the essays, not us."

"It does not work like that," Hondros replied. "In battle, the failure of one brings the ruin of many. The death of Galen Teresi should have taught you that."

I sank in my seat, cheeks burning with shame. A glance at Alexander made me jerk. He was finally looking at me, and the expression on his face was more terrible to behold than Drakos.

Bloodshot eyes, washed-out skin, and eight tiny marks on his forehead like he'd get from clutching his face. This wasn't the unruffled, swaggering bastard I met on the road. I finally did to him as he did to me.

I broke him.

"You are responsible for each other now as you will be when you march side by side. Galanis had trouble reading. I'm certain you're all now motivated to help her learn what she must know before she enters my class again."

I could feel the hostility like a restricting band across my throat. I wanted to believe he wasn't inciting them to do what it sounded like, but this man didn't look naïve to me.

"Galanis," he continued.

I stifled my groan.

"Why are all harpies born insane?"

Tears stung my eyes. I never felt shame for the life I lived in the cave with Iris, Evangeline, and Chloe. Why should we be shamed when we'd done nothing wrong? And still I felt no shame after I escaped her clutches and found myself back in a world I didn't know anymore. There was no time for it while I was running as fast as I could to the border.

But right then, sitting in that room and being forced to say, "I don't know. I don't know" over and over as they heckled and called me stupid... I hated it more than a millennium in the reflection room.

"Galanis." Hondros's voice sharpened. "Answer me."

"I do—"

"Harpies are born mad because they're trapped here in Olympia with us." All heads swiveled around. "In the ancient times, they had the whole world as their hunting ground. A veritable buffet of evildoers to capture and torture as they hauled them screaming to Tartarus. Now there are only us demigods, and we fight back. They enter life knowing they'll spend their entire existence unfulfilled and unsatisfied," said Sebastian Barba. "Wouldn't that drive anyone mad?"

"Though your answer is correct, Barba, it was to come from her mouth, not yours. Do not speak out of turn again."

Sebastian tipped his head. "I'm confused. Didn't you just say we're all responsible for each other? She clearly didn't know the answer, so I helped out my fellow sister-in-arms."

"Be silent," he snapped. "Now, Galanis—"

That time I didn't stifle my groan. Daciana squeezed my hand under the table.

"I'm sorry," she whispered. "He'll just keep picking on you until you answer correctly. He put me through the same torture on the first day."

"Excuse me, wolf." Hondros stalked toward us. "Did you speak?"

Daciana stared him dead in the face. "Yes. I said you'll just keep picking on her like you did on my first day."

His face hardened. "Is that what you believe I'm doing? *Picking* on her."

"Absolutely," Sebastian called.

"I will not tell you again," Hondros roared, whirling on him. "Be silent."

Sebastian made a show of buttoning his lip. I blinked at him, eyes huge. What was with this guy? Hondros looked ready to tear that expensive cooling unit off the wall and beat him with it.

"The purpose is not to pick on you," he said, leveling us with that glare. "This information is vital. You cannot defeat a monster you do not know. Something as simple as knowing what the smell of sulfur means will save a life. Don't you agree, Galanis?"

My glare heated to destroy his. "Yes, Captain," I forced through gritted teeth.

"Next question. What do the three heads of a cerberus represent?"

They represented something? Mama only ever told me that the first one guarded Hades, and now his descendants guard places of importance—whether the locals wanted them to or not.

"I do—"

"The past, present, and future," said a voice becoming all too familiar with me. "That's why they're near enough to impossible to kill. One head sees everything you plan to do. You're dead from the moment you decided to attack."

If I thought his vein was jumping before, it was out of control then. "You're trying my patience, boy."

He shrugged. "You're trying mine. We all know she didn't do the reading because she spent the last week locked away in the reflection room. It has nothing to do with her work ethic and everything to do with the lack of light.

"You are picking on her, and my guess is it's because torturing students is the only thing that gets your blood pumping south ever since the battlefield chewed you up and spat you out."

Someone gasped. It was me. This was a different world from my schoolhouse. Back there, no one dared speak to an instructor that way.

"Out! Out of my classroom!"

Smirk hanging off his lips, he spread out his hands. "I'm sitting right here, waiting for you to make me."

Hondros advanced on him—fist raised to unleash a punch or his power, I couldn't tell.

"Stop!" I jumped up, toppling my chair. "It's my fault. I should've found you after I was released and asked what the assignment was. It's been a while since I've been in school— I didn't think," I rushed out. "I will answer the next question right, or I'll do ten scrolls for each one I've missed."

He turned on me, eyes bulging. I couldn't even be sure he heard a word I said. "You, your *protector*"—he spat the word—"and the entire class will give me twenty scrolls if you respond incorrectly."

"Oooh. Mean little son of Anteros, isn't he?" She laughed a strange, *tsk*ing chuckle. *"Fitting that a man of such misfortune should be host to the god of unrequited love. I'm sure torturing my sweet pet does make his blood run south. Surely no man or woman has given him the honor."*

I tried to mute her nastiness, focusing on the question that would seal my fellow novices' hatred. "Agreed."

"Where do mermaids make their home?"

I ran the question five times through my head before it penetrated. This couldn't be real. Of all the questions, he asks this of a girl who grew up by the sea.

"Mermaids do not exist. Olympia was founded by people from many lands, and their history, myths, and traditions molded with those of ancient Greece to create something that is entirely our own. But there were never mermaids in Olympia. The closest creature is the half-woman, half-bird sirens who build their nests on rocky, uninhabited islands."

A tense silence followed my response. Though we were locked on each other, I felt the eyes pinging from me to Captain Hondros.

"Correct."

I didn't have to breathe a sigh of relief. Half the class and all my friends did it for me.

"That just leaves the twenty scrolls on the monsters Barba answered for you." My chest tightened. "That applies to everyone. On my desk first thing tomorrow morning. Dismissed!"

"Fuck's sake," shouted a boy I didn't know. "You weren't satisfied with getting Galen killed. Now you're messing everything up for the rest of us."

Me? They were blaming me for Barba's rebellion and Hondros's power trip?

Nasty, poisonous glares trailed me out the door. I didn't need help for that question. The answer was yes.

My friends practically hustled me through the halls, carrying me back to the dorm. We burst in and slammed the door like a mob was coming for us.

"What the hell?" I burst out. "Is every instructor like that? Will every class be like that?"

"That was our fault," Nitsa said. "We thought they'd give you a break 'cause they all know you've been in the reflection room. I underestimated what bastards they can be."

The guys nodded in agreement. Seems they were all like this.

"Have they really been treating everyone like this all week?" I asked, flopping on the couch.

"Not everyone," Tycho corrected. "The Sisypheans. One week and we got the hint. The Titans can do no wrong. The Sisypheans can sit down, shut up, and just be glad we're here."

"That's awful. I'm sorry, guys. All I did was walk in there and make it worse. Forty scrolls in one night? That's impossible."

"Course it is," Theron said. He dropped his head against the door, gazing resignedly at the ceiling. "When we show up more than a few scrolls short, it just gives him an excuse to pile more punishment on us. But you can't blame yourself, Aella. That was all Sebastian."

"Does he always speak to teachers like that? I thought my eyes would fall out of my head and roll out the door."

"Oh my gods." Nitsa dropped down beside me. I had no idea why she was whispering. "The guy is unreal. Most days, he just sits there, staring off into space like all of this is a waste of his time."

"And we were lucky for it," Ionna threw in. "It's when he speaks... That's when there's trouble."

They didn't have to explain further. I saw it for myself. "Did he finally reveal his power? Is it as mind bending as everyone thought? Is that why Hondros put up with him for as long as he did?"

Nitsa tossed her head. "It's been nothing but smoke creatures. At first I thought it was cruel, but now I know why they make us reveal our powers to everyone on the first day. Sitting next to someone in class and having no idea what he can do to you..." She trailed off, expression grim.

"Demigods only get one power," I reminded. "That power can take different forms like it does for a shape-shifter like Sirena, but it's still just the one. He isn't lying about playing with smoke. The question is, what else can he do with it?"

"Maybe he'll tell you," Ionna replied.

"Me?"

"This morning was the first time he came to someone's rescue. He didn't speak up for Daciana."

"I doubt that was about me," I said, pushing up. "I wasn't looking for a rescue. More likely, Hondros pisses him off and he jumped on a chance to humiliate him. Speaking of, we should get started on those scrolls. And I need to get caught up on the week, so we don't get any more."

We buckled down and passed the next hour studying, reading, writing, and prepping me for what was coming. Sirena, the Titans, and Hondros caught me off guard. I wouldn't walk in with my head down again.

"Next is history, then self-mastery," Daciana murmured to me. We molded into the crowd of novices shuffling out of the dorm wing. "Afterward, the mess hall opens for two hours. Once it's closed, it's closed and we don't eat again until it opens after the day's lessons."

"That leaves combat and field medicine for the afternoon. Not so bad."

"Think again," Nitsa said, falling in step with us. "After that, we have mountains of coursework and studying to do. They really pile it on in the first couple months to prepare us for the culling."

"The culling," I repeated. "They mentioned that in the welcome book. It's a test to determine if we're ready to move on to the second part of our novice training. Did they tell you guys more about it while I was *away*?"

"No, nothing," Daciana said. "I asked our history instructor because she's less horrible than the rest, but even she was cagey. She said something like 'knowing too much about the test will change it.' Whatever that means."

"We already know enough," Nitsa added. "Anything called the culling can't be good."

Neither of us had a response for that.

The trek to the history room was less eventful than the throbbing, bleeding wound I had courtesy of my run-in with Sirena and the Titans.

Our crowd of Sisypheans turned left down the wall where it split around the reflection room. Light spilled through a rare window, casting a warm gift on my cheeks as I passed through. I stopped for a breath, just soaking it in.

I wasn't afraid of the dark. Eight years in a cave rid me of such childish things, and instead gave me an appreciation for the light. If life awaited me after the coming battle with the goddess, I'd build a home that was all windows, even the ceiling. All day the sun would shine on me. All night the stars would watch me sleep.

"Aella?" Daciana snapped me out of my daydream. "I said she's less horrible than the rest, but that doesn't mean she's cool with latecomers."

"Coming."

I left the sunlight behind, trailing my friends into the history hall. My lips parted but nothing came out.

Books. Books as far and wide as I could see. We came out on the second-floor loft—students breaking up to make for the two spiral staircases leading down to the lecture floor with its desks, and those desks piled with more books.

"Wow," I breathed, moving to the gold-and-iron railing to look up, not down. Another loft of bookshelves going all the way around promised the knowledge of fifty lifetimes. The true name of the goddess was here. It had to be. I couldn't believe there was a secret that escaped this temple of knowledge.

"Down in front. Down in front."

I snapped around as my instructor exited a side door hidden behind the shelves.

"Fill in the front rows first," said Madame Remis. "Come, now, novices. The rumors that I bite are greatly exaggerated."

I watched Sirena lace her fingers through Alexander's and tow him to the front row. A band of gorgeous, strutting Titans packed in around them. I watched two of the girls who said they'd back Sirena up if she mauled Nitsa, set her books in front of her and fuss with her hair—making it more perfect than it already was.

What are they? Handmaidens?

I was not looking to make more trouble for my friends, so if Sirena and her group were front row, it was the back row for me.

My friends and I settled on the Sisyphean side, far enough back that Sirena would have to crane her neck tossing smirks my way.

"Good morning, everyone. I trust you all have scrolls for me," Remis began.

I studied her as she moved a pile of books off her desk, then perched against it. She was quite pretty. Thick, dark hair cut short above her shoulders in a cut as severe as her sharp cheekbones. Should've made her seem severe, but she was softened by large, fawn-brown eyes and a tiny little coin of a mouth. I put her in her early thirties. Twenty years younger than Vasili at the very least.

Mixed feelings swirled in my chest. I wasn't sure what to make of her. She led me like prey into a trap, misleading me about the Tantalean bread and standing silently by while her boyfriend rendered me unconscious and locked me in a torture device. But the fact remained they were following the orders of the pompous, soft-bottomed schoolteacher who now hates me. If they didn't do it, Drakos would've done it himself.

"Pass them up."

There was shuffling and murmuring as everyone passed up their summary of the first chapter in our textbook, History of Olympia. I took out mine.

"Madame." I raised a hand. "It's not a full scroll, but I wrote down everything I know about the founding of Olympia."

She waved me down. "There's no hand-raising in my class, Aella. We're all adults. We know when to speak and when to listen. As for the assignment, of course I don't expect that today. Review the chapter first and hand it in to me next week."

Daciana shot me a look. *See? Not so horrible.*

"For the rest of us," she continued. "Did you learn anything that surprised you?"

"I learned my village teacher lied to us," said Kristopher Aetos, a Titan. "She said Olympia was formed because monsters were attracted to the divine in our blood. We came here to fight and defend each other."

"She was right and wrong," Remis replied. "Some monsters can sense the god or goddess within our souls because they're descendants of gods themselves. But as for the rest—the cursed—they see a human and only a human. No, the creatures that sensed the divinity in our blood and made life impossible for us... were the vampires."

A sharp crack turned my head. A snarl peeled back Daciana's lips as she tossed away her now broken writing reed.

"Vampires smell blood. One sniff and they knew instantly that we were special. Human blood has an amazing restorative and drug-like effect on them, but demigod blood..." She whistled low. "It was like eating bread and cheese your whole life, and then discovering a world of cakes, sweets, meats, and wine. They couldn't get enough, so everywhere in the world we lived, whole covens hunted down demigods."

She paced the length of the aisle, meeting my gaze, then flicking away as she passed. "Divine blood runs in families, not neighborhoods. Back then, you could be the only demigod family for a hundred miles. Who would come to help you when the vampires came?"

We were quiet mulling over that horrible thought. Just a family. Mother, father, and child—lying safe in their beds one night when bloodsucking beasts burst through the door. Life was never simple for us.

Never.

"Everywhere our people were dying and the gods were dying with us," Remis said softly. "The vampires were bringing to an end what the humans started. The end of the Olympian gods. The end of everything."

"Why would that have been the end?" asked a girl sitting in front of me. "The essence would just leave our bodies, right? Find a new person."

Remis was shaking her head before she was done. "There's a reason the choice to scatter was made in a last desperate attempt after they lost the war with the Christian god. Your heart is a part of you. If it's removed from your chest, it dies and you die. It's the same for the godly essence. It dies with us."

Spine straightening, my eyes narrowed to slits. The goddess laughed in my ear.

"*Now she's starting to get it.*"

"So, what did they do?" Sirena asked. "How did they overcome the vampires to found Olympia?"

"Children of Hermes." Remis ended her stroll before her desk. "Those with the power, sent messages far and wide to the demigods of the world to come together and fight. Thus began the first Vampire-Demigod War."

"A war?" Sirena cried. "An entire war we never heard about?"

Remis inclined her head. "A war fought in the land that became the Americas. The destruction of that battle remains to this day. Nothing but a massive crater that goes on for miles and miles. How much kinder it would've been on the mundane population if this was the last cross-species battle.

"But there was another in the southern region of the Americas. Two in Europe. *Three* in Africa, and then two more devastating wars in Asia."

We sat quiet and spellbound. This was definitely a time to listen.

"Two wars in, demigods formed alliances with the vampires' natural enemies: the werewolves."

Kristopher snorted. "So you dogs can be useful." He twisted around to smirk vilely at Daciana. "You should follow in your ancestors' *tracks*. Fight some monsters or get the fuck out."

My retort was hot on my lips. "Shut—"

"Kristopher Aetos," Remis snapped. "You will keep a civil tongue in your head, or I will remove it. The body breaks easier than it mends."

"Yes, ma'am," was his mumbled reply.

I checked on Daciana, but it didn't appear that she heard the exchange at all. She was shaking—her head down and fists balled tight on the desk. "Are you okay?"

She didn't answer or look up.

"As I was saying." Remis resumed walking up the aisles. "The werewolf packs joining us had a brutal impact on mundane casualties. Werewolves and vampires are evenly matched. Both have superhuman strength. Both are superior trackers. But werewolves and demigods had an edge. Our fight doesn't stop when the sun comes up."

"They started turning humans to keep up their numbers, didn't they?" Nitsa said.

"They did indeed. Wiped out entire villages. Thus, mundanes were forced to fight for their lives, or become a puppet in death."

"How did all of this end in Olympia?" Nitsa asked. "This sounds like the start of the end of the world."

"It very nearly was." I twisted in my seat, tracking her path. "Until the final species could sit out of the battle no longer."

"The fae."

I didn't know who said it, but Remis's pleased cry said they were right. "The fae, my young novices, the fae. They joined the side of the mundanes, and the last and final interspecies war was over in a fortnight."

"Why did they join the side of the mundanes?" Sirena asked.

"For the same reason they stayed out of the conflict for so long. Fae are beings of nature—born from the primordial gods to become creatures all their own. They never obeyed the Olympian gods, and the Olympian gods never had the power to make them. Their only loyalty is to the balance and protection of the natural.

"Whereas we demigods, vampires, and werewolves are not natural. We're mundanes perverted by magic, curses, and gods. When we became a serious threat to the survival of the mundane species, they stepped in, ended the war, and crafted the Five Dominions Treaty."

"That, I know of," Sirena said, nose high in the air. "The Five Dominions Treaty designated the sovereign land of the mundanes, vampires, werewolves, demigods, and fae."

Remis snapped her fingers. "Correct, but did you all know that because of the treaty, we got the short end of the stick?"

"By being granted Olympia?" I heard myself say. "How?"

"Oh, it's not the land. It was magnificent even back then when it went by another name: Atlantis. No," she said. "We got the bad deal... because we got the monsters."

"Got the monsters?" Nitsa repeated slowly. "Are you saying the monsters live in Olympia because of the treaty?"

"That is exactly what I'm saying, Miss Castellanos. When it came time to determine what species monsters were, and therefore which dominion they should live, the other four representatives voted ours unanimously.

"These creatures were the descendants of Greek gods, the creations of Greek gods, and the enemies of Greek gods. If they were anyone's problem, they were ours. Back then the very first council was ordered to enter this land with the monsters and seal the barrier behind us. If a single monster escaped to wreak havoc on the other dominions, it'd be a violation of the treaty and the war would begin anew with every being magical and mundane descending on Olympia."

No one spoke for so long, I wondered if we lost the ability.

"I don't understand," Sirena said. "How can any of that be true? Why is this the first we're hearing about this? If the fae or the whoever forced the monsters on us, it'd be known. It'd be taught."

"Would it?" Remis said softly. She leaned against a bookshelf, running her fingers along the spines. "Between the pages is a safe place, isn't it? There can be no lies, no half-truths, no missing information in the books we trust to tell us the world. I'm sorry, my dear novices, but the first thing you'll learn about history is that it's like everything else—subject to bias. Do you think the history books in vampire academies paint them as the villains or the heroes?"

A low growl escaped Daciana's lips.

"But then why?" I asked. I laid my hand over Daciana's, comforting her like she did me in the face of Captain Hondros.

"Because look around you." She swept out her arms. "We're trapped in a land with monsters that eat our flesh, devour our children, sing us to our deaths, burn down our villages, and wipe away everything we love in a single day.

"In the early days after the treaty, demigods attacked the barrier daily. Bands of Hecate's children went after it looking for weaknesses. The council weathered more than a few assassination attempts for agreeing to the terrible terms in the first place. Keeping control got ugly and violent very fast. As a result, the wars and the true terms of the treaty were stricken from the history books. Here we are two thousand years later, and no one remembers."

"Why can we know now?" a guy in the third row spoke up.

"Because there's been a recent change in the curriculum." Madame Remis's smile swept over us. "Me."

"You?" Sirena repeated. Did she hear the disdain in her voice, or was it just natural at this point? "You're going against council law to teach us banned information? You have no right."

"This is my classroom, Miss Cirillo, I have every right. You'll find Deucalion Academy is autonomous of the council. Here, I tell you what the laws are."

A choked noise came from Sirena's throat. "Nothing and no one is autonomous of the council. You—"

The gong sounded, signaling the end of class. I jerked like it snapped me out of a dream. An hour and a half passed already?

"That's all for today, ladies and gentlemen. Your assignment for tonight is to read chapter two, *The History of the Gods*. Tomorrow, I'll tell you what's missing."

"I doubt there's anything missing," Sirena snapped.

She flashed her a smile as pleasant as the one that beamed on me in the reflection room. "You'll find out tomorrow."

Sirena was at the front of the class, but managed to shove her way through and storm out the door first. Daciana was right on her heels, ignoring our calls.

"Is she okay?" Ionna asked.

"I'm not sure. I got the feeling she's not a fan of vampires."

"None of us are after that," Theron put in, shuffling up between us. "Think all that stuff's true?"

Nitsa slung her arms around our shoulders. "I mean, it does make sense. Mother told me the monsters came to Olympia because they could smell the divine in our blood. If that was true of all of them, there's nowhere we could hide. But we do and we can. When I was nine, I was playing with my brothers in the woods when I stumbled into the path of a gorgon. I dove under a bush and hid there until my brothers came to find me. If she could sense me, why aren't I dead?"

"Nitsa, I never felt more stupid than I do right now," Theron said gravely. "It's so obvious now that you say it. Why didn't we notice that before?"

Nitsa, Ionna, and Tycho echoed him.

"I know why." My books crushed against my chest. "Because we believe in our mothers, and the sweet stories they tell us as we drift to sleep. We believe in them stronger than we ever will the gods."

"That's true," Ionna whispered.

"—tell my mother about this." Sirena echoed through the hall. "It's an outrage that this information was kept from members of the imperial household, but it's even more disgusting that she shared it for every pig-stinkin' peasant in there to hear. She should've held a private class for those with the right to know."

I passed by her, barely keeping hold of my tongue.

"Mother will be furious when she hears about this."

Her handmaidens chimed in on cue.

"You're right, Sirena."

"Madame Remis went too far."

"I bet none of that was true anyway. No way would the first council let a bunch of beasts and mundanes dictate to demigods. The whole thing makes no..."

Their voices faded as we headed out of the lecture wing, making way for our last class of the morning. The guys told me a little about self-mastery class, but I was curious to see it for myself. I was even more curious about what the instructor had planned for me.

Together we gathered in the stadium arena, circling the lone man on the platform. Everyone except Daciana.

"You have all heard my speech, but for the benefit of our latecomer"—Instructor Kazran cut eyes at me so I didn't mistake who he was speaking of—"I will repeat myself. Self-mastery is power combat training. Here you will train to improve your speed and accuracy."

Kazran was a young man. I put him at early thirties, maybe late twenties. According to my friends, this should impress me. He was young, fit, and built. His spiky red hair caught beams of sunlight between his locks, drawing your eyes up for the slight second you could stand to look away from his cornflower-blue eyes and the tawny dusting along his nose and cheekbones.

Young, fit, handsome men such as he were serving their army sentence with no hope of getting a teaching position until they were much older and slower. For Drakos to get him assigned to the school proved how much power the headmaster had, and how impressive Kazran was.

"A long time ago," he continued, "self-mastery class was sending novices off the grounds to face whatever crossed their paths. Some came back, some did not."

I wonder if that was left out of the history books too.

"Eventually, monsters got wise. We weren't sending out snacks. We were sending out hunting parties, and like us, some survived. Most didn't," he said. "As a result, they moved farther out of the area. Too far to send you out and back in half an hour. So, we make do."

I raised my hand.

"Put that down," Kazran said. "You're not a child."

Down it went. "How do we make do, Instructor?"

"With proficients." Kazran clapped and ten men and women broke off from the circle, and joined him on the platform.

I was learning slower than the others, but I did know proficients were students in their third year at the academy. Theron impressed upon me the weight of graduating to proficient. By the third year of training, fifty-five percent of the average starting Sisyphean class was dead. Thirty percent of the starting Titan class was gone.

We were looking at survivors.

"These men and women have powers closest to the kind of dangers you'll face while protecting Olympia. Fire wielders, hypnotic abilities, shape-shifting tricksters, regenerators, speedsters, fliers, iron skins, magic bearers, elemental molders, and seers. What you'll do is simple," he told me. This was only for my benefit.

"They will attack. You will defend. This should go without saying, but I'll say it anyway. You cannot move to another opponent until you've defeated your first. The same applies in battle because out there if you cannot defeat your monster, you won't move on... since you'll be dead," he deadpanned. "Any questions?"

I braced myself as the question hit the air. "How do I do this without a power?"

Jeers assaulted me immediately.

"Still a lying traitor," Kristopher scoffed. "She hasn't learned her lesson."

"No one's buying your shit, coward. Stand up and fight like the rest of us."

"Quiet." Kazran kneeled on the platform, boring over me. "You do have power, Galanis." He spoke slowly like he was talking to a child. "You just haven't figured out what it is yet. Lucky for you, this is your first step toward finding out."

"How so?"

He swept a hand over the proficients. "What if you're a daughter of Hephaestus and impervious to fire? Can't find out until you get burned. What if you sprout wings and fly? Won't know until you jump off a cliff. By the culling, we'll know without a doubt what your power is or..." He clicked his tongue. "Or fate will have granted you a more merciful end than what awaited you during the culling. Either way, this class is your salvation."

Gaping, my bugged-out eyes watched his retreat. I wished there was ambiguity in what he said, but his meaning was unmistakable to everyone listening. Self-mastery would throw everything it had at me until I was either killed, or a power suddenly appeared and saved me. If a power did not appear, the culling would finish what this class started.

"Don't let him scare you," Nitsa whispered. "We've all got your back."

"Break into groups of ten," Kazran called. "Newcomer, hang back. I'll tell you where to go."

I watched my friends shuffle off with guilty looks and mouthed "sorrys." So much for that. No one would have my back.

The group split into packs of ten and each followed a proficient to their own corner of the stadium. There was only me waiting beside the platform, asking myself if Instructor Kazran was planning to see me burned or thrown off a cliff.

"Galanis," he barked, waving me over. "Here."

I turned toward him and froze. A group of five stood in front of Kazran and a tall, long-haired woman with battle armor and a bored expression. It was Alexander, Sirena, and her handmaidens.

"Why?" I asked, not moving a muscle. "What's her power?"

"You'll find out soon enough. Come. Now."

I considered arguing, then I considered what Kazran's punishment would be for disobeying him. Scrolls or worse?

I'm not going to find out. I walked up to the group, stiffening with each step. Alexander's stare was a thousand needles digging into my skin.

"I'm not without mercy," Kazran said. "You'll go last to see how it's done. Learn from them and formulate your plan for defeating Proficient Catherine."

I glanced at my simple white tunic and brown pants. "Can I have armor or gear—?"

"Have you had a single combat class?"

"No."

"Then what would you do with gear?" he asked, brows cocked. "Throw it at her?"

Sirena and her friends burst out laughing, heating my cheeks. "But what if—"

"Try not to kill her," Kazran said, turning his back on us. "Begin."

It was just the six of us.

Try not to kill her? Was he talking to our group or to Proficient Catherine?

"Move aside, traitor." Sirena came straight at me, forcing me to jump aside or get mowed down. "Kazran said you're last and least—where you've always belonged and who you'll always be."

I barely heard her. Closing the distance between me and Alexander, he tracked my approach like a predator. I just wasn't sure if the predator was him or me.

Sirena said Galen's death destroyed him. A brief moment seeing them together and I believed her. Alexander was so light and free that morning, laughing with Galen in the stadium. A freeness I didn't see during that long journey with his brothers-in-arms or the string of women going in and out of his room.

"Alexander," I began. "I should've come to you before. Said this sooner. I'm sorry about what happened to Galen."

His face was chipped in stone.

"I didn't know him but, in that short while, he was kind, brave, and strong. He was someone I believe would've made me better for knowing him, and I'll carry the pain of never getting that chance for the rest of my l-life." I stumbled over my words, growing more unnerved by his stillness. But this had to be said.

Mama used to tell me that it was our duty to apologize when we'd done wrong. Whether or not that apology was accepted. Whether or not forgiveness is given. The true shame was not admitting your wrongdoing at all. She would say a person who goes their whole life without apology was not someone she wanted to meet.

Mothers give more lessons than they do examples. But this is one I can keep on my own.

"I know you don't have the highest opinion of me, but know if I could take back what happened, I would. I—"

"Come closer."

A second passed before it penetrated that the words came from his lips.

"Closer," he repeated, raising a soft hand dotted with calluses. A warrior's hand. "Aella."

Maybe it was my name. Maybe it was the way he said it—caressing it on his tongue like he'd done every time since he tricked it out of me.

I moved closer and he came to meet me—the tips of our boots brushing together. My breath caught as he palmed my cheek, skin molding to me as though it was meant to be there all along.

Alexander leaned over me, brushing the tip of his nose against mine as gentle as the ghost of his exhale on my lips. I stopped breathing altogether.

"Uh, Xander," trembled one of the handmaidens. "I don't think..."

She faded in the background as everyone did when Alexander brought me closer still. Not a hair could sneak between our bodies, and I blushed at my breasts flattening against his chest. Eight years in a mountain cave did not prepare me for this.

Swirling ponds of lily pads, his eyes were alive with heat, passion, and electricity. Gazing into them, I saw the king of the heavens.

"Why?" I whispered.

"Because." His lips caressed mine in the barest brush of a kiss. "I think you're going to keep talking, and skin-to-skin contact makes it hurt so much worse."

My eyes bugged. Tearing away, my feet tangled and dropped me hard on my ass—jarring pain up my bones. The handmaidens burst out laughing while Alexander eyed me on the ground without interest. In his arms or in the dirt, it made no difference to him. I was nothing.

"Ready?" Proficient Catherine called, flicking my attention to her.

Sirena adopted another pose. "Naturally."

I blinked, and Catherine was gone. A blur streaked toward Sirena, who shifted even faster. Shooting off the ground, a magnificent creature with the body of a lion and wings of an eagle spread them wide, and flapped a gust of wind that blew my tunic over my face.

It was Proficient Catherine's turn to be popped off her feet. The blur became a woman, and she sailed through the air only to twist at the last moment and slide across the arena on her feet.

"Excellent," she said, unfazed by her unscheduled flying lesson. "Who's next?"

Sirena touched down naked as the day she was born and made sure to give Alexander a kiss on the cheek before getting dressed and sidling up to her friends. The three handmaidens huddled around her, whispering and pointing to me and Alexander. Her eyes narrowed to slits.

Our lone guy took his place as I peeled myself off the ground. "Ready."

Catherine streaked toward him.

"Ahhh!" She jerked to a halt so suddenly, she flew off her feet. Sliding across the limestone, her screams echoed through the academy.

Alexander dropped his hand—the torment over as soon as it started, but Proficient Catherine lay there in a sweaty pile, her chest heaving and breaths ragged.

"Amazing, Xander." Sirena draped herself on him, trying to blink up into eyes that were once again watching me. She actually tried to tip his chin, then she slid between us when that didn't work. "You're next, Galanis," she barked. "If you haven't figured out how to beat her by now, then watching Rue, Tessa, and Hyacinth put you to shame won't make much of a difference."

Biting my tongue, I crossed to Catherine. I was starting to get real tired of this random woman barking orders at me while the stinging cuts throbbed on my cheek. There was nothing more important than freeing myself from the goddess's clutches. I could guess why she was bound and determined to be a distraction, but that didn't make it any less irritating.

Catherine slapped away my outstretched hand. "I don't need your help," she snapped. "Take your place, novice."

After just being dropped on her backside by another novice, I let the hostility pass. I took my place across from her and ran through my options.

How do I defeat someone with such incredible speed? The lamia was fast, but nowhere near as fast as Proficient Catherine.

"Ready?"

The only way is to be clever in the millisecond I have before she's upon me. Hunching down, I nodded. "Ready."

I flung out my arms as she disappeared. *Be clev—*

A hand seized my wrist. There was barely a chance to scream before Catherine sent me flying over her shoulder. I bounced off the limestone and landed smack on my back—dazed.

Sirena and her crew laughed uproariously. "What did you think you were doing, Sisyphean? Trying to swat her away like a buzzing fly?"

I pushed myself up and a blur streaked across my vision. I was flying through the air again to the tune of Sirena's delicate, snotty laugh.

Catherine waited for me to be ready once, but all mercy was rescinded once she left her mark. I skidded across the limestone, tearing the sleeve off my shirt and groaning as a layer of skin went with it.

Clutching my shoulder, I imagined how it'd go over if I asked for a minute to get on my feet—think of a new plan.

"A monster wouldn't give you a minute. Suck it up, novice."

You wouldn't think it'd take me a week to figure out what all my friends did.

This place was horrible.

Come on, Aella. Think of something clever. Think of something!

Flicker of movement out of the corner of my eye. Clenching my teeth, I swung my aching body around—sweeping my legs. Catherine appeared five feet from me, stumbling to a stop in front of Alexander.

"Almost, novice," she said, flashing a grin. "You didn't trip me, but you forced me to veer off course. A point in your favor that you can carry with you to Asphodel Meadows."

Sirena's giggling grated on my ears. Asphodel Meadows was the realm of hades dedicated to ordinary people who lived ordinary lives. There were worse places she could've sent me, so I didn't take it personally.

"You're done for the day," Catherine continued. "We'll pick this up tomorrow. But just know, that trick won't work twice."

I scraped myself off the ground, hugging my chest tight. My unwanted limestone back-scrubbing tore holes all throughout my tunic. I felt as exposed as Sirena after a shift.

And I'll have to do this all over again tomorrow. And the day after that. And the day after that until I defeat a woman who runs faster than I breathe.

"Gods, you're pathetic." Sirena crashed into my musing. "Why that beast didn't rip out your throat and do the world a favor, not even the Moirai can answer."

My cheeks flushed under the pressing heat, popping pinpricks of sweat on my aching body. It invaded the cuts on my skin and cheek, stinging worse than ever. Alexander tracked my approach—expression revealing neither pity nor anger. Was he hoping I'd get close enough to make it hurt?

"Do everyone a favor and volunteer for hard labor before they have to drag your worthless ass out of here." She knocked my shoulder shoving past. "It's the kindest sentence you deserve for daring to live when Galen died."

"Enough."

Sirena halted, muscles in her back tightening. I noticed this out of the corner of my eye. Alexander brought me back to him with that scorching, intense stare.

Something deep inside told me he was making his mind up, and it wouldn't serve me well to have my back to him when he came to a decision.

"Excuse me?" she hissed.

"I said enough. You get to know a lot about monsters when you've lived with one, and deep down, they're all lashing out because they're broken inside. If you think you're currying favor with your cheating boyfriend by attacking and cutting me down, I suggest you try a new tactic," I said to her, but gazed at Alexander. "If he cared that much, he'd be staring at you, not me."

His eyes narrowed to slits. Ever so slightly, his fingers twitched. *I think he's made up his mind.*

"How— I'm not—" For the first time since I met this unpleasant woman, she faltered. "You can't talk to me like—"

"No, you can't talk to me like that. I didn't trade one miserable existence with a monster to come to another prison and put up with your garbage. You want all of Alexander's attention? You can have it. It won't be missed."

His lips peeled back, sounding the warning bells in my head. But under that blazing sun, clutching my aching body while the echo of Sirena, the handmaidens, and the goddess's laugh rang in my ears, I couldn't stop.

"I've got bigger things to worry about, so stay out of my way and I'll stay out of yours." I said it to Sirena, but my gaze was still on him. Always on him. "Trust me, you won't be missed either."

Giving them my back, I limped out of the stadium.

"Hey— Hey, come back here! Don't walk away from me, bitch! No one speaks to me that way."

Sirena's shouting, fussing, and carrying on followed me out onto the grass.

"How I admire your fire, my little pet. Even though your attempts to defy my will displease me, I will enjoy watching you make enemies along the way." That strange *tsk*ing laugh. It would follow me to the day I died. *"The harder you try to save them, the more they'll prove they don't deserve to be saved."*

I DIDN'T MAKE IT TO the mess hall that afternoon. After the beating I took in the arena, I dragged my battered body into a hot bath and soaked until I wrinkled. All my friends were lounging on their beds or in the common area when I returned to the dorm.

Daciana wasn't among them. I had no idea where she went after leaving history, but she was entitled to stay there while she worked out what she was going through. It wasn't like they could execute her for skipping training for an army she'd never join.

"We've got to spend every spare minute on these scrolls," Ionna explained. "We brought you something to eat though. Hope you like sausages and artichokes with poppy seed pastries for dessert."

I more than liked it. I scarfed it down in between picking up my own books and getting to work on my scrolls about harpies.

Our textbook only had two chapters on the creatures. I ran out of things to say five scrolls in.

Eventually, we put aside our impossible task and headed out to the grayed-out section of our schedule. My friends led the way to the atrium, where they turned right instead of left. My eyes drifted against my will, finding the spot where I held Galen as he died. Memories took me, leading my mind away though I continued on and outside.

I bumped into Nitsa's back, nearly sending us both toppling down the marble steps.

"Oh, sorry. I didn't realize everyone had stopped."

"We had to," she said softly. "Look."

I looked down, following where she was pointing. The entire novice class stood on the steps, waiting respectfully as the procession passed. Madame Remis led the way, speaking and gesturing to the two men carrying a stretcher across the lawn. A sheet lay over them, but there was no questioning they were carrying a body.

A band tightened around my throat, knocking me off-balance. *Galen?*

"Can't believe it," Nitsa continued, unaware of what was happening behind her. "Another life lost during training. It's so senseless. Why can't they make these lessons safer?"

Tycho's response floated over her head to me. "Because they don't care if a few or more Sisypheans die. It's only further proof we don't belong in the army. Better we die here with some semblance of honor than be a liability out there."

Nitsa quieted while I got my breath back. My prayers were with that poor soul and their family who did not think them worthless—no matter what class they were in. But it wasn't Galen. I couldn't have borne if it was Galen.

Only when Madame Remis and her silent bearers were gone did we continue to class. Whispers trickled through our group, passing the news on.

"His name was Giles Nanos." I didn't recognize the girl talking to Ionna. "Son of Alectrona, the goddess of sun and morning."

"Was he killed during training?"

"Worse," she replied, dropping her voice. "I heard they found him at the bottom of the southeast tower. He either fell or..."

Jumped, I finished for her. *Dear gods, they think the poor guy jumped.*

"That's awful. Can't imagine what kind of pain he was in to... choose to go that way."

"Who knows. He was a Titan, so it's not like he had it as bad as us. They're saying he could conjure a beam of light as bright as the sun, blinding anyone who saw it."

"No one's life is perfect—Titan or not. My brothers lost so many friends in the academy. None of us are stronger than grief..."

Their conversation faded as I hung back, letting them move farther ahead. I couldn't stand this talk of death and grief. Was this to be our life now? Every moment of every day in and then out of the academy?

No wonder the instructors and headmaster were hardened to the point of breaking trainees on impact. You can escape grief... when you stopped caring.

Morose thoughts plagued me through the trek around the academy to one of the many parts I was seeing for the first time. The stretch of freshly cut green went as far back as I could see. It'd be beautiful as a place to picnic under the open air, enjoying the breeze and sunshine while working on assignments with friends. But of course, the academy put it to more practical uses.

Platforms of the same type, but much smaller than the one in the stadium, were scattered about the lawn. A row of stands stretched in a neat line alongside them, and among them all—waiting for us—was Commander Vasili.

"Titans, find your groups. Sisypheans, find a seat."

The next ninety minutes were as boring and tedious as Tycho promised. The commander made us sit on the stands, rays beating down on us while we watched the Titans train, practice, and form battle strategies with other children of the same god. He wouldn't even let us work on assignments for other classes. I knew because the girl who was speaking to Nitsa about Giles Nanos tried, and he confiscated it and made her do a lap around the castle.

"I don't get why you guys can't practice with them too," I said, leaving myself out. After the humiliation of self-mastery class, I had no delusions that I had anything to contribute. "They keep saying we fight together and we die together. You'll have to do this in the army, so why have you sitting on your butts?"

"I hate to say it, but I'm not sure we would be much use off this bench," Theron said. He couldn't write on it, so he used a piece of parchment to fan himself. "My powers are violent and unpredictable. There's no measuring the scale of my destruction like there's no hating something a little or halfway. I could take out half the green and for what purpose?"

I inclined my head. "True, but Ionna, Nitsa, and Tycho, you could—"

They were all shaking their heads.

"If my gift of prophecy was more focused—more accurate—Commander Vasili would pair me with the other children of Apollo. Otherwise, who wants me out there confusing them, shouting out the dozens of possible futures I see with no idea which one is right, or if they're all wrong?"

"Nothing for me to do either," Tycho said. "Unless someone dies."

He didn't need to say more. The commander would be a twisted person indeed to send him out there to fight with animated corpses.

Nitsa just shrugged. "How many famed battles do you know that involved a cow? For once, I don't think they're being cruel. They're just being realistic. Sisypheans are destined for positions in the army that don't see a lot of combat. The medical battalion, messengers, sentries, border watchers, trackers, weapons-making. We'll still do our part, Aella. But not right now. Not today."

"So... we sit here."

They all leaned back against the stands, glistening sweat shining on their foreheads.

"We sit here."

At the end of time, it was a relief to march inside the cool castle and head to field medicine. Tycho, Nitsa, Theron, and Ionna took me inside the lecture wing, down the hall, and up a spiral staircase. Two doors awaited us at the top. Sirena and her feathered companion disappeared through the door on the right.

That was reason enough to turn and drag my sweaty body into another bath. She was too busy barking orders at her group and making all the decisions to worry about me sitting in the stands, but now that we were in close proximity again, I had a feeling she'd finish what she stuttered to say that morning in the stadium.

Squaring my shoulders, I went in and stopped—mouth hanging open.

"Beautiful."

Was I dreaming? I couldn't be. I wasn't hot, sticky, and achy in the dreams where I imagined the home I'd build of windows, windows, and windows—spreading warmth and freedom through all four walls and the ceiling.

This room was my imagination come to life. Double-paned windows let the light in, but the heat out. Matter of fact, a cool breeze enveloped me as I stepped over the threshold—soothing my burnt skin.

Hugging the windows were potted trees of all types, bearing plump, delicious fruit. Some of them I'd never seen before. In the middle of the room, the space was cleared out to make room for ten desks. My friends gathered around one, settling into a routine now familiar to them.

"A greenhouse. Why can't every classroom be like this? It's amazing."

"It's actually an orangery," said a melodic, feminine voice. "But I thank you for the compliment."

A short, stout woman with a shaved head and russet skin brushed past me and plucked a reddish-pink fruit off one of the trees. She was dressed unlike anyone I'd ever seen in or out of Deucalion. Flowing floral silks covered her in layer upon layer that moved as she did. "For you, dear."

I fumbled to catch the tiny, bumpy thing. "What is it?"

"Lychee. They're exclusive to the Isles of Paradise, and this room." She clapped. "Come, come, Aella Galanis. With you here, our little flock is finally complete. Take your place anywhere."

I took my place between Ionna and Nitsa. Standing directly across from me, Sirena did her best to telepathically explode my head.

"Forgive me while I repeat a few things for our latest arrival's benefit. My name is Cassia Moralis, daughter of Demeter. There are very few of us in Olympia. It is my honor to be chosen, and to pass on her gifts and knowledge to all of you." Instructor Moralis plucked another fruit off a tree and tossed it at Cleon, one of the Sisyphean boys. "Identify."

"Elderberry," he replied. "It's used to treat coughs, burning throats, and flu."

"Well done." Moralis fixed on me. "In an ideal world, there would be so many children of healing gods, we'd have a dozen tasked to each mora, or unit. As it is, there are only thirty alive now with the power to heal serious injuries. Two are employed at the academy, most are in the private employment of noble families, five are with the medical battalion, and the rest reside within the Imperial Palace.

"I tell you this so you'll have no delusions. When you're out on patrol and tragedy strikes, help is *not* close by. Do not make the mistake of believing this class can be taken lightly." Among the silk and sweet-smelling fruit, I did rid myself of a delusion: Moralis wasn't someone to underestimate.

"Out there, the only help you'll find is from the ones who've always been there for you: Mother Gaia and Mother Demeter. They grow the medicines that will heal you, soothe your pain, and grant you that little extra time to get to the medical battalion. So, do not disrespect yourself and your comrades by slacking off in this class. My life does not depend on your attention. All of yours do."

She was still looking at me, so I said, "Understood, Madame Moralis. I'm excited to learn."

Her face changed so suddenly, the beaming smile made me step back. "Ooh, madame. So formal. Cassia will do, dear." She clapped, cutting off my reply. "Now. Last week, we talked about the medicinal properties of bark. This week, we'll discuss the benefits we get from certain leaves. Take your books out if you must, but I want you walking around, seeing them, feeling them, committing their scent, sight, and feel to memory. Starting here with the neem tree..."

We settled in, taking notes on her lecture, and then moved around to study the plants as she requested. Believe it or not, most of what she said I knew. The lamia would hardly take us to a village healer when we got ill. If she was to track down medicine without risk of attack, that left the forests, groves, and fields as her shopping ground. I learned what black cohosh was the week I got my first monthly bleed. How bittersweet to finally not be the clueless one in the room.

I rounded a bilberry tree, making note of the small differences that set it apart from a blueberry.

Flapping tipped my head up, alerting me to the arrival of Sirena's bird. The little owl preened, fluffing out her beautiful feathers as if on display for an admiring audience.

"You are lovely." I couldn't help a smile when she hooted in response. "Shame you don't keep better company."

Tawny hopped on a lower branch, coming closer. She cooed a sweet sound to me, fluffing her feathers out again.

"How is it you're allowed here? I don't see anyone else with a pet riding their shoulders." I snorted. "Must be another rule that doesn't apply to her."

Tawny flew down to a branch eye level with me and gently bumped my nose with her beak. If she spent her days in the Imperial Palace, she was likely used to compliments coming with treats and pets.

I looked around for Sirena. She was across the room—within two feet of Alexander as usual.

"Okay," I whispered. "But this is just between you and me." I reached out, running a finger through—

"Caaaah!"

Tawny flew at me. I whipped my arm up, snapping across my face. Vicious sharp pain lashed across my forearm. My cry bounced off the windows.

"Tawny? What are you doing to her?!"

I didn't have a chance to reply to Sirena's idiotic accusation. Screeches and cries assaulted my ears, heralding the berserk animal's outrage. Screeches almost as loud as mine as she clawed my forehead, scalp, and ears.

"Galanis, get down!"

I heeded the unfamiliar voice, dropping flat to the floor. Just like that, the screeching stopped.

Thud.

Peering through my fingers, I squinted at a ripe bundle of green grapes. Sirena's scream shattered my eardrums worse than the owl.

"You monster! What did you do?" She knocked Rodion aside rushing to me. Completely ignoring the person bleeding from multiple head wounds, Sirena cradled the grapes, her eyes welling with tears. "You killed her. She was just defending herself." She kicked me in the side spinning around. "When I'm done with you, Sarris, you'll wish I had dropped you from the highest peak into the deepest ocean."

"It's not dead," he snapped, kicking his way out of the trees' clutches. "I turned her into grapes, I can turn her back."

"Do it. Now."

"Love to. Once you get that insane animal in a cage."

"She's not insane. She's never done that before. That Sisyphean did something to her and if you don't turn her back now—"

"Enough," Cassia barked. She shoved through the gathering crowd and came to me. A sharp hiss whispered through her teeth at the sight. Bad sign. "Rodion is right. You will take that owl outside before there's any thought of changing it back. And it's never to enter this classroom again."

Sirena harrumphed. "I'm telling you, Tawny's never done anything like this before. That twisted bitch provoked her. She's had it out for me since the day she got here."

I was in too much pain to shout back at that bald-faced lie. It felt like I groomed my hair with a comb of scimitars. A pool of blood grew beneath my head.

"Get it out. Now."

Sirena stood up to go. Over Cassia's shoulder—so quick I might've missed it—she winked at me.

That bird's attack was no accident.

There's my answer to if she intends to leave me alone. It would appear when Sirena Cirillo makes an enemy, she carves her revenge in blood.

Class was over for me.

Cassia had Ionna and Nitsa help me to the infirmary—a soothing place of brown limestone walls and two rows of soft beds resting beneath its own stained-glass windows. They cast a myriad of colors on me as my friends helped me onto a bed.

"I'll look for Healer Helena." Ionna ran out, calling her name.

"Don't." Nitsa stopped me reaching for the mirror on the bedside table. "Look after she heals you. Trust me."

"Good idea," I rasped. "I can't believe she had that creature attack me. That bird went straight for my eyes, Nitsa. What kind of psychopath does this?"

"Sirena Cirillo is a special kind of psychopath with one mission: marry Alexander Damien and get rid of anyone who gets in her way."

"I'm not in her way."

Nitsa moved down to help me out of my boots. "Neither was Eliana Filo. She was a maid who worked in the Imperial Palace to save up some money for her family before she entered the academy. Alexander took up with her last summer. It was just a bit of fun for both of them. Eliana wasn't looking to get serious at sixteen, and she had no delusion that the son of a councilman would promise forever to a maid."

"What happened?"

"Rumors spread through the palace is what happened," Nitsa said, perching on the edge of my bed. "They weren't walking the grounds hand in hand, but they weren't hiding it either. More than a few guards watched her slip into his room at night. Anyway, it got back to Sirena. She isn't so reckless as to announce an engagement that Alexander doesn't know about, but she made her stake on him clear since they were twelve.

"People were laughing at her. Or so she thought. They were smirking at the fool who thought she tamed the heart of a Damien. Or again"—Nitsa cut me a look—"so she convinced herself. To punish this slight against her, she hid her mother's priceless pearl necklace in Eliana's quarters.

"Eliana was sentenced to five years in prison," Nitsa dropped dully.

"What?" I cried, shooting up. Pain raked across my scalp. "Why— How could she do that?"

"Psychopath. Remember?"

"But she was framed. Didn't anyone speak up for her? Didn't Alexander?"

Nitsa eased me back down. "It's because Alexander spoke up for her that she got five years instead of fifteen. Sirena's mother wouldn't hear of it being reduced any less, and she was not only the 'victim' but also on the council. There was nothing more he, or I, or her family could do."

"But if you knew it was Sirena—?"

"I didn't have proof. One of the maids told Eliana that she saw Sirena slip out of the servants' hall that night, but all of *Sirena's* maids swore up, down, and sideways that she never left her room. Who was the council going to believe?"

"That's just... evil," I whispered. "She ruined her life for nothing."

"Yes, she did." Nitsa slipped her hand under mine. "Now she'll try to ruin yours, because whenever your back is turned, Alexander looks at you. Not her."

Warmth stained my cheeks for no good reason. "No, he doesn't— I mean, not in a romantic way. Alexander hates me and the feeling is mutual."

"Eliana and Alexander didn't have feelings for each other either. I told you how that worked out."

I sighed, sinking into the pillows. "Probably wasn't a good idea to taunt her about 'cheating boyfriends' and their fixation on me."

She choked. "You said that? Now I understand why you're bleeding from the head."

I almost chuckled, but the thought of it rippled torture through my forehead. "I'll be smarter from now on. Watch my back around her."

"*I* will watch your back from now on," she corrected. "And Tycho. And Theron. And Ionna and Daciana. Sirena is used to everyone skirting her in the halls, keeping their heads down. Sadly for her, we're not in the Imperial Palace anymore. They may favor Titans, but a novice is still a novice. With a class fatality rate of forty-seven percent, no one expects us to get out of this place unscathed."

I studied the deep lines around her eyes, and the hand tightening on mine. "You really hate her, don't you? Were you and Eliana close?"

"I was close with her brother. He and I..." She ducked her head, flush creeping up her neck. "When she was imprisoned, the entire family was cast from the palace. I haven't seen Nikolas since."

"Didn't he report to the academy?"

If possible, her flush deepened. "No, he... He already did his time in the academy. He was— He *is* a bit older than me."

My brows climbed up my forehead, and it did not feel great. Didn't stop them. "How much is a bit?"

"Not that much. Just six years."

"He's twenty-four," I cried.

"Shh!" Nitsa flapped her hands—head whipping around, scanning the empty room. "It sounds more scandalous than it was. He was a soldier stationed at the palace. That's how Eliana got the job. At first, all we did was talk about the books I'd catch him sneaking out of the library.

"He was such a gentleman, he refused to act on the feelings growing between us until I was out of the academy. I was the one who snuck into his room the night of my seventeenth birthday and..." Her blush was in full force. "You know."

"Uhh, no, I do not know. Spill it, young lady. I want every sordid detail."

Nitsa burst out giggling. It made me feel better just for making her do so. "Surely not every detail."

"Don't worry. You can rest safe knowing I won't have a clue what you're talking about. My knowledge of sex amounts to the pair of dogs I saw rutting by the pier when I was nine."

She scoffed. "I don't believe it. You're so beautiful it makes my eyes hurt. Men must carve your name on their chests for want of seducing you."

"They do, as it happens. It's revolting. Explains why I'm still in maidenhood." *That and the twelve-foot monster that brought lots of things to the cave, but suitors were not among them.*

We both cracked up.

"—owl?" Voices came down the hall. "How did such a thing get in here?"

"You'll have to hear my sordid past some other time."

Nitsa moved away as Healer Helena bustled in. The woman took one look at me and cringed. "Gods above, child. Be brave just a moment longer. I'll get something for that right away."

Maybe it was a good thing no one would let me look.

Sirena

"You did very well, Tawny." I kissed my sweet girl, then handed her to Rue to have her talons cleaned. The poor thing was covered in that wretch's blood. "Do that on the balcony. I just swept the room for feathers."

Well, to be accurate, Tessa swept my room for feathers, but I was kind enough to not see her have to do it again.

Toeing off my boots, I spread out on my lounge. Hyacinth was there in an instant to rub my aching feet. The best room in the Titan wing. The only one with a balcony and the biggest shower, and it was still a manure pile.

I was forced to replace the tacky, scratchy sheets. A cloud of soot assaulted me the first time Rue lit a fire. The carpet didn't match. The cooling unit wasn't the latest model, and it was so small, it was like living in a servant's water closet.

"It's not enough making me live in this hovel. They put on the final flourish with this beastly schedule. Every day the same thing and I'm learning nothing new. As if these instructors could match the superior education I received at the palace."

"They're lucky to have you," Tessa spoke up from my desk.

"Keep working," I ordered. "No one else will have those forty scrolls done except me. Everyone will receive another ridiculous assignment, except me."

"Of course, Sirena, it's just..." She flicked to Hyacinth. "Maybe the three of us could trade off on your scrolls, so at least I have a chance to work on my own?"

"Stupid. What will Hondros think if it's written in three separate hands?"

"If we're careful, we can match—"

"No."

Tessa wisely shut her mouth and went back to work. Gods knew what she was so worried about. She was a Titan and daughter of Lethe, but despite her ability to steal memories, she'd never rise higher than imperial clerk like her father. I, on the other hand, would sit on the throne of Hera—serving as high councilwoman alongside Alexander. It was vital that one of us sail through the next tedious four years. Hint: that one was me.

Anyway, the three of them had the far better deal. I wasn't allowed to bring my maids with me, so I had no choice but to remind the clerk's daughter, maid's daughter, and advisor's daughter who were entering at the same time, that it was far better to be my friend than my enemy.

"Alexander did well today," Hyacinth ventured. "He took down Proficient Catherine in milliseconds. He truly is the most powerful son of Zeus today—barring his father."

"He was magnificent. It's rare for a god to choose members from the same family. Even rarer for them to choose a father and son, but the Damiens prove they have a bloodline so strong, the king of the gods continues to honor them. I cannot conceive of the heights our children will reach. They'll be the most powerful in all of Olympian history."

"Never has there been a match that makes more sense."

Grinning, I pictured Xander on our wedding day—standing tall and proud before the richest, strongest, and most envious of Olympia. Of course we made a perfect match. I didn't need her to say it, but it was nice to know others saw the facts as plainly as I.

My grin vanished as quickly as it came. "If only Xander didn't insist on these games. Men today all think that if they make no verbal promises, there is no commitment. He thinks I'll stand for it while he bed-hops with every whore from the Myrtle Mountains to the Isles. Once it's out of his system, he'll come crawling back to me like nothing happened." I kicked her away, dropping my feet to the floor. "I'm not putting up with it anymore. We will be married by summer's end."

"What if you nudged him along?" Hyacinth said, picking herself off the floor. "It worked with my sister and her now husband."

I snorted. "Your peasant sister and her soot-stained blacksmith are nothing like me and Xander."

"Okay." Hyacinth wandered off and busied herself making my bed.

Jaw grinding, I bore a hole in her back. "But out of interest," I said slowly. "How did she nudge him along?"

"She got to his best friend. Once Kostas started courting her, all those women down at the tavern lost their bedmate. Panos made promises and commitments to her quick."

"Hmm. I guess it is true what Mother says. Men don't know what they have until they lose it. That's why they need us to do their thinking for them." I crossed to the mirror, thoughts churning on the way, and mind made up by the time my reflection winked back at me.

"Xander knows the only woman worthy of being his wife is me. He may even believe he's doing me a favor by granting me freedom before marriage binds us forever. Sweet, but like Mother says, this is what happens when men don't have a woman doing their thinking for them. I will nudge him along."

I picked a dress off my bed, picturing how it'd hug my curves, and how Xander would follow those curves as they sashayed to another man.

"What do you think of coral and gray for our wedding colors?"

"Beautiful, Sirena."

"It'll be the event of the century."

"Yes." I smirked. "It will."

Aella

"Can't believe I missed another lesson. Anything interesting happen in combat training?" I tossed over my shoulder.

"Depends," Theron whispered. "Do you find striking the same spot on a monster training dummy for over an hour interesting?"

I shrugged. "More interesting than staring at a wall while waiting for the healing potion to kick in."

"Looks much better now. Better than it did twenty minutes ago."

Theron and I wandered the library. We were the volunteers to search out and bring back everything the school had on harpies and cerberi. From all the students from our class that we ran into in the stacks, we weren't the only ones.

I touched the healing scars on my temple. They were still a bit tender, but like Theron said, they hurt less than they did an hour ago. And an hour before that.

"Aella, why don't you check upstairs in the bestiary archives? That's where they keep the pre-Olympian history books." He pointed up. "I'll keep looking down here."

"Sounds good."

Like everywhere in the academy, the library was larger—and more impressive—than any life I've lived. This place was the same style as Madame Remis's room with the spiral staircases leading to stacks upon stacks on floors over floors. I climbed one to the very top, stepping off among the archives.

Cerberi, cerberi, cerberi.

A creature that can see the past, present, and future. What could one tell me if it wasn't hell-bent on killing me? It could start with how I ended up in the goddess's clutches. What went so wrong that horrible night, but also, what went right that I was able to stop her completely taking me over mind and body? And most importantly, was there victory in my future... or the end of everything?

I trailed down my desired section, running my fingers along the spines. *If only I could find one and ask. That they're hideous hellhounds didn't mean they're mindless beasts. They'll have a way to communicate, and if I could speak to one and ask if I defeat the goddess and how—?*

Great idea, Aella, another voice broke in. *We'll just pop through the gates and have a chat with one of the deadliest, unkillable creatures in Olympia.*

Cursing, I sank to the floor. What was the point of coming up with theories if I couldn't leave the grounds to find the answers? The dryads said I had to break the link to break the spell, but they also insinuated there was another barrier after that.

I did not delude myself that I could make another deal with them to get past the rest. I still had no sensible plan to get out of here, and every second I wasted, Olympia was brought closer to danger. I didn't see her coming the first time. Why would I be forewarned the second?

"What are you planning?" I whispered. "How can you possibly complete the ritual?"

She was there in an instant—speaking from nowhere and everywhere. *"It's no fun for either of us if I ruin the surprise."*

"I hate surprises. Trust me, telling me now will be so much more fun for me."

She faded away, her laugh lingering behind.

Thud.

I shot up. "Who's there?"

A voice drifted through the stacks. "I was going to ask you that."

Picking myself up, I peered around the column, gazing into the bowels of the archive. Darkness shrouded at the edge of the torchlight, and within it, I heard movement.

Slowly, I crept closer. "Hello?"

"Hello," they replied, light and playful.

Hairs rose on the back of my neck. *What is this? Why is someone lurking around up here?*

"What are you doing in there?"

"Waiting for you." The alarm bells chimed at maximum. "Did you bring me something sweet?"

Carpet, couches, and a small table littered along the back wall. Squinting, I spotted a moving shadow passing over an armchair. "This isn't funny. Stop fucking with me and show yourself."

"Whoa. No need to get abusive," said that soft, slithering voice. "I've got your coins. Give me what I need and I'll be on my way."

Rounding the last stack, I lit on the figure bent over the table—face pressed to the wood. He inhaled a sharp, short sniff and then snapped up, making me leap back. Something hard and sturdy jabbed the back of my knees, collapsing them and dropping me into the couch's waiting arms.

Whipping around, he locked on me. For a breath, we both just stared.

I'd never know what was going on in his head, but I was taken by what rested on top. Long, copper waves flowed from the roots and ended in soft curls. It framed a face that it tried to soften and feminize, but for his full down-turned lips and dreamy eyes, soft wasn't what I'd call his thick brows, diamond jaw, or his dimpled chin. The guy was molded in clay by divine hands, gifted the kiss of life, then sent to earth to put the memory of Adonis to shame.

He swiped his hand across the table and quickly wiped it on his pants. The act tipped him off-balance and bumped him into an armchair. "Who are you?"

"That's what I've been asking you."

"Are you Calypso?"

"No," I said, righting myself in the chair. "Who's that?"

"All that matters is it isn't you." Clicking his tongue, he came a little closer—body swaying oddly like we were on the deck of a ship rolling on stormy seas. "Seems you don't have what I need." With closer steps, his dreamy eyes focused. "But you..." He whistled. "You are something sweet."

"And now we're back to fuck off." I shoved off the couch. "Have fun lurking around in the dark."

"Whoa, there we go again with the abuse." His words were slowing—slurring. His legs weren't.

I bounced off his hard chest, surprised to find him suddenly in my path.

"You could be nicer to me, you know. Someone should be nice." He rested his head on my shoulder, yanking a choked, squeaky noise out of my throat. "My brother in all but blood was buried today. I wasn't allowed to attend his funeral."

I stilled. "Funeral?"

"Mmmm hmmm," he drew out. His fingers tangled in my hair, popping goose bumps on the back of my neck. "He was killed last week... by a fucking demon."

Oh no...

"I wasn't there... Should've been there..."

"At his funeral or... when he died?"

"Both," he said so softly, I nearly missed it though his lips were inches from my ear. "When it mattered, I wasn't there..."

He took such a long pause, I thought he fell asleep on my chest.

"...now I can never be again."

"That's not true." Hesitantly, I cupped the back of his head—strangely pleased to find his hair was even softer than it looked. "You were there when he needed you. You were his friend. His brother."

That day came into sharper clarity. Alexander wasn't allowed to go to his friend's funeral. Instead, he had to spend all day, staring at the girl who got him killed. That would put rage in my eyes too.

"Friend." His tapered, calloused fingers traveled along my shoulder to those goose bumps. A shiver rippled down my spine as he traced slow, lazy circles on them. "I need a friend tonight. You'll do that for me, won't you?"

"Uh, we don't know each other." With that reasoned statement out of my mouth, it opened the door for more to come in. "Don't stay up here alone. Go down and find your friends. They're who you really need now."

I grasped his hands, untangling from his grip. "I have to go down and find mine. I hope you get through this and... I'm sorry."

"Don't go, something sweet. You're exactly what I need right now."

"Creepy," I said, sidestepping him. "I am going and you are too. Get out of this place and find Alex—"

The mysterious, beautiful man waved his hand and an even prettier cloud of pale pink smoke appeared. A tiny gasp escaped my parted lips, and closer I drew, eyes widening at the sparkling silver flecks glinting within the cloud. "What is it?"

Saying nothing, he puckered his lips and blew. The cloud enveloped me, racing into my mouth as I opened it to protest.

Sweet, placid calm blanketed me like a lake's still surface. All my worries, fears, pain, and doubts sank into the depths—buried where the sun would never reach. All that mattered now is—

"You."

He smiled, and I did too. A wide, beaming smile for how happy I was to have pleased him.

"Call me Calix, sweet one."

"Call me sweet one." Grasping his chin, I guided him back to my bosom. "Call me whatever you want."

"You'll be my friend tonight, won't you?"

"Yes."

"Cater to my needs?"

"Yes."

"Warm my bed?"

The fog thickened in my mind—so nice and soothing as I would be to him tonight. Taking all his troubles away. "Yes."

"And above all, we won't talk. We'll do anything, but talk."

"Yes, Calix."

Suddenly he was gone—ripped from my arms. I cried out, chasing after him.

"Calm yourself, sweet one." Calix reclined on the armchair. "Sit on my lap."

I did so happily. Snuggling against his chest, I asked myself if a moment could ever be more perfect than this.

"Look at me."

Our gaze locked—his capturing mine though I ached to trace every part of him. The cute wrinkle between his thick brows. The cloudy, unfocused haze in his citrine eyes. The curve of his lips as they closed the distance.

Calix kissed me. Gentle, honeyed, and teasing, he nipped for entrance and it all rushed in.

Crashing, coursing, exploding—heat erupted in my chest, my soul, and the very core of my being. He was melting me. His tongue tangled with mine to turn up the furnace and melt me from the inside out, so I'd always be his and his alone. That was the only explanation for the wetness pooling between my legs.

Who knew after eight hellish years and the worst night of my life, something amazing was waiting for me?

It was Calix.

It was love.

"Hey, Cal? Are you up here?"

Who was that? I thought, pulling my love closer still.

"Cal, man. Speak up. I know you're here."

I frowned into our kiss. *Why wouldn't they go away?! Didn't they know Calix had everything he needed? Me.*

"Cal— What the fuck?" Rough hands snaked around my waist, tearing me away from Calix.

My scream echoed through the rafters.

"What the hell are you doing!"

I thrashed in his grip, fighting and straining to get to Calix. My love straightened in the chair, his perfect lazy grin as lopsided as his wonderful hair.

"What does it look like I'm doing? Don't judge me, Xander. We should've been at the funeral. Ajax needed us. Galen needed us! Even if it took burning these fucking ward spells down, we should've been there." He shrugged. "If I need a distraction to get my mind off the unforgivable betrayal to our brother, then you can just fuck off and slam the imaginary door on the way."

"I know what today is," snapped my captor. "Galen's dead and you've got your tongue down the throat of the girl who did it. Dammit, Cal. If you had taken a break from putting that shit up your nose for one fucking minute, you would've connected the face to the name." He shook me. "Aella Galanis. This is her."

My love's smile vanished. "Can't be," he croaked. His beautiful, foggy eyes sharpened. "This skinny little treat? She's the one you've been ranting about? She got Galen killed?"

"Yes."

"Calix." I clawed the air reaching for him. "Calix, my love."

"Get out of here."

Calix looked into my eyes—reading my pleading, my agony, my absolute love for him.

Then he walked away.

"No! Calix, please. I—" The fog vanished. Rocking on my heels, my head smashed into his chest as those worries, concerns, and the real me exploded through the lake's surface. "Oh my gods," I breathed. Horror deadened my bones. "What was that? *Who* was that? What did he do to me?"

"Nothing you can't forget, since believe me, he is paying for it as we speak." Alexander spun me around. His grip was iron around my arms. "What were you doing up here anyway? Everyone knows what goes on in the archives. Were you looking for milk or nectar, Galanis?"

Incredible that even though he kept his word to call me only by my name, he still made it sound like an insult. "I have no idea what you're talking about. Let me go."

"Sex or drugs," he hissed. "What pain do you need numbed? On the day they put a good man in the ground, how have you made yourself the victim?"

I gaped at him. "Victim? I wasn't looking for either of those things. This is a *library*. I came up here for a book."

"Really?" Anger scorched through him, burning me where our skin connected. Or at least that's what it felt like so close to his rage—his heat. "Tell me something, Aella." He spat my name out like a curse. "Did you mean a word you said today? Are you truly sorry your ignorance and stupidity got Galen killed?"

I swallowed past the rock in my throat. "Of course I am. What do you think of me, Alexander? How could I not be sorry?"

"You weren't sorry about the border watchers who risked their lives following you into a pack of typhons," he dropped, tone flat. "You weren't sorry about the man you tore to pieces."

"That was different!" I ripped out of his hold, backing to where the torchlight didn't reach. Anything to make it harder for him to see my filling eyes. "I had to get away, but you and the border watchers didn't have to follow. You made your choices like I made mine. And Nico," I cried. "How dare you throw him in my face? You know what he tried to do to me. I know you know."

"I do know," he said, following me into the dark. There wasn't time to run as his hands slapped the wall on either side of me. "I'm not shedding any tears over the man, but for such a seemingly naïve, sweet little thing, neither were you.

"You ripped a person into shreds and it didn't disturb a minute of your rest. The cool, logical calm of a killer." Alexander bore over me, pressing me flatter against the wall. Gently, he caught a tear off the tip of my nose. "As cool and logical as this little performance. Tears on cue."

"This isn't a performance, Damien. Gods, what's become of you?" I burst out. "What made you so hard and distrusting? Some-times— Most times, an apology is an apology. And tears are just tears. I don't relish the pain you're in now." I couldn't stop myself touching his clenched jaw. "I don't relish it, and I had nothing to gain from it. Galen's death was such a senseless, terrible tragedy. I mourn him."

I claimed the tear staining his finger. "I cry for him."

He stared at me for a long time—the body molded to mine stiff and unmoving. I didn't mistake this for passion. As he said, skin to skin made it hurt worse.

"I want to believe you, Aella. To trust his death was an accident, and not the act of the brass, unrepentant traitor you've always been."

"Of course it was an accident. Why would you think other-wise?"

"Are you saying I have no reason to?"

"Yes," I replied without hesitation.

"I can trust you to tell me the truth?"

My head bobbed. "Nothing I've hidden is because I've wanted to. I want to be honest with you. Honest with everyone."

"Okay, Aella." He tipped my chin—his callus both tender and scratchy on my sensitive skin. "I'm going to ask you something, and if you tell me the truth, it can all be simple from here on. You and I will know where we stand."

"All right. Ask me."

"Were you out in the woods that night because you were trying to escape?"

The world narrowed, converging on a single point and crushing around it... until I stopped breathing.

"Answer me."

"Alexander—"

"Answer me," he whispered.

"*It can all be simple from here on. You and I will know where we stand.*"

Yes, we will.

"Yes." The word singed leaving my tongue. "I was looking for a way past the barrier spells. That's why I was out that night, and why I ultimately crossed paths with that demon."

His hands slid down the wall, swinging down by his sides. I couldn't say why the move left me feeling exposed. His stepping back and peeling off my body was the same as him removing my clothes.

I was bare before him, and neither one of us liked what we saw.

"Thank you, Aella." His tone was dull—emotionless. "You found the last shred of honor in your soul and told me the truth. Now, I will do what I promised."

"What does that mean?" I squeezed my arms where he grabbed me. My only shield in the face of that true still lake within his eyes.

"People have guessed what you are from the armed escort that had to bring you through the doors, but I haven't confirmed it because even though you think I'm a bastard, I believed you deserved a chance to prove yourself without the chains of your mistakes holding you back. Making you do your duty was punishment enough.

"And you know what? Maybe a softhearted part of me felt responsible for locking you in the dark and dirt with Nico Xenakis. Leaving you be for the next four years was my way of making up for failing in my duty."

My lips parted but nothing came out. Alexander felt guilt over Nico's attack? How could I have known that when immediately after he sentenced me to this place?

"All of that's changed now."

"Why?" I didn't mean to sound so stricken. "Yes, I was trying to get out, but that doesn't change the fact that I didn't know what that baby really was. It was an accident, and I won't let myself stop paying for it."

"No." Bright green pools glowed through the dark. "But I'll do a much better job."

My body went cold. "What are you saying?"

"I'm saying you killed my brother," he growled. "Any guilt is gone. Any softheartedness is dead. Any sense of duty is over. I will no longer hold back what's coming for you." He laughed. "Hold it back? I'll be leading the charge.

"It is my solemn swear and promise to you, Aella Galanis, that I will make the rest of your days hell. Anything and everything you love I'll personally and with great pleasure grind beneath my boots. I hope you do find that way out," he said, turning to leave. "Run away until you hit the border and throw yourself off so many times you finally snap your neck. That's where I'll find you to say our final goodbye. Otherwise, I'll never stop."

Alexander disappeared around the stacks, his awful promise lingering behind to keep me company.

I never got those books or finished that paper. I didn't leave the lonely archives at all until the torchlight paled under the sun.

I TRUDGED INTO THE dorm late the next morning. My friends were all inside—exactly where I didn't expect them to be.

"Hey. Shouldn't you be in class?"

Ionna poked her head out of her alcove. I guessed it was the familiarity of being around friends that made her comfortable walking around in nothing but her breast band and undergarments. "None of us should. There's a memorial for Galen Teresi today. We're all required to attend."

"I know what you're thinking but no," Theron spoke up. He was also bare-chested while he chose between formal tunics. "Morning lessons aren't canceled. They're pushed back. Did you get to finish your scrolls?"

I shook my head. "Hopefully Hondros punishes me and just me this time." A flicker of movement drew my attention to the space beside mine. "Where's the memorial?"

"Near the southwest tower. By the lake. There'll be signs telling you where to go."

"Okay, thanks." I took a step and stopped. "Theron, have you ever heard of a guy named Calix?"

He dropped his shirts, brows snapping together. "Yes, but I hope you haven't. He's a son of Aphrodite with a nasty power."

"To make people fall in love with him."

"To make them fall in love with the first person they see," he corrected. "Doesn't matter who. An eighty-year-old man with rotted teeth. A murderer. Your own brother. One look and you're so helplessly devoted, you'd jump off the top of the Imperial Palace tower if they asked you to.

"Wait. Why do you ask?"

"No reason," I said, moving toward the alcove. "I just overheard some girls talking about him."

"I hope everyone's talking about him and warning others to steer clear. He's close with Damien and the rest of the imperial heirs. All those guys think they're untouchable because they're next in line for the council seats."

"Thanks, Theron." I took everything he said and filed it away. Alexander said I wouldn't need revenge against Calix because he'd do a fine job punishing himself. I didn't think he was lying. No, I was certain Alexander Damien meant everything he told me the night before.

But that didn't mean I'd do nothing against the man who... stole my first kiss.

"Daciana?" I tapped on her desk, drawing her head up. "Can I come in?"

"Sure."

She looked okay. Daciana was bright and beautiful as she was every morning. Her wavy two-colored crown was brushed till it shone and that always present smile hung on her lips. Dare I say something that would take it away?

"I just wanted to make sure you were okay," I began slowly. "You disappeared after history class yesterday. I was worried about you."

"Disappeared," she repeated, rolling it on her tongue. "What a nice thought. Back home, I'd have to run for miles through mud and lakes for my pack to lose my scent. Kinda nice to be somewhere I don't have to run far for peace.

"It's not as nice that I worried you. Sorry about that. I just wasn't expecting to hear about vampires here of all places."

I joined her on the bed. "You didn't know about the wars either?"

"No, I knew. Knowledge can't be hidden from the pack. The history of our ancestors is a gift from the goddess that's meant to grant us wisdom. Seeing the lessons they learned and the mistakes they made, makes each generation stronger."

"What does that mean? Seeing the lessons?"

Daciana gazed off into the distance. "It means I've lived a thousand lives, Aella, and nearly all of them were ended brutally and painfully by a vampire... including my mother."

It was the second time within hours that I was struck speechless. *She can't be saying... Please, Hera, mother of all, don't let her be saying what I think she is.*

"Do you mean you saw it all in a vision? Like Ionna?"

"I wish they were visions. Those would be easier to bear." She tossed her head. "We see it all as if we're walking in their shoes. Looking through their eyes. On the longest night of the year, we pray for the goddess to unite us—binding us together, and to her, forever. In return we are blessed"—she let out a small laugh—"or maybe we're humbled to see, hear, smell, and *feel* those who came before.

"I felt his teeth sink into her throat as she screamed for my father to run with me. I heard my own fading cries as she died alone on the cold floor." Daciana flashed me another smile, but there was no mirth. And it wasn't that pleasant. "So, you could say I'm not particular to vampires. There wasn't mention of them in the chapter we were assigned. Madame Remis blindsided me with the true, unedited version."

"Oh, Daciana." I threw my arms around her. "Everything I think to say sounds silly and trite. I'm so sorry for your mother, and that you've had to relive the pain of her death in the worst way. Whatever you need, I'm here for you. Even if it's just someone who'll run through the mud and lakes by your side."

"You couldn't keep up, Olympian." She nudged my shoulder, smiling a real, true smile. "But thank you. There was nothing silly or trite in that."

We sat in silence for a little bit, but we weren't alone. The space was filled with our demons paying call.

"Hey, guys?" Nitsa stuck her head inside. "We're going down to the memorial. Are you coming?"

"Yes," I said. "I have to pay my respects."

"I'm coming too."

Quickly, I ducked into my bare, undecorated space and pulled on gifted clothes—a wool dress tunic, black undershirt, and soft black boots. It wasn't as formal as Theron's or Ionna's, but it would have to do.

Together, our group exited the academy and joined a scattered line of people heading for the back of the castle. As we veered off the lawn and skirted near the tree line, the reason this area was chosen became clear.

Fairy slippers, larkspurs, mountain bells, and wildflowers I couldn't name smattered about the clearing, breaking up the green with patches of pink, purple, white, and crimson. Resting beneath the tallest oak, the crowd encircled a stone plinth, and the golden plaque it was honored to carry.

We neared closer and my gaze drifted over the heads, through the patch of trees where I spotted the shining reflection of fractured sunlight dancing on the lake.

And Sebastian.

He leaned against a cherry blossom tree—close enough to hear, but far enough to set himself apart from us.

"—gathered here to honor a fine young man." Drakos dragged himself out into the sunlight, but only so far that it got him under the shade of the oak. His tunic, pants, and overcoat were from expensive fabrics in the most stylish pattern, and all of it black. "Even though it wasn't my pleasure to know Galen Teresi, I was looking forward to seeing him achieve the greatness he was destined for."

His eyes scanned the crowd, and stayed just a tad longer on me. "The academy is a hard, unforgiving place. Many have lost their lives on these grounds and many more will in the days to come. By now, you'll have heard of the loss of Giles Nanos. Another tragedy before the year has truly begun.

"Know this," he said. "Though every lost trainee will not receive a plaque, they all are remembered with the highest respect for their sacrifice. Without the academy. Without all of you, Olympia is no more. Thank you."

Applause broke out among the trainees and staff. Subdued but sincere.

I found myself joining in. It was a good speech and a nice message for the "many more" who were fated to snap their thread within these gates. I've always had respect for the army and the protection they'd provide. What troubled me was as we sat there with condolences for Galen and Giles, we had no idea if the latter jumped to his death to escape the place that didn't offer another way out.

"Galen's brother, Ajax, will now say a few words."

Ajax broke away from the line he, Calix, and Alexander formed beside the plaque. I traced his face while he spoke of growing up in the palace with his twin brother and closest friend. You'd only know they were twins if you were told. Ajax's eyes were dark brown whereas Galen's were light. His cheekbones were softer. His jaw rounder. But what they did share was a handsomeness as effortless as the confidence in their stance.

Galen was going on to do great things, and Ajax planned to be right by his side.

"—senseless death of my b-brother." His voice cracked. "Imperial Hecate Enchanters were personally employed by my family. This week, they will strengthen the ward spells in and around the academy. In Galen's name, the academy will be made a safer place. Nothing like this will happen again."

Heads turned to me, eyeing me up and down. Their thoughts were plain on their face. So plain, my friends moved in closer.

"If anyone else would like to come up and say a few words for Galen..."

A dozen people stepped forward, including Alexander and Calix. One by one, they shared sweet and funny stories about Galen. By the last person, my eyes were dry, because the goddess laughed the whole way through.

"What a lovely day for a funeral."

I ground my teeth, anger turning my vision white. Her horridness was incomprehensible.

"Thank you for coming, everyone." Drakos brought me back. "The mess hall is open. Please eat, relax, and continue sharing memories of Galen. Afterward, lessons resume on the hour."

My rumbling stomach told me where to go. Instead I stepped to the side, hanging back to let others pass. "You guys go ahead. There's something I have to do."

They nodded like they knew what that was. When almost everyone was gone, I approached the silent figure standing before the plaque. Alexander looked up from his conversation with Calix. They both stopped talking as I tapped Ajax's shoulder.

"Ajax?"

Facing me, the taller boy's red-stained orbs beheld me without a hint of recognition.

"I'm Aella Galanis," I offered. "I was with your brother the night he—"

Alexander snapped to our side. "Leave it, Galanis."

Though it was hard not to look at him, I went on like Alexander hadn't spoken. "The night he died," I finished. "This offers no comfort, but I'm sorry for the part I played in his death. If I had recognized the demon for what it was, none of this would've happened."

Ajax's expression wiped blank. I couldn't be certain he was hearing me.

"If there is anything I can do for you or your family, please let me know. He spent his last day on earth showing kindness to me. I will never forget that. The name Galen Teresi will always live in my heart."

I waited.

And waited.

And waited.

Ajax did not twitch a muscle.

"Okay," I said in the end. "Thank you for hearing me. I'll leave you in... peace..."

Ajax raised his hands. Slow and coordinated, he waved them in a mirrored dance—holding them apart and as high as his chest. Within his swirling fingers, a tiny water droplet took form. Before our eyes it grew—an undulating watery orb that held my shifting reflection.

"Beauti—"

He jerked and the orb flew at me, swallowing my head. Water gushed into my nose, eyes, and mouth.

"Hey!"

Gasping, panic overwhelmed my senses—choking me faster than the liquid rushing into my lungs. I thrashed, swiping desperately at the bubble. My hands passed harmlessly through the water.

Shifting, moving, shouting. All of it tried to reach me as Ajax dragged me to hades. None of it penetrated, but the black bleeding into my vision did.

No. No!

My feet tangled and I crashed to the dirt. Dull pain prickled my toes and nail beds. I was dying... and I was afraid.

Flipping onto my front, I had half a clear thought to hide my blackening fingers under me. Strong hands grabbed and flipped me back—slapping at the water and pumping my chest.

"*Change! Change!*" the goddess shrieked. "*Kill them! You cannot die, my pet. My pet.*"

I stopped flailing. Ceased gasping. Giving in to the dark, I let go.

"WAKE UP. WAKE UP, CHILD."

I cracked an eye open, squinting under the harsh sunlight. "Wha happened?"

"You came back from the brink of death is what happened." Healer Helena bustled over and tipped an elixir down my throat without preamble. I sputtered—hacking half the nasty thing up.

She tsked. "What were you thinking?"

"About what?" I shifted, feeling cushion and blankets under me. I was in the infirmary—again. I was hurt—again.

How was I...? Ajax's blank face floated through my mind.

It all came back.

"He tried to kill me," I said flatly.

"He did indeed. It's a good thing Madame Remis ran and got Commander Vasili in time. He put the boy to sleep and ended his attack. A few minutes more, and I'd be looking for your next of kin."

I just nodded. "Where is Ajax now?"

"Trying to kill a fellow trainee in front of the headmaster earns you time in the reflection room, which is why I suggest you be careful from here on." The grim set to her lips quieted me. "If he's reflecting on anything down there, it's how next time he can get away with it without getting caught."

"Next time? You think— I mean, it wasn't wise to approach him while he stood over his brother's memorial. But if I give him space from now on. Let him cool off, then..." I trailed off at the look in her eyes.

"I've worked here for sixteen years, Miss Galanis. Most of the students I've lost were because of training mishaps, but the deaths that haunt me are the accidents." Her gaze drifted over my head. "In our world, you can never truly know. If you and Mr. Teresi were alone this morning, and he tossed you in that lake ten feet from him after using his power, what would everyone think?"

"That I drowned," I whispered through numb lips. "An unfortunate accident."

"I don't want to say this academy is a dangerous place. I *can't* say it. Foul play has only been proved a handful of times in the hundreds of years since this institution was formed. But I've seen the damage of great power in irresponsible hands."

Nico and the power that overwhelmed me in seconds haunted my mind.

"Galen Teresi was the son of a powerful family and their friends are even more powerful. Fair or not, you've made enemies." She squeezed my wrist. "Watch your back in the days to come. It's my sincere hope that I don't see you in this room again."

I thought about what she said on the walk through the empty halls to my room. I was hopelessly naïve about too many things, but the fact that I had pissed off some powerful people wasn't one of them. How could it be when, deep down, I understood why they hated me. None of this would've happened if I hadn't been out in those woods looking for an escape.

But then of course, it also wouldn't have happened if an evil deity hadn't captured and turned me into her puppet. It wouldn't have happened if I wasn't ripped out of reality at age ten and kept in a cage to be a lamia's replacement daughter.

I could spiral down the list of random and connected events that led to this senseless tragedy, and there'd always be someone to blame, but Ajax, Alexander, and Calix would never see all of that. All they knew is the one to blame was me.

I got through my delayed morning classes intact, but not unscathed. None of my classmates, or owls, tried to attack me, but Hondros was less than impressed when I showed up short on my scrolls. He assigned the class ten more that night even though I wasn't the only one who didn't complete the assignments. The glowers following me out of class made me keep my back to the wall.

History was better. Madame Remis spun us such a fascinating tale about the birth of the Titan and Olympian gods, and why the birth of the fae and wolf gods were left out—that no one had time to do anything but listen and, in Sirena's case, hotly question every word out of her mouth.

"So if there are wolf-shifter gods, are there other shifter gods too?" I asked Daciana on the way to self-mastery.

"Not that I know of. But the goddess teaches us that the universe is infinite and our brains are smaller than a watermelon. We shouldn't pretend we know everything."

I laughed. "I like your goddess. She's wise."

The laughing stopped when we arrived at the stadium. Instructor Kazran sent me back to Catherine. The good news was I didn't have to deal with Alexander, Sirena, or her handmaidens because they all moved on to another proficient. The bad news was Catherine tossed me around like a doll all over the arena. I didn't get close to stopping her attack.

"Galanis." Kazran's shadow fell over me. "You're dead."

I groaned, straining to flip onto my front. "Certainly feels like it, sir."

He hauled me to my feet. "I suggest a new approach. Standing there and taking a beating doesn't seem to be working for you."

Aren't you a sarcastic smartass? I penned in the reply. Eight years in a small space with three people and a monster, sharpened my tongue. My sisters and I fought a lot. Rather than get involved, the lamia crawled out of the cave to get some peace. We didn't have that option, so all the frustrations in our hearts and the meanness that sprouted from it was said.

But here there is somewhere to go if I go off.

The reflection room.

My teeth ground. "I'm open to any tips, Instructor."

"Here's the only one you need: If they're faster, you need to be smarter." He strolled off, leaving me to trudge to my friends.

"How'd you guys do?" I asked. It was hard to tell because they were all in various states of disarray. Ionna was covered in dirt. Theron had a deep gash on his forehead. Tycho was cradling his arm. Nitsa was banged up from top to bottom, and Daciana was in the middle of changing into her clothes. She was stronger than all of us put together in her human form. Any opponent that forced her to shift had to be tough.

"I'm ready to throw myself off the tower," Tycho griped. "That's how I did."

"I'm next."

"Me too."

"We'll hold hands on the way down," Nitsa returned.

I passed Daciana her breast band. "Did anyone move on?"

Everyone shook their heads except Daciana. "I did but only because my mind is so alien as a wolf, her attempt to control it failed. She ran pretty fast when I charged her."

"Control your mind?" I squeaked. "They can do that?"

"Not the way you read in stories." Nitsa leaned on me to make up for her limping left leg. "They don't control you, but they can make you see and hear things that aren't real. Children of Dolos have the kind of powers that make you pray there's a good person behind them."

"I know that prayer."

The end of self-mastery brought the beginning of lunch. All of us were late since a stop in the showers was vital. Freshly washed and free of ripped and soiled clothes, we headed into the one part of the building where everyone—Titan, Sisyphean, Novice, Competent, Proficient, and Expert came together.

I found my head tipping up to the ceiling as it did every time I came in here. Unlike the other murals on and under the ceilings around the castle, this one didn't depict the gods or a battle. It was us.

All the different peoples and cultures and histories that came together when we formed Olympia, painted in all the colors I could and couldn't name. It was a reminder that we were telling the story now. In the future when they told the tale of the Olympian gods and what became of them, it will include us.

"Move." Rue elbowed me out of the way. She, Tessa, Hyacinth, Sirena, and even that vicious bird smirked at me strutting past with their trays.

Again I bit back a sharp reply about wiping Sirena's boot prints off her back. Healer Helena told me to be smart, and the first start was to not pick a fight with someone before I knew their power. Thank you, Ajax, for driving that lesson home.

Our group joined the line, carrying our plates between two long tables loaded with food. Our society was a blend of cultures, but that wasn't something a young girl living in an isolated town and eating mostly fruit, fish, and the occasional honey cake as a treat, got to know. Here the variety of Olympia was displayed in a universal language: food.

I loaded up on lamb stew, something Nitsa called tamales, rice covered in curry lentils, and a mug of watered wine.

Small tables like the ones gathered in the courtyard of the inn Alexander stayed in that fateful night, scattered about the hall. We weaved through the columns separating the food area from the seating, and joined the wide-open space of laughter, studying, and bellies satisfied.

Theron pushed two tables together and we settled in. I looked up as my butt hit the seat and locked eyes with him immediately.

Directly across the hall at a row of tables pushed together in the back, Alexander sat with Sirena, Calix, Tessa, Rue, Hyacinth, and four other people I recognized from the first day loitering on the lawn.

Calix shook his shoulder, then followed where he was looking to me. He blew me a kiss.

Cheeks flaming, I snapped my head down and resumed stabbing my tamale. His power didn't have the decency of causing amnesia too. I remembered every second. Every thought. Every rise and fall of my heaving chest as our tongues tangled and eyes watered. In that hidden corner with him, I would've given him anything if only he asked. My maidenhood. My hand in marriage. My firstborn bearing a crown of wavy locks and deceptively tender eyes. It was all his for the taking.

Why was Ares the most hated Olympian god? Surely that was Cupid and his ill-fated arrows.

When I looked up again, Alexander and Calix were coming straight at me.

"Guys," I hissed. "Guys, look."

Theron, Nitsa, and Ionna ceased talking as the two planted themselves in front of our table.

"Something wrong, gentlemen?" Theron asked.

Alexander didn't take his eyes off me. Gods, why did I ever think those molten orbs were beautiful? They were two molten rivers burning me alive. "With you? I don't have the millennium it would take to rattle off that list."

"Jackass." Damned my tongue. "Your list of failings would crush the earth under its weight. If you walked over here just to insult someone, you can take that acid tongue back to your gorgon betrothed. She's dying for someone to burst that oversized, snake-ridden head."

He chuckled. "Oh, Aella. Always the clever comeback. Let's see what you have to say about this," he said, leaning over the table. "You, and the traitors who unwisely chose to align with you, are banned from this hall.

"You're not to eat where Galen should've eaten. You're not to walk the halls where he should've walked. You're not to laugh while he doesn't breathe. Should you break any of these rules, the consequences will be... unreasonable." The threat ghosted over my lips. "Stand up and get the fuck out if you understand."

A hand gripped my chair and shoved it back like I weighed a hair. Daciana planted herself in front of him—their faces so close their noses bonked. "I've lived a thousand lives and died a thousand deaths, demigod. Neither your threats nor that little power intimidates me. Return to your table. You will not bother Aella again."

Breath trapped in my lungs, I peered around her for his reaction. Any second I'd be pushing her aside to take the full blast of his blood-boiling.

"Hmm," he drew out. "So you're Galanis's protector?"

"That's right."

Alexander cut eyes to Calix. "What do we think about that, Cal?"

Clothes rumpled, hair messy, and shoulders slumped like holding them up was more effort than it was worth, and still Calix was as gorgeous as the object of my fever dreams. I wanted to find fault in his looks—in *both* of their looks to prove the gods were not so cruel as to gift a monster flawless beauty. But the bastards wouldn't let me.

"What I think..." Calix drawled, draping an arm over Alexander's shoulder. "Is that you're a high priestess, correct? Eighteen years old, you're too young for the ascension, but like a good little wolf you've kept and will continue to keep yourself in *pristine* condition to make the goddess happy."

Daciana's shoulders set in a hard line.

"We're not all ignorant fools who can't bother to pick up a book on the other dominions. Some of us took advantage of the best education money could buy."

It was odd seeing Calix then. The man I met the night before was funny, slow, and sad. So very sad. But this cold, smirking twin was nothing like that. Watching him, I wasn't sure which side was worse.

"I know what would happen if I helped you pop the cork off that bottle," Calix said. "You may not fear Xander, but you definitely fear that."

"You can't make me do anything," Daciana growled.

He jerked a chin at me. "Ask your friend if that's true."

"Why?" I said, getting to my feet. "What are you talking about?"

Neither Alexander nor Calix acknowledged me. "Is standing against me to protect *her* honestly worth it?" Alexander asked. "She won't be coming with you when you leave in four years. She won't repay the favor and protect you against your pack."

The silence stretched between them, our group, and the nearby trainees openly listening.

Turning her back on them, Daciana took my hand and led me out. Her head was high and back straight, but even so, we were leaving. Those two had won that battle and I didn't know how it happened.

"Daciana, what's going on?" Chairs scraped back, alerting me that all of my friends were leaving too. "Why did you give in to them? Even if I deserve their wrath, you, Theron, Tycho, Ionna, and Nitsa don't."

"Answer me this," she said, voice low. "Can that man make people do things against their will?"

The corners of my lips tightened. "He can... make you believe it's not against your will."

"That's why we gave in."

It was a subdued, quiet group that returned to the dorm to await the next period of sitting in the heat while the Titans trained. More than once I felt I should say something. "*Thank you.*" "*You didn't have to do that.*" "*I promise I'll get Alexander and his Titan comrades to leave you alone.*"

The first two were inadequate and the last was an empty promise. So, I kept my mouth shut and worked on Hondros's scrolls in my tiny corner of room.

Eventually, it was time to head back out to the south field.

"Titans, form your groups and be prepared to show me what you've been working on. Sisypheans." Vasili motioned to the stands. That was all he had for us.

"Let's sit over there," Nitsa said. "There's a little shade."

"Thank you," I blurted, turning everyone's heads. "You guys should've said 'I barely know that girl. Do what you want with her,' and kept eating. Instead, you tried to defend me and you walked out with me."

"Course we did," Theron said. "Xander's surname is Jackass, but none of us share the same father."

"Still. I'm going to make it clear to him that if he has a problem with me, he deals with me. I won't let them bring you into the war that's brewing."

Nitsa snorted. "We were already in it, Aella. A line was drawn in the sand between us and them from our first day in imperial school. They would've come for us—for all the Sisypheans—no matter who we befriended. Don't think you have to do this alone." She gripped my shoulder, drifting to Sirena. "Alone you can't beat them. No one can."

I smiled mirthlessly at Daciana. "You're probably wishing you kicked the messenger that brought you your acceptance in the interdominion program."

She chuckled. "Not at all. Father encouraged me to go. See another part of the world and experience life outside the pack before it became my whole life. If what I learn is that everywhere I go there's always another self-proclaimed alpha who needs a lesson in what happens when they underestimate me, then it's experience that will only serve me when I lead in the goddess's name.

"Do not worry about this Cal." Daciana flapped a hand like he was a gnat buzzing in her face. "I will find his weak point and rip it out with my teeth. Let us see him try to control me then."

Daciana glided away—long hair swaying and gorgeous smile on her lips once again.

"She's tough," Theron mumbled.

"She's amazing."

All eyes swung to Tycho, who promptly reddened. "I mean— I'm just saying she's cool, you know. A good friend. What!"

"Nothing," Nitsa breezed. "Let's get under those trees before the seats are taken."

We followed after Daciana, skirting the groups of Titans unleashing on practice monster dummies. They were all roughly the same size even though they were modeled after manticores, ty-phons, hydras, gorgons, and griffins.

The trainees are in for a surprise when they face their first typhon in real—

Something hooked my ankle, holding fast. I dropped flat on my face—forehead bouncing off the ground. Raucous laughter went up around me.

"Shit, Aella." Theron and Tycho lifted me under the shoulders. "Are you okay?"

"I'm okay." A blunted ache pounded my temple. I'd have a lump there within the hour. "What happened?" I asked, twisting my neck. "Was that there before?"

"No." Anger leeched into Tycho's voice. "It wasn't."

I flicked from the root that suddenly appeared from the ground, to the open smiles and malicious laughs. Yes, it was a mistake to leave the stadium after my placement. Having everyone's power out in the open put us on equal footing. Without that footing, I'd be getting used to falling on my face.

"Let's go."

We continued on carefully, our eyes on the ground. I didn't relax until I joined my friends on the stands, and we settled in for ninety minutes of tedium.

"We should play a game to pass the time," Nitsa offered. "Ionna, what was that one you were talking about last night? Guess the God? Ionna?"

Our crimson-haired, freckled friend stared off in the distance. I was beginning to understand what that meant.

"Oh, okay." Nitsa let her be and faced us. "Basically, I think what we do is describe one of the many crazy godly tales, and then the others guess the god involved. The trick is you have to be vague. No obvious details that would give it away. Okay, like this." She clapped, getting excited. "I say pride made her boastful, arrogance made her challenge, hubris made her fall. Who is this story about?"

"Hmm." Tycho stretched out on the seat behind, resting on his elbows beside Daciana. "You said her, so that takes a few people out of the running."

"And it's punishment for hubris," Theron added. "Is it—?"

"Guys!" Ionna jerked up, startling Tycho into falling on Daciana's lap.

"What?" I said. "What is it?"

If she heard me, she gave no sign. Ionna scanned our surroundings, eyes narrowing. I looked where she did but didn't see anything.

Her shoulders slumped. "Nothing. Just another wrong vision." Shaking herself, she tried for a smile. "What were we talking about?"

"We're playing your Guess the God game." Red-faced, Tycho righted himself and looked everywhere but at Daciana. "My guess is Arachne and Athena."

"Correct. Now it's your turn."

"Guys." That time the interruption was mine. We ceased our game as a group of Sisypheans seated on the lower benches got up and climbed the stands, circling us.

Kosma Ariti drew ahead of the pack. I recognized the short brown hair cut above the nape, along with the long face that got longer when Commander Vasili said *Sisyphean*. "You six are in our seats."

She's the daughter of Poseidon. The one who speaks to horses.

"We're not," Nitsa said. "We got here before you."

Kosma folded her arms. "I don't think you heard me. You're in our seats. Get up."

"Move on," Theron said, turning his back on her.

She came around and planted herself in his face. "I don't care who your mother is, Theron Zervas. We're not in the Imperial Palace. Here, you're just a traitor's bedmate, and we don't want any of you near us."

"We weren't near you," I replied. "We were over here minding our own. If you go back where you came from, we can continue to not be near each other."

"Don't talk to me, bitch."

"Hey," Nitsa barked. "What's your problem, Ariti? She's right. You guys got in our face, not the other way around. Fuck off."

Kosma sniffed. "What's my problem? My problem is you guys think you can cozy up with a traitor and a murderer and no one gets to say anything about it. I want you out of my sight. All of you. You can find a spot in the dirt and shit where you belong."

"No one gets to say anything about it because I'm not a traitor or a murderer," I said.

"Don't try it. *Everyone* knows the truth about you now, Aella Galanis. You were picked up by border watchers for trying to flee Olympia. They gave you a choice between death or duty, and the first thing you did when you arrived at the academy was try to escape—again. Did she tell you that?" Kosma flung at my friends. "That's why she was out in the woods that night. It's why Galen ended up dead."

"Who told you that?" I rasped, though I already knew. Alexander said he wouldn't protect me any longer. Everyone would know what I was, and let the ruin fall as it may.

The man worked fast.

"Everyone knows," she repeated.

Pressure built on my chest. "You don't know a thing. I love Olympia. All I want to do is protect my home, and everything I've done is to see it safe. Whoever said otherwise is full of typhon dung."

"The one who said otherwise is the son of the *Zeus council-man*," she drew out. "I'll take his word over yours any day."

"The one who said otherwise is the typhon's anus the dung came from."

Kosma and her friends gasped, gaping at me. "Treason! Are you listening to this, Zervas! She openly disrespects the council. I bet she plotted to kill Galen Teresi."

Theron got to his feet. "Ariti, I'm not sure if you noticed, but you're a Sisyphean like the rest of us. You may think carrying out the imperial heirs' vendettas will curry favor with them, but they don't care about anyone but themselves. If Aella says she didn't try to desert, then I believe her. It wouldn't be the first time one of those guys lied or framed an innocent person to get their way."

I dropped my gaze, lips pressed tight.

"Once they've got their satisfaction out of torturing Aella, they're not going to kiss your cheek and invite you into the inner circle," Theron said. "If anything, you'll be next."

Her lips pressed into a thin line. I wasn't sure what nerve he hit, but he definitely got one of them.

"This isn't about currying favor. It's about right and wrong. It's wrong for her to strut around the castle with those of us who didn't shirk our duty, and didn't get anyone killed in the process. Go," she shouted at me, flinging out her hand. "Stay the fuck away from all of us. Same goes for you who dare to defend her."

"Fine," Ionna said before I opened my mouth. "We'll go."

"What? No." I stepped away from her outstretched hand. "I won't be run off by Damien's poison. I'm truly sorry that Galen paid the cost for my ignorance, but I've done nothing else wrong and I won't be punished for imagined slights."

"Imagined? Did we all imagine the army escort that pushed you through the gates?"

"You imagined that was any of your business. We're not going any—"

Ionna tugged sharply on my arm. She mouthed something to me, eyes bugging.

"I'm not going to tell you again!" Kosma rushed me. "Fuck off." She grabbed my tunic, ripping a tear in the neck as she shook me. "Traitor!"

"We're going," Ionna cried, shoving her away. "Dammit, Kosma, are you trying to bring Vasili down on all of us? Cuddle up to a child of Harmonia and calm the hades down." Ionna had a tight grip leading me away. "And Theron's right," she called over her shoulder. "Alexander's still going to ignore you after this."

"Bitch!" Her insults followed us off the stands and across the lawn.

"What was that, Ionna?" I asked. "Why did we walk away again? They're Sisypheans too. They don't have the power to make us do anything, so why give it to them?"

"Because I saw it," she hissed.

"Saw what?"

"Saw you!" She spun me around, grasping my shoulders. "I had a vision of that fight, Aella. Normally, I ignore them because they rarely turn out to be true, but then everything was happening the way I saw it, and she grabbed you, and I— I couldn't—"

"Couldn't what?"

She tipped her head, stricken. "Let you die. I had a vision she was going to shove you too hard and push you off the stands. You would've... fallen and broken your neck, Aella. She was going to kill you."

"By the goddess," Daciana breathed.

"We'll stand up to her next time," Ionna said. "When we're not high above the ground."

I didn't argue with her. That was the second time my friends had to save me. And the second time that day I was nearly killed. What was coming for me tomorrow, or the day after, or next week? Alexander was determined to turn the whole academy against me and he was doing a great job. The headmaster was no friend to me. Commander Vasili stopped acknowledging my existence.

I had only my friends to rely on, but the fact remained we'd known each other for less than a fortnight. It wasn't their responsibility to protect the mundane girl with a goddess's monster parasite burrowed in her soul. It wasn't and I didn't want to be. Why should they be tormented for the next four years of their lives because on the eighteenth day of my birth when the lamia brought me to the cliff's edge—

"They shall be tormented either way, sweet Aella. At least they'll have the honor of spending their last days protecting my pet. All that matters is what we must do," she whispered. *"Surely you see that now."*

I cut eyes to my friends sitting on the last stand by themselves. I shot beneath it and slipped into the trees.

"I don't know that at all. I don't know what you want, why you're doing this, or even who you are. Why won't you tell me, huh? Is it because the more I know, the easier it'll be for me to stop you?"

"You cannot stop me." Even without seeing her, the act of her speaking in my mind hurt. Each word was a pound on the nail piercing my skull. *"No one can now. Events are already in motion to complete what we've started. Soon, I will have total control over my pet. Then I'll reign over a wasteland of blood and bones."*

"Why would you want to! Of all the gods I know, none of them were harpy-shit insane," I shrieked in the direction of a tree. "Who are you? Why are you doing this?"

She hummed. "*Come, come. I shan't tell you my secrets until I have your assailable loyalty. Even though you know the consequences, you're still thinking of a way to warn your little demigod friends that they're in danger. So sweet. So foolish.*"

I whirled around on nothing. "I will find a way to warn them, or I'll kill myself. I swear by the boiling acid pits of Tartarus where I'll watch you burn forever, you will fail."

"*What a nonsensical reply. A goddess cannot die. Not as long as the embodiment of all I am lives on.*"

"I will stop you."

"*You will do no such thing.*" My head pounded harder as she laughed. "*You can't. You won't be killing yourself either. Remember what happened the last time you tried? You want to live, Aella Galanis. So much of your life was stolen from you. For years you dreamed of freedom. Of light and love and that home of windows with a loving family inside.*"

A pang pricked my heart. Lips trembling, I fought to not see that home. To reject the hope of that dream.

"*You can't,*" she whispered. "*That's what so fascinated us about you humans. It's why we just couldn't stay away. Gods don't dream. They do not hope to be anything more than they are. Prometheus did not know when he made you... that you'd surpass us all.*"

Tears painted my lips. She hurt. She hurt so much.

"*Your dream of freedom is buried deeper in your soul than any curse can reach,*" she said. "*You will not kill yourself, and you will not roll over and expose yourself to the many pests here who are willing to complete the task for you.*

"*While there's a glimmer of hope in your heart that you can defeat me, you'll hold on to the dream. So let us continue our dance, pet.*" Her *tsk, tsk, tsk* laugh was an anvil smashing my skull. "*We will see what wins: a child's dream or a goddess's wrath.*"

"I will," I rasped. I took a step and stumbled. "I will because I fight for something bigger than my dream, or your insanity. I—"

I spun around, and landed on the raised brows of Sebastian Barba.

"Please continue," he said, legs crossed and leaning on the tree that received my abuse. "You were saying something about insanity?"

"How long have you been standing there?" I pressed the heel of my palm to my temple, furiously racing through everything he might've heard. *Did I say anything that could give her away? Could he tell— No, no!*

That familiar pain sprouted in my fingertips. *Don't get scared, Aella. Don't let it through, or he dies!*

"Long enough. I heard you were in here shouting to yourself, and I fancied eavesdropping."

"You heard? How—?" I peered through the trees at my friends. None of them were looking in this direction. "Doesn't matter. Go."

"Did you hear me?" I swept out my hand and stumbled. Sebastian blurred in my vision. "Go away... or..." Deeper, deeper, deeper drove the nail. "Or... I'll..."

"You'll what? Be quick about your threats."

I stumbled again, and Mother Gaia dragged me into her arms. The last thing I saw were his boots coming toward me.

Alexander

"Our attack would be simple," said Zoe, the only daughter of Zeus in our training group. "I would unleash rain on the beast and Timon"—she gestured to the final member of our team—"will unleash his lightning. When it's down and disoriented, Damien will finish it off.

"What do you think? Damien? Alexander, are you listening?"

"I am." I squinted as if it would make it any easier to see through wood and leaves. "Here is the revised plan: I kill the beast. We all go to the tavern for cards and drinks."

She blew out a breath. "That's your *revised plan* for everything we come up with. We're supposed to devise strategies that use all of our strengths and powers."

What are they doing in there?

Galanis and her band of misfits moved to the stands in the back, but for some reason, she didn't join them. She disappeared into the forest, then Sebastian Barba went in too. Did they think nobody would notice? Was this some kind of prearranged plan to sneak away?

My fists balled. "Tell you what. Here's a plan that utilizes your strengths and powers. I'll kill some fucking monsters, and you two will sit on your ass and watch it done right. Any questions?" I was already marching off, making fast for the trees. "Good."

Barba had no business going near my traitor. The guy was barely a step away from one himself. He disappeared out of sight and off all records when he was nine years old. Almost everyone believed the rare, prized, *feared* son of Hades was dead. Then two years ago, he resurfaces.

Multiple palace officials questioned him about his whereabouts and he refused to answer. Even more demanded a demonstration, and he wouldn't give so much as that ludicrous performance with the smoke birds. As it was, he told those officials, and the council giving their orders, that he'd never live in the palace, claim the empty seat of Hades, or live as a puppet for a bunch of... many expletives were removed from the report.

Ever since, he's dodged the spies sent to trail him and discover where his actual loyalties lie. All I needed to know was that they didn't lie with the council.

Is that what the two of them bonded over? Barba was quick to defend her against Hondros despite not giving that much of a shit about anyone else. Traitor finds traitor. They could be in there figuring out how to escape the grounds.

I picked up the pace, shoving through the fools in my way. *But why would he do that for her and how did she know he was an ally?*

Did the two of them disappear into the same place? Have they known each other the whole time?

Are they lovers?

The thought slammed me to a halt, rocking me off my heels. Did what I actually see was the two of them sneaking off for an hour and a half romp in the woods?

My lips peeled back from my teeth. *Unacceptable.*

Just like that, I was sprinting past Theron and his weakling friends—bursting through the trees. She would not dare to laugh and fuck and have herself a good time on the day we said *goodbye to Galen.*

Visions bombarded me unwanted. As clear as if they were before me, I saw her soft skin dripping with sweat as they rolled through the leaves and grass. Fevered moans peeled from her pouty, irritating mouth while it gifted him more kindness than anyone else who'd been on the other end of it. He tangled in her messy curly hair. She raked her nails down his back.

Vision Aella lifted her gaze, fixing on me with that holier-than-Hera smirk as she kissed a trail past his blond crown and wrapped her lips around his—

I'll kill them!

Power rushed to my fingertips. No, I'd kill him slowly and painfully, extracting each scream on beg of merciful death. Aella would watch her rebel lover die, then maybe she'd know a fraction of the destruction her selfishness left in her wake.

Growling, I shoved through the trees—searching for them, listening for the moans.

"Galanis!"

Aella

I'm not sure what woke me. One moment I was staring at the split figure of Sebastian Barba, then next my eyes opened again, coming face to face with... a mushroom.

"It's about time. You sleep like the dead." *Chuckle, chuckle.* "And I would know."

"Wass going on?" I mumbled, pushing myself up. "Where— My gods, where am I?"

Elysium? Did she finally do it? Did the goddess burn my human mind past the point of no return?

It was beautiful. Any place painted with the gods' own hand could be nothing but.

A bed of foxgloves cradled me, tickling my skin with tiny purple fingers. They surrounded the lake with friends of cornflower and poppy—each of them delighting the lake's shore in a myriad of color. Gazing over the water, I saw the lily pads floating on their still bed, and felt the last traces of my headache melt away.

Tree branches hunched over me, reaching for their lovers across the lake. It had gotten late according to the reds, golds, and purples fleeing across the skies with the setting sun, but the trees enclosed me in my own little world—safe, quiet, free.

It's my dream.

"Where does it look like you are?"

I shot Sebastian an irritated look. No, this was not paradise. That place didn't come with strange, silent stalkers who follow you into the woods and—

"Kidnap me," I cried. "You brought me here, didn't you?"

"Wasn't anyone else around to haul you out of the dirt." He jumped off the boulder that was his throne. "You're welcome, by the way."

"I didn't say thank you."

He chuckled at the snap. "We're deep in the forest, but still on academy grounds of course. A friend of mine told me about this place."

"Why would you follow me into the woods?" I broke in, blunt as a spoon. "Who exactly told you I was talking to myself?"

"That's not what I said." Barba adopted the same cross-legged, leaning stance on the rock. His hair hung loose and free, draped around strong shoulders that carried me through the forest. Poised like that, I could almost believe he was holding still for the dryads to freeze and watch him be—forever in awe of his beauty that they'd waste away and turn to stone rather than look away for a moment.

"I said I overheard you talking to yourself. Surely I wasn't expected to walk away from such a spectacle."

"Yes, you were," I said, getting to my feet. "Even a madwoman deserves a little privacy."

The corner of his mouth curved in a grin. "You're funny. No one said you were funny."

"No one has business saying anything about me to you."

"You're quite touchy this evening."

I rounded on him. "I get that way when I'm lied to. You weren't anywhere near me when I ducked into the trees. I saw you all the way across the lawn, in a staring match with a stuffed manticore."

"Well, there wasn't anything else for me to do with the thing. Vasili gets strangely angry when I use my power on them, all the while barking at me to use my powers." He shrugged lightly. "Mixed messages."

"Really? Because the message is clear to me. He's pissed that you're downplaying your power instead of showing everyone what you can really do."

Hooded eyes peered at me through his lashes. "What can I really do, Aella?"

A shiver went down my spine. The way he said my name reminded me of Calix calling me sweet one. Did all men have this power of rolling your name on their tongue and releasing it with a kiss? No wonder Nitsa was so smitten with her soldier love that she took matters into her own hands.

"What you can do is distract and deflect," I replied, voice steady. "One minute you were across the green and the next you were behind me. Did you follow me into the forest? Is there something you want to ask me?"

He tipped his chin, smiling, smiling—still smiling. "There're quite a few things I want to ask you."

Goose bumps popped along my arms. "I'm listening."

"What..." he began, peeling off the rock and circling me, "can you really do?"

I kept my expression blank. "What do you mean?"

"Are you really not a demigod?"

"Yes."

"Not a drop of power within you?"

My neck craned following his path. "We're in the same class. You've watched Proficient Catherine fling me to and sunder. If I had power, I'd have used it by now."

"Would you? Some secrets are worth pain."

"And others are worth mercy." I held out my arm—not a quick or demanding movement. Just a gentle raise that halted him against my skin. "Why do you hide yours? To spare others pain or yourself?"

"Hmm." It was neither a quick or demanding movement from him as he moved down my body and paused in front of me—so close I breathed the air that left him. "Did you ever ask yourself why it's so important that they not only know what each of us can do, but that they also control every aspect of our lives until we're either old or infirm?"

I dipped my chin. "Yes."

"You have?" A wrinkle marred his brow. More than that, I thought I detected a hint of surprise.

"Yes," I repeated. "To have absolute power, you must control absolutely."

"Huh." I didn't imagine it then. A wide grin revealed a dimple in his cheek.

I looked away—embarrassed to see it for no good reason.

"You are a rare find, Aella Galanis."

"This is true. Now put me back where you found me."

He swept out a hand. "The way is through there. I'll show you."

"I think I can find it. It's the huge, soaring castle in the distance, yes?"

That earned me another chuckle. "Goodbye, Aella. I hope we speak again soon."

Sebastian returned to his boulder, his gaze prickling the back of my neck long after he was out of sight.

He and I would not speak again soon. He was quite good at it. So good, maybe I wouldn't have noticed if I hadn't spent the last few months under thrall of the goddess.

Sebastian didn't answer a single question I asked about him, but he did follow me. Across the green and into the trees, he watched for the moment I slipped away alone.

But why?

I WAS LATE TO FIELD medicine class and earned four scrolls on the medicinal uses of aloe. I could have told her I passed out in the woods, and a random smirking demigod decided to carry me deeper into it instead of telling my friends what happened to me. But for some reason, I didn't want to mention that strange interlude with Sebastian. The same Sebastian who opted not to show up for class.

"What happened to you?" Nitsa said in my ear. "You just disappeared. Did Ionna's vision rattle you that much?"

"It was sobering to find out I escaped death twice in one day."

"A possible future. Ionna sees a hundred of those a week. What matters is she stopped that one from happening, and next time, we'll get her out of our face before the shoving starts."

"I guess I must accept that there will be a next time." I knew he was looking before I peered over her head. Alexander was watching me, and he looked madder than ever. "Maybe even as soon as tonight."

"Now, everyone, spread out and take a look at the black currants," she called. "This is a lovely little berry that can treat the skin afflictions that flare up after long days riding under the beating sun."

We left the table behind, me heading in the opposite direction of Alexander. Standing over the thriving bush, I inhaled the sweet scent of the currants. My eyes fluttered open and connected with Damien.

"Oh, Hera." I peered at the ground. "How did my shadow get over there?"

"So witty," he gritted.

My mouth lost the mocking twist. "Is something wrong?"

"I thought I told you you're not allowed to walk these halls, or stand where Galen should've stood."

"Yes, you did, but you didn't mean lessons, because you can't have. I can't sit in my dorm all day."

"Don't play to me like you care about lessons. You never wanted to be here. You don't give a shit about training, and I'm certain you're still plotting an escape."

"What?" I hissed, brows shooting up. "No, I'm not, and you have no reason to think so. I've either been in lessons or in my dorm, buried under scrolls."

"You were neither place an hour ago when you snuck off into the forest."

My brows climbed higher. "Stop. Watching. Me. Damien."

"Would you like that?"

"Yes, I would."

"That makes me disinclined to give it to you."

I turned to leave. Damien was in my path between blinks.

"How do you know Sebastian Barba?" he demanded.

"How do I know him? We're in the same training class, Jackass."

He nodded. "But you knew him before." It wasn't a question.

"Uh, no, I didn't. Never seen him before that first day in the arena." I tried sidestepping him, but he moved with me.

"After that day, you spent a week in the reflection room." A heady mix of musk, earth, and scented soap filled my nose. The gods already made him too beautiful. Did the man have to smell so good too? "Your first day back, he almost takes a punch to the face defending you from Hondros. Today he's meeting you in the woods. If you didn't know him before last week, you bed your lovers awfully fast." He smirked. "Maybe Calix didn't use his power on you."

As Alexander often remarked. My tongue was quick and I had a sharp wit. I knew when I was being insulted.

Snatching a handful of berries, I smashed them in his face. Damien roared—surprise knocking him off-balance. He pitched onto a desk, half his face a mask of purple.

"There you are. Those berries cure mind-bending stupidity, and the humiliation cures my need to kick you in that typhon's anus of a mouth!"

"What is going on over there?" Cassia shrieked. "Is this how two serious, sensible trainees conduct themselves?"

The glare he bore me as he straightened was not that of a serious and sensible anything. "Stay away from Barba. I don't care if you're fucking, or plotting, or both. You're done with him."

"I'm done with you," I said louder than intended. "So why don't you pull another girl out of a jail cell and stalk her?"

"Don't be silly." Alexander closed the distance, forcing me to hold firm between him and the berry bush. "You've got my full and undivided attention, Aella. I dare not give another woman my time." I was too thrown to stop him encircling my shaky fingers and bringing them to his lips. "I will shadow you until one of us leaves this earth. But I promise you," he whispered, lips ghosting over my knuckles. "That won't be long now."

"Xander!"

The screech jarred me free of his hold. Sirena came up on us quick. Ripping away from him, I shot to the side as her changed and taloned left hand swung through the air my head had just occupied. She could get me with that once, but she wouldn't get me twice.

I ducked away and was across the room before she let loose.

"Alex, are you okay?"

"You didn't need to get involved," he said, searching me out. Sirena grabbed his chin and swung him back.

"Course I did. Look at what that hay rat did to you." She was all sweetness and light wiping the berry juice off his cheek. "I told you, you can sit back and let the others handle her. That bitch will be the next to throw herself off a tower. I give her a week..."

Her bile faded the further away I got. I couldn't say if her assurances reached him, but Sirena certainly kept a tighter hold on Alexander through the rest of class. If he moved in my direction, she was a step behind him. If he looked at me, she popped her head in his line of sight. I was almost grateful to her by the end of class.

"What was all that about?" Daciana asked while we packed up and headed out. "I turn my back for one second, and you're smashing berries in his face. Good job, by the way. That look of surprise will sweeten my dreams for years to come."

I giggled. "That was funny, wasn't it? I thought his own head would explode."

We busted up, lightening the mood immensely. "But honestly, I don't know what that was. He came out of nowhere saying these vile things. I've gone from a maiden to a tumbler after one missed class, and I have no idea why."

"What's a tumbler?"

"Oh, right." It was so easy to talk to Daciana, it felt like we'd known each other our whole lives—despite the fact she lived in another dominion. "That's what my mother used to call the painted women who stood outside taverns, shaking their skirts at passing men. It wasn't an insult. People shouted much nastier things at them. I'd hear it even though she covered my ears."

"Tumblers. Hmm, I kind of like that too. It is what you do with a mate—tumble into bed." She cocked a brow. "Who are you supposed to have tumbled?"

I snorted. "Theron, according to Kosma. And he twisted Calix's sick act of mind manipulation into a wanted stolen moment."

"Ugh, how dare he. I know he's lost a friend, but his hatred of you scares me, Aella." She tapped her ear. "I heard what Sirena said about 'letting the others take care of you' and 'jumping off a tower within a week.' You don't think... Could that be what he wants? To make things so bad for you here, that you give up?"

"I'm pretty certain… that's what he just told me."

"I won't let that happen." She slipped an arm around my waist, resting her head on my shoulder. "No matter his power, he'll never be stronger than all of us together."

I held on to that. I didn't know if I, or we, or anyone was strong enough for the real challenge I had ahead, but I held on to it anyway.

"*Events are already in motion to complete what we've started.*"

What was Alexander's plot for revenge in the face of the goddess's plans to kill us all?

Together we trekked back outside to the green and Commander Vasili. The last lesson I had yet to start. I had a passing thought that it'd be hard to train since the sun beat its final retreat and set about shining on Mother Gaia's other side. That thought vanished as my boots touched the ground.

Hundreds of bright, glowing orbs floated above our heads, illuminating every corner of green. The academy was prepared for anything.

"Novices," Vasili barked. "Grab a staff and continue practicing the high, mid, and low strike."

The setup behind him was free of platforms and stands. No point asking in a school full of demigods how they broke it down so fast. In its place, two rows of practice monsters stretched all the way down the lawn. There was enough for each of us to do as Theron complained—whack them over and over again for an hour and a half without letting up.

On my right, wardrobe-sized weapon cases held staffs and other more dangerous weapons of death. I joined the line to retrieve one.

"Galanis, over here."

I broke off and jogged up to him. "Yes, Commander."

He gave me a long, leveling look. Only when I was thoroughly uncomfortable, did he speak. "This is your first combat class. Safety and the proper order of things are paramount on this field. No one moves on until they've mastered the task before. Is that clear?"

"Yes, sir."

"Your first task is learning the proper way to hold and wield a staff. Retrieve one."

I did so—choosing a long, smooth rod that let my fingers curve around and meet my palms." I jogged back. "What now, sir? Should I watch what the others are doing and copy them? Or maybe one of my friends can show the proper way?"

His frown deepened. "What nonsense are you speaking, girl? Why would a novice teach another novice? Is your instructor not standing right before you?"

"Oh. I— I didn't—" I pressed my lips together to stop something unwise coming out. There was only one thing to say. "Yes, sir."

"Show me a standard hold."

I held it out, placing my hands in the middle of the—

"No. Again."

Shifting, I spread them further apart.

"No," he said, tone as flat as his expression. "Again."

I adjusted my left hand.

"No. Again."

Frustration welling, I glanced over his shoulder and tried to see what the others were doing.

"Galanis, your fellow trainees are distracting you. Turn your back."

The message finally sunk in. *So this is what we're doing.*

Rigidly, I gave my back to the green. Vasili rounded me, then planted himself shoulder width apart and hands behind his back.

"Show me a standard hold."

It took great effort to keep my tone respectful. "Sir, this might go faster if you demonstrate what a standard hold is."

The grizzled, hard jaw ticced. "Are you questioning my methods?"

"Merely making a suggestion."

He stuck his face in mine. "When I want your suggestions, I'll ask for them. Standard hold. Now."

Inside, I shrugged. If he was content to waste his time like this, so was I. Nearly half the lesson block frittered away while he barked at me for the wrong hand placement. When I finally got it right—one hand facing up, the other face down, and both placed at the one-third points—we moved on to the narrow hold and he spent the rest of the time coldly making me feel stupid for not knowing that.

I practically ran off the field when he finally called time. I assumed the goddess hated me for how mercilessly and thoroughly she was destroying my life. But no.

True hatred lived in that man's eyes. I understood as I watched his body ripple with barely contained rage—he wished I did not exist, that I never came to Deucalion, and that the Fates would correct their mistake and cut my thread... before he did it himself.

"We saw everything," Tycho said, catching up with me just past the doors. "That was brutal."

"He hates me," I dropped flatly.

"Why would he? Far as I know, he never met Galen before we all entered the academy."

"It's not about Galen." I cast a look over my shoulder. Vasili was still on the field, and he was fixed on me. "I made him doubt everything he thinks he knows. Now he's in an impossible position of wanting to go out on a quest that may ultimately be futile, or stay here and do his duty of training the girl who made him relive the worst time in his life."

"Pretty specific. Should I ask?"

I shook my head. "It's fine. I can handle Vasili. Trust me, I've handled worse."

Tycho thankfully let it go. We held up in the back corridor to wait for the others, then tramped down to our dorm. Daciana, Theron, and Nitsa volunteered to hit the mess hall after we all changed. The last thing any of us were interested in was another run-in with the Titans or their eager-to-curry-favor lackeys.

I would not back down, but I also wouldn't go looking for trouble. Ajax attacked and I started to turn in front of him, Alexander, Calix, and Drakos. That could not happen again.

"One thing I can't complain about is the baths," Daciana said. "Soaking in bubbling, scented water is the only fix after days like this."

"What do you do in your dominion?" Tycho asked.

Nitsa nudged his shoulder. "Are you asking her how she bathes herself? Want to know if she starts with the front or back?"

"What— I wasn't—! Shut up, Nitsa!"

Daciana and I muffled snorts. "It's okay," Daciana said. "I know what he meant. In my wolf form, I bathe in freezing cold lakes and streams. I don't feel the cold, but I know I'm not in a hot spring. In our natural form, we need shelter but the need to move and run free is ingrained in us. That means trailers—" She noted our blank looks. "Moveable homes. Homes on wheels."

"On wheels?" Theron repeated. We neared the dorm wing and my waiting bed. "How do you put them on wheels?"

"Well, they're these rectangular, metal... uh... boxes," she said, motioning with her hands. "Beds, food, and bathrooms are inside, so we have everything we need."

"But you live in metal boxes," Ionna said, alarmed. "No wonder you want to be free."

"No, I— I'm not explaining this right." She blew out a breath. "Honestly, they're quite comfortable. The point is we can take our shelter everywhere we go, and when the wolf needs to run free, all we have to do is open the door. What we don't have are swimming pool–sized baths fed from an underground hot spring."

"What's a swimming pool?"

Daciana laughed. "You guys all have to visit me one day. I have a feeling it will be a mind-blowing trip."

"I wish we could," Nitsa said. "We're not allowed to do the interdominion program. Nothing's more important than us receiving our training, and then we're bound for army service after that. Only the council and council representative are allowed to leave Olympia without a death sentence. They're the ones sent to foster relations with other dominions."

"What about after you leave the army? Even when we are old and gray, my friends." She hooked her arm through mine. "You'll be welcome among my people."

"I really wish we could." Ionna grasped her other arm, dropping her head on her shoulder. "Even out of service, we have our powers. Powers that are always needed to defend our homes and family, no matter how old we are. No one leaves Olympia, Daciana. That's the way it must be."

"Doesn't that... bother you?" she asked carefully. "I mean, to not be able to leave even with the promise of coming back."

"Anyone could say they just want to leave for a short visit and then never come back," Theron reminded. "This is our home. This is where we belong. It is our duty. None of that bothers me."

Nitsa, Ionna, and Tycho nodded sharply. It never crossed my mind to include them in my escape plans, and seeing them then, it never would. They weren't like Alexander and his friends, but their loyalty and obedience were to Olympia in every way that counted.

I could not get them to understand why I had to drain these libraries of knowledge, and then bust through the enchantments at all costs. At least, I couldn't tell them without filling in the *entire* story. I believe they'd understand in the brief spell before the goddess made me kill them.

We arrived at our dorm and filed in. Neither one of us made it farther than the common area. Stiff and blinking, we beheld an incomprehensible sight.

Headmaster Drakos reclined in Ionna's preferred seat, finishing off a golden apple. Behind him, I heard shuffling in one of the empty nooks.

"Um, Headmaster," Nitsa began. "Can we... help you, sir?"

He glanced up like he just noticed we were there. "You cannot, Miss Castellanos, but it's polite of you to ask."

"Was there something you needed of us, sir?" Theron asked.

Drakos took another bite of his apple. He didn't answer until he slowly chewed, swallowed, then had another bite. "I'm merely here to oversee the smooth transfer of Lysandros to dorm eleven. There were disagreements between him and his dormmates, and classmates, and instructors."

My brows furrowed tighter and tighter.

"Discussions began on if the academy was the best place for him, but then I heard of you."

"Of us?" Ionna repeated.

"You're quite the tight little unit. All of you supporting and sticking up for each other despite your"—he flicked to me and Daciana—"differences. It's wonderful to see."

Then why does it feel like you're thinking the opposite?

"I believe Lysandros will thrive among this group. He's also being transferred into your lecture class, so you can help him focus, complete assignments, and interact more positively with those around him. I'm depending on you for his successful completion of training."

We traded looks. I read on their faces that they heard the subtext loud and clear too.

"Why does he need this support?" Nitsa asked.

"Lysandros Scala is a son of Eris." Drakos got to his feet. "Speaking of, his apples are delicious, but I wouldn't recommend trying one. Good evening, novices." He zeroed in on me brushing past. "Good evening, Miss Galanis."

"Good evening," I forced through a dry throat. My muscles didn't untense until he was out the door and his footfalls faded.

"What was that about?" Daciana said.

Tycho swung an arm out, stopping her in her tracks when she tried to move. "Nothing good," he said under his breath. "A child of Eris? Here?" He eyed the alcove with a strange look on his face. "He wasn't there that first day when we displayed our powers. I never thought I'd meet one."

"Why?" I whispered. I figured if he was doing it, I should too. "What just happened that I didn't understand, Tycho?"

"Eris is the goddess of chaos and discord," Nitsa breathed—also fixed on the narrow opening. "That drop of her essence in a human soul is no gift. The power she grants them is no prize. Children of Eris cause problems everywhere they go. Fighting, betrayals, love soured, friendships broken. They spark... Well, chaos."

"And Drakos transferred him here to our dorm and made him our responsibility despite being told he should send him from the academy," I stated.

"Go ahead and run, little Aella. There are worse things within these walls."

"I have to apologize to you again." Frustration shook my voice. "Seems like all I've done since I got here is make the academy harder for you."

Ionna inched along the circular walls. "Why are you apologizing? You didn't move him here. This isn't your fault."

Oh, but it is.

"Let's not jump to conclusions about him," Daciana said. "Maybe the issues he had with his dormmates and instructors were because they heard *Eris* and prejudged him. I'm sure he's—"

Lysandros jumped out—boots thump-slamming on the floor.

"Ahhh!" Tycho's and Theron's shouts were no softer than ours.

The new boy's head jerked, swiveled, and bobbed between the six of us like one of the hinges came unscrewed in his neck. "Hell-llooo." The greeting slithered out of his throat in a low, deep baritone. "Wouldn't happen to be talking about me"—he snapped to me—"would you?"

I shot back, smacking hard against the wall. It wasn't that he was frightening— Although jumping out like that did nothing good for my pulsing heart. Lysandros was pleasant-looking, dare I say handsome. A crown of auburn hair swept from back to front and fell across impossible light, golden eyes. His ears stuck out and curved at the top, coming to pointed tips. The elven shape aided to his air of mischief, but the slightly crooked, once-broken nose completed it.

I swept down, falling on twitchy fingers. They moved constantly as if striding along a lyre. No, it wasn't these odd, jerky movements that were frightening. They unsettled me because they were so... chaotic. If there was another word, I'd use it.

Daciana stepped forward. "We were talking about how pleased we are to have you here. Welcome, Lysandros."

A huge smile stretched across his face, revealing all his teeth. "The wolf lies."

"I'm not—"

"Always lying, lying wolf. The peacemaker. The priestess," he rasped, head cocking sideways. "Never saying what you want. Never doing what you want. Can't even fuck who you want."

Daciana jerked like he slapped her. "How— How dare you. You don't know me."

"Don't know you. Don't know you," he sang. Lysandros rocked side to side, dancing closer to us. "Nobody knows you. Nobody ever will."

"That's enough," Tycho ordered. "We're not rising to your bait, son of Eris. Access the normal part of you, and we'll be happy to welcome another comrade. Otherwise, you can get the fuck out and I don't care what Drakos says about it."

"Ooooh, the Death Dancer. I've made him angry." Lysandros laughed loud and sudden, shooting my heart back up my throat. "Can't have that. Don't want that. Very happy to be among comrades. I will stay with you."

Lysandros reached behind his back and came away with six golden, plump apples. Bowing, he presented them to us—his smile growing wider. "A gift for you, my new friends."

"Even if I knew where he pulled those out of, I wouldn't eat that," Theron said under his breath.

"Very nice of you," I said. "But I won't. Thank you."

My friends all chimed in saying the same.

The smile melted off his face. "Spurning my gift. Rejecting me!" he shouted, pulling a cry out of Ionna. "Seems we will not be friends after all. Not friends. No comrades." His apples tumbled to the floor. "*Tsk, tsk.* Such a shame."

"Don't say that," I tried. "We can still be friends. I'd say we'll be better friends now that you didn't play whatever trick you intended with those apples."

Smirking, he backed into his alcove. "It is a child of Dolos who plays tricks, Aella Galanis. Who lies and deceives and keeps secrets. They do it as well as a child of Maia."

I froze—still and pinned to the spot.

"I am no trickster," he whispered. "What you see is what you get." Lysandros slipped out of sight. "Good night... friends?" A laugh floated out. "We'll see."

None of us moved or spoke for a solid minute.

"I want to change rooms," Nitsa announced.

"Agreed," Ionna said. "Drakos wants him in dorm eleven. He's in dorm eleven. Doesn't mean we have to be."

Theron edged toward his space—right next to Lysandros. "I doubt he'll make it that easy for us."

"Who? Drakos or him?" Tycho asked.

"Take your pick."

A silent communication passed between them, and a decision seemed to be made because Daciana and Theron went into their alcoves, while the others went to get dinner.

I didn't move from my place—gaze still fixed on the spot where he disappeared.

"How?" I croaked. "How does he know my mother's name?"

Sebastian

"It is confirmed, my lord."

I leaned against the windowsill, gazing out at the cascading stars. I once knew them and their constellations all by name. I once knew the feel of the grass tickling my neck as I lay with Mother in the fields, delighting in the stories she told me of the figures in the sky.

Those days were over. The last place my enemies would catch me is on my back.

"How certain are you?" I asked.

"Certain," Linus said firmly. "She did not lie. Aella Galanis spent eight years of her life trapped in a mountain cave with a child-devouring beast."

"Tough girl. Did something happen while she was imprisoned? Something that explains what's happening to her now?" I turned away in time to see him shake his head.

"No. As yet, there is no explanation for the infection in her soul."

"Now is the part where you tell me that you're working diligently to find that explanation, and will have it for me the next time I see you."

Linus snapped to attention. "I am working diligently to find all the answers you seek, my lord. I shall not return until I've fulfilled my duty."

"Better. With every passing minute, the sense grows that she will one day be a force to be reckoned with—if she isn't already. She will be on my side. Fight for my cause, or she will die before the council ever knows what she is."

"We don't know what she is. But we will," he added quickly at my look. "I will not fail you, Lord Barba."

Bowing deep, Linus vanished from the spot. There wasn't so much as an indent in the carpet to prove he was ever there. With him gone, I had no reason to delay.

I stepped lightly, padding from the bedroom into the bathroom. Expert Avram Rossi relaxed in his steaming bath—head resting on the rim and hot towel laid over his eyes. The blue-and-purple bruises adorning the parts of him I could see, told of his hard day of training.

I grasped his head.

"Wha—!"

Down I shoved, holding him underwater. Rossi kicked and flailed, swiping at my hands and sending desperate, gurgled shouts to the surface. Teeth gritted, I held firm—ruthlessly continuing our battle of whose strength would win out first. How much easier this would've been if the guy preferred heights like Giles Nanos did.

Soon, Avram's thrashing slowed. I didn't let up until he kicked for the last time. His ankle slid off the rim, hanging off the side as I pushed him down a little farther, then arranged his limbs.

I stepped back, observed, and nodded to myself. Anyone would believe he drifted to sleep and drowned. *Especially after I'm done.*

I went to work wiping up the spilled water, refilling the bath, neatly hanging the towels, and checking for a trace of anything out of place.

My last touch... I withdrew a bottle of powder from my pocket and carefully tipped the crushed nectar out along the wash basin.

Poor fool. Just another soul lost to the hazy dream world of nectar.

I left the dorm behind, my mind already drifting back to the strange girl shouting to herself and passing out in the woods.

What are you, Aella Galanis? And how will you be of use to me?

Aella

I huddled at the back of the cave, clutching the blanket Evangeline left behind. It had long since stopped smelling like her, but every now and then, I found a blonde hair tangled in the woolen threads.

Evangeline was real. Chloe and Iris were real. My sisters and I once filled this dark hole with laughter, stories, and promises of hopeful days to come. I would hold on to those memories, keeping my sisters alive, until my dying day.

Until tomorrow.

A shadow fell over the cave mouth, outlining an enormous six-limbed figure.

"Cora, come."

"What is it, Mother?"

"Just come, dear. I have a present for you."

Bile rotted through my gut. She had given me more and more presents in the days following the murder of Evangeline, Chloe, and Iris. As if she thought her heartless cruelty was something I could get over with more books, dresses, jewels, sweets, or games. Another present on my last day of life would surely sweeten my thoughts as I hurtled to the bottom of the mountain.

I glanced at her last gift—a green-and-gold dress that could've been woven by Athena herself—and spat on it.

Any trace of the human mother left was long ago devoured by the beast. There was nothing good in her anymore.

"Cora, did you hear me, darling?" Impatience crept into her voice. "Come."

I shoved up, trudging out to meet her. She would only come and retrieve me herself. I knew from experience that fighting was futile.

Rounding a natural curve in the wall, she came into view. All these years later, neither age, weight, nor the burning sun touched her. She was the same pale, red-eyed, scaly beast bearing the upper half of a pretty young woman.

I remember the night Iris broke her beautiful, gold-inlay hand mirror and plunged the shard in her sleeping chest.

It was a spell of wild, desperate insanity. Back then, we were all alive and had hope she'd bring us down the mountain and free us. We woke to her cries and the lamia's booming laugh.

The beast plucked the shard from her chest, blood gushing down her abdomen and said, "You missed."

Now, there wasn't even a scar to mark the first time one of us fought back. That was the sum total of our eighteen years. We left no mark on the world. We made no impressions.

I plastered on a smile. "Yes, Moth—" She snatched me up, scurrying out of the cave. "Wait! Hey!"

My feet dangled miles above the ground, and me getting farther, not closer to it. "Where are we going!"

She ignored me. Cutting right, her claws burrowed sure and true in the mountain. The cliff came into view.

"What? No," I screamed. "No! It's not time yet. My eighteenth year begins tomorrow." I bit and pounded at her tough flesh. "It's to-morrow!"

"I know, darling," she said almost sweetly. "Mother told you she had a surprise. It's for your birthday, Cora. Look."

She repeated it twice before, nauseous and trembling, I peered through her claws. My lips parted, dropping in time with my widening eyes.

"Who is that?"

A lone figure waited on the cliff, sitting astride a black stallion pegasus. A slim hand poked out of their long ebony coat, and stroked the

majestic animal. It tossed its head like it could no more stand to be pet-
ted than it could to be treated like a common pack animal.

"Here she is," the lamia said. She dropped me on the ragged stone
before the flying horse and rider. "Safe—as promised. Ready and will-
ing to serve the goddess—as agreed."

"You've done well."

The blood drained from my face. That voice. I knew that voice.

"The goddess will be pleased with this vessel," the rider said. "Fi-
nally, after hundreds of thousands of years of waiting, she will rise,
overthrow the usurpers, and claim this land for her glory."

This wasn't real. It can't be happening!

Crossing an arm over her chest, the lamia bowed. "For the glory
of the goddess."

"For the glory of the goddess." The rider hopped down and caught
a blast of breeze that blew off her hood. She smiled at me like no time
had passed.

"Hello, Aella," said Mama. "Are you ready to fulfill your destiny?"

"Ruff! Arf, arf, arf!"

I bolted up in bed, ripped viciously out of sleep and dreams.
"Ahh!" Losing balance, me and a tangle of sweat-soaked sheets
crashed in a pile on the floor.

Lysandros raced out of my alcove.

"Lysandros!" I chased after him and tripped—feet snagging in
the sheets. Kicking them free, I tore after the barking, creeping lunatic. "What the fuck were you doing! Stay out of my alcove."

Lysandros jumped over the armchair and beat it for the door,
laughing himself sick. I grabbed the only weapon on hand and pelted him. The first apple bounced off his head. The next caught his
elbow before it slid out of the door.

"What's going on?" Nitsa stumbled out, rubbing the sleep from
her eye. "Aella, are you okay?"

"No, I'm not okay." My heart raced a mile a minute. Chest heaving, I rocked back and collapsed in a chair. My too-early morning wake-up was enough of an unwelcome surprise, but that nightmare—

No, that memory. Where had it come from? I pushed what happened that day down and refused to think about it. For months, it hadn't pierced my thoughts or dreams, so why now?

Because of him, a voice supplied. *Because Lysandros said my betrayer's name after I all but struck it out of existence. How could he know about her?*

And what else did he know?

My grip tightened and droplets of juice coated my nails. I glanced down and noticed I was clutching one of my missiles.

These apples did look delicious. They were plump and firm with juice, and all I had to do was take a bite.

I was hungry—also Lysandros's doing. Because of his final remark, I was so distracted I barely ate my dinner. An apple would be good right then. It would tide me over until the mess hall opened—

"Aella!" Theron snatched my wrist, stopping the apple a breath from my lips. The fog broke, fleeing back into the depths of my mind.

"Oh my gods." I opened my hand, letting the horrid thing hit the floor. "What just happened? I was going to eat it. I didn't realize what I was doing."

"They're made of power. That power must've drawn you in." Theron tugged off his nightshirt and dropped them over the apples. "Maybe touching one did it, or maybe we just need to get these things the fuck away from us."

"What do you think would've happened if I...?"

"The goddess Eris kicked off events that led to the Trojan War, Aella, and it all started with a golden apple. Whatever those things do to people, I can promise you it's nothing good."

I had one thing to thank Lysandros for. Focusing on how pissed I was at him, took my mind off the nightmare. I spent the rest of the time working at my desk until my friends returned with food from the mess hall. Fed and showered, we headed to Hondros's class.

"This has been the longest week of my life and it's only halfway over." Nitsa rolled her neck, grimacing. "Can you imagine four more years of punishment scrolls, endless drills, early mornings, and dealing with *him*?"

"Dealing with who?"

I jerked, nearly dropping my books. Lysandros strolled behind us like he was always there—twitching and popping his lanky little body.

"Hondros," I replied. I was still pissed at him, but it wasn't worth antagonizing someone who stood over me while I slept. "Where did you come from?"

He grinned. "Where did you come from, Aella Galanis? Do you even know? Do you want to know? Are you afraid to know? What will you find? What will you find?" He rapid-fire shot the questions at me, pushing me farther away until Theron, Nitsa, and Ionna were between us.

We were a tense group heading into the lecture hall. Having all eyes turn to us when we went inside did not help.

Stiffening, I kept my head up as the smiles turned to glares.

"Weren't you told you weren't allowed in these halls?" A girl I didn't know at all pushed through her friends, getting uncomfortably close. "Go in through a window, traitor."

She tried to knock our shoulders and I twisted at the last second, tripping her up. We ignored her furious squawking and continued on.

"Don't let them get to you, Aella," Nitsa whispered. "They'll get bored of this soon. We've got bigger things to worry about. Like surviving training."

I put my foot down, and it slid away from me—rocketing into the air. The six of us went down like a manticore training dummy.

Falling flat on my back, the air punched out of my lungs and an icy chill claimed its place. Dazed, I didn't move for a solid spell—just lying there as guffaws pelted my ears. My vision cleared on a figure standing above me.

"Oooh. We found your power," Lysandros said, chuckling. "Aella can fly. And fall." Moving fast, he grabbed one of my books and flung it across the room.

"Ow!"

"Don't hurt Aella. My Aella! Mine, mine, mine!"

"Eris freak!"

Over my head, I heard scuffling, straining, and muffled curses. "No, not him," someone snapped. "Trust me, you don't want to fight him."

I pushed up as the commotion ended. Everyone had their backs to us, all filing into their lecture halls. It gave me a chance to study the sudden and unnatural ice patch that appeared beneath us.

"You just don't learn, do you?" Alexander smirked from the doorway, watching me get up, fall, and try to get up again. "To think I once admired your stubborn streak."

"You're going to admire my aim next!"

He laughed. "These halls are off-limits to you, and the rest of them. I won't say it again. You got a very helpful suggestion to use the window. You'd be wise to listen, because if I catch you where you don't belong again, I'll start with him." Damien leveled a finger on a wobbling Tycho. "See how long you can stand his scream before that sharp tongue is licking my boots."

"Trust me." I flailed on splayed legs, losing dignity fast. "You don't want me that close to your favorite appendage."

His grin was a terrible thing to see. "Like you'd know what to do with it if you were."

"Give me a knife and I'll figure it out."

Hondros appeared behind him, startling me off my feet. "What is the meaning of this delay?" he asked, though it was obvious. "You seven are late. If you do not respect my time, you do not respect this class. You will report to me after the day's lessons. Let's see if scrubbing the atrium floors on your hands and knees teaches you to take your training seriously."

"But, Captain," Nitsa cried.

"Make that tomorrow as well." His tone was colder than the ice biting my palm. "Do I hear more complaints?"

"No, Captain," Theron gritted.

"I thought so."

Alexander trailed him inside, but not before tossing me a wink. With difficulty we finally went inside. Everyone was seated and staring at us, whispers trailing as we walked past. Alexander found a spot in the second row because Sirena was in his seat and—

My brows blew up.

—Kristopher was in hers.

Sirena leaned in close, cleavage pressed against his arm as she whispered and giggled in his ear. In the ten seconds I watched the scene, she checked to see if Alexander was looking half a dozen times. The guy was too busy fishing out his books and scrolls to notice.

Shaking my head, I drew out my chair and sat. My butt plopped on a soft, bony lap.

"What the—?" Jumping up, I spun on Lysandros. The guy blinked up at me—head cocked and expression trying to pass as innocent. "That's my seat. Get up, please."

"No, it's my seat. My seat. Mine." He beamed. "I will sit with my friends. You sit somewhere else."

"You—"

"Galanis, take a seat," Hondros ordered. "Now."

Swallowing a retort, I left it alone and crossed the room, making for the last empty seat. Sebastian did not stir from his apparent sleep when I sat down.

Arms crossed, eyes closed, and head hanging over the back of the chair, he looked like he was getting the peaceful rest that nightmares and Lysandros denied me.

"Listen up," Hondros said. "Today, you will form groups of four and plan a strategy for one of three scenarios. First, the four of you are separated from your mora when a giant corners you. Second scenario, a cerberus makes its home before the gates of the garden of Rhode where the children of Hecate guard their most treasured spell books. Third scenario, your boat is low on supplies and taking on water when you're attacked by a seven-headed hydra.

"Form your groups. Begin."

There was shuffling, chairs scraping, and murmuring as people got up, found a group, and set to work. I grabbed the back of my chair and headed to Daciana.

"Leaving so soon?" Sebastian cracked one eye open. "Not you too, Galanis. Refusing to mix with someone from another class."

"That's not it. I'm just going to sit with my friends."

He held out his hands. "Are you not with a friend now?"

I goggled at him. What nonsense was he spewing? "You're not my friend. You're my kidnapper."

"You are no kid, and I am no napper. You're a woman"—sliding his fingers through mine, he guided me onto the seat—"and I claimed you. What's the word for that?"

I swallowed as Sebastian pushed in my seat, putting me back where I came from. How did that happen? I was there and I didn't witness it.

"Deranged," I whispered. "Deluded? Lunatic?"

Amused, he grinned into my too-wide eyes. "I'll let you decide."

Slam! "What is she deciding?"

I jumped, penning in a cry. It was only Sebastian's hand on my chair that stopped me tipping over.

Alexander followed slamming his books down by dropping a chair in front of us. "The scenario we do is certainly not up to her."

Seems we had our third member of the group. The comment was no sooner out of his mouth than Sirena was rushing over to us, plopping her seat next to Alexander. So much for Kristopher.

"What have I missed?" she asked tightly, narrowing on me.

No, no, and hades no.

"I should really get to my..." But it was already too late. Daciana, Theron, Ionna, and Nitsa huddled up while Tycho and Lysandros pulled up seats beside two other Sisyphean boys. Everywhere I looked, the groups were set.

"Alexander Damien and Sirena Cirillo," Sebastian chimed. "This is a pleasure. Welcome to our humble group."

Damien flicked to the hand Sebastian still had on the back of my chair. I wondered if Sebastian felt the heat under his gaze, because I did.

"We're doing the cerberus," Alexander announced. "Hondros is expecting everyone to choose the easy scenarios. We won't be so predictable."

A giant and a seven-headed sea monster is easy?

"Fine with me. Aella?"

"Sounds good," I replied.

Alexander's gaze was making me more uncomfortable than usual. Why was Sebastian's hand still there?

"You two are quite chummy." Alexander leaned in, filling my nose with pine-scented baths and the smell of the earth after rain. "When did you meet?"

"We've been over this," I forced out.

"I've learned to treat everything you say as a lie."

"I've learned those apples you love so much make you pass wind in your sleep. Loudly." Sebastian barked a sharp, startled laugh. "But we shouldn't hold one's faults against them."

Sirena shifted and pain blossomed in my calf, making me cry out. I stuck my head under the table in time to see her talons retract into her ripped boots. Blood began seeping through the shallow cuts on my leg.

"You will not speak to your betters that way," Sirena hissed.

Growling, I snapped up. "Should I come across one such better, I'll keep that in mind."

She moved again and the sound of two limbs colliding echoed under the desk.

"Enough," Sebastian said, that light, jovial lilt vanishing. "Let's finish this."

I glanced under the table to check if he was okay. Sirena rubbed her foot, but I didn't know why. There wasn't a mark on Sebastian.

"I expect a detailed plan that utilizes the power of each member of your team," Hondros called. "And by detailed, I want a full scroll by the end of class—from each of you. They will be corrected and returned to you tomorrow morning. You will need those notes as the starting point for the essays explaining how and why you went wrong."

Wonderful. The man has us failing before we begin.

"And if we create the perfect battle strategy?" Daciana asked.

Hondros looked down his nose at her. "You won't."

I got a fresh scroll out of my pack. I reached for my reed, but Sebastian was already there, passing it to me. Alexander's lips peeled back from his teeth.

"We've got a shape-shifter, blood boiler, smoke conjurer, and a mundane," Sebastian said, unaware of what was brewing on the other side of the table. "What's our strategy for taking down a cerberus?"

"*We* will decide our strategy and let you know," Sirena said. "Unless you're finally willing to share the full extent of your power?"

"I'm starting to feel bad for how much I've disappointed all of you." Reclining in his seat, Sebastian draped his arm over mine again. "What you see is what you get."

I frowned, flicking from him to Lysandros. Such an uncommon phrase to hear twice in less than twelve hours.

Eyeing the son of Eris brought Maia and the nightmare into sharp focus. I quickly looked away.

"Then you, and the hay rat, can stay silent."

"I do not take orders from you." Sebastian's icy blues gave nothing away, but his tone said enough.

The corners of her mouth tightened. "Yet."

I pointedly slammed my scroll down. "Okay, so in the story of Heracles, he grabbed the first Cerberus around the neck and strangled him until he passed out. Just because one of the heads can see the future, doesn't mean they can stop it. I say we don't bother trying to come up with something clever, and just go in for a full-frontal attack."

"Do you?" Alexander said. "Well, I say you speak when you're given permission."

My response was an obscene gesture that made Sebastian laugh again.

"I agree with her," Sebastian said. "Any tricks or traps the beast will see coming. Better to confront and force surrender." He pulled out his own scroll and reed. "Or do you disagree?"

Alexander's stiff jaw said he desperately wished to disagree for the mere fact it wasn't in his nature to be accommodating. "No," he finally replied. "Full-frontal assault. Galanis"—he dismissively gestured to me—"will be the bait and distraction. Naturally we'll have to conclude that she dies, but it'll be a noble death for a supposed mundane and known traitor.

"Sirena will attack from above. Barba, you attack from the flank. If it sees the future, it'll know what I'll do to it, so it'll try to come for me first. All you need to do is hold it off long enough that I can get close."

"Great idea, Xander," Sirena said, draping herself over his shoulder. She shot me a self-satisfied smirk for no reason that I could name.

"Fine by me," Sebastian said, easily swallowing my death. "Let's write it up."

"It's not fine with me," I protested—outraged that they both picked up their reeds and started writing without a question. "My only option is not to die. I can lead it on a chase or—"

"I will be detailing your graphic and gruesome death," Alexander said. "You're welcome to put something else down, but Hondros will have something to say about our scrolls not matching."

That unpleasant man would have something to say. He had not warmed up to me since that first day. Truthfully, he acted like my ignorance was a personal insult to him, and that if I didn't do better, I'd get someone else killed. I would never forget about Galen. Hondros, Alexander, and the Titans would make sure of it.

Sirena and Alexander talked around us while Sebastian focused on his scroll. The three of them were Titans, and that did nothing to dispel the thick air of dislike between them. Alexander would not be sitting here if it wasn't for his insane notion that the two of us were plotting something. Or tumbling.

"Galanis, you have something on your cheek." Sebastian flicked a thumb across my cheekbone, brushing it away as my hand came up.

"Thanks," I muttered, getting back to work. I was in the middle of describing Sirena distracting the three-headed beast by shitting griffin dung on his head.

My concentration broke again when Sebastian pinched my strands. "Got a bit of lint," he explained.

Nodding, I got back to it. Five minutes later, he rubbed my earlobe—shooting goose pimples down my arms. "You flicked some ink—"

"Enough." Alexander punched the table, surprising me into kicking the wood and toppling the inkwell for good.

"Ahh, there it is." A grin stretched Sebastian's lips. "I thought I picked up a direct correlation between my hands in proximity to Galanis, and that vein in your forehead picking up speed. Theory tested and proved. What's the problem?" he asked. "This whole hating-her thing a cover? She secretly your girl or something?"

Alexander, Sirena, and I sounded off all at once.

"Fuck no."

"Of course not!"

"I'd be in a secret relationship with an actual jackass before him."

Sebastian flashed amusement on us all. "So what exactly sent you running over here when Galanis sat down?"

"Simple," Alexander said. "You're a disloyal agitator that refuses to reveal his powers or report to the council. That Galanis found and attached herself to you immediately is as innocent as your motives. I believe the traitor latched on to another traitor in the hope you'd help her escape. I won't let that happen."

"Is that what you believe?" All those accusations thrown at him and Sebastian didn't spare a grimace. Actually, he just looked bored. "Well, you do have to be cautious. You're the one who picked her up, reduced her sentence, and brought her to Deucalion. If she escapes, you'll be executed in her place."

"Wait, what?" I cried. "Executed in my place? Damien, is that true?"

"No, it's not true." Those piercing eyes flayed me. "You will never escape me, Aella. Even if you get beyond these walls, I told you how our story ends. With your death," he hissed, "not mine."

"Then you have nothing to fear," Sebastian cut in before I opened my mouth. "Doubly so because our acquaintance is perfectly innocent. No plotting going on here. So this"—he snaked around my waist and tugged me squawking on this lap—"has no reason to bother you."

Alexander kicked his chair over shooting to his feet. His hand was up and pointed at Sebastian's head in a blink.

Throwing his arms off, I snatched up my scroll, bag, and chair, and marched across the room. I dropped my stuff next to Daciana's surprised group and returned to my work, not so much as sparing those idiots another glance.

There was tension between them and they were using me to fight it out. I had enough problems with Alexander without him inventing another reason to hate me by thinking I'm plotting with a rival.

But now I understand why I keep plumbing Alexander's depths and finding the hatred just goes deeper. I admitted that I was trying to escape that night. My failure caused Galen's death, but success would've caused his. If I'd known...

The thought trailed off. I didn't know where it could go. I didn't want to cause *anyone's* death. Not even Alexander Jackass. But the fact remained that I was putting the academy trainees in more and more danger every day I was here. I still remembered the goddess in my ear, urging me to murder the demigods coming up the steps the night I changed to kill the demon.

What if shock hadn't brought me back? I would've killed them all while she cheered from the pocket of Tartarus where she resides.

I had to go as soon as a way out presented itself, but I couldn't sentence Alexander to die because of it.

Where does that leave me?

I wrestled with the question all through class. Finishing my scroll only gave me more time to stew. Sacrificing everyone in the castle to save one guy who hates me? That math didn't add up. But then, how was I any better than the goddess if I went around deciding who got to live or die?

"Aella, are you okay?"

Shaking myself, I focused on Daciana as we lined up to hand in our scrolls.

"Something on your mind?"

"About a million things," I muttered. "Can I ask you something? How does your pack handle traitors? I mean, if someone is acting outside the interests of your community, what's done to protect everyone else?"

"If such a thing happened—and it's rare—but if it did, they'd be judged by the goddess. If she deems them guilty, she'll remove her gift."

"Remove her gift? Does that mean they won't be a werewolf anymore?"

She tipped her chin. "I'm told it's a painful experience... that almost always results in death."

I looked away, grip tightening on my scroll. Werewolf or demigod. It seemed there was never mercy for those under the whim of a goddess.

"I see."

"Why are you asking?"

"It's just... I wonder how Olympia got here, Daciana. The executioner's blade drops so swiftly on a dissenter's neck—all to protect a land, legacy, and life the gods chose for us. Is this really what's best for everyone?" I asked, sweeping out my hand. "Or am I too weak to accept what needs to be done? Two thousand years and Olympia still stands in the face of the monster scourge. Eighteen years of age, what do I know?"

"You know your own mind, Aella, and that's enough." Daciana dropped her voice. "It is not normal to happily swallow every choice someone makes for your life. The happiest place on earth will still have those who think it can be better, more can be done, and those in charge don't have what it takes to lead.

"Whatever it is that you believe is wrong, you're not weak for thinking it." She pierced my gaze. "And you're not weak if you did something about it. Following our sense of right and wrong is the only way to live. I've seen the damage of those who blindly follow someone else's."

Somewhere through the conversation we took a shift to a place I didn't mean to go, but was glad we did. She heard all the same rumors that I was a deserter and traitor. My demigod friends dismissed them, assuming Alexander was lying and I was too good of a person to do something so horrible.

They could not know that I did it for the most unselfish of reasons, but Daciana didn't either... and she believed in me. Believed in my judgment instead of assuming my goodness.

I didn't know until then how much I needed someone to tell me no matter what I did or why, I wasn't a monster.

"Thank you," I whispered.

She squeezed my fingers, saying nothing. One after the other, we handed in our assignments, grabbed our things, and headed out. Lysandros attached himself to our group as we headed for the door. *His* motives were ones I questioned. He laughed when I fell, then pelted books at the guy who did it. He called us friends but left his apples to tempt us.

Son of chaos and discord. We may never understand why or what he's doing.

"Stop," Hondros called. "I am missing one. Cirillo, where's your scroll?"

Sirena hitched her bag up her shoulder. The blue satchel matched her robin's-egg gossamer dress perfectly. I asked myself how many scrolls I'd be made to write if I traipsed in here out of dress code.

So much I'd get buried under them and no one would find my body for weeks.

"You have it," she replied. "Alexander and I wrote one scroll and signed our names. You don't need two scrolls saying the exact same thing."

His face hardened. "I will decide what I need. Your scroll is to be in my hand within the next minute, or this assignment is considered incomplete."

Scoffing, she rolled her eyes. The novices heading out the door suddenly found reason to stay. "Then consider it incomplete. It's ridiculous to ask us to write the same thing four times." Sirena marched off.

"Cirillo, report to this room after the day's lessons. The atrium floor awaits your scrubbing."

"Excuse me?" she cried, whirling around. Even Alexander—who from what I observed paid her little attention—halted in packing away his reeds to flick between the two of them. "I will do no such thing!"

"Then you will ponder your insubordination and its consequences in the reflection room."

My eyes went round. After all the rules she flouted without shame or reprimand, it's one blank scroll that winds her up here—on the verge of an evening with an iron maiden.

She sputtered, cheeks flushing deep red. Someone who wasn't used to people telling her exactly what they thought of her, couldn't be used to consequences either. This had to be the first time in her entire life that she found out the rules applied to her too.

And she didn't like it.

"How dare you threaten me, you self-important, three-limbed *toova*!"

My jaw dropped. I said there were more cruel, insulting words to call the men and women selling a tumble in the sheets for coin. Toova was the worst of them.

"My mother, Aphrodite *council*woman, will have your job, your head, and then the academy for this. I've already informed her that council money is funneled to Sisyphean instructors who pass tedious busywork off as teaching, in between exposing banned information, but when she hears about this..." Smirking, she shook her head. "You can scrub those atrium floors yourself tonight. Might as well get a taste of your new career."

Sirena flounced out the door, leaving us all gaping in her wake. All but Captain Hondros. His face chipped from stone during her entire speech.

A pregnant silence smothered the room as Sirena's footfalls disappeared down the hall. With slow, controlled movements, Hondros packed the scrolls away in his desk, grabbed his overcoat off his chair, and left.

We shoved each other rushing out the door. If we thought we would be treated to another showdown, we were disappointed immediately. Sirena headed in the direction of history class. Hondros went the opposite way.

"I can't believe that just happened, and I was there to witness it," Theron breathed. "I will tell my children about this one day. They won't believe it either."

"Gods above, what was she thinking?" Nitsa cried. "You can't talk to an instructor like that. In his own lecture hall. With dozens of people watching."

"Apparently you can do it and think you'll get away with it," I said. We set off for history but were in no more rush than other students slow-walking to give them plenty of time for gossip. "Will she, Theron? Your mother is a councilwoman. Can she have instructors fired?"

Theron blew out a breath. "Don't get me wrong. The council is powerful even without the weight of their authority. They're the most powerful son or daughter of their Olympian gods. But Deucalion Academy stands as its own entity, and laws were put in place hundreds of years ago by another council to protect it from interference.

"Once, a particularly paranoid son of Zeus got it into his head that the headmistress at the time was assembling a force to overthrow the council. He tried to pass a law that every student put into the Titan class had to swear an oath of fealty to him, and him alone.

"Another generation and another council, they tried changing the army's mandate from protecting Olympia to protecting the founding city. Everywhere else the people could fend for themselves. Then, another council repealed the law that the academy had to be free to everyone. Still mandatory," he said, "but not free. Families that couldn't afford to send their sons and daughters, still said their goodbyes at the academy gates before the parents were sentenced to hard labor paying off the debt."

"Goodness," Daciana said. "Tell me that one didn't last long."

"It didn't," he replied, loosening my shoulders too. "It's about two thousand gold coins a year for one student to attend the academy. Only nobles and the Imperial Palace have coffers that big. But greed is greed, and that council couldn't help counting up all the coin that would flow to them if it wasn't being siphoned by the academy.

"After all that, it was ruled the headmistress or master alone makes decisions for the academy. Same for the army and its high commanders. They bound that law up so tight, plugging every loophole and stamping out any misinterpretation, that hundreds of years later it can't be repealed. Training and keeping Olympia's only fighting force strong is more important than politics." He threw an arm around me.

"That's my long-winded way of saying no. Sirena's mother can make his life difficult in other ways. I certainly would not want to be caught alone in a darkened hallway with the woman, but she can't fire him or stop him reprimanding her. Sirena just made a mistake."

"A very big mistake."

Those grave words were the last said before we passed over the threshold, descending onto the history lecture hall floor. Sirena was already seated at the front, pulling out her books, reeds, and paper like nothing happened.

The class had never been so quiet as they claimed their seats and followed her lead. Madame Remis remarked on it.

"You're a subdued group this morning. Have you learned to fear my historical revelations?"

"We had one shock," Eladio, one of the Sisypheans, said. "What's another? Surprise us, Madame Remis."

She chuckled. "I'll do my best. Now, yesterday we were— Oh, Leonidas. Is something wrong?"

Our heads swiveled around and up as Commander Vasili and Captain Hondros entered the room. How fitting that we were in the history hall. We were about to witness another scene for the history books.

"Forgive the intrusion, Stavra," Vasili said. "We're here to escort Miss Cirillo to the reflection room. Bear with us for a minute of your time." They planted themselves in front of Sirena. "Miss Cirillo, on your feet."

Sirena pretended not to hear.

"On your feet. I will not ask again."

"We'll see what my mother has to say about it." She flapped a hand. "You can go."

"Your mother has no power here," Hondros said. "I urge you not to make this worse."

She snorted. "*You* have no power here. That's why you had to run off and get Vasili to handle me for you. What's wrong, Hondros? Afraid of a woman half your size?"

I pinched the bridge of my nose, stifling a groan. The potential to do a lot more damage than Sirena lurked within me, and it wasn't enough to save me from the reflection room. An iron will steeled my resolve during eight years in hell, and it shattered like glass within that iron maiden. Sirena did not understand what she was getting herself into. So much for me being the ignorant one.

Alexander rose to his feet. "She said she's not going with you. End this power trip before you piss me off too."

Sirena blinked up at him—the quickest gleeful grin twisting her lips before she caught herself. She not only had his attention, but he was rising up in defense of her. I did not need to ask if this was her dream come true.

"That's right. I'm not going anywhere," she snapped, finally deigning to look at them. "You are. Walk out now and I won't remember this when I'm ruling the council and you worthless toovas are—"

"Sleep." Vasili snapped his fingers and Sirena's head hit the desk. She was out cold.

"Hey!" Alexander lurched forward.

"Sleep."

The son of Zeus crumpled, hitting the floor hard. Once again, we were the quietest bunch of stunned novices in the history of the academy.

Without a pause, they dragged Sirena's and Alexander's unconscious forms up the stairs and out the door. No one had to ask where they were going.

I didn't have a clue what Remis talked about for the rest of the lecture. I just kept imagining two of the class's strongest Titans force-fed Tantalean bread and shoved in an iron cage. Did it matter that they couldn't die in there? The torture they were about to endure was beyond cruel. Our language hadn't come up with the word for it yet.

If they can do this to novices who commit insubordination, what became of soldiers who mouthed off or didn't obey their captains? Whatever it was… not even the council could stop them.

Whispers about what happened to Alexander and Sirena passed through our lecture group and filtered into everyone's ears as classes ended and we all piled into the halls. No one looked sideways at me or my friends. This was much more interesting.

"Not one, but three Titans sent to the reflection room? Damn. Did they all try to kill someone? Titans don't fucking get punished for any less."

Snort. "Yeah, they did worse than try to kill some Sisyphean. I heard they called Hondros a toova."

"I heard Sirena ripped up her scroll and tossed the pieces in his face."

"I heard Xander was about to unleash his power and pop Vasili's head like a grape. He was too slow by half a millisecond."

"I heard Sirena clawed him and almost took off the other arm."

The story reached grander and bloodier heights by the time our group got outside, and broke off for the stadium. Instructor Kazran took news of our missing training mates in stride.

"Fine. Scala, you're with Proficient Catherine." His gaze sharpened on Lysandros. "I won't have any of your tricks in my stadium. You walk in, do the work, and get out. Is that clear?"

Lysandros responded by laughing so long and loud, Kazran walked away halfway before he was done. The two of us fell in line behind the eight other novices. They weren't like me who was facing Catherine because they had yet to beat her. They already defeated their first proficient and moved on.

"He was a mind-bender. An illusionist," Kristopher taunted me. "Much harder than a speedster. If you can't even beat her, you might as well lie down and die right now."

"Go first. Show me how that's done."

He smirked. "With pleasure." Kristopher shoved through the line, moving to the front of the pack. Catherine didn't comment on his rudeness. "I'm ready. Let's do this."

"Whatever you—" Catherine blurred.

Dust blasted over our group, and Kristopher followed its path—soaring over our heads. He hit the ground in a crumpled heap, wheezing and clawing for air into his stunned lungs.

My shadow fell over him. "Ahh, so that's how you lie down and die. Thanks for the demonstration."

Lysandros howled and I couldn't help joining in. Maybe Chaos Boy wasn't so bad. He couldn't help that the goddess made him this way any more than I could. Plus, he seemed about as fond of bullies as I was. That was a good starting point for a friendship.

"Fuck off!" Kristopher bowled me over running up on Catherine. "Again."

"You'll get your chance tomorrow. I've got other novices to throw around before the day's end."

"I said again!"

Her shifting expression dropped the temperature twenty degrees. "I said stand aside. You're in my way."

"You cheated the first time. You were supposed to warn me so I could be ready. A cheat is no winner. I go again."

"Are you kidding me? You think a bronze bull or a dragon is going to give you a warning? Maybe sit back and stretch their haunches while you warm up? Get some sense, Sisyphean."

"I'm not a Sisyphean."

"Then you have no excuse," she shot back. "You're an embarrassment. Step aside."

I didn't love her bringing my class into it, but I wouldn't deny my satisfaction at the humiliation on his face. Kristopher stepped aside, and stormed all the way out of the arena.

"You." Catherine gestured to Lysandros. "You're up. What's your power?"

"Speedy, speedy, daughter of Hermes wants to face me."

"It's the other way around," she said. "What's your power?"

I stepped forward. "He's a son of Eris."

"Hmm. That's new." She crouched, getting in her runner's stance. "Prepare yourself, son of Eris."

Lysandros shrugged off his stuff, letting his pack hit the ground with no care that his books spilled out. He squared off with Catherine, though that might not be the word for it. He was looking everywhere but at her—scanning the skies like something more interesting was happening up there.

"Are you ready?" she asked, a tad impatient.

"Are you? It only gets harder from here, *proficient*, and for all that you've been lucky during training, you know your luck is running out. So many monsters are faster than speedy, speedy Cath—"

Catherine disappeared from sight, and Lysandros hadn't taken his eyes off a slow-moving cloud. A blur streaked across our vision. I winced even as it happened.

Lysandros went flying—his legs and hands spinning out like he was revolving on the tip of a finger. He struck the ground with an audible thud that ripped hisses out of me and three other people.

That hurt. A lot.

"Lysandros?" I called. "Lysandros. Are you okay?"

The red-haired boy didn't move or raise his head.

"Whoa. Is he dead?" someone whispered.

"Lysandros?" Worry crept into the name. "Say something."

Catherine appeared next to me, making me jerk. "He's fine. And he's done for the day. Next!"

"I don't think he is fine." I ran over and crouched down beside him. His face plastered to the dusty, arena stone. "Hey, can you hear me?"

I brushed his hair back, and Lysandros's head snapped up. I scrambled away so fast I scraped my palms on the ground, leaving smears of blood.

His mouth peeled back from his teeth, revealing sharper than normal canines that leaked with increasing spine-chilling snarls. Gone was the vaguely handsome face and mischievous smiles. I did not know this man. No one did. This mask of pure rage and hatred wasn't human.

"Lysandros, you're okay. Please, calm—"

Roaring, he shot to his feet—arms raised to the sky.

"Nooo!"

Apples burst forth. From everywhere. Anywhere. They rained from the sky and shot from the ground. They pelted me across the face, head, and arms. More rolled harmlessly on my lap. In the space of a breath the entire stadium was covered.

"Run!"

"Don't eat them!"

"Get away!"

Shouts came from everywhere. One of them from Theron, but it was already too late.

Catherine was devouring an apple like she hadn't eaten for months. My whole group jumped on the pile, fighting each other for apples even though they had half a dozen tucked under their arm.

Everywhere I looked they were eating, eating, eating, and Lysandros lowered his arms... and laughed.

"You." A Sisyphean girl from my group spun on a Titan girl. "I know you're fucking Lukus. You know I like him. How could you? We've been friends since swaddling."

She spat in her face. "You were always jealous of me. Wanting everything I have. Face it, you're nothing but a worthless Sisyphean dog."

The supposed worthless dog punched her dead in the face. Blood spurted from her busted nose.

"It was all l-luck." Catherine hugged her knees, rocking on the ground as she bawled her eyes out. "I won't make it in the army. What do I do? What do I do?"

"Scala!" Kazran leaped on the platform and nearly fell tripping on an apple. "Put them down. Don't eat those!" Making fists, he flexed them toward the heavens as if raising a heavy burden. Snakes slithered out of the shiny, golden menaces.

I screamed.

Raising a smooth, diamond-stamped head, the snake tangled me in its gaze—tongue scenting the air. I froze. Not breathing, not moving, not thinking.

It lunged.

"Ahh—!" The snake latched on to the apple, tearing it out of my hands just inches from my lips. I hadn't noticed I picked one up.

"*No,*" the goddess shrieked. "*Eat it. Change. Kill them! Kill them all!*"

So powerful, her voice in my head was a clanging gong that chased the last trace of Eris's power out. I was clear, and I had to run.

She wants me to eat them. Reason enough for me to get as far away from them as possible.

Scrambling over the apples and snakes, I tore for the exit. The entire stadium was pandemonium. Fighting, screaming, and powers flying. And those were only the people consumed by rage.

Theron slumped against the platform, covered in writhing snakes. My stomach heaved even though I knew they were under Kazran's control. I skidded to a stop. He was my friend, I couldn't leave him.

"Theron?" I approached him, scream leaking through my teeth. I was not fond of snakes. "Come with me. Please, I'll get you out of here."

"*Eat it! Eat the apple!*" Her screams just helped me focus.

"—am worthless," he sobbed. "Even my mother is ashamed of me. She— She hesitates every time someone asks if I'm her son."

"Oh, Theron, that's not true." I stuck my hand out, praying against hope he would take it and let me pull him out instead of me having to get closer to those venomous, slithering creatures. "That's the apple talking. They do something to people. Brings out their insecurities, their pettiness, their jealousy and then makes it ten times stronger. You know your mother loves you."

"*Yes,*" the goddess crowed. "*Change, my pet. They'll never know it was us amidst this carnage.*"

Her happiness finally made me look at my hand. My talons reached for Theron—crowning a black-scaled fist twice the size of my own.

The snakes.

"Theron, please!" I cried, snatching my hand back. "You have to come with me now." I ran to him and my knees bent, dropping me on a pile of apples. Unnatural, inhuman legs strained my pant legs.

Time's up.

"I'm sorry," I screamed, scrambling away and leaving my friend trapped in hellish mental torment.

I was close. So close. I just had to get out, be free of the snakes, find help!

The archway loomed ahead. I stumbled on foreign legs, hobbling as fast as they allowed me. "*No, stay!*"

A powerful hit struck my spine, propelling me off my feet. Groaning, I flipped over as Cow Nitsa charged to do it again.

"Nitsa, stop," I bellowed. "It's me. It's Aella."

She changed and my naked friend crouched before me. "I know exactly who you are, bitch." The venom blew me back. "Gorgeous, innocent Aella with the pouty lips and acid tongue. Even the men who hate you have lust in their eyes."

I gaped at her. What was she saying?

"You can have any man you want, while the one man I want won't answer my letters!" She flung an apple at my head. "What hope do I have of finding someone else when I'm always standing next to you? Why didn't Theron leave you where he found you!"

"I—" She shifted before the protest landed on my lips. Mirrored in my widening eyes, she charged.

"Argh!"

We both whirled around. Nitsa's hulking form lost its balance and tipped over. I saw it out of the corner of my eye, unable to help her even if she would've hurt me for trying.

Bones popping, shifting, melting—Daciana roared her transformation. Where my friend once stood was a fearsome, black wolf standing three rows high. The demigods descended on her.

"Beast!"

"Monster!"

"You don't belong here, half-breed mongrel. Die!"

A ball of fire struck her side. The wolf's whimper tore my heart to pieces. Turning away, I ran.

Out of the stadium, across the law, bounding up the steps, and bursting inside. "Help! Someone help."

I bleated all through the hall, screaming for someone—anyone—to help. Kazran's snakes stopped them from eating apples after it was far too late. It wasn't just insecurity and jealousy those disgusting things amplified. It was hate.

And that hate was focused on Daciana.

"Help!" I tumbled into Drakos's office, human once again, and snapped the man's head up—I assumed. It was difficult to make out more than a moving outline in the gloom. "Sir, y-you have to come now," I wheezed. "Everyone... in the stadium ate his apples. They're going crazy, sir! Fighting, arguing, crying, and attacking Daciana. Someone's going to get killed. You have to—"

"Move aside," he barked, sweeping out of the darkness and nearly knocking me out. I tripped running to keep up with him.

In the short time I'd known the unsettling man, I hadn't seen him display any excitement, urgency, or a sense that he wasn't in control at all times. To race behind him as he ran struck me deeper than the horrific chaos I left. This was the same person who casually spoke about our low chances of survival. If he was running to save my friends and classmates, this was bad.

I was a heaving, sweating mess staggering up the hill to the looming stadium. Piercing the shouts and sounds of battle, were those crushing whimpers.

If she's whimpering, she's alive. Drakos will save her. He has to.

Because I can't. Furious tears streaked my cheeks. Sisyphean wasn't an insult; it was what I am. Useless in a fight. Useless to my friends. Useless when people I love need me the most. Even if I was freed from the goddess's curse, I didn't belong here. What good was a frightened little child who only knew how to run.

I collapsed against the wall, not trusting myself to go farther than the arena's covered entrance. There were snakes all over the place, and the goddess had every intention of making a bad situation worse.

Drakos didn't slow. He charged into the stadium, throwing apart two grappling Titans without slowing down. He was a dark shape jumping on the platform beside Kazran.

"RISE!"

The ground rumbled beneath my feet.

"What is this?" I backed up. "What's happening? What—Ahh!" Limestone exploded, showering me in rocks and rubble that split seams on my skin. I hacked, waving the dust and dirt from my face.

The haze cleared, and our eyes met. My talons ripped out, bursting forth faster than the scales rippling up my arms.

Hunks of flesh still clung to his bones, stubbornly hanging on along with its swinging jaw. Round, shrunken eyes rattled in sockets that did not shrink with it. It bent its head, and those eyes popped right out.

I screamed—legs bending, feet elongating, torso growing, wings bursting from my back. Terror I'd never known dragged me deeper than I'd ever gone as the dead ripped through the earth, and attacked.

The skeletal army seized, tackled, and pinned demigods all over the stadium. Stephanie Papamichael, the fire wielder, incinerated two that came her way. A dozen more poured out of the earth, swarming and burying a screaming Stephanie under bones and decay.

Hades.

Drakos dropped us in the pits of hell itself, and the only thought in my fading mind was to get away.

I clawed the ground, dragging my too-heavy body across the rocks. Three dead soldiers broke off and came for me. Fear pushed my consciousness deeper, giving way to the goddess's pet.

A figure stepped out of the entrance to the stands. "What are you?"

Kristopher's pale face shone stark in my sharpening gaze. "What the fuck are you?!"

No, I raged. *Please.*

The goddess's laughter held me under. Appearing in her horrible, scorching, wonderful, soul-shredding glory, her morphing feet touched down beside me. The last thing I saw was her smile.

I TRUDGED THROUGH THE forest, picking up dirt and rocks in my torn boots. I barely noticed.

"*Why are you so upset, pet? It is I who should be upset.*"

"Shut up." The command lacked heat. I didn't have the strength to yell at her. There was nothing left in me at all. "Just... shut up."

She hissed. "*That's no way to address your goddess, insolent girl. Further proof we must complete the ritual. After you changed, you ran the opposite direction and went there of all places. There was no one there! Not even that Hades spawn.*"

"*I cannot do what I must when you continue to defy me.*"

"There" was the beautiful, serene clearing Sebastian took me to just the day before. It was there I woke up... covered in blood.

A band tightened around my throat, pushing down sobs. I drained myself of those as I washed furiously in the lake. All that was left standing in my ruined boots was a soaking wet, red-eyed murderer.

"*He had to die,*" she whispered, clenching my teeth. "*They all do. It's not for mortals to understand the will of a god.*"

"Stop it."

"*I existed before the birth of man. Before time. Before the sun graced the sky. Everything must rise and fall. Even gods.*"

"I said stop." Not because it hurt. I deserved worse pain. She had to stop because I couldn't stand to hear her justify what she made me do.

"Their precious humans rejected them. They tore the Olympian gods from their thrones and forced them to their knees. Instead of accepting their fate and letting those who must come next take their place—they invaded the souls of hundreds of thousands of humans, changing the course of their lives for generations to come.

"You look around and see demigods in need of saving. What you don't understand— What eighteen measly years of existence hasn't given you the wisdom to understand, is that your people need saving... but it's not from me."

"Please," I burst out, nearing a scream. "I've asked you for so much that you've refused to give me, but you can give me this. Give me peace. Just for one day. Peace," I whispered.

I waited for a response. And waited. And waited longer as I tramped through the woods. No more divine words grated against my skull.

In silence I walked. A silence inside, not without. Dryads marked my path—throwing twigs and dirt at me, and hissing their unreserved feelings. They knew now that the child was a demon. Didn't mean they warmed up to the lying, faithless thief.

I paid their insults no remarks. What were they saying that wasn't true? I was lying to everyone I knew, putting them in danger, and walking right back to the castle to do it again.

The dryads were being kind. The word that described the cowardly piece of dung that was me was not known by god or man.

The castle was quiet, my echoing footsteps the only sound reaching back to me. I couldn't say it was a noisy place, but after the stadium, shouldn't instructors and staff be running around, losing their heads over the havoc one novice brought down on the academy?

There was no such scene as I made my way down that long hall and entered the dorm wing.

"Hello?" I croaked. The door swung shut behind. "Theron? Daciana? Nitsa, are you here?" Empty alcoves looked back at me.

I dropped my aching body in a chair, summoning tears that wouldn't come. The only proof of what I'd done to Kristopher washed away in the lake. I didn't remember what I did. I didn't remember the first time either. That night, I just came to next to the pieces of the first person to be kind to me in eight years.

A sob broke the peace, and my silence. The dam broke.

Soon I would dress, go out, and find my friends. Make sure Daciana was okay. Tell Nitsa I forgave everything she said. But then, I would cry for mean, smirking Kristopher whose family and friends would never know why he died.

"What do you have to cry about, sweet one?"

I jumped, snapping up straight in the seat as Calix stepped into sight—leaning against the entrance to my space. "What...?" Words faltered under my brain's failure to understand what it was seeing.

Calix in my dorm... waiting for me?

I tensed. *But why?*

"What do you want?"

He shrugged. "Lessons were canceled. Some big emergency sent all the staff running to the arena. Seeing as you killed one of my brothers, and the others are locked in the reflection room, there isn't much for me to do right now."

Again I was struck by the way he talked, looked, and held himself. The dreamy boy in the stacks was nothing like this deep-voiced, dead-eyed, swaggering twin of Alexander.

"I figured now was a good time to get to know my enemy," he said, peering into my room. "A waste. You don't have a single personal item in your desk, shelves, or hidden under your bed to warm your nights and heat those lips."

I heated then wondering what he was talking about, but knowing all the same it was filthy.

"Something sad about that," he mused. "Or maybe it's wise. Which is it, Galanis? Did you shed your past to hide it, or because there's nothing worth remembering?"

"Get out."

"Oooh, not very hospitable," he said, chuckling. A loose tunic and tight pants rode his body—both tantalizing and teasing every wandering eye he passed. Iris once read a love tale to us where the writer said there was nothing worse than a handsome lad who knew it.

I didn't know what that meant until that moment.

"I'm sorry. How about this? Fuck off."

"Hmm." Calix took a step, then another toward me. "Something's different about you today."

"Like you would know," I snapped. "You know nothing about me."

"I know I didn't call you sweet one that first night because of your pillow lips or plump bosom."

A strangled noise squeaked out of my throat. Who was he to speak so casually of my body?

"No, it was because of your eyes." He stepped again and I did too, maintaining our distance. "There was an innocence in those seafoam jewels. A kind of softness like the world hadn't destroyed you yet.

"It's gone now," he said bluntly. "Now your eyes look"—one corner of his mouth curled—"like mine."

"Get out, Calix." My voice didn't shake though the rest of me did. "You won't find what you're looking for in my dorm or from me. All you need to know is that I'm not your enemy."

Lie. Lies, lies, and more lies, Aella.

"Aren't you? Alexander said you were in the woods that night because you were trying to escape. Makes you a traitor as well."

He moved closer and I sidestepped, keeping the couch between us. "You've already made up your mind about me, so why bother sneaking in here or asking me questions?"

"Because—" He came around the couch and I darted away, shooting into my entranceway. Calix raised a brow at my escape. "What's this? Are you refusing to let me near you because you think my power can't reach you from a distance?" That beautiful pink-and-silver smoke clouded his hands. My heart jumped in my throat. "Well reasoned. You do need to be just a bit closer."

"I'll never get near you again!"

Calix cocked his head. "Why so angry? I'm told my power is the best kind of euphoria. Love in its purest and most lethal. Not even nectar compares."

"Why am I angry?" I goggled at him. "I was fawning and falling over a man I never met, behaving like a cotton-stuffed fool. You stole my first kiss!"

Emotion leaked into his eyes then—surprise. "First kiss? How old are you?"

"That's not the point," I said, face warming. "I don't care if a thousand women before me dazzled under your power, then thanked you for the privilege. My kiss wasn't yours to take."

He laughed. "Oh, look. My sweet one is back. So innocent. So naïve."

"Excuse me?"

"Your kiss wasn't mine to take? No, it was yours to give, and how did that work out in the end? It was taken from you anyway. By the gods, how are you still clinging to the illusion that there is such a thing as choice?" Slowly, deliberately, he advanced on me. "Life isn't something you decide, it's something that happens to you. The bad, the ugly, the tragic, and the fatal, we don't choose how it's doled out and no one up there gives a shit if some of us get more than our share."

I tripped over my feet, falling onto my bed. Calix lunged and dropped over me—hands planting beside my ears.

"Want to know why?" he whispered.

I think I said no, but if I did, the whimper faded before it reached either of us.

"Because there's no one up there, sweet one. They're in here." Calix tapped my chest. "We're the gods now. Aphrodite saw fit to make people clay in my hands, so I ask you, if it wasn't mine to take... why did she give it to me?"

"You can't blame Aphrodite. You have a choice, Calix." Kristopher's stricken face scraped harder than her speech across my mind. "You don't know what it is to truly be at a god's mercy. Everything you've done is wholly and pathetically human."

"And again, you're wrong. Were you not listening?" Somehow he was getting closer, heavier, burrowing me deeper into the mattress. "There's no such thing as choice or control. If there was, Galen would be alive. If that's not proof this is the pointless, random realm of hades we're all forced to suffer in until we move on to worse, then what is?"

"Get off me." I put my hands on his chest, but the strength to push didn't come. "I want you to go."

"And I want you to see what I see," he hissed, urgency lacing his voice. "I want to ruin you, sweet one." His lips ghosted over my cheekbone. "Your eyes will forever be like mine."

I should throw him off. Run. Hit him. Something. Maybe I would've if not for one thing I knew for certain. I wasn't scared.

"What does that mean?"

"It means that now I know my enemy and her weakness." His lips were still tracing patterns on my cheek. "Alexander will break you. Ajax will kill you." Calix stated this as fact, not a question. "And I, in vengeance of my brother in all but blood, will ruin you.

"There will be no trace of your sweet, tempting innocence when I'm done. And when I am, you'll bow before the true gods that rule your fate."

Just like that, he was gone—up, off me, and slipping out the door.

"Goodbye, sweet one."

I didn't know how long I stayed there—gazing up at the ceiling as the feel of him lingered on my skin. I stirred when my door banged open again, part of me believing Calix had returned to keep his promise. Ruin me.

"Aella? Are you here?"

"Theron?" All thoughts of Calix washed away and I ran to him. "Oh my gods, Theron. Are you okay?"

I regretted asking the moment it left my mouth. Theron was covered in bruises. His left arm hung in a sling and his right eye was purple, blue, and rapidly swelling shut. But it was the left eye that stole the stupid questions off my tongue.

I'd spend no more time wondering how Calix saw a change in my eyes. It was there in Theron's clear as day. He was not okay.

"Theron, I'm so sorry," I whispered. "I should have gotten you out of there."

He smiled. It didn't reach his eyes, but still, a smile. "I heard you calling for me in... the place I was. Heard you trying to help me. I've got about eighty pounds on you, Aella. You couldn't have carried me out of there, and I wasn't going any other way, so don't blame yourself."

"Still, I should've done more."

"You brought Drakos, didn't you? That was plenty." He absent-mindedly rubbed his arm. "For years I heard whispers there was a son of Hades out there that could summon an army of the dead. Just didn't know that son was not Sebastian."

A shiver climbed my spine thinking of those rotted, eyeless corpses bursting through the ground.

"Speaking of Drakos, we've got to go. He wants to see us all in his office."

I frowned. "See us? Why? He doesn't need to ask us what happened. Lysandros's apples were all over the place."

His fist balled at the name. "I didn't ask why. We just have to go."

Nodding, I followed him out and across the hall to the administration wing. I shuddered walking into Drakos's office for an entirely new reason. I finally understood why he liked it dark.

Nitsa, Ionna, and Tycho lined up before his desk. Nitsa glanced at me, then looked away, dropping her gaze.

"Ah, Miss Galanis. Thank you for joining us." He gestured for me to take my place in the line. You wouldn't have known that hours ago he commanded an undead army to attack and restrain fifty-nine out-of-control demigods, and the laughing son of Eris amidst it all. Drakos reclined in his high-backed chair with not a salt-and-pepper strand out of place.

"Is something wrong, sir?"

"I would say so," he said lightly. Softly. Commandingly. "Last night, I not only warned you about Lysandros Scala's apples, but I made it clear that you're responsible for keeping him in line. Twelve hours later, your training group descends into madness, a high priestess of our ally dominion is rushed to the infirmary, and a novice is dead. Would you say you five failed in your task, or would that be putting it gently?"

I stepped forward. "How is Daciana? Is she okay?"

Drakos held up a hand, then pointed. The message was clear. *Step back.*

"Sir, we did fail," Theron said, "in a task we weren't prepared for and shouldn't have been given in the first place."

"He's right, sir," Nitsa added. "We didn't know he could rain apples like a thunderstorm, or that they're enchanted to make people eat them. We didn't stand a chance from the start, but that's not the point. We're not his keepers. If he can't control himself, it's not up to us to do it for him."

"Is that what you believe? As you stand side by side with the men and women of your mora, will you tell yourself that their lives and deaths are not your responsibility? Will you say the same to desperate villagers under siege by monsters? 'Sorry, if you can't handle this yourself, it's not up to us to do it for you.'"

Nitsa flinched like he slapped her. "I... No, sir." Defeat slumped her shoulders.

"Don't do that to her," I blurted. "Don't turn her words around like she's selfish or uncaring. Because it's not about that." I lifted my chin. "We both know that you put Lysandros in our dorm to punish me. This is a task we were *meant* to fail so you could justify what you're going to do next."

"Aella," Theron hissed.

"No, I won't stop because I'm tired, sir." Kristopher's face. His fear, his bloodless lips, his wide eyes. Over and over again. "Tired of shouldering the burden of others' vendettas. We don't see Lysandros as our responsibility because he's not. He is, and will remain for the next four years, your responsibility. You are to blame for today."

I ended my final word quickly, chest heaving with rapid pants. It was impossible to talk to him like this when I didn't know what he could do. Now I wanted to crawl under his desk and hide, before they burst through the floor.

Drakos did not raise his hands. He didn't call "rise" or move from his seat. What he did was worse.

He laughed. "Oh, Aella, how I admire that fire. You aren't afraid to speak your mind even when you're wrong. Some have more negative opinions of that characteristic, but I respect it. It is a weak man who wishes to be surrounded by conviction-less sycophants. Such a desire says that deep down, I can't handle being challenged, but neither you nor I have that issue.

"That's why you'll hear me when I say I did not set you up to fail with Lysandros to justify punishing you. I do not need justification." His confident smile found me through the dark. "I can do whatever I want with you, Aella Galanis. Tomorrow I can commute your sentence and carry out that execution.

"Today, I can change the rules and send you out monster-hunting with nothing but the clothes on your back and the insistence that you're not a demigod. This is Deucalion Academy, novice. I am the law."

I swallowed with difficulty, but my chin didn't dip. Our gaze did not break. "Will you do those things, sir?"

"I will reserve that answer for the time being," he replied. "We're here to discuss Mr. Scala. His placement in your dorm was a last resort, not a punishment. He's been moved three times in less than two weeks. His dormmates banded against him which did nothing to alleviate the tension.

"You're an accepting group—from an imperial heir to a werewolf to a *mundane*." Skepticism continued to lace his reference of me. "I figured you'd relate to him better, and if he stopped seeing himself as surrounded by enemies, he'd thrive. You are here now to tell me if that's not the case. If you're not willing to support your fellow brother-in-arms, my next move becomes very simple.

"Lysandros will be expelled."

"What!"

"No."

"Sir, you can't do that."

Theron, Nitsa, Ionna, and Tycho sounded off at once. All looking at him like he threatened to execute Lysandros too.

Drakos flicked to me. "By the confusion on your face, you don't understand what that means. If Lysandros is expelled from this academy, he will be taken into custody by imperial forces and sentenced to hard labor. These are tasks too dangerous for civilians and too risky to waste good soldiers.

"Clearing out arachne nests, cutting down poisoned fields, going out ahead of the mora to face sphinxes. The difficulty of these jobs is in the name. It's a rare few that survive to see the end of their sentence."

"I understand." *All too well.* "You can't put Lysandros through that. Either Eris's essence changed him, or she chose him because he was different. Either way, you can't slap another kind of death sentence on him for being who he is. Don't expel him, Headmaster.

"Expel me."

"What?" Theron cried. "Aella, what are you saying?"

I didn't look away from Drakos. "I'm the one who doesn't belong here. I'm not a demigod. What I am is a d-danger to everyone around me." Kristopher's blood weighed heavy on my hands. They stained as deep as Galen's. "I've already gotten one person killed in trying to protect me. Now I'm causing more problems for my friends and among the novices than Lysandros ever could.

"Send me away, sir. I'm not a demigod, but Lysandros is. And he's certainly not the most dangerous one in this castle. Life can go back to the way it belongs after I'm gone."

"Aella, don't do this," Nitsa said. "You're not causing problems for us. You—" Tears filled her eyes. "Please don't think we want you to go."

"She's not going anywhere," Drakos said, flapping a hand like he was waving my painful, honest speech out of the air. "You're not yet familiar with Miss Galanis's bouts of nobility. They're all smokescreens to get her out of army service."

"That's not—!"

"Silence." Once more Drakos didn't raise his voice or glare, but the command snapped my mouth shut. "You will remain on these grounds until death or graduation releases you. By all your protests, the same will be said for Mr. Scala, yes?"

One by one, my friends nodded.

"Good. One last thing," he said. "As for today's disaster, dorm eleven will clean and repair the stadium beginning this weekend and all the weekends to come until it's finish."

"That's all," he said ahead of our protests. "You may go."

We turned to leave. The door swung open as Tycho reached for it. Madame Remis didn't come in past the threshold.

"Matthias, Avram Rossi's family is here to claim the body. They're asking to speak with you."

We filed past her, none of us speaking until we reached the main hall. There I broke off. "I'm going to check on Daciana," I called over my shoulder. "See you guys later."

"Aella, wait." Nitsa ran after me. "Healer Helena closed the infirmary. Too many people pretending they wanted to check on friends, when they were really looking for gossip on what happened." She said that, but her grip on my arm was tight, leading me away from our friends. "Aella, I am so sorry about—"

"You don't have to do this, Nitsa. I know—"

"No, I do." We entered the atrium and stopped. She gripped my shoulders under the towering figure of Aphrodite. "I can't— The words to describe what it was like under the influence of those apples…" She faltered, chin trembling. "It was like every stray mean thought that ever popped in my head, came roaring back to scream at me. Just screaming and screaming that if I didn't do something about it, I'd never have peace.

"When I first saw you, I thought 'oh, look. Theron's got another outcast to add to the group.' But it was just for a second," she said, voice rising. "Half a second. And then later that day, you were so kind to me, saying my power wasn't useless and I should be proud of it. From that moment on, all I've felt is lucky to have you as a friend. I swear."

She shook me. "Please say you believe me. Children of Eris destroy friendships everywhere they go. Tell me ours isn't one of them. I'm sorry, Aella. I didn't mean to attack you or say those awful things. I take it all back."

"Nitsa, stop." I grasped her shoulders in turn. "I'm not mad at you. I never was. Trust me, I know what it's like to say and do things you don't want." I smiled real, wide, and genuine. "Besides, I've been called much worse by people who were like sisters to me. Evangeline once said I was a toothless toova who couldn't charge more than a copper because I was so damn ugly. After I slapped and bit her, she pulled my hair, then we made up like it never happened."

"Wow. Sisters, huh?"

I hugged her tight. "Sisters."

"Thank you," she whispered. "You wouldn't really have let Drakos expel you, would you?"

My smile dimmed. *That was just one desperate plan to save you and everyone here from me. Now I'm back to the first.* "No one is getting expelled. Didn't you hear him? We're in this together until death or graduation."

She laughed. "They should remove the stag and put that on the academy crest."

"No! Get off me!"

Hooded figures lashed me to the altar—the leather restraints may well have been iron for my useless struggling and straining.

"Let me go!"

Go where? I didn't know where she brought me. The mother I believed long dead flew us across the skies in complete silence, ignoring every question and demand I shouted at her back. Hours later, the pegasus touched down beside an abandoned temple with rust on the hinges and a pile of dead, unswept leaves on the steps. Three cloaked persons waited to greet us.

"What do you want from me?" I shrieked, thrashing on the cold, unforgiving marble.

It was obvious this temple was never an inviting place. Horrific depictions covered the cracked walls and ceiling, telling stories of death, human sacrifices, and the same face—beautiful yet monstrous—painted over and over. Like the lamia, the traces of her beauty remained, it was just overshadowed by the glowing eyes; cavernous, sharp-toothed maw, and streaks of blood for tears.

This was not someone you worshiped. It was a god you appeased for fear they'd come back and do worse.

"Mother! Mama, please!"

She pretended not to hear me. "Sisters, let us prepare."

My screams were a backdrop to their lighting candles, sprinkling unknown liquid, and ripping the clothes from my body. I kicked and flailed as they dressed me in a plain, undyed cotton gown.

"Sister of the Sky, bring the dagger."

One of the cloaked stepped out of sight. She returned carrying a curved blade covered in ancient characters. She bowed handing it to my mother.

"Sister of the Sea, bring the anointed treasure."

Something set down on the altar above my head. I twisted my neck trying to see.

"Sister of the Void, prepare yourself," said Mother.

Another figure stepped forward and removed her hood. The middle-aged woman bent over me, letting her long, gray-streaked waves fall on my stomach. "For the glory of the goddess," she said through thin lips.

My mother gathered the woman's hair on top of her head. Tipping her chin up, she sliced her throat without a moment's pause.

"Nooo! Oh, gods! What have you done!" Blood gushed from her neck, soaking me in warm red liquid. I twisted as far as the restraints would let me and vomited over the side.

Mama threw the body away. "Sisters, silence the vessel as I pray."

Hands clamped over my mouth. Mother began chanting in a harsh, guttural language that didn't exist as far as my limited knowledge knew.

"For the glory of the goddess." Centering the knife over me, my wide eyes reflected in the blood-soaked blade as she brought it down.

I jerked up in bed, chest rolling with rapid pants. Throwing off sweat-soaked sheets, I patted myself down—feeling for blood, itchy cotton gowns, or the wound in my abdomen that healed hours later without a scar.

Nothing.

Why? Why were these memories invading my sleep after months where the only peace I got was when I closed my eyes?

Swinging my legs over, I padded to my desk and lit a lamp. A pile of books on barrier enchantments and Hecate spells awaited me. There was no getting back to sleep after that. At least when awake, the demons that haunted me didn't wear my mother's face.

Alexander

Scant light pressed on my eyelids, calling me to open them. Slowly I did, meeting the shocked faces of Remis, Hondros, and Vasili. The latter trained himself not to give away surprise or an emotion he didn't have complete control over. It filled me with twisted glee to blow that commander training to hell.

Lifting my feet, I stepped out of the iron maiden maw—not a scratch on me.

"Not the best woman I've spent the night with," I drawled. "But not the worst."

"How...?" Remis trailed off, scanning me up and down like I couldn't be real.

"He flouted his punishment," Hondros sputtered. "Someone let him out and then let him back in before we came."

"'Fraid not. I was insubordinate and did my time. I did not learn my lesson though," I said, matter of fact. "Next time this happens, come up with something better. This little toy was never going to break me." I cuffed Remis's hanging jaw, making her jerk back. "Close your mouth, madame. My ego can't take your awe."

Brushing past them, I walked the stairs alone, coming out in the east wing of the proficients. Who knew they had multiple reflection rooms stashed all over the castle? Made a guy wonder what other secrets lurked in its depths.

I moved to the window, peering out into a starless night. The Tantalean bread prevented hunger from marking the hours, but I was relatively alert. More than two nights and the no-sleep sickness would've messed with my mind.

My boots clomped in the empty passage, heralding my arrival to the dorm wing. The entrance to the Titan wing and my trek up three flights of stairs awaited me at the end of the hall. I didn't make it that far. Pausing before dorm eleven, I let myself in.

Hondros and Vasili forced me to let my traitor out of my sight. What an over-punishment it would be if I stepped out of the reflection room to find out Galanis was gone, and the imperial guards were waiting to take me to my execution.

Soft snores filtered out two of the alcoves. Otherwise, dorm eleven slept soundly.

I passed by Zervas's space and scoffed. Shame the way that one turned out. A little teasing when we were kids, and the guy renounced the other imperial heirs and took up with the staff's children. There was no reason he couldn't be the Ares councilman. All he had to do was get over his weakness and kill the man sitting in his seat.

Naturally, there was no other way for a child of Ares to claim ownership of the seat. They all had the same power, so how could one claim to be stronger? If one of them wanted among the Twelve, they had to kill the person standing in their way.

But Zervas never would. He did not have the strength to rule, or the willingness to do whatever it takes.

Which is why it's strange how taken he is with you.

I closed the distance between me and Aella, my clomping boots soundless on the steps. Aella Galanis was nothing like Theron Zervas. She was ice and fury. Iron and brutality. She betrayed Olympia without remorse. She marched to her death without regret. And she eviscerated a man and handed me his heart without a tear. Aella was nothing like the band of weaklings she fell in with. In another life, she'd be my soulmate.

Aella lay tangled in her sheets—one slender foot poking out and the top cover bunched and resting from one shoulder to the opposite hip. The rest of it pooled on the floor.

Moving away from the bed, I drifted to the desk, shaking my head at the tiny boxes they stuck the Sisypheans in. My horse's stable was bigger than this.

I picked up a few books and read their spines, brows rising higher. They were all books about spells and enchantments. I had the displeasure of being in the same lecture class as the woman. These weren't for any assignment that I knew about.

My jaw clenched. Still trying to escape even though Galen died during her last attempt. What was it about this place that made it worse than death? She couldn't be afraid of dying in army service because she certainly wasn't afraid to die in the traitor's noose.

She claimed not to know or have anything to do with the Children of Eirene, and I was inclined to believe her. Nico got what was coming to him in that cell, but someone who hated violence wouldn't have gone as far as she did with his body. She did not stop after he was dead.

I tucked the books under my arm, planning to return for the rest. When she woke up and saw these gone, she'd get the hint.

Or maybe she wouldn't. Galanis was proving to be the stubborn type. The only thing that's been consistent with her is that she would not name her power or god. Day after day, everyone in the stadium watched Proficient Catherine toss her around. Those hits were real and painful. She was doing nothing to protect herself.

Just like that Barba. She—

I stiffened, back bent over the desk. *Is that it? Was the answer that simple the whole time?*

Aella is a daughter of Hades.

It would explain everything. The reason Barba deigned to acknowledge she existed. The gruesome power that made shredded meat out of a powerful son of Zephyrus, and her unwillingness to share it.

Children of Hades were rare, and they were all given gifts that can topple kingdoms. Over fifteen hundred years ago, one did exactly that.

King Midas amassed an enormous fortune with just the touch of his finger, and used it to buy the palace guards that slit the councilmembers' throats while they were sleeping, then threw open the doors for him to stroll in. He was eventually assassinated twenty years later by a daughter of Dionysus as revenge for the murder of her mother.

After his death, it took decades to untangle his monarchy, reinstate the council, regain control, and pass laws that applied to children of Hades and them alone. Laws that were for the good of them and the people of Olympia. Not that most of them saw it that way.

Drakos clawed his way to the top of the army chain where he could pick any assignment he wanted. Now he sits on high as headmaster of Deucalion where the power of his position trumped the laws enacted to control children of Hades.

But what's a girl from a tiny port trapped between the sea and stone to do if she doesn't want to be hauled before the council, and bound with spells and enchantments that secure her loyalty—forever?

Eternal servitude, escape to the mundane dominion, or death. This stubborn, hot-tempered menace would never choose the first. And now it all makes sense.

"Mama... no," Aella burst out.

Years of training stopped me jerking in surprise. Setting down the books, I crossed to the bed—standing over her. The little traitor frowned—forehead, brows, and lips scrunching up tight. She fisted her tangled sheets, still very much asleep.

"What have you done?" she rasped.

A nightmare about her mother? The copy of the report I received from Jason said Aella and her mother were both presumed dead from a lamia attack. That report clearly got some things wrong, but if her mother survived too, there was no record of it.

There was entirely too much about my traitor that I didn't know. Not that it matters.

My fingers found her neck, tracing a gentle line across her damp throat. I didn't need to know her history to kill her, and I gave her my word that's how this would end. Like continuing to call her Aella even though the names in my head were nowhere near as pretty as her Amazonian namesake. I always kept my word.

"Glory," Aella whispered, kicking under her tangled sheets. "Godd... ess."

"It's right that you have terrible dreams." I skated over her pursed lips. "When I close my eyes, blood is all I see, too."

Aella flipped—arm coming up and hooking around mine. My eyes bugged as she turned over, and took me with her.

"Shit—!" I flew off my feet, landing flat on top of her. My face buried in the hair-covered pillow, inhaling deep the scent of sweat, sunshine, and jasmine-scented skin oils. Molding to her, my body plastered to her back—my middle finding and fitting to her ass like a puzzle piece.

Moaning softly, Aella nestled my arm between her bosom—holding her prize tighter.

I panicked.

Scrambling off the sheets, I yanked my arm free and bolted out the door. I heard a sharp gasp and the top cover finally hit the floor. I was out and running faster than the time the imperial chef caught me salting the desserts for the annual Olympian Ball.

Aella

I trudged behind my friends, barely keeping my eyes open. The final days of the week passed in an exhausted blur. Most of our novice class ended up in the infirmary nursing minor to near-fatal wounds. Those that could still walk were sent to lecture halls to study in a room with forty empty seats. This bought us no sympathy. Our instructors piled work on us from scrolls on breaking mind enchantments, to endless drills under Commander Vasili's watchful eye. I stayed late every night for not getting it right.

Weekend brought an end to lessons, but it did not bring me rest. From sunup to sundown, we worked in the ruined stadium—clearing out the rubble, filling the holes, and beginning the long process to put it back to rights. Two days and twenty-four hours of work, we hardly made a difference.

All of it could've been bearable if Hypnos, the god of sleep, would keep me in his grip, but every night he surrendered me to the nightmares.

Every night I dreamed of Mama, and Kristopher, and Dimitri.

The night before, I was granted two hours of sleep and six hours of reading long, dry texts about magic. All I had to show for my night were dark circles under my eyes and theories on the principles of ward spells. Not a word on how to undo them.

The dryads said I had to break the fence to break the spell that wouldn't let me over it, but it could not be as simple as taking an ax to the thing. Hundreds of demigods with destructive powers have entered these gates through the years, but never has there been a successful escape from the academy. One would have to believe at least one of them battered these gates with everything they had.

They did not get through, or they did and then stumbled into another spell.

There was also the dryads' final advice. Get the person who put up the spells to take them down.

That is not a plan. It's not an option. With what power would I force a child of Hecate to break the highest law of our land, and free a traitor? With what defense would I stand against them when they turned those spells on me?

If I changed, I'd kill them while the goddess looked on with approval. In the end I'd wake up covered in blood and still trapped.

No, I had to find the answers on my own and do this as Aella. The goddess could not control my mind or actions—a fact which brought her great displeasure. She couldn't stop me fleeing to the border. She couldn't prevent me crawling to the edge for that final, fateful try. All she could do was exploit that crack in my emotions where the fear bled through.

I would do this as myself. After the lamia. After the terrible night my mother lashed me to the altar. Aella Galanis would fight back, and free herself.

"Aella?" Ionna drifted next to me. "Are you okay?"

"Fine. Just tired." I tried for a smile. By her deepening frown, it wasn't working.

"We'll check on Daciana after morning lessons. I'm sure she's feeling better now. Healer Helena takes care of everyone who walks through her doors."

Goodness, I wasn't even thinking of Daciana, but now she was all I was thinking of. The stadium. The apples. The demigods fighting with all they had to kill my first real friend. Desperately running for help. Drakos's army of the dead.

Kristopher.

Lysandros shoved between us, knocking Ionna aside and jarring the memory deeper into my brain.

The look on Kristopher's face when he saw what the goddess made of me. Surrounded by rotting, skeletal corpses, and the one who scared him... was me.

"What will we do third block with the stadium closed down?" Nitsa cut Lysandros a sharp glare. "Did anyone say?"

"I heard Kazran ended up under Healer Helena's tender care too," Tycho said. We cut through the main hall, heading for the lecture wing. "Madame Remis might know what we do after her class. I doubt she'll say we're getting a break to relax for an hour and a half."

"Wouldn't that be..." Nitsa trailed off when we entered the lecture room. A dozen other conversations did too.

Titans and Sisypheans—they all stopped rifling in their bags, talking over assignments, gossiping, stealing the last few seconds before class started, and shifted to us. For the first time since I entered the academy, they weren't looking at me.

Lysandros strolled beside me, head rolling on his shoulders—his gaze everywhere but on the trainees fixing on him. The hall was fuller than it was the Friday before. Our class was back.

"Twisted," someone hissed.

"Crazy."

"Killer."

Twisting, I searched out the person who said that last hissed word. But I didn't need to.

"Murderer." Kosma pushed through the crowd. A healing burn covered the side of her face and down her neck. "Because of you, Kristopher is dead."

My breath stopped.

"Because of you, half my face melted off! You could've gotten more people killed. You could've gotten us all killed!"

"I got no one killed," Lysandros said to the ceiling. "The apples only bring out who you truly are. Small, weak, insecure"—he snapped on the crowd—"hateful. You did what you wanted to do deep, deep down."

He laughed, ripping tense shoulders through the crowd. His head swung to the right. "Kill the half-breed." To the left. "Attack the rival for his dicky dicky prick," he said to the Sisyphean girl who screamed at her friend for sleeping with *him.*

Lysandros rounded on Nitsa. "Make the girl who's so much prettier than you, not so pretty."

Nitsa shook, eyes welling. Lysandros only laughed louder.

"If mean, vicious Krissy is dead"—he shrugged—"it's 'cause one of you wanted him that way. Not my fault," he sang. "Murder in your hearts. A monster in your soul."

Vision blurring, my nails pierced half-moons into my palm.

"Too bad!"

"What is wrong with you?" someone—all of them—shouted.

"It's us against the monsters. We're supposed to have each other's backs."

"One of your own is dead and it's your fault."

The words were daggers in my chest. Lysandros tilted back up to the ceiling. Just like that, none of us were there or worth his time.

"Drakos should've expelled you." An inkwell came flying at his head. "Die in some swamp doing hard labor, traitor."

"Stop," I shouted. "It wasn't his fault."

"Wasn't his fault?" Kosma jabbed at her face. "This wasn't his fault?!"

"He— He— He didn't mean for anything to happen to Kristopher." *That was me. It was all me. And Lysandros can't pay for a crime that was mine.* "You don't—"

Kosma slapped me across the face. "Shut your fucking mouth. You're next."

I snapped around, fist coming up and flying before I could think. My knuckles smashed into her healing skin. Kosma's scream smashed my eardrums.

The crowd surged forward, surrounding me and my friends in a blink. Lysandros snaked out of the fray, grasped my shoulders, and shoved.

I went flying, shooting past four people who jumped aside to let me bounce off the marble. Strong arms stopped my descent.

"You know." Sebastian's dry voice slipped between my ears. "If you want me to carry you everywhere, you could skip the fainting and falling, and just ask."

I just gaped at him. Whether I was shocked to find his arms around and pulling me to his chest, or the words that came with it—I couldn't tell.

"That's enough," Sebastian called. "Fight's over."

A guy in my class, Venedict, came forward. "Who says? You?" He scoffed. "My girl's in the infirmary because of *that*." He jabbed at Lysandros. "So I say the fight's not over. He's dead. The traitor's dead. And the worthless Sisypheans protecting them are going the same way. Fuck off before you're added to the list. We all know you're not going to do shit to stop us."

"Do you know that?" A low, deadly rasp whispered through his lips. "Are you so sure I won't do shit?"

Before my eyes, his brilliant blue pools disappeared—drowning in a flood of black.

"Is today the day you want to find out what I will do?"

Venedict paled. His jaw and fists flexed as he weighed his Phobos-gifted power, striking fear in the hearts of man and monster, with the unknown power of the son of a god who always grants a gift to topple kingdoms.

Giving us his back, Venedict walked away. He knew better than most that some creatures were deadlier when they're afraid.

Coal-black eyes beheld the silent, unmoving crowd. "One of you, then?"

They broke apart—hissing threats to Lysandros, me, and my friends—warning that Sebastian wouldn't be around next time.

Sebastian set me on my feet. He blinked and his eyes were back. "You're welcome."

"I didn't say thank you," I replied, but smiled. "Why are you so—?"

"Ahh! Ahhhh!" Tycho collapsed, screaming and writhing on the floor.

"Tycho!"

"Didn't I say...?"

I jerked to a stop in the middle of running to him. Alexander came into the hall—his hand up. Calix loped in behind him. Locking on to me, the son of Aphrodite tossed me a wink.

"I told you what would happen if I found you where you shouldn't be one more time." Damien closed his fist, and Tycho's screams ratcheted to inhuman. "Aella, Aella," he tsked. "There isn't a single rule you won't break. Even if it means"—his fists tightened and so did Tycho's scream around my heart—"getting someone killed."

"Alexander!" Theron charged him.

Damien dropped him with a careless wave of his left hand. Crying out, Theron dropped on hands and knees. He raised his head and Calix kicked him in the mouth. Theron flopped flat on his back, blood weeping from his lip.

And the vengeful, stirred-up crowd that finally walked away came running back. Two boys seized Nitsa, tossing her across the room and smack into the wall. She crumpled as they rushed the guy who was standing behind her.

Lysandros roared as two—five—ten novices grabbed him. All the while, Tycho convulsed beneath a sobbing Ionna.

"Stop it," I screeched. "Stop! Please!"

"Is that what the dryads said?" Alexander bellowed over the noise. "When they begged you to return their disgusting demon babe? Did they tell you to stop as you went running straight to Galen?!"

"You didn't stop." Tycho jerked so hard his back nearly snapped in half. Blood spurted from his throat. "Why should I?"

I ran at Alexander and Calix moved in the way, bouncing me off his chest. "Don't do this! Hurting me isn't worth killing Tycho and getting expelled."

Alexander smirked over Calix's shoulder. "Why would I be expelled? No one will recall what happened."

Horror stunned me. Everyone would lie for him?

The question answered itself. A Sisyphean and friend of a traitorous mundane, walking the halls with an insane, poisonous apple-bearing demigod. No one would get in the way of him teaching us all a lesson.

"What did I tell you, sweet one?" Calix pecked the tip of my nose. "Gods don't get punished."

"No," I rasped. "No!"

Sebastian. He's here. He won't lie for them. He'll stop this. Whipping around, I searched for the blond-haired demigod as it came swinging at my face. Kosma's backpack—heavy books and all—smashed into my cheek. I hit the ground and she turned on Lysandros, pummeling him over and over again. Vines like the one that snagged my ankle that day on the green, lashed around his hands. He wasn't summoning any apples.

Lysandros barely visible under the powers and boots stomping him. Nitsa groaning on the floor. Theron's face a mask of blood. Tycho hoarsely gasping as his body ran out of screams. And Ionna in the midst of it all, eyes wet and glazed as visions took her.

I knew without doubt that she was seeing how this terrible, one-sided fight would end—if I didn't do something.

"Alexander, please." I staggered to my feet, clutching my aching face. Sobs wrecked my throat. "I'll go. I won't walk these halls again. Just stop this!"

I knew he heard me... because his smile widened.

Theron stirred. Flopping over, he struggled to get his hands under him. Alexander dropped him again.

My gods. Where were the instructors? Where was Drakos? Help!

"Argh!" A tan-and-white streak shot past me. Nitsa charged Calix, her shoulder down and head angled to ram through him to Alexander.

Moving fast, he bent and blew a pinkish-silver cloud before him. She ran straight into it, and stumbled.

"Calix?" She straightened, unsteady on her feet like a drunk. "Oh, Calix, my love."

"Come to me," he purred, arms as wide as that vain grin. "My moon eyes."

She leaped into his arms. The two started kissing so passionately, my stomach heaved.

Theron tried to rise again. Lips curled, Alexander raised his other hand, keeping him down for good.

Theron's screams bled my ears.

"Oh yes. I do like this one. Even for a host of Zeus, he's very entertaining."

Her laughter battered me as I ran. I launched at Alexander, grasping his wrists. Holding them tight, I held them between my bosom—over my heart.

He jerked so violently I might've smashed another palmful of berries in his face. "What—!"

"Damien, please." Tears streaked my face. "You can stop this. They'll listen to you. End it and I'll do what you say. I'll obey all your rules."

Alexander gazed at our hands, shocked anger twisting his mouth. I wasn't sure if he heard me.

I weaved my fingers through his, holding him tighter. *He needs to hear me. Dammit, Damien, listen.* My other hand cupped his cheek.

"Please," I whispered, tasting wetness on my lips. "This isn't you. You're in the business of killing monsters, remember? Not of hurting your own people because your pain is too great to be satisfied with hurting me.

"I did wrong, Alex. I don't deny it." I drew him closer, not heeding the growl leaking through his teeth. "I will obey your rules if you promise this stays between you and me from now on. I... I can't have one more person hurt because of me."

"Get off."

Alexander yanked back. I held on and bumped against his chest, catching the slightest brush of his lips on my forehead.

"Promise me," I said, eyes glowing as intensely as his.

"You—"

"Stay down, Zervas," Calix barked. "Moon Eyes, take care of him for me."

"Yes, Calix."

A resounding hit, then a grunt. I spun as Theron crashed against the wall, clutching his stomach. He dragged his head up, and the look in his eyes made me step back.

"Theron, no!" Ionna screamed. "You'll kill us all!"

Kill us all? The thought no sooner passed my mind than the air bent. Haze warped my vision, as sudden and unwelcome as the pinpricks of sweat popping on my neck and forehead.

"Theron, calm down," Ionna cried, fighting through bodies to get to him. "You can't— I saw it—"

Slowly, Theron turned on Calix and Alexander... and me standing in front of them.

"*No*," the goddess shrieked. "*Get away from him. Get away from him now!*"

She screamed as the air heated to boiling. Blisters erupted on my skin. I was going to die.

We all were.

"Aella!"

Breaking free, Alexander grabbed my waist and spun—putting himself between me and Theron.

"*Run, pet! You can't—*"

Theron exploded, sending a wall of fire over Alexander's shoulders.

All the screaming stopped.

Alexander

Heat blasted my back, tightening my jaw and my grip. The great son of Maximos Damien. Heir to the seat of Zeus. Burned alive by a Sisyphean. Kharon will laugh so hard, he'll fall out of the boat carrying me to hades.

I waited for his laugh. The cold grip of his hand around my neck. The demand for payment. My welcome into Tartarus. Causing the death of dozens of novices could land me nowhere else.

We're going together. Aella was warm and panting in my grip. *A pair of killers—headed where we belong.*

I waited. And waited.

"What's going on?" A whisper broke through.

"How did we get here?"

"I don't understand."

"Alexander." Her voice was soft. "Let go."

I peeled my eyes open, blinking at a pair of dryads peering at me from behind their trees. Waves of green hair fell around their cocked heads.

We were outside on the green, not far from the ruined stadium. All around, the novices that were in the hall gaped at their surroundings. Lysandros Scala broke free of dumbfounded hands and slipped away, giggles floating behind even as he limp-walked through the side entrance.

I twisted to Galanis but she was already gone. Wisps of her long, flaxen hair disappeared around a corner.

I WOKE EARLY THE NEXT morning and passed by her dorm, slowing for only a fraction of a beat.

Thump-thump-thump-thump-thump. Gritting my teeth, I pushed on to the training room.

The dorms, food, and lecture halls all left much to be desired, but there was nothing I could say against the training rooms. By proper order, the academy funneled its obscene budget into the best weapons and equipment children of Hephaestus could craft. Not a handle was scuffed. Not a single blade was dull.

Though, that wasn't what impressed me. It simply met the standards of the Imperial Palace. No, this was the only place in the building worth being because at that time of the morning, no one else was around.

I pushed into Training Room Eight.

"Ahh, yeah." Moans hit my ears. "Jace, just like that."

Tangled up on my practice mat, Sirena and Jace Rojas rolled across the floor with bits of clothes on their bodies, and the rest flung around the room.

"Oh, gods," Sirena cried, pulling him closer to cover herself. "Forgive me, Xander. I didn't know you were released already." She ran her fingers through his hair, smiling seductively. "Jace and I were celebrating my freedom. And the letter I just sent to Mother detailing the graphic and violent punishment awaiting Vasili and Hondros."

I inclined my head. "Carry on."

"Wait—"

I crossed to Training Room Five. *Empty.*

My hands wrapped around ash wood. So light, but so deadly—the iron tip slashed effortlessly through the closest typhon dummy.

Practice began, and the calm settled. My mind emptied out. Thoughts cleared. Nothing penetrated except the steady routine of my practice.

At least it was that way for the first ten minutes. All too soon, the problems I avoided with six hours of sleep came rushing in.

How did we move from the hall to the green in the blink of an eye? What god even granted such a power? Children of Hermes sent messages with such quickness, but not people.

A power like that is formidable. They could whisk a monster to the depths of the sea before they know they're gasping on water.

They could do the same to a demigod. Could this be the power Aella hides?

I shook the ridiculous thought from my head, sprinkling drops of sweat on the mat. The single drop of divine essence grants only one power. A mortal with all the powers of a god is a dead one. Our bodies cannot handle more. Ancient, and now banned, experiments to extract the essence from other demigods and put it into another proved that. Both groups died—painfully.

No, whatever Galanis can do relates to shredding creatures to pieces. She can't transport them. And Barba wasn't even there when Zervas lost control. He found something better to do with his time when I entered the hall.

As a son of Hades, he avoided me as a rule. Son of a councilman, I watched the slippery traitor even when I had other demands on my attention.

There was someone else in that hall with a power they are downplaying. Whipped out when lives were at stake, but certainly not revealed that first day in the stadium.

I'll find out who it is. Father will want to know—

Phantom fingers laced through mine. My strike went wide, knocking me off-balance. I stumbled on the mat and nearly stabbed a wall of broadswords.

"Fuck!"

The woman was a disease. A plague. Since she entered my life, she's done nothing but wreak destruction. Father swore off his protection, promising to uphold my execution if she escapes me, so naturally that's exactly what the infernal woman continues to do even with the death of Galen in her wake.

She flounces around, laughing it up with her Sisyphean friends, loudly and often calls me the jackass, flaunts her books on spell- and barrier-breaking for all to see, and then has the manticore's boulder-size balls to touch me familiarly and say my actions "weren't me" as if she knew a damn thing about me.

Where the hades did she get off saying she would obey me as long as I left her friends alone? As though her obedience was something she'd give and withdraw, instead of mine to have by will, right, and force.

A warm palm caressed my jaw, and then my hands gripped hers—pulling her from danger. Shielding her body with mine. Molding her to me as perfectly as the night she pulled me into her bed.

A disease. A plague. A menace. My brother's killer. And in that moment when I thought she would die... I tried to protect her.

Roaring, I flung the spear across the room. Training was over for the day.

Moving through the dorm hall, I didn't try to stop myself from going into Aella's room. Of course they kept it locked. Of course I stole a key.

My boots were soundless on the stone, passing by more than the usual empty alcoves. Many of her dorm mates found a new place to sleep in the infirmary.

Tossing and turning in the alcove with the largest window, Aella lay under a blanket of moonlight. Her only cover thanks to the crumpled ball of sheets at her feet.

More nightmares. I gathered all her books on spells and enchantments. *What visions do you see that finally wipe the arrogance off your face?*

I didn't wait around for an answer. Carrying out her books, I left the traitor to her torment.

Three hours later, Sirena and I joined the line of Titans trudging out of their rooms.

I got out of the shower earlier that morning to find her climbing into my bed. It had been years since she'd done that. Mostly because the other side of my bed was usually occupied. But before I discovered the benefit of being me was that I never had to sleep alone, nightmares of her mother reducing her father to nothing would send her running to my room. Beneath the covers, she'd cling to my arm—sniffling as she asked if one day her mother would wipe her away too. Every time I promised her that would never happen, because I would protect her.

A child's vow, but I meant it as much then as I did that day.

"They won't trap you in that room again, Sirena." I climbed in, thinking nothing of her once again clinging to my arm. "I swear it."

Her thin rasp found me across the pillow. "I couldn't change, Xander. I kept trying, and trying, and trying but... I couldn't fly."

"You can always fly." It was me who drew the covers over us. "Away from her. Always."

She didn't reply. Soon, Sirena drifted off to sleep, leaving me to stare at the canopy, lost in the thoughts training was supposed to give me a break from.

"Xander." Sirena drew a line between my brow. Her way of warning me I was wrinkling it again. "What did he say?"

"Don't pretend my brow told you that," I said, clomping beside her down the stairs. "You saw the crumpled letter in the bin."

"Maybe I did. Maybe I didn't. Tell me what he said."

"The same thing he said in the last one." I drifted over combed and uncombed heads, landing on that bobbing blond mane. "Acquire him at all costs."

The smile melted off her face. "He's smart to keep tossing around those smoke birds. No one can safely approach him without knowing what he can do. Except maybe for Aella Galanis." I met her cocked brow. "She seems to get very *close*."

"I have my theories on why that is," I replied simply.

"He's bedding her obviously." Scoffing, she flipped her hair over her shoulder. "I had her pegged as a two-copper toova from the second I met her."

A pounding heart fluttered beneath my hands. Sneering, I forced the conversation away from her. "I've broken into his room twice late at night. Or at least the room that's supposed to be his. Both times the bed was empty and, except for the clothes, there was nothing personal lying around. I suspect he lays his head elsewhere, for the very reason that grants him late-night visitors."

"Where could that be? The castle is hundreds of years old with the secrets, hidden rooms, and concealed passageways to go with it, but even those only get you as far as the barriers around the academy."

"Who needs to get beyond the academy if you can hide for a lifetime within its walls?" I bore into the back of his head. "He knows we can't publicly make a move against him. The time to bring him under council control was before he turned eighteen. Now he's under Drakos's watch and no law supersedes training. I bet that's why he came despite his obvious contempt. He knows he just bought four years of freedom from the council."

"Or so he thinks," Sirena corrected. "He may have found places to hide, but there's nowhere for him to go. Children of Hades are dangerous. They're strange, unpredictable, and filled with power no one person should have. The council was formed because the other demigods understood that.

"They knew the strongest had a duty to come together for the good of Olympia, and lead the weak on the right path. Those like Barba can serve that purpose by pledging their power to the council, and the fact that they continue to rebel is reason enough they must be held down, or put down.

"Barba did not buy himself four years of freedom. What he did was trap himself with the people who will extract his allegiance by any means necessary, or send him to the hell he belongs in."

I nodded slow as Sebastian turned his head without reason and locked on to me. Smirking, he winked.

"Everyone lays their head somewhere," I murmured. "Find his hiding place, Sirena. I do hate to keep denying him the pleasure of waking up to my boot on his throat."

Our smirks mirrored Sebastian's.

"This'll be fun."

Our group melded with the Sisypheans headed to class, though we didn't take the usual route. The novice wing was closed for renovations. Children of Hades were quite fearsome if only most didn't take such a limited view. They couldn't stand the effect constantly stewing in hatred had on their lives, so they chose to live as worthless Sisypheans in and out of the academy.

Hatred was not a disadvantage. It was fuel, purpose, and power. We weren't out there day in and day out fighting those monsters because we loved the fucking things.

We found ourselves in a wing of unused lecture rooms. The fine layer of dust on the desks and chairs drove the point home.

Filing in, I passed a glance over Hondros shuffling scrolls across his temporary desk and flicked off. I bore no ill will toward the man. I was insubordinate. He acted within his confines to reprimand me. I would do the same when I was the first son of Zeus in history to rule as councilman and rank as High Commander of the entire Deucalion Army. Gone would be the days the army and palace commanded as separate entities. Gone would be the days people questioned whether the son could rise higher than the father.

Sirena constricted on my arm. She glared at Hondros hard enough to grant her another stay in the reflection room.

"—better, Daciana?"

My head snapped around. Aella's crowd piled in—short Theron, but regaining a member with the werewolf. There wasn't a scratch on her.

"I'm fine," the wolf confirmed. "My people heal fast. Truthfully, I was fine to leave yesterday, but the healer insisted I stay longer to be sure. Everyone fears an interdominion incident," she said with a laugh, though I did not understand the joke.

Fear of that very incident is why my father's letters didn't order me to acquire her too. Pity. The woman was a high priestess, readying to take the most powerful position in her pack. All we had to do was capture her, use her to lure the rest of the pack, and then force them all to fight for the good of Olympia. If Remis's history lessons were to be believed, the people of the other dominions owed us that and much more.

They all found their seats. Watching the door, I waited for Galanis to walk in behind them. It swung open.

Incredible. She begs for her friends' lives, then goes back on her word at the first—

The thought cut off at the knees. Banging the opposite wall, the door swung back and caught on his palm.

"Ajax." I went to my brother, grabbing and pounding him on the back. "You're out."

He didn't grin, smile, or say "course I'm out, idiot. I'm standing in front of you." Any of which would've been a standard Ajax response.

"Yes," he replied, face blank. He flicked over my shoulder and stepped back, nearly out of the room.

Tap. Tap. Tap.

Every head swiveled to the window. Galanis stood there red-cheeked, brows crumpled, and glare leveled on me. She locked on to my gaze and mouthed one word. "Jackass."

I grinned right back. She knew her books were gone, and she knew who had taken them.

Galanis flashed me an obscene gesture to remove all doubt.

I blew out a breath. "Thus answers the question of if the woman's learned any humility."

"What's this?" Ajax asked while her friends rushed to the window.

"I made it clear to her she isn't to walk, sit, or enjoy a moment's peace in the places where Galen belonged."

He gave no outward reaction. "I see."

The wolf and cow girl helped her up and over the ledge. Hondros just glanced at the scene without interest and returned to his preparation. Without Theron, there was an empty seat on the Sisyphean side. Galanis went where she belonged, bypassing Barba. She dumped her bags and came straight for me. When she saw who I was with, she ground to a halt.

Ajax brushed past me, walking down the aisle where Galanis stood still as a statue. The whole room fell silent. Even Hondros looked up from his scrolls.

Three steps.

Two steps.

One.

They were a hand's breadth away from each other, and mine rose in readiness. It was his right to kill her, but not in front of a room full of people. A second time, and it wouldn't be the reflection room that Drakos sent him to. I would not lose another brother to this walking plague wrapped in that pretty paper.

Ajax walked up to her, sidestepped, and continued on. A collective sigh, or perhaps disappointment, spread as he claimed the seat that was usually mine. Aella watched him go, then snapped to me.

"Damien," she hissed, planting in front of me. "Were you in my room last night?"

"Why would you think that?"

"Because you stole my books!"

"Ahh, of course. Yeah, that was me."

"Give them back."

I bent, putting my face in hers. She didn't back down an inch. "I thought I gave the orders."

"I could put a please at the end, but it won't change the meaning. You don't understand what you're doing. Give me back the books."

"What else is there to understand? You're trying to escape. The only way I'll let you do so is if they're carrying your corpse through the gates. We both understand the situation just fine."

"If you—"

"Now let me make my situation clear," I sliced in, bearing closer on those intense, unwavering green-blue eyes. "Your life is tied to mine. If you escape, I die. If you stay, I'll kill you or ensure the one who does"—I glanced at Ajax—"gets away with it.

"Choose the first option, and I'll kill every traitor-loving friend of yours before the imperial guards haul me out of the academy. If you choose the second, and my favorite, option, your friends only suffer and die when you piss me off." Grinning, I flicked her chin. "Do you see now why option two is best for everybody?

"Your life was forfeit from the minute you tipped off that gorge. Every day since has just been borrowed time. The next fall is going to kill you, Aella Galanis. It's your choice whether you jump alone."

Moving in closer still, Aella pierced my stare and said, "Option two will not end the way you think. Not for any of us. You're fighting on a foggy battlefield, Damien. You can't see who you're swinging your sword at, or even who your enemy is. By the time you realize it's not me, it'll be too late."

Confusion tried to break through my confidence. What was she talking about? Why did nothing this woman said make sense?

"I agreed to obey your rules to protect my friends and *I* keep my word." She said that like I didn't. "You can keep the books."

She turned away as if she gave the final word. As if I was dismissed from her sight.

"If you get more, I'll take those too," I warned.

"Naturally," she tossed over her shoulder.

Irritation blazed into an inferno. I lurched and grabbed her arm, spinning her back around. "I know what you are and what you're running from."

Aella's confidence broke. A sudden flash of panic chased away her defiance. "What? How—? You couldn't."

"You should've made it a little less obvious." Movement flicked out of the corner of my eye. Hondros was bearing down on us fast. "I will see you meet your fate, Galanis," I whispered in her ear. "I keep my word too."

I let her go before Hondros opened his mouth. Taking my seat, I felt nothing close to victory.

"You're fighting on a foggy battlefield, Damien."

What did that mean? And why through all my death threats and promises of violence against her friends, did she only look scared when I said I knew the truth?

Sirena

Alexander glared over at that Sisyphean traitor for the tenth time in the last hour and a half. It was everything in me not to fly her up a hundred feet and let go. That morning we finally made progress. Xander held me in his bed like he used to when we were children. Now he was back to hushed arguments and tense stares with *her*.

Even though he claimed to hate her, and even though I believed he did, there was something about her that was staying his hand. He should've killed her a long time ago. When he picked up her traitor ass at the border, and certainly after she got Galen killed. For some reason, he's refusing to simply pick up his hand and end it in the seconds it would take to explode her head.

The only explanation I could think of for why he hadn't is that she presented some kind of challenge to him. Alexander didn't meet with those often—or ever. In the palace, everyone bowed as he walked by. His sparring partners held back for fear of injuring a councilman's son. Guards followed him everywhere despite his frequent and loud orders to fuck off. No one said what they truly thought of him. No one uttered a word that might upset him.

Damien was one of the strongest demigods in Olympia, but only by title. No true opponents have ever risen up and made him prove it.

By the way that toova spoke to him—insulting him to his face, rolling her eyes, staring him down, and completely ignoring that every slight could be her last—maybe Xander thought he finally met his match.

In the wrong woman.

My fists balled beneath the desk. *I* was the one who challenged him. *I* was the one who told him the truth. *I* was the one who looked at him and saw more than Maximos Damien's son.

My mother wanted our pairing for the unstoppable match we'd make, but I just wanted him. I was Xander's soulmate. Everything he needed he would find in me.

We were both glaring at the back of Galanis's shining crown then. *This bitch would have to go.*

Chairs scraped across the stone, signaling the end of class. I hooked through Damien's arm, holding tight to him as I gathered my stuff. We were going everywhere together from now on. Fuck Hyacinth's stupid plan to make him jealous.

"Miss Cirillo," Hondros called. "Stay behind."

Xander slipped out of my hold, following Galanis to her window and exit. I barely bit back a frustrated scream.

The one-armed waste of blood, skin, and power stood at his worktable, shuffling through scrolls. I didn't attempt to hide my disdain as I climbed the steps and faced him. "Yes, *Captain*."

"I'm not one to beat around the bush and that won't change now."

I frowned. "What are you talking about?"

"After your sudden and unnecessary outburst over turning in your own scroll, I grew suspicious and decided to take a closer look at the other scrolls you've handed to me."

My muscles went rigid.

Unfurling a scroll, he read, "It's important to never give an empousa leadway. They will change form the minute they're out of your sight." He picked up another one and read, "No leadway. No mercy." Hondros dropped the paper, eyes hard.

"What?" I snapped. "Am I supposed to know what that just was?"

"Leadway is known to be confused with the correct word—leeway. For the same spelling mistake to show up in two scrolls on the same topic would be a coincidence, if I believed in them." He tossed both scrolls in the direction of the trash. "I've gone through both your and Tessa Madden's assignments and found several instances where the rewritten sentences were just close enough to match."

My pulse quickened. Sweat beaded on my temple. *No, no...*

"I needn't ask who holds the power in that dynamic. It's clear you've had Tessa complete all your assignments since the beginning of the year."

"That's a lie! How dare you accuse me? A couple of misspelled words isn't proof." My voice grew louder and louder, shouting over the internal scream to do something. *Now!* "I wrote every word on those scrolls in my own hand. Ugh, like I would let an illiterate clerk's daughter put my name on some garbage she wrote. What kind of idiot doesn't know leadway isn't a word?"

"So you're saying Miss Madden is the one who copied your scrolls?"

"She must've," I said, shrugging. "There's no other explanation. It's disgusting, Captain. I deigned to be her friend. Allowed her in my room while I wasn't there. I can't believe the whole time she was using me to get out of doing her own work."

Hondros leaned away, crossing his arm over and grasping his stump. "This is a very serious offense."

"As it should be."

"Cheating not only deprives you of training, but it also displays a contemptible lack of integrity that has no place in the army. Any trainee caught cheating will be expelled. No exceptions."

I blinked lazily. "Are you waiting for me to tearfully beg for the cheater to stay? Expel Tessa. What's it to me?"

"Hmm." Hondros gave me a long look. "I will not expel Tessa Madden."

"Why not?"

"Because it wasn't Miss Madden who refused when I demanded she do her own work. You're a liar, Cirillo. I would expel you this very moment if my suspicions were enough. As it is, Headmaster Drakos would require more proof."

A smile pulled at my lips. "Then I guess we're done here."

"Not quite," he said, halting my retreat. "You will complete the scroll you refused to do and all future assignments here. In this room. Under my supervision."

"You can't—!"

"I assure you I can. While Drakos may not share my suspicions about the previous assignments, he will certainly find it suspect if you continue to fight this simple request. After all, whether you do these assignments in this room or your dorm, it should make no difference, yes? Unless..."

I opened and closed my fists, mentally cycling through the host of flying creatures with talons sharper than blades. *Threat of violence won't work any more than threat of the council. Everyone heard him call me to stay behind. If he spends the rest of the year in the infirmary, they'll know it was me.*

"No unless," I forced through clenched teeth. "Of course it makes no difference, but that doesn't mean I'll happily go along with your persecution. This has nothing to do with cheating. You're just getting off on the modicum of power you have over me."

"I assure you I'm doing nothing of the kind, Miss Cirillo." He didn't sound defensive. If anything, he sounded bored with me. "Report here after your final lesson of the day. Dismissed."

I walked out calmly. On the slam of the wood, I ran. Tearing through the halls, I blew past shouting fools and indignant wastes of my time. *Where is—!*

Her head bobbed among the crowd. Tessa reached the staircase, making her way up to the new location of our history lecture hall. My griffin's claw snatched her from behind, constricting around her neck. I hauled her around, her bulging eyes reflecting my snarl.

"We need to talk."

Alexander

"You missed a lot. Compared to these first two weeks, the rest of the year will be dull."

Ajax grunted something in response. He strolled next to me, eyes glazed and unfocused as if lost in thought.

"Drakos transferred a son of Eris into our lecture group. The Sisyphean went berserk, poisoned everyone, and kicked off a riot that destroyed the stadium. Or so I'm told."

"Pity."

"Zervas found the balls to tap into his power. He almost killed dozens of people, including me and Calix. We made it out alive, but I couldn't tell you how or who did it."

"Interesting."

"All right, what's up with you?" I got in front of him, forcing him to stop. "You're—"

"Leave the Galanis girl alone."

"Hold on. What?"

"Forcing her out of the hall and mess. Making her climb through windows." He shook his head. "I know you're doing this for Galen. Avenging him because Drakos gave her a free pass, but I had nothing to do but think while in that cage. If he didn't die protecting her, he would've done it while defending a village from typhons or rooting out a nest of gorgons.

"This is what we signed up for. Hating her for his death won't change it, but it will cheapen his honor. He died a hero." He shook his head. "Whether the person was worth saving or not."

My jawline stiffened. "What are you saying? Some traitor gets an imperial heir killed while trying to escape, and we just let that go?"

"She didn't get an imperial heir killed," he growled, eyes flashing. "She got *my brother* killed! This isn't about the fucking council. Her death is mine to claim. Her punishment is mine to decide, and I say it's over. Leave her be."

I clamped his shoulder, stopping him from sidestepping me. "I've got my own scores to settle with that girl. Your mother didn't spit me out on the same nursing bed, but he was my brother too. That night, Galanis tried to escape and get me killed, instead she killed Galen. That cannot stand."

He shook me off, that strange dullness taking hold of him again. "She's a mundane undergoing the most brutal training program in all five dominions. We both know we won't have to wait long," he said, walking off. "Whatever business you've got with her, handle it. Just don't do it in Galen's name."

I watched him go, eyes narrowed. What the fuck did they do to him in that reflection room? Ajax once drowned a guard into a heart attack for grabbing Galen from behind and trying to drag him into an empty room.

He did not forget. He did not forgive. And he did not show mercy.

Something was up with him, but the stubborn ass would admit he was in love with the nobleman's son from Kuna City before he let anyone inside his head. I didn't know he wanted Aella dead until she was flailing on the floor, drowning on dry land.

Galen was his twin. His brother to avenge, but she was my traitor. Peace was not hers to have. Forgiveness wasn't something I gave.

That morning, I spoke the truest words I ever said. Our lives were linked now, but our paths were opposite. Going her way would get me killed. Going mine would strip her of right and freedom—two things she's already proven she'll die for.

Phantom fingers brushed my cheek, drawing me closer. I smacked across my jaw, wiping her touch, her memory, her everything away.

This wasn't over. Not until one of us was dead.

Aella

T*hunk.*
   Thud.

I jolted upright, jarring out of the dream as my claws shredded Kristopher's liver.

Alexander kicked back in my chair, boots resting on my scrolls for Madame Remis. I watched him paw through my desk while my breaths slowed. The sweat cooled on my chest, my pounding heart evened out, but the nightmarish memories lingered to stay.

"Hello, Damien." I wasn't surprised to see him. He made a late-night visit to steal my books once. Why wouldn't he drop by again? "To what do I owe the displeasure?"

"Came to deliver a message," he replied. The guy had no shame riffling through my pack and checking my reference books.

I drew my twisted sheets up to my chin. Long, fitful, sweaty nights made sleeping in my cotton nightdresses uncomfortable. I'd taken to sleeping in nothing but my breast band and undergarments. I didn't let myself think about how often Alexander saw me barely clothed.

"What message? That you have all the morals of a bilge rat? Your skulking around in a woman's private space while she sleeps already told me that."

He chuckled. "Now don't be mean when I'm giving you a treat."

"A treat?" I edged away. "What treat?"

"Your punishment is lifted. You're free to walk the halls, eat in the mess, laugh with your friends, and all the rest. I won't hurt you or them for it."

His beaming smile only deepened my frown. "What the fuck is wrong with you?"

Alexander wheezed trying not to laugh loud and wake the dorm. "Don't rush that thank-you off your tongue, Galanis."

"Why would I thank you for playing mind games with me? You *tortured* my friends to get me to obey your rules, and now you're here saying never mind?"

"Mmm. Tortured is a strong word," he breezed. "Trust me, they would've screamed much louder if I was going for torture."

"You're a bastard." The blunt decoration got me another laugh. "You're not easing up on me out of the goodness of your heart, so get to the end of your message. I can walk through the halls but I have to do it naked? Or you'll let me eat in the mess as long as I wear a sign saying whatever your evil, twisted mind comes up with?"

"All excellent suggestions. I will keep those in mind for when Ajax comes to his senses."

I stilled, sensing the hairs rise up on the back of my neck as they did that morning when Ajax closed the distance. "Ajax?"

"He's the one who called your punishment off. Hating you won't bring Galen back, and he rather remember his brother for dying a hero… instead of sacrificing his life for an ignorant deserter."

I held his gaze for all of a second. My eyes flicked down, flashing their shame to my see-through sheets. Alexander wasn't being a jackass or a bastard. He was telling the truth. Galen died for my ignorance.

"He says I'm not to torment you in Galen's name, so I won't." He paused, waiting for me to speak. No reply came. "I'm serious, Aella. Go back to life as normal. I won't make it difficult anymore.

"Other than preventing your escape, of course." Damien got to his feet. "I don't share your death wish, so excuse me if I don't let you book a date for my execution."

"So that's it," I blurted. "You're done torturing me just like that?"

"Like I said," he replied, strolling off. "If I was torturing you, there'd be more screams."

"We don't have to be enemies—you and I."

Alexander paused in my entrance.

"I don't expect your forgiveness, and you shouldn't expect mine. But maybe we can go back to how it was in the beginning?"

"How was that exactly?"

"You ignoring my existence while I count the dandelions."

He made a sound that might've been a laugh but I wasn't sure. "You mean back when I thought you were nothing more than a cowardly deserter. Before I realized you're hiding something you'd rather die than let anyone know."

I fisted the sheets. "That's not true. I didn't want to go to the academy. I refuse to serve in the army. That's why I ran. There's no reason bigger than—"

"There you go again," he burst out, spinning on me. A sharp grunt sounded from Tycho's space. "You just keep *lying*. By the gods, woman, are you capable of telling the truth? If you are, show me." My eyes grew round as he leaned over me. "Tell me. Everything. Right now. Do it and I'll grant any request—whether it's to keep my distance or shower you in imperial gold. Go on," he whispered. "Be honest for once in your life."

And I thought you didn't want me to book a date for your execution.

That time, I had no trouble meeting his eyes. "I told you the truth. I don't have powers, Alexander. I don't belong here. The law says I must come here to fight, or do hard labor and die. I decided to take my fate into my own hands."

"I don't believe you," he sang.

It was my turn to tilt my head, studying him. "Why? Why is it so hard to believe that living and dying on my own terms is worth fighting for? Have the laws of Olympia been driven so deep into your soul, you don't see what you're giving up to uphold them?"

"Have the tales of woe from the likes of Sebastian Barba been driven so deep into your soul, you believe hoarding your powers is more honorable than using them to protect your people?"

My brow wrinkled. "What does Sebastian have to do with this? You can't still think I'm tumbling the man. You know better than anyone where I spend my nights."

"It's bigger than you fucking him. You're the same, aren't you?" He glared hard as if trying to see into my thoughts. "You're both children of Hades. That's why you ran from the academy, and why you're still trying to run. If anyone witnesses your power and reports you to the palace, there's an oath of fealty and a life serving the council waiting for you at the end of training. Live and die on your own terms," he repeated.

"*Ooh, he's a clever one. He's right that you're hiding the god that bound your life in chains. Just wrong about which one.*"

"Admit it," he said over her fading chuckle.

"Why do you need me to, Damien? Why is it so important for you to understand the traitor's motives?"

"Why do I need to understand why Galen's dead?" he growled. "Why do I need to know what's so important on the other side of that gods damned wall that you're *still* trying to get over it after everything you've done?"

I flinched. "You're right. That was a stupid question. There's a heart in there somewhere." I laid my palm flat on his chest. "I know that I broke it."

Alexander moved so fast, I was left blinking at my hand hanging in the air. He curled his lip from the other side of the alcove.

"Don't flatter yourself. Break my heart? Whatever power you're hiding, it's not that."

My hand fell to my side. "There's nothing I can tell you. Nothing that you'll accept."

"You have no honor, Aella Galanis." The declaration was an arrow through my chest, springing sudden tears on my lids. "But I do. I will respect Ajax's wish that I take no more revenge in Galen's name."

I ducked my head so he wouldn't see all that he already knew. I did have no honor. If I did, I'd have escaped Alexander long before he got me through these gates. If I had honor, Galen and Kristopher would be alive.

That's the truth I owed him, but it hung unsaid in the air as the door swung shut.

"THAT'S IT? JUST LIKE that?"

I shrugged. We were steps away from the mess hall, though I was the only one inching toward it. "Yeah, I guess. He told me Ajax ended the war. I'm free to go where I want. He won't harm you guys for it."

Nitsa, Daciana, Ionna, Tycho, and a banged-up but healing Theron exchanged looks. Lysandros was busy whistling to himself and doing a strange swaying dance. He already grabbed and spun me off my feet twice. I let it go in stride. He wasn't a bad dancer.

"Did you ever consider he was lying through his teeth?" Tycho asked. "It's no fun for them when you stop fighting back. Now they're thinking of a new way to torture you."

"If that's true, tumbling through windows won't change anything."

"Aella," Ionna cried. "This is serious. We all nearly died because the imperial heirs don't know when to stop."

Theron flushed under his bandages. I didn't see after I walked away from Alexander, that the crowd of demigods that nearly became red mist in the novice hall, turned and beat Theron to a pulp.

"Alexander will keep his word," I said. "It's that absolute sense of certainty that he's always right all the time that makes it easy for him to do what he says he will."

Still, no one took a step. The last time we went up against the heirs, Theron and Tycho ended up on the floor. Nitsa threw herself at Calix in a power-fogged lust. And Daciana almost became the only surviving member of our group. It had been a hellish few weeks, I could understand why they wanted some peace.

They'd have peace if they didn't befriend me.

"Guys, look. This all happened because of me. Alexander warned me, and I didn't listen. All I can do is promise I won't make that mistake again. If he and the imperial heirs are coming up with something else, I'll take the brunt of it."

Scoffing, Theron moved around me. "Getting the shit kicked out of me didn't dislodge my honor. I'm not putting my head down and shuffling past whenever they get in your face. I'm just saying there's no way this is over. So we better be ready."

My friends all echoed him as they headed into the mess hall. I watched them go, feeling a wave of gratitude mixed with something else.

"These are the people you want dead?" I whispered. "These are the horrible hosts corrupted by parasites? Demigods are better than you say they are. They're definitely better than you."

"I am a goddess, pet. I am not bound by your morality, therefore I cannot be defined by it."

"Is that what you tell yourself to justify your mad plan to rule a world of death and pain? That right and wrong don't apply to you?"

"It's not a justification when it's the truth. Laws are only obeyed when someone stronger than you enforces it. There is no one stronger

than me. All your precious gods have scattered like seeds in the wind, hiding out in their human pets while they long for the days they ruled."

I gritted my teeth under the pain. But I would finish this. It's time she listened to me. "If you're so all-powerful, why are you hiding out in a human pet, cursing the day this same girl who's barely out of nursing strings ruined your grand plan? Seems like there is someone strong enough to stop you. Me."

She hissed—the sound a sharp spike through my mind. *"Insolent girl. Why my faithful Maia brought me such a blasphemous offering, I'll never know."*

Sweat beaded my forehead, and it wasn't just for the pain. Flashes of my violent fever dreams roared through the peace of morning, sending me right back to the nightmares behind my eyes.

"The day is coming when I'll be freed. I will wipe out every trace of the Olympian gods and stand on the turn of the universe as its high ruler. You cannot stop this, child. So ask yourself if you'd rather stand as my ally, or whimper in chains as my enemy."

"Enemy," I rasped. "Definitely enemy."

Her voice faded. *"Insolent girl..."*

I collapsed against the wall, breathing heavy. Sebastian trailed past me, brows riding up to his hairline. My cheeks reddened. Why was this guy always around at the worst times?

He went into the mess hall without saying anything and I found myself behind him in line for food. Staring at his broad back made it seem like I didn't notice the dozens of pairs of eyes on me. But I did.

The noise fell to a dull roar. The murderer. The traitor. The mundane. Was back.

Just focus on what you need to do. I was getting closer to the answer with those books. They all said no enchantment is absolute.

There's always a way to break them. A big reason why children of Hecate guard their spell books with their life.

After I eat, I'm going straight to the library to find the books Alexander didn't take from me. They didn't need to worry about the traitorous mundane. Until I found the answer, the library stacks were my home.

I fixed firmly on Sebastian while eyes crawled on me. He poured himself a bowl of porridge and topped it with honey, nuts, raisins, and olives.

"Ugh. I was going to follow you until you added that last bit." He flashed an amused grin on me as I held up my bowl of porridge with nuts and raisins as proof.

"This is how my mother used to make it," he said, piling sausage on the side.

"Ahh. Did she not like you much?"

A short, startled bark of laughter slipped through his lips, and then he couldn't stop. Sebastian threw his head back—shoulders shaking as he guffawed. The entire mess stopped talking, and they stopped looking at me.

His entire... everything... changed. Gone was the bored set to his jaw. Light warmed his icy blues. Pleasure made his handsome face *lethal*. If you told me he could put you under a Calix-like spell with his laugh alone, I wouldn't question it for a second.

"Try it first." Sebastian cupped my hand under the bowl. Again I was powerless to stop him bringing me closer and sprinkling olives on my porridge. "There's something about an imperfect pairing. The wrongness just makes it... right."

I squeaked a reply at his back as he walked off. My fingers tingled strangely where he touched me. Maybe this was the normal way of the world. Tycho, Lysandros, and Theron walking around bare-chested in the dorm. Alexander gazing at me in my breast band without a shred of shame. Calix calling me pet names with my kiss on his lips. Sebastian casually leaning in to whisper in my ear.

I'd have built a defense against it if I hadn't spent eight years in a cave with three girls and a woman that long since stopped being one. As it was, my extreme dislike for Alexander did not stop me noticing it was a miracle he didn't lose himself in every mirror he walked past. The night before in my room when he said he had a treat for me...

I flushed, head dizzying on my scurry to my table. I couldn't admit even to myself the thoughts I had. Did I picture him glistening under orb light as he wielded his staff on the green—muscles rippling with every perfect strike?

No.

Did I see the way he worried his hair while he worked on assignments, carding his fingers through and revealing those secret curls?

No.

Did his voice come through the wall in my mind—husky and panting as he pleasured another random girl in another random inn?

No.

Did I, for the barest second, think my treat was to discover what the last eight years denied me of men, pleasure, and *tumbling*?

Absolutely not.

I did not want Alexander Damien in any way, let alone that one. I felt for the pain I caused when that demon jumped out of my hands and killed Galen, but the fact remained Alexander set himself against me from the moment he boiled my blood in the mud. I despised him from that smirk, to his vicious taunts, to the frightening bloodlust.

Eventually I would build up my shields against handsome men and their too-green eyes. Until then, I was wearing my nightdress to bed from then on.

THE DAY PASSED QUICKLY after that. We went on with our lessons in the wrong rooms and the wrong stadium, but the instructors fell into their routine of normal. My friends and I could not say the same.

Theron, Nitsa, and the guys stared harder at Ajax, Sirena, and Alexander than Alexander stared at me. When they weren't keeping an eye on them, they were weathering the usual crap from the Titan class and Kosma's constant hissed insults. They already hated Lysandros for the apples and the stadium. Theron wasn't getting any nice looks either.

Then, of course, there would always be me. The traitor and mundane who never belonged here in the first place. I should've been executed. Or at least that's what Kosma whispered to me as our group made for the green and the final lesson of the day.

The only one who didn't have something to say to us was Alexander and Ajax. Sirena didn't come near us either, though she had great fun smiling knowingly at me whenever she picked lint off Alexander's shoulder, ran her fingers through his hair, or found an excuse to touch him.

I barely contained an eye roll when Damien and Sirena pulled ahead of us and she curled through his arm, shooting me a wink.

What does this woman think our relationship is? She can paw him to her heart's content. It's got nothing to do with me.

We got in line, each of us grabbing a staff and taking our place. I finally graduated to my own dummy and no longer had to deal with Vasili's one-on-one instruction. That didn't stop the man from hovering nearby and criticizing everything I did from the way I held the staff to the way I breathed. Literally, the day before he berated me for breathing through my mouth.

I stepped up and took a staff under Vasili's watchful eye. It followed me as I got as far from him as possible, claiming the gorgon dummy near the end. Maybe I was naïve for believing he'd eventually stop hating me for being the child of Hermes that brought him the devastating news. That was clearly wishful thinking.

Vasili must not believe there was any hope of finding his son alive, and he despised me for giving it back to him for however long it took for it to be crushed again.

"This evening we're mastering the downward strike," Vasili called. The enchantment on his voice made it easy to hear from all the way down the green. "To perform this maneuver, you will raise the staff above your head parallel to the ground, spin, and bring it down sharply with your left hand. Begin."

I got to work lifting, spinning, and striking. After a few wide and clumsy misses, I found my rhythm. *Thunk, thunk, thunk* across the typhon's head each time.

"Terrible."

I stumbled, startled to find Vasili behind me.

"Your foot placement is wrong. Your hands are too close together, and you're losing your center every time you strike. Do it properly or get off my field."

Clenching my jaw, I fixed myself and readied to—

"No. Again."

A scream bled through my teeth. There was no getting out from under his hatred. Why did I let myself hope?

"Do you have something to say, girl?" Vasili asked, bearing down on me. "Speak up."

Across from me, Daciana gave me a supportive smile. I hadn't shared my time with the lamia with anyone other than Drakos, Remis, and Vasili. By then it was obvious they didn't tell anyone else either. She didn't know why he despised me, but she was used to getting crap from students and instructors. At least someone was on my side.

Which is why I'd much rather moan with Daciana in the mess hall after lessons instead of staying out here running laps around the castle because I mouthed off to the commander.

"Nothing to say, Commander," I replied. "I just stepped on my toe."

"A clumsy soldier is a dead one. Get your head out of your daydreams and focus."

"Yes, sir."

I tried again, bringing my arm down and—

"No. Your feet, girl," he barked. "Fix your feet."

"Commander," Daciana called. His frown snapped off me. "I mastered the basic bo staff strikes when I was six. I noticed you gave half a dozen Titans permission to move on to advanced techniques. I would like the same."

"Would you?" He stalked up to her, leaving me in blessed peace. "Those novices demonstrated perfect mastery of those strikes. I assume you're prepared to do the same. Now."

"Yes, sir." Turning to her dummy, she tossed me a wink. Words could not describe how much I loved her.

I blew out a breath and found my stance, falling back into my easy rhythm. The day could not come that I fought on a battlefield. I wasn't dense enough to believe that four years of training could rid me, or anyone, of the fear of facing my death against every monster that crossed my path. If I wasn't rid of the goddess by then, the most dangerous creature my mora would face is me.

No, this training was me biding my time to keep out of hard labor. In the meantime, the repetitive motion allowed my mind to wander.

I ducked into the library between breaks, reading *Principles of Magic* in pieces. So far, nothing gave specifics for breaking through barrier spells, but that didn't mean I wasn't learning a lot about them. A spell caster had to be the one to take them down and erect them, but people still found ways to slip past. Either by the power granted them by their gods, a failsafe in case of danger, or a situation the caster didn't think to cover when they created the spell.

I already ran into that situation with the demon. The barrier both had to keep the demon out and let me in because my life was in danger. In the end, my life was held above all and that clever, filthy demon found his loophole.

What if I was in danger again? If I stirred the dryads to anger again and they chased me to the gates, the spells would let me over to save my life.

I clunked the typhon's head, running out of steam physically and mentally. A good plan but how would I recreate that situation? I doubted there were any more demon babies lurking in the woods. The only other way I knew to become an enemy of the dryads was to cut down their sisters.

I swung wide at the very thought of that, my stomach twisting. Killing the tree killed the dryad. I couldn't do something so horrible to normally peaceful deities. Saving myself from killing *by killing* made no sense.

Think of another way. Some way to force real danger, but that doesn't put anyone at risk.

My brain did not supply an answer for me.

"Enough."

I glanced up. All my failed planning ended at the sight of Alexander.

"I can't watch this anymore," he announced. "You're terrible at this, Galanis, and since Vasili hates you, he can't resist spending the entire block badgering you."

"Thank you for telling me. I wouldn't have had a clue what was going on without you."

He chuckled at my sarcasm. My sisters didn't like my sharp tongue and the arguments it kicked off, but Alexander just found it amusing—when it didn't enrage him.

"All the time he spends on a mundane is a waste for everyone else. Here." Alexander tossed his staff down between us. "I'll show you how it's done so when he's finished with the wolf, he'll finally move on to someone else."

"Her name is Daciana."

"And I care why?"

"Jackass," I muttered.

"Stop talking." Alexander grasped my hips and I did just that. My cheeks lit on fire as his fingers settled on the space between waist and thighs. My *bottom*. "Your hips should be square like this. Solid and stacked over your feet. Your feet change placement depending on the strike, but you always return to this resting position. Understood?"

My pulse thrummed loud in my ears. Alexander did away with his tunic in favor of the tight, white sleeveless undershirt beneath. White quickly became translucent as he worked up a sweat. By then, he could've done away with that too because it was doing nothing to hide his hard, bronze chest or the dusky nipples crowning it.

"Well...? Do it, Galanis."

The bark jarred me awake. "Oh, right." Following his instructions, I squared my hips and placed my feet where he told me. "Like this?"

"Yes. Now chin up." He propped his finger under mine, tipping my head level with his pursed mouth. I didn't dare look over his shoulder and find Sirena. One look at her and I'd turn to stone. She had to be spitting mad. "Focus on your target."

Releasing me, he backed up. The burning handprints on my hips and backside didn't go anywhere. "Give me your staff. I'll show you where to put your hands."

"I'm not sure I like this," I said slowly, handing over my staff. "You being nice to me."

A grin twisted his lips, panging my already battered shields. "Is that what I'm doing? I told you my reasons are entirely selfish."

"Yeah, of course. You wouldn't tell someone they were on fire unless there was something in it for you." He laughed. "But the result is the same. Your helping me to help yourself is still helping me."

"Hmm. Should I stop?" I didn't reply as he held out the staff, placing his hands at the one-third points. "The first thing to remember is—"

The wood flashed. In one clean, smooth move, Alexander snapped the staff over his knee. My eyes bugged, jaw hanging open and words stalling on my tongue. Alexander popped the pieces on my palm looking so damn smug as shit, I would've hit him over the head if my body was responding to my brain.

Whistling, he loped off.

"Yes, you rantallion, puss-covered shit brick! Stop helping me!"

Alexander's howling rang over the green. The only one louder than Vasili.

"Galanis! What did you do to that staff? A soldier who doesn't care for their equipment is—"

"—a dead soldier," I sighed.

"No, an out-of-breath one." He jerked his head. "Five laps around the castle. Now."

I didn't bother arguing. Dropping my half staffs, I jogged off—shooting a poisonous look at Damien on the way. He saluted me, then went back to his practice, muscles glistening in the orb light.

Sirena

"Sirena, I don't know about this." Tessa bleated at me all the way across the green. "We could get expelled for this. We can't—"

"Shh. Not so loud," I hissed. "We'll only get expelled if we get caught." I got in her face. "And may I remind you we almost did because of you?"

She shrunk back.

"We wouldn't be in this mess if you hadn't screwed everything up in the first place. I told you to make sure our essays weren't similar."

"I did— I tried," she stammered. "But if we do this—"

"What are you so worried about? I'm taking all the risk. If we do this right, no one will know you're involved."

"But it's..." Her face crumpled. "It's wrong. What we're doing is wrong."

Rolling my eyes, I walked off. By the gods, these common people were naïve. Tessa should know better from growing up in the palace, but it seemed she wasn't paying attention. It's a cutthroat life in Olympia. The strong and powerful decide what's right and wrong.

With her dismissed, Hyacinth and Rue fell in step with me. We approached the line of novices putting away their staffs in time to see Aella Galanis huff and puff on by.

"Pick up the pace, girl," Vasili bellowed.

I grinned at her plight until I saw Alexander. He was staff-free but he was still there, leaning against a battered dummy while he watched her. Visions of him pawing her, tickling her chin, and laughing louder at her than he had with me in months flashed through my head.

I shoved my staff at Rue. "Put that away."

"Yes, Sirena."

"Hyacinth, I'm going to need you to do something for me." I narrowed on Galanis's shrinking back. "And you can skip the part where you moan about how wrong it is and you couldn't possibly. Do this and whatever you want, name it and it's yours."

"Do what exactly?"

I told her, studying her close for her reaction. Hyacinth gave nothing away. She just nodded once and left.

"Tessa," I called. "Let's go."

She trailed behind me, dragging her feet across the green, through the back entrance of the lecture hall, and up the steps to the second floor. I arrived as Calix's lecture group left their field medicine class. That damn fool Tessa was still waffling on the third step.

"Calix." I snapped my fingers. "Over here."

"Fuck off, Sirena," he drawled, breezing past. "I'm not one of your lackeys to be summoned."

Snatching his arm, I tried hauling him back and got dragged off the top step. I shrieked losing my balance. Legs flipping over my head, I reacted fast—sprouting phoenix wings. They pumped true and strong, catching the air and placing me lightly on my feet. Calix's class didn't know whether to laugh or clap. They did both.

Marching up to Calix, I slapped him across the face. He burst out laughing.

"Gods, Cal, you're such a bastard when you're off nectar."

He cracked his jaw, shrugging. "They say I'm a bastard when I'm on it too, so what can you do?"

"I need you to do something for me."

"What's in it for me?"

Classic Calix. Doesn't ask what it is first. He asks what he can get out of it.

I motioned for us to move away from the crowd. "What do you want?"

"Mommy Dearest has been vague about when she's naming me as her successor. I want an official declaration and the celebration to go with it by summer's end. And I want that promise signed, sealed, and blood-marked by the end of the week."

I clenched my fists behind my back, fighting the temptation to slap him again. Calix went straight for the jugular every time. A side of him no one got to see because he was either concealing himself in Galen, Ajax, and Alexander's shadows, or so high on nectar he forgot what an insufferable dung pile he was.

I loved Xander. I didn't have to love his friends.

"How am I supposed to get her to do that? When and who she names is her choice."

"Walking away is my choice." He loped off. "Good luck."

"Okay. Hold on. Stop!" I cried, spinning that smirk back on me. "End of the week. It's a deal."

Mother will have to go along. She knows we don't have a choice. Besides, there's no one she could name other than Calix. It's rare for a child of Aphrodite to receive a defensive power, and what stronger defense than turning your enemies into simpering fools who'd jump off a cliff if you asked?

"That's what I like to hear. What do you want?"

"Not what." I flicked to Tessa wringing her hands and shuffling in the corner. "Who."

Calix listened to my plan without reaction. "Easy. Just tell me where."

I smiled for the first time that day. Okay, maybe I didn't hate Calix. There was something wonderfully refreshing about a guy who understood what the rest of Olympia was still getting their thick heads around. The council and those of us chosen to one day step up in their place were the blessed few to be granted the highest gifts from our gods and goddesses.

It's us they chose to reign. It's the peasants and Sisypheans they placed below us. We were beholden to no one's rules.

We were gods.

"Let's go," I ordered. "We have to get there first."

"Lead the way."

Together the three of us descended the stairs and made for our new wing. Tessa broke off to go back out the way we came. I didn't worry about her though I followed with slitted eyes. She would do what she was told.

"Hold on," I whispered.

I sidled up to the third door on the left and stuck my head inside. *Empty.*

"Okay, we're good." I motioned for him to go in. "You know what to do."

Calix entered Hondros's room and found his place behind the door. I took a seat on my usual table, then moved over and three rows down, then got up again and propped myself against Barba's space. I was fixing my skirts when I heard footsteps coming down the hall.

Hondros stepped into the doorway and landed on me right away. "Ahh, Miss Cirillo, thank you for being prompt. We'll—"

Concealed behind the wood, Calix tipped his chin and blew a pink-and-silver cloud into the air. Hondros breathed in deep, blinking at the first person his gaze found—me.

"Sirena," he whispered.

I couldn't shrink my smile. "Evening, Hondros. I've been waiting for you. What took so long?"

His face fell, horror flooding his eyes. "I'm so sorry. I never meant to make you wait," he cried, falling to his knees. "Forgive me? I love you so much."

Calix slipped out the door, shutting it softly behind. His job was done.

"Hmm. Maybe I'll forgive you but..." I trailed my fingers along my collarbone, caressed my dress's right strap, and brushed it off my shoulder. "You'll have to do something for me first."

"Anything." Hondros crawled on his knees to me. I raised my boot and he kissed it without being told.

I wondered if Mother refused to acknowledge Calix not because she wasn't impressed by his power, but because she *wanted* it. The power to bring men literally to their knees... and it was wasted on a man. The council may seem like one body working together, but power was weighted by the seat.

The king and queen of the sky were Zeus and Hera. Therefore, their children had final say over every law and motion made. If there was a tie between them, the Poseidon councilman broke it. Otherwise, the other councilmen and women were only in charge of matters relating to their god. With Calix's power, Mother could—and I had no doubt she would—unseat the Hera councilman and elevate her position as high as Maximos's.

But that's up to me now, I thought, pushing Hondros back down with my boot. *I will claim one of the highest seats in the land, and with my love by my side, we will remake Olympia in my vision.*

I peered at Hondros through my lashes. *No one will get in my way. Least of all you.*

"Hit me."

His eyes rounded. "My love and light?"

"You heard me. Hit me," I ordered. "Hard. It'll make me so happy if you do."

Shooting up, Hondros slapped me soundly across the face. My head snapped around—ears ringing, pain singeing down the side of my cheek.

He beamed at me in hope. *Did I make you happy?*

"Perfect. Hit me again."

Hondros backhanded me, slicing my lip on my teeth. Blood coated my tongue.

"You know what you get for that?" I rasped, blowing him a blood-stained kiss. "Take off your pants."

The man fell over trying to tear his pants off one-handed. I hiked up my skirts as he righted himself. My underwear slid down my knees to hang off my ankle. He half wept as I fell open for him.

"Sirena, I'm sorry for everything. Forgive me. You can turn in blank scrolls if you desire. Whatever you wish, my heart, it'll be yours."

I fisted his tunic, drawing him closer. "Yes." I hissed as he pushed past my folds—the sudden prick of pain tugging a wince. "It will be."

He started pumping, the elation on his face telling wonders of the mediocre sex this man enjoyed during the forty years of his dull life. He should thank me after this. To touch the future queen of Olympia was the highest honor.

I struck—slicing eagle claws across his face. Crying out, he almost fell out of me.

"My love?" he cried, cupping his dripping wound.

"No, don't stop." I bent him over me and whapped his ass with my foot to get him pumping again. "Wrestle with me. I like it rough."

That stupid lovesick grin returned. "Yes, my love."

Hondros slammed me on the desk, straining to pin me down as I bucked and rained smacks on him. "Oh no, please stop," I bleated.

Through our flailing limbs, I winked and licked my bloody lips for him. "Don't do this, Captain Hondros. Don't—"

"What on earth is going on in here?!"

Healer Helena burst inside, slamming the door into the wall hard enough to splinter wood. Hondros whipped around—

—and the spell broke.

"What— No, I—" His skin flushed a sickly pale as he looked at me, and I erupted into tears.

"Help me," I sobbed. "P-please. Get him o-off me."

"Get away from her, Timothy! How could you!"

"No! I didn't—!" He backed away so fast he crashed over the desk—his pale, hairy legs flying over his head.

Tessa darted inside. Coming up behind Helena, she reached toward her head and whispered, "Forget."

Helena's eyes rolled up in her head. She collapsed in a heap on the floor while Tessa ducked back out.

"Helena?!" Hondros was kicking, scrambling, twisting to get his pants up. "What did you do? Dear gods, what have you done!"

Smirking, I hopped lightly onto the floor and neatly fixed my skirts. "What did I do? What did *you* do, Hondros? I warned you of the consequences of crossing me time and time again. Your mistake was thinking my power ended with my mother." My eyes hardened. "I can eliminate threats all on my own."

"Oh, gods. Oh, gods." Hondros peeked the damp on his cock and heaved. I grimaced as vomit splashed on the limestone.

"Rude," I breezed. "You're gonna make a girl feel bad."

"What did you do to me?" He finally got his pants up. Touching his face, he gazed at the blood on him and me. A deep, piteous groan poured from his soul, doubling him over. "Why?"

"I already told you why, but the how isn't important. All that matters is Healer Helena just saw you beat and shove your cock in a pleading novice." He groaned louder. "I've had the memory taken away from her, but I can make her remember whenever I want. And when I do, you'll be fired, stripped of rank, clamped in irons, and forced in front of a tribunal headed by my mother." I winked. "Ask me if she'll go easy on you..."

"You... You... Argh!" Hondros ran at me.

Basilisk wings sprouted from my back and shot out, pointing like lances at his body. He froze, chin balancing on the edge of my wing. "These feathers are razor sharp. A flying, molting basilisk can kill dozens of innocents walking below. Imagine what they'll make of you."

"What do you want from me?" he gritted. Beads of sweat dripped off his nose.

"Too many things to name off the top of my head, but we'll start with the first. You're to forget whatever you think you know about the assignments I've turned in. From now on, you'll accept every scroll I put in your hands with a smile, and give them the grade that reflects the fact I have your balls in a vise."

"I can't do that. I won't!"

My wing poked him, piercing his skin easily. Pinpricks of blood stained a line down his tunic. "You will, or I pop that memory back in her head and your life as you know it is over."

"I'll tell Helena what you've done. She'll know it's all a lie."

I scoffed. "You're going to bleat that you're innocent of a crime she doesn't even remember, and swear up and down that anyone who says otherwise is lying? Ha! You'll raise her suspicions so high; she'll call the guards just to be safe."

"I'll—"

"Stop trying to think of a way out, because there isn't one. You'll do what I say from now on. End of tale. Is that understood?"

Hatred burned in his bloodshot eyes. He didn't say a word, but it was written all over his face.

He was beaten.

Aella

An hour later, my muscles screamed for mercy. I staggered the last lap around the castle—falling and forcing myself up every five feet. Stumbling onto the green, I fell to my hands and knees before Vasili, sucking in air but not breathing.

"You're done," he said. "Get off my field."

He left me in the dirt, cursing his name. My arms buckled and dropped me flat on the grass. I didn't bother to move.

A shadow fell over me. "You've got to breathe through your nose when you run."

My withering glare was less effective from the dirt.

"What's a rantallion, by the way?"

"It's a man whose wrinkled, ugly balls are longer and thicker than his cock will ever be. Certainly explains your anger issues."

"Now you know that's not true. You listened with your ear pressed to the wall enough times to hear my bedmates' favorable description of my cock."

"All I heard were those fake, exaggerated moans," I huffed out. Gods, how could there be no air outside?

"Stop angling for a peek, Galanis. No matter what you say, I won't drop my pants to prove you wrong."

I choked, body lighting on fire. "There's a special place in hades for you, Damien."

He crouched beside me, admiring his handiwork. "Not too worried about that. No gods on Mount Olympus, no Hades in hell. The inmates are running the prison down there. You can bet like everywhere else—the strong rule."

"Do me a favor? Jump off a cliff and find out for me. No rush on reporting back."

Alexander cracked a lopsided grin. "Your sharp tongue is less stinging when you're a sweaty heap on the ground."

"And you're even less of a man now that you've proven your word is shit."

He cocked a brow. "I've kept my word."

"You said you were done tormenting me!"

"I am," he said lightly, shoulders lifting. "I will not lay hand or power on you or your friends. But I never said anything about letting others do it for me." He tsked. "You've pissed off a lot of people. All I've got to do is set the right trigger, and step back."

I forced myself up. "Why can't there be a real truce between us, Damien? Nothing you're doing will bring Galen back." His eyes flashed. "It won't bring you peace."

"Peace is a lie. It's another word for compromise, and in those, someone always gets less than they want. I don't settle for peace." Damien curled his finger under my chin. "When vengeance is so much more satisfying."

Anger flared hot and fast. "I won't do this with you anymore! I'm sorry, Alex. I'm sorry, I'm sorry, I'm *sorry*. If I could take back what happened that night, I would. You think I wasn't punished harshly enough, but I can promise you there's nothing anyone can do or say that'll make me hate myself more than I do!" The scream ripped out of me. "I didn't want this life. I didn't ask for *any of it*. I've been doing the best I can with the shit-covered, tangled thread the Fates wove for me, and still I know it's not enough."

My chest heaved—stunned lungs screaming out for air it wouldn't receive, and rest I'd never have. "If I had been strong enough to do what I must..." The knife pressed against my heart, as clear as if it wasn't just a memory. "No one would've died because of me," I rasped. "I know I've been a coward. Take comfort in knowing I'll punish myself for that long after you've stopped—"

"Blah, blah, blah." Damien rolled his eyes skyward. "I'll take your acid tongue over this pathetic whining any day. I swear, whenever you're called on your bullshit, you roll out the tears and vague sob stories. Play this tune for someone who doesn't see through you."

Open and vulnerable, my heart shrunk back into my chest to wither and die. "You're such a..." I blew out a breath—suddenly more tired than an hour run could make me. "You're not even a jackass, Damien. What you are is full of the same crap as me. You don't hate me for trying to escape that night. I did exactly what I'd sworn, shouted, and promised to do while you hauled me across Olympia. The person you hate is yourself."

His expression changed, the smirk vanishing as quickly as the light behind his eyes.

"Admit it. We both know that if you listened to Jason, or Castor, or fuck, even *me* when we said not to bring me to the academy, none of this would've happened. You don't blame me for what happened to Galen. You blame yourself."

He shot forward.

I held still, my heart pounding out of control at his nearness. When would he stop having this effect on me? When would I stop drowning every time I looked in his eyes—dragged down by all the lies and wrongs that kept us on opposite sides?

"That may be," Damien growled. "But I'm not a masochist. I'm a sadist. So I'll be taking my guilt out on you."

I waited until he was well and truly gone before trudging inside. There was still time to bathe and grab dinner from the mess hall. I leaned toward taking it back to my room, stretching out on my couch, and relaxing while surrounded by the only people in the academy who didn't hate me.

Alexander was right about his not needing to lift a finger. He removed his ban on the mess hall, and here I was avoiding it, and the people whispering murderer and traitor behind my back and to my face. Everyone loathed me. I had no doubt they'd continue on in the imperial heirs' place.

I hopped in a quick bath, washed the sweat and grime from my skin, dressed in an empty dorm, then booked it to the mess hall. Rounding the corner, I chanced upon Sebastian and Lysandros talking outside the double doors. Lysandros handed him an apple.

"Hey!" Tearing down the hall, I shot between them and smacked the thing from his fingers.

Howling, Lysandros took off running into the mess hall.

"That was rude," Sebastian said mildly.

"Rude?" I spun on him, hands planted on my hips. "I just saved your ass. You're welcome."

He grinned. "I didn't say thank you."

"Haha. Very cute. I know it amuses you to skip lessons, but you shouldn't ignore destroyed stadiums and novices carted into the infirmary by the dozens. Didn't you hear what his apples did?"

"Yes. That's why I was curious."

I pulled a face. "I'm sorry. Did you say curious?"

"His apples bring out the worst side of you and heighten it to a hundred. Although, it's said someone with a balanced mind—who knows who they are, good and bad, and accept themselves fully—can eat the apples and they'll have no effect on them." He flicked to the shiny, golden treat. "Can't blame a guy for wanting to know if he's balanced, or if he's got some deep, dark side of himself he's still afraid of looking at. Can't blame anyone for that actually. I bet that's what makes them so tempting. Deep down, we all wonder who we really are."

I shivered—not because of what he said, but because I finally understood why the goddess wanted me to eat that apple. Deep down, I was a coward. Heighten that fear a hundredfold, and the destruction the monster inside me would wreck on this castle would go down in our history as our greatest tragedy.

"Is it worth finding out if you're balanced?" I asked. "You're so determined to hide your true power. The apple could give you away."

"Once again"—Sebastian bent and pocketed the apple—"what true power?"

I watched him disappear down the hall. Whatever Sebastian Barba hoped to discover about himself, he wasn't doing it with an audience.

Explains why Drakos munched on that apple without consequences, I mused as I passed into the mess hall. *He certainly has an air of confidence I've never seen on anyone else. Does that come from knowing no one can stand against him?*

An army erupts at his feet, ready and willing to do what he commands without hesitation or fear of death. If he marched on the palace right now, who could stop him?

Is that why everyone is both afraid of and in awe of children of Hades? Maybe, but to take it so far as to chain them in servitude to the council?

I'd bet children of Hades weren't that rare. They just learned a long time ago... to keep their mouths shut.

"Aella? Aella, over here." Ionna waved from a table in the back.

I was wondering where my friends got to. Nitsa, Ionna, Tycho, Theron, and Daciana sat around their pushed-together tables, hanging out and waiting for me. Lysandros was busy sneaking around the hall, coming up behind people, and scaring the crap out of them. He made Kosma spill a mug of wine down her white tunic, so I didn't bother the man.

I crossed to meet them.

"Heard you got a reprieve, sweet one."

Turning my head, I fell on Calix and his tablemates. It wasn't Ajax, Alexander, or Sirena. Hanging off, under, and around his arms were Rue and three other Titan girls. The four of them served him in various ways. One girl finger-combed his waves. The other fed him his dinner. One rubbed his shoulders. And Rue rubbed his crotch.

Plain in the middle of the mess hall, she stroked his erection through his pants, then slipped under his belt.

"Fuck's sake, Calix." I veered left, coming up on him fast. "Do you not have a shred of shame? What the hell is wrong with you?"

He blinked lazily as he tipped his chin for a grape. "Me? What have I done?"

"Enchanting these women to *service* you for all to see? What kind of muck-sucking pig does that!"

Rue scoffed. "Excuse me? We're not enchanted, Sisyphean. We're not all so weak-minded that a little puff of smoke can tell us what to do." Her hand jerked furiously between his legs.

"Yeah," said Grape Girl. She leaned over and planted a searing kiss on Calix's lips. "So take your prude ass somewhere else. We're busy."

If Calix was a muck-sucking pig, he was one with the biggest self-satisfied smirk on his face. Better I didn't forget that with a face like his, he only had to use his powers for fun. Plenty would fall down at his feet just to get him to look their way.

"Gladly," I said. "Oh, and you can take this." I tossed my plate on their table, ignoring Rue's shrieking when fish sauce splashed her sleeve. "I've lost my appetite."

"What did you do to call Ajax off?"

That made me pause. "I didn't do anything. He decided to let go of vengeance."

"Did you threaten him?"

"What?" I cried. "Of course I didn't."

"You must've done something," he replied in that slow, lazy way of his. Rue was giving it all she had and it wasn't putting a speck of pleasure on his face. I wondered if he was even enjoying their attention, or if he simply liked proving to everyone he could do what he wanted, whenever he wanted. Like a god.

"Ajax never learned to forgive when it comes to his brother. Xander says you're hiding a lethal power. You threatened him with it after getting his brother killed." He shook his head. "Doesn't get much lower than that, sweet one."

My eyes bugged, heat welling up the back of my neck. "I'm low? I haven't said a word to Ajax since he tried to *drown* me. Ask him yourself."

"He wouldn't admit the truth and neither would you. I've known the guy too long to believe you're not behind this." He clicked his tongue. "Obviously, I can't let you strut around, gloating in Ajax's face."

I stomped over and yanked Rue's hand out of his pants.

"Hey!"

Calix let out a low hiss—the single sign that it hurt.

"What do you want from me?" My voice shook. "Is it to kill me? Go ahead." I threw out my arms. "Do it, Calix. Your friends here can all give witness that I gave my permission.

"I never wanted to come to the academy, and I accepted my punishment for running away. If execution is what it had to be then... then maybe it's what it has to be now."

The boredom leached from his face as a frown tried and failed to mar his perfection.

"Kill me and end this, Calix. Give Ajax peace. Free Alexander from his guilt. End the threat I am to everyone here."

As the words left my lips, I knew they were right. All I had were escape plans I couldn't execute, blood on my hands, and no way to rid the goddess's parasite from my soul even if I got beyond these walls. My only hope had always been to leave Olympia behind forever and make it impossible for the goddess to carry out her terrifying wishes. It was the coward in me that ever believed that home made of windows was still out there waiting for me.

"Go ahead," I said. "If you use your power, I won't be scared." *She won't be able to stop me.*

A snarl echoed from the back of my mind. *"Don't you dare. Remove yourself from him immediately. I command it."*

Stony faced, Calix untangled himself from his tablemates, eating the distance between us. "You're an interesting one, Aella Galanis. I'm finally beginning to understand what's tripping Xander up about you." He blew out a breath, rocking back. "But you have me all wrong. I'm a son of love, darling. I only kill as a last resort. Although, when I think of Galen's last moments, I'm definitely tempted. Still, I only made you one promise... to ruin you."

Warning bells chimed. I shot away from him too late. A glittery pink cloud enveloped me.

"Seeing as I'm such a muck-sucking pig..." Calix relaxed into the welcoming arms of his harem, kicking back as he spread his legs. "You already knew this was coming. If you want back into the mess hall, it'll require *servicing* me."

I grinned sloppily. "Yes, Calix. Whatever you want."

"That's my favorite phrase, sweet one. I'll take a dance." Calix patted his lap. "Lose the clothes while you're at it."

The fog settled on my mind, pushing away all stupid, pointless thoughts and problems, and leaving room for complete clarity: there was nothing on this planet that mattered more than Calix and making him happy.

I'd die for him. I'd kill for him. I'd turn back time and erase all the pain I caused him if only he'd asked. Calix was my life.

Gripping my tunic hem, I ripped it over my head.

I'd do anything for him.

Wining my hips, I danced to an old tune from my child-hood—fun, fast, and bawdy. One an eight-year-old wasn't sup-posed to listen to, but came singing through the square on Eros Night, teasing a young girl pretending to sleep.

Now I would dance for Calix like those young lovers danced in the square. How perfect our lives would be now that we'd found each other. That home of windows would be mine, and I'd share it with Calix.

I stalked toward him. He hummed as I gripped his knees and rolled my waist between his legs.

"I said to lose the clothes."

My breast band was off in a blink. I dropped it on his lap—leaning over to capture his lips.

Our mouths clashed in an explosion of sparks. Tongues tan-gling, noses bumping, moans echoing. Kissing Calix was like walk-ing across a bed of coals—dangerous, burning, *thrilling*.

"Calix?" A grating voice broke into our world. "Cal, enough. What about us?"

We broke apart, but I grasped his jaw, keeping him firmly on me.

"Whoa ho! Look, guys. The traitor's putting on a show."

"Shit. Nice tits."

"Where is *everyone*? They've got to see this."

Chairs scraped back, people stampeded, whoops and cheers went up around the room, but there was only me and him.

My grip was firm drawing him forward, up, and away from those handsy bitches who would find me standing over their beds that night. No one touched what's mine.

But he touched me.

I laid Cal's palms under my breasts, and rolled his fingers over my nipples. There wasn't pleasure on his face when that filthy toova Rue strangled his cock, but there was now.

Smirking, I dropped to my waistband—unbuttoning and loosening my pants. I hooked through two layers, readying to remove the last barriers between us.

"Yeah!"

"Take it off, mundane!"

My underwear slid off my ass.

A black-and-white blur streaked across my vision. In the space of a breath, Calix's hands disappeared from my body—vanishing as suddenly as he did. I blinked at the figure in his place.

A cow.

"Uh, ow…" Laughter sounded to my left. "Damn, that was a good hit."

"Oh, gods," I breathed. I looked down at my bare body. "Oh gods!"

The enchantment was well and truly broken, and I was standing bare-assed in the middle of the mess hall with a man's touch lingering on my breasts.

"Aella!" Daciana shoved through the crowd, sending two guys twice her size flying. Tearing off her overcoat, she threw it around me, holding me tight to her as we took off running. A wall of Sisypheans and Titans blocked our way.

"Not so fast," Kosma taunted. "It's not fair to end a show halfway."

"Get out of the way," Tycho shouted. He and Theron got out in front of us as Ionna piled more clothes on me.

"Who's going to make us?" someone shouted back. "She goes when she finishes her dance."

I shrunk in their clothes, tears hot and stinging on my lids.

Theron shoved a guy who tried making a grab for me. "If you think I don't got the hatred to burn us all the fuck up again, then you better pray to the gods for another miracle. *Move!*" The command boomed from his chest—belied with the power of Ares.

The crowd lurched back, flashes of panic shattered their vileness. They were seconds too late to comply. Nitsa came charging through.

Scattering demigods like dice, she cleared us a path. We beat it out of there, racing from the mess hall and not stopping until we slammed, bolted, and shoved a couch in front of our dorm door.

Nitsa, Ionna, and Daciana carried me into my alcove, holding tight to me as I cried.

I BURST THROUGH THE doors, red-rimmed vision blurred, but not enough to stop me finding the staircase I was looking for. Narrowing, I charged up flight after flight, carrying me away from the murmurs on the occupied library floor to the quiet of the stacks.

Calix wasn't in the dorm I shoved into twenty minutes before. Despite my friends warning and begging me to steer clear of him, after the tears... came the rage.

I couldn't say why I knew to check for him there, but if I stumbled on him in this hidden spot for milk and nectar once, why wouldn't he be there again?

The thought drifted through my mind as I peered around the shelves, falling on him just as he snorted a line of powder off the table.

"Oh, sweet one? What are you—?"

I slapped him with every ounce of strength in my body. Calix's head snapped around, taking his body with it. He toppled onto the floor. "Whoa," he breathed—slow and dreamy. "You're mad."

I jumped on him. "You— I—" Everything I wanted to rage and shout at him fled my mind. I just started hitting and hitting, raining blows that wouldn't stop falling.

Calix made a half-hearted attempt to shield his face. I yanked his arms away and he didn't try again.

My knuckles cut on his teeth, bloodying him and me. I ripped out strands of his hair. Punched his eye. Grabbed his shoulders, lifted, and slammed his head on the carpet. Through soul-wrenching sobs and gasping heaves, I beat Calix as savagely as I was able.

Calix gazed at me through eyes beginning to swell. "Feel better?"

"Shut up!" I smacked his chest, my cry breaking on a sob.

"It's all right... sweet one." Blood dribbled down his chin. "I hurt people to feel better too."

"Don't you dare compare what you did to me." Straddling him, I bent over, wrapping around his neck. "You humiliated me. *Violated* me. I didn't deserve it. You do," I hissed, squeezing.

"Don't... you?" Glaze heavily coated his amber eyes. Whatever world nectar sent him to, hadn't let him go. "Anyone who begs their enemy for death is looking for punishment. Deep down, you believe you deserve it."

I trembled, willing and shouting at myself to squeeze harder—silence his horrible words for good.

"Why, sweet one? Why don't you think you're worth anything? Why—"

"Shut up," I rasped, fingers constricting. "Shut. Up."

"—do you want... to take the... pain away? Why are you... giving up?"

I shook him. "Stop it. I said stop!"

"Why are you... like me?"

Wetness dripped off my chin and painted a line down Calix. I hated him. I wanted him dead. Wanted the memory of his touch on my skin burned away. Wanted all the firsts he'd stolen *back*! Never did I get to choose.

I couldn't choose my life, or my fate, or my actions. I couldn't choose a mother who would love and protect me, instead of trading me in for eight years of hell and then servitude to a psychotic deity. I couldn't choose to save the lives she forced me to end, or bring back the ones I lost trying to free myself from her.

My life was not my own... so why shouldn't I let the imperial heirs end it?

"It's okay, sweet one."

I hadn't noticed that I released him. That I was slumped and crying as I held my face in my hands. Calix gently pulled them away.

"Whatever it is, you don't have to say. We don't talk up here," he murmured. "And we don't hurt. Say the word. I'll take it all away."

I couldn't be sure what he meant. I couldn't be sure of anything anymore as I looked him in the eye... and nodded.

I didn't fight or lean away as the pink cloud floated toward me. Breathing deep, the fog blanketed my pain and worries. Mother, Kristopher, Dimitri, Galen, the goddess—it was as if they'd never been.

Calix wrapped me in his arms. I clung to him happily, soaking in his love and attention. How could I ever be angry with him? How could I ever be angry again? Everything was perfect now.

I had Calix.

"Sleep, sweet one." He tucked me under his chin, holding me close. "The dreams don't follow us where we're going."

Lacing my fingers through his, I let him take me where he will.

CLINK.

My eyes fluttered open, peeling apart as two boots walked away from me.

Calix disappeared around the corner, leaving me on the pile of cushions and overcoats that was our bed.

That feeling of lightness, love, and freedom was gone. All that remained in me was the rage, grief, and a new layer of shame for the night before.

Calix didn't make me do anything. The opposite, it was him who held me, stroked my hair, and whispered sweet, nonsensical things in his nectar-induced haze.

What sense did it make that I came here to hurt him, and wound up spending the night in his arms? Was he right? Had I developed such a self-destructive, worthless sense of self that I handed my enemy another humiliation? Calix was off to Alexander right then, laughing about how after he made me strip in front of the entire academy, I just went running back to him for more.

It was a long walk back to the dorm. My friends were all up and getting ready for classes. A bowl of porridge sweetened with honey waited for me in the common area.

"Aella, there you are." Nitsa ran and hugged me. "We were so worried when you didn't come back. We went out looking for you, but nothing."

"I'm fine." Nitsa drew back, but I squeezed her tighter. "Vasili's an idiot for putting you in the Sisyphean class, Nitsa. You're a fucking hero and I'll correct anyone who says otherwise."

She pressed her cheek to mine. "I just wish I was faster."

"If you're not up for lessons today, I'll skip with you," Daciana said, moving in to hug me from behind. "The last thing you need is Hondros's badgering or Vasili's bullying."

I shook my head. "Everyone expects me to hide my head in shame like I was the one who did wrong. I won't give them the satisfaction."

"Fuck everyone else and their satisfaction. It's what you need right now, Aella."

A crack appeared in my armor. "I... could use a day," I croaked.

"Then we can too." Ionna tossed her pack back in her alcove and got comfortable on the couch. My friends all did the same.

"Won't we get in trouble for this?" I asked.

"Heaps of it." Tycho held my hand bringing me to the couch, wrapping me in a blanket, and passing over my breakfast. "But we'll deal with that tomorrow."

"Thanks, guys." My voice was so small, I wasn't sure they heard me. From their supportive smiles, they did.

"What are we going to do today?" Daciana spoke up, nuzzling in beside me. "I've been dying for a full tour of the castle."

"Or we could get away from everybody and explore the grounds," Nitsa offered. "I heard there are hidden lakes, streams, and waterfalls all tended by naiads, so you know they're beautiful."

"My suggestion was going to be we all crawl back into bed and wake up after dawn for once," Ionna said. "But it looks like you don't need it, Aella. You look good this morning. Like you finally got some rest."

I froze, spoon halfway to my mouth. It wasn't until she said that I realized for the first time in weeks, the night before I didn't dream.

Hours later, the seven of us found ourselves laughing and splashing each other in the waterfall-fed lake about half a mile into the forest. It was easier to find than we expected. Theron asked a dryad and she pointed him in the right direction. As for me, she threw a stick at the back of my head as we tromped off.

Ionna rolled her eyes at the guys. "They're enjoying themselves."

I giggled—a miraculous sound after the night before. Lysandros, Theron, and Tycho were all sunning themselves on the pebble shore while their naiad admirers all nuzzled, cooed, and draped themselves over them.

Our welcome was nothing like that. Instead of praise and kisses, the naiads either ignored us girls or popped out of the lake and spat water in our faces while we swam. They raced off giggling to our sputters.

Only the guys knew what beauties they were in their other form. To us, they looked like a bunch of fish-like, gargoyle-looking creatures.

Tycho flushed deep red when one grasped his chin and kissed him. It was not as sensual a sight from our point of view. We smothered laughs.

"Look what we did," Nitsa mourned. "They're never going to want to leave this place."

"They can have their fun." Daciana floated on her back, drifting lazily in the water. "I'm just glad we're finally having some. Even with all the classes we've missed, we haven't had a real break since we walked through those gates. Is this our life for the next four years?"

"Oh no," Ionna replied. "It'll get much worse."

"She's not even kidding," Nitsa said. "We still have the culling, the nemean trials, the quests."

I poked my head out of the water. "Quests?"

"Oh, yeah. When we're proficients. That's when they start sending groups of us out of the academy to complete different tasks—Labours of Heracles style. Bring back the head of a bronze bull. Steal a treasure guarded by a cerberus. Stuff like that. It's battle strategy class in action."

"Wait," I said. "They send us out? We're allowed to leave the academy?"

She nodded. "They've got ways to make sure we return though. Even if we're... coming back a corpse."

"Wow. If they send proficients to face bronze bulls, what do they make the experts do?"

Nitsa grimaced. "My brothers didn't talk much about their expert year. Eventually, I stopped asking."

That sobering response silenced us all for a beat.

"Let's talk about something else," Daciana said, floating back our way. "Like how you'll all be my lookouts when I sneak into the Titan wing, and bite Calix's head off in his sleep."

My smile didn't reach my eyes. "That sounds good to me, but I have to deal with Calix on my own."

"We keep telling you that you don't." Ionna hugged me from the side. "You're not alone in this, Aella."

"I know that. I really do. But someone—a very blunt, unpleasant man—pointed out that I started running a long time ago and never stopped. I've let a lot of people get away with hurting me and controlling my life. It's easy to say I didn't have a choice because I don't have powers, but there's a whole dominion of people without powers. It'd be a wasteland if they all just bent over and took it. So why do I?"

"Why, sweet one? Why don't you think you're worth anything?"

I swallowed hard. "I just don't want to run or hide behind anyone this time."

"We get it," Nitsa said softly.

Ionna and Daciana nodded. "We do."

Nitsa peered over her shoulder. "No one should be in the mess hall at this time. Let's send the guys to get food and we'll have a picnic. They could use a break from the naiads anyway. I swear they're all about to stain their pants."

"What?" Theron said when we burst out laughing. "What's funny?"

Eventually our day by the waterfall had to end. We didn't think to change into bathing clothes before we headed out, so that left us to tug pants and tunics onto our sopping wet bodies, and trudge back to the dorm where our towels and warm blankets awaited us.

"We've got to make this a regular thing," Tycho said.

Daciana tossed him a teasing wink. "Oh, I bet."

"That's not what I meant," he cried, face lighting up. "I was talking about all of us blowing off the bullshit and just hanging out. It's been nonstop since the first day. I mean, think about it. After we graduate, we'll be assigned to different moras, and Daciana's going back home. If we don't do stuff like this now, we won't get another chance."

We exchanged looks—the truth of his words sinking in. Life would soon split us all apart, and going by the frequent reminders of the academy death toll, we may not even have those four years.

So much was stolen from me. The goddess plans to steal more, from all of us. This may be as close as I ever get to the future I dreamed of. Tycho is right. I can't let the goddess or the imperial heirs drown every day in misery.

I thought the words, but deep down, didn't believe. Alexander and Sirena trained a few feet from me every day. Drakos forced his own version of hard labor on me every weekend. Calix was everywhere I looked. And at night, the nightmares were always waiting.

What happiness was there for me to find outside of these stolen moments? They couldn't happen every day or all the time. I'd just have to be thankful I got one night and one day of peace. Hera knows I prayed eight long years for it.

Ionna bumped my shoulder. "You've gone quiet."

"Just lost in thought. I'm okay." I plastered a smile on my face. "Let's keep the good day going. Theron, I saw you're hiding dice and cards in your room. I've always wanted to learn how to play."

Nitsa, Ionna, and Tycho sounded off at once.

"No, you don't."

"Whoa."

"Think about what you're saying."

"What?" I asked. The grand staircase loomed in front of us. "What'd I say?"

"Theron is a beast at dice," Tycho said. "Fifteen years old, I watched him take half a dozen palace guards for everything they're worth. This isn't a game to him. It's war."

"Stop scaring our lovely friend." Theron's grin was wolfish. "I'll go easy on her."

"Run," Ionna deadpanned. "Run and never stop running, Aella."

I cracked up. "I still want to learn, but maybe we'll have Theron sit in the corner for the first few rounds. Until *I* learn how to take *him* for everything he's worth."

"I like her." Theron tossed an arm around me. "She's a dreamer."

We clomped up the steps, laughing and joking.

"I'll teach you some card games from home," Daciana said. "But I warn you. If you think a son of Ares plays to win, then you've got no idea what you're up against with a wolf."

"Mmm, half wolf," Tycho corrected. "So we're only half intimidated."

Daciana swatted his shoulder. He ducked her and came back tickling.

Shrieking, Daciana took off running up the stairs, Tycho on her heels.

We shared knowing looks but were kind enough not to say anything. Even Lysandros shook his head at them, rolling his eyes like he was thinking, *get on with it already.*

Theron and I climbed to the top step, deep in the rules for the game.

"The dice are everything. It seems like chance but don't be fooled. It takes skill. You guess the number your opponent will roll and bet on if it will be higher, lower, or the same. The trick is, you can't bet higher or lower than the number cards in your hand."

"Okay, so if I want to bet twelve, but I only have as high as a ten. What do I—?"

My foot hit the top step, and slid. I went flying.

"Ahhh!" I slipped out of Theron's hold, tumbling the long, long way down the marble steps.

"Aella!"

"...THIS HAPPEN..."

"...get the... quick!"

"...oh, Aella..."

Voices pounded on the dark, dreamless space carrying me. What did they want? Why wouldn't they let me be?

I groaned, making a noise to send them away as words failed.

"Zeus above. Aella? Aella, are you okay?"

I cracked a lid open, letting in the stabbing prick of evening light. Four heads hovered over me. "What... happened?"

"Don't get up," Nitsa said. Salty wetness rimmed her eyes. "Holy fucking gods, Aella. We thought you were dead. You fell down like a thousand steps."

Peering past her, I glanced up... and up. It all came back.

Me screaming as I tumbled, hitting each step on the way down. Then the hard smack to my temple that extinguished the lights.

I tried to get up and cried out. Everything hurt.

"Stay still," Daciana said. "Tycho ran to get Healer Helena. She'll take care of you."

"Okay." I gave in to that request all too easily. I was more than happy not to move until the healer's pain potions arrived by the dozen. "I can't... believe it. How?"

"We were all wet and dripping." Ionna took my hand and let it go when I hissed. "You slipped on the water. I'm so sorry, Aella. We should've been more careful."

"Wasn't your fault," I rasped. "I'm lucky... to be alive. When Healer Helena comes, I'll be happy about it too."

They waited with me, keeping my spirits up until Healer Helena arrived with Madame Remis in tow—both of them fussing, pushing my friends aside, and wincing over the nastily banged-up body that was me.

My history instructor skipped the potions and rested her palm on my forehead. A cooling wave of power spread through me, knitting my sprained bones back together, snapping my dislocated fingers back into place, and shrinking the boulder-sized lump on my head.

So much for a fun end to a perfect day, but as that week bled into the next, we kept our promise to find stolen moments to enjoy ourselves.

One month to the day since we entered the academy. I couldn't believe we made it—though we couldn't say the same for everyone in our class.

"Andino died this morning," Theron said. Our pack followed behind the rest of our novice group to Madame Remis and her always interesting history lesson. "His instant darkness power was no good against Proficient Myron. Son of Hephaestus. The guy has iron skin. Can literally walk through an inferno without a scratch. Andino came for him in the dark, Myron swung too hard, and an iron fist to the head..."

He didn't need to fill in the rest. The guy basically took a hammer to his skull, and we knew the result. Alexis was dead.

"That's three novices lost in one month," Nitsa said. "And just in our lecture group. Others have lost up to five trainees."

"Maybe that's why no one will tell us what the culling is," Daciana said. "We're already in it."

That chilling remark followed us into the history hall. We made for our usual seats.

"Move." A hard hit from behind propelled me off my feet, spilling me and my books across the table. Sirena flounced by with that bird on her shoulder. Her other arm was securely around Alexander. He didn't even glance at me.

Why should he look back and observe the damage? He was just pleased that his friends, followers, and worshippers were handling it for him.

I straightened in time to turn and come face to face with Ajax. I held my tongue, not daring to voice the many apologies on my lips after the last time I dared.

But it didn't matter.

He slid off me like I wasn't there and continued on.

That distraction was all Lysandros needed to take my seat *again* and stick me next to Sebastian *again*. Sebastian grinned at my approach as if I planned it.

Tossing my head, I sat down, then flicked to Alexander—seeing what I expected to see. Him glaring at us, also as if I planned it.

"Settle in, everyone," Remis called. "Today, we're discussing the short-lived reign of King Midas."

Nitsa cleared her throat. "Before we do, Madame Remis, will you answer some of our questions about the culling? No one will tell us anything and we don't understand why."

Leftover conversations ended quickly. Everyone wanted to hear this.

Remis sighed. "I apologize for all the secrecy, and the anxiety that secrecy has caused you, but there is a reason we can't discuss the culling. Giving you any details will change the ordeal."

"You said that before, but what does that mean?"

"Let me put it this way," she said, propping her elbow on her podium. "Say I tell you your next exam will be on the rise and fall of the Olympian Golden Era. That single generation where the collection of the strongest council members in our history were enough to beat the monster population to near extinction, and we achieved something close to peace for the first time in our history.

"For weeks you study, then on the day of the test, the questions change before your very eyes. Everything about the golden era disappears, and suddenly the exam is about some obscure historical event you've never heard of." She swept over us. "That is the inevitable fate of anyone who tries to prepare specifically for the culling. It will not allow you to be forearmed, so there's no benefit in being forewarned."

"It won't allow," Tycho repeated. "You say that like the culling is... sentient."

She gave him a steady look. "Yes, I do."

A shiver climbed my spine. What kind of test was this?

"Can we at least know the day?" Sirena asked. "Next month? Next week?"

Remis shook her head. "The culling will choose its own time and place. It will choose who goes first and who is last. My goal is to prepare you to the best of your and my ability until that time comes." She clapped. "Now, onto King Midas."

She shut down the conversation, but not my curiosity. What kind of challenge administered itself? And how could we ever be prepared if Remis just admitted the culling won't allow us to be? Everything we're learning will be useless on the day.

"King Midas's reign was a fascinating time in Olympian history," Remis went on, uncaring of my wandering mind.

"The *usurper* Midas," Sirena stressed, "was a traitor and assassin. That psychotic Hades spawn is a black stain on our history. Nothing more."

Remis smiled patiently on Sirena. The daughter of Hera was making a habit of arguing with her, and getting loud when Remis shared banned information with us. None of this stopped Remis, though, who wasn't afraid to put Sirena out of the room when she was at her most belligerent.

"No one is arguing the man's morality left a lot to be desired," Remis said, "but when he unseated the council and named himself king, he repealed a fair number of laws. Including the one that didn't allow regular Olympians to come and go from our dominion as they pleased."

"Really?" Delia, a Titan, asked. "He brought down the barrier?"

"He didn't bring it down. Such an ancient and powerful spell, he couldn't. But he did command the children of Hecate working in the palace. They guarded the spell that let council members pass through and return. Midas made it so anyone with a reason or request could take a jaunt into the human dominion."

"Wow," Daciana said. "So that's why even mundanes know the legend of King Midas—the man who turned everything he touched to gold."

"That is why exactly. With the lid popped off our hidden world, mundanes learned of Midas, and that's not where it stopped. Of course, mundanes already had a concept of gods, demons, and magic from before the scatter and the treaty of the five dominions. Gods they still believed in, but the rest faded into legend and scary stories.

"When we powered demigods suddenly reappeared in their lives, it set off a wave of hysteria among those who couldn't believe we were real, let alone meant no harm. To be fair, it's possible quite a few demigods did do harm." Once again, we were a rapt audience. "True magic performed before their eyes. Fatal illnesses healed overnight. Men taking the form of animals. Women controlling people with the snap of their fingers.

"Mundanes quickly determined that we were demons sent by Hades, or poor mundanes possessed by such a demon. Naturally, the only solution was to hang, stone, or burn every suspected communer with Hades."

"Rhea and Cronus," a guy behind me said. "Savages."

"Looking back, their actions were certainly cruel and barbaric, but they were scared. Everything they thought they knew of the world was turned on its head. All of a sudden, they were seeing impossible things wherever they looked. Many thought they were going mad. Many deemed others mad when they told tales of men who wielded fire with their bare hands. Too many people to name were locked away in asylums for sharing the truth of what demigods could do.

"Yes, they were wrong to kill out of fear. Although I ask you, my young novices, were we not wrong too? We could've been passive observers in their world. Instead, we blew in, had our fun throwing our powers around, and then blew out leaving them to deal with the consequences," she said.

"Around the time mundanes started hunting for 'witches,' they stumbled on vampires by accident. This gave birth to vampire hunters that drove their covens deeper into hiding. Of course, we were blamed for reawakening them to humans with extraordinary abilities. It nearly kicked off another interdominion war.

"King Midas appeased the vampires by giving them gold. As much as they desired," she said, motioning to an invisible pile taller than her. "From then on, vampires went from living in crypts and abandoned buildings, to occupying castles and buying out entire out-of-the-way towns. One ill-conceived act led to another, and as a result, we made an enemy stronger than they ever were."

I flicked to Daciana. Did she know this particular part of history, or was she learning about it for the first time too? Knowing her hatred of vampires, she can't be thrilled to learn demigods had a hand in making them stronger.

"Why are you telling us this?" Sirena didn't ask a question politely when rude and demanding worked just as well. "Midas was stupid to break council law, but you can't expect much more from a psychopath. Everything else that happened with the mundanes and the vampires is just too bad. Their weakness and ignorance wasn't our fault."

Remis picked up her feet and walked the room as she did. The lady was never behind her podium. "I don't aim to assign fault. My goal is to teach you history and hope you learn more than facts and dates. I won't tell you what the lesson is to be learned in this instance." She turned her enigmatic smile on us. "You tell me."

We spent the rest of the class discussing the other dominions, and the rare times the demigods visited them. Maybe the council had good reason to keep us all on this side of the gorge. We seemed to kick off war and death wherever we went.

"Excellent discussion today." Remis brought class to a close. "Our last order of business, pass your scrolls up. Today we talked about what wasn't in the book about Midas's reign. Last night, you were supposed to write two scrolls on what was."

Bending over, I riffled in my pack for my scrolls. My fingers hit on nothing.

I frowned, yanking my bag open and sticking my head inside. *Where are my scrolls? I put them in my bag last night, right before Theron and I went another round over cards.*

I shoved everything around twice, then dumped the contents on the table. Nothing. My scrolls were gone.

I don't understand. How—?

Looking up, our eyes locked. Alexander winked.

"Of fucking course." Alexander had not let up in his campaign to ensure others carried out my punishment in his place. Putting as much distance between us as possible made it hard for him to mess me up in combat training, but it looked like my midnight visitor found another way.

I shoved my seat back and stomped over to him. Alexander watched me coming with a widening grin.

"Good morning, Galanis." He reclined in his seat, arms folded. "To what do I owe this visit?"

Cleon shoved his shoulder from behind. "Maybe she's going to put on another show for you, eh." He gyrated disgustingly. "Take it all off this time, Galanis."

"Fuck off." Sirena forced her hand under his arm. "You're not welcome in our presence, Sisyphean. You're not welcome anywhere."

I ignored everyone that wasn't him. Locking our gaze, I plucked his scrolls from the pile, unfurled them, and then slowly and deliberately tipped his inkwell over the pages.

"Aella," Remis shouted. "What do you think you're doing?"

Alexander's only reaction was to smirk wider.

"I'm shocked at you. You will report here after lessons. Am I understood?"

"Yes, ma'am."

I picked up my things and left, leaving Damien to enjoy his victory. I was already finishing up various punishments for the stadium and the day we skipped lessons. Didn't he enjoy watching me get myself another.

At this rate, I'll be scrubbing the atrium, doing extra assignments, cleaning the cobwebs from the rafters, and hunting the forest for litter for the next four years.

That last one was Cassia's punishment for skipping her lessons. The dryads deeply enjoyed using me for target practice. So much so, they hunted for trainee-dropped litter on their own and lobbed it at me while they giggled in the trees. It actually made it a lot easier to find since Cassia had us going out there with nothing but an orb light and the long-since-set sun.

All of that was worth it to have one great day with my friends, just sharing a picnic on the shore while the sun dried the cool beads of lake on our skin. It was also worth it to cost Alexander another night of redoing assignments.

The rest of the day passed quickly, ending with my least-favorite lesson. Walking out onto the field, Vasili's glittering, fixed gaze reminded me he disliked me just as much.

"You'll notice the practice dummies were removed from the field," he began. "Today, you'll pair up and spar. You won't fight demigods in battle, but you will fight moving targets. As such, the natural progression is that you move on from stationary dummies.

"You will not, I repeat *not* use your powers at this time. You may be novices, but you're all at different stages of combat readiness. Only when you master one stage, will you move on to the next. When I see that you can defend against an opponent without your power, then you will graduate to combat with your powers.

"But not before," he stated as if trainees forced him to repeat himself often. "Do not presume to test me on this. Whipping out your power on an opponent who is suspecting you to fight honorably, is considered cheating." Vasili looked his nose down at us. "I hold cheaters in the highest contempt."

He didn't have to fill in the blanks on what he'd do to cheaters. The welcome book bolded and underlined the words *zero tolerance* and *expulsion*.

"Sir," Cleon spoke up. "Why do we need to master combat without our powers? When we're fighting in the army, we're always going to use our powers."

"That is a valid question and I will answer it to rid you of such inaccuracies before they make it onto the battlefield. There will be times that your god-given gifts may as well be holes in a spoon. Useless to you.

"If you must see to aim your power, how will you defeat a medusa? If your powers only work on living creatures, what will you do in face of undead demons? Being demigods does not make us all-powerful. Not even the Olympian gods themselves were all-powerful. They feared gods older and stronger than them.

"Training, boy. No matter the situation, that's the one thing you'll never be without."

"Yes, sir," Cleon muttered.

"Pair up and find a platform. Now."

I peeked Alexander bearing down on me out of the corner of my eye. Sirena was fast on his heels. *Great. He's looking to get me some extra laps around the castle before I do ten scrolls on an assignment he stole out of my pack.*

Maybe it was a good thing his sabotage made me late to bed every night. Since that mistake with Calix, the nightmares returned with a vengeance.

I spun around, making for Daciana. A hook through my arm nearly popped me off my feet.

"Commander, Aella and I are partners."

"Fine. Get your staffs and a platform."

Rue dragged me off to the weapons hold. I wrenched free of her. "What are you doing? We're not partners."

"If you pass me over, I'll tell Vasili it's because you're afraid to fight me. He hates a coward even more than a cheater."

I ground to a halt, flicking between her, Vasili, and my friends who were starting to take notice. If Rue spouted that lie in his ear, he'd force us to pair up, and then make me run laps carrying a fifty-pound shield over my head. He added that torture the other day when Alexander dropped a mangled shield at my feet. Vasili didn't question how I could even pull that off.

"What's your game? Skip the bullshit and tell me now."

Beaming, she picked up two staffs and tossed one at me. "No game, Sisyphean. I just want to see what you can do."

I gestured to my friends, mouthing that I'd be okay, and followed her onto a sparring platform. With the dummies cleared out, there was plenty of room for padded stages, each rising four feet off the ground. We climbed up and squared off.

I stepped to the right and she moved left, mirroring me. My grip tightened on the staff, finding the right position that Vasili drilled into me.

Rue was better than good with a staff. I watched her beat the stuffing out of her dummies enough times to figure she learned from the same imperial instructors that made these early lessons laughably easy for Alexander, Ajax, and Sirena. No matter what she said, she wasn't standing across from me for the hell of it.

Be ready.

"You're really good at all this." I moved again and so did she. "How long have you been training with a staff?"

"I mastered the staff when I was eleven. When did you perfect being a two-copper slut?"

"Excuse—"

She flashed. Darting forward, her staff cut through the air, striking my left thigh hard.

My leg buckled and I dropped to my knees, crying out.

"There you go again," Rue crowed. "You're either on your knees or on your back."

"What is wrong with you?" I shoved up and away from her, edging as far back as the platform let me. "You can't seriously be mad that Calix enchanted and took advantage of me? What sick twists and turns did your mind take to put the blame on me?"

"Save it," she snapped. "You pretend you hate the imperial heirs, but whenever anyone turns around, you're all over them. You just can't leave Calix and Xander—"

She struck—swinging a downward strike on my skull. I barely got my staff up in time to block.

"—alone."

Pain sung in my palms. I did my best to beat back a grimace. "You know everything you're saying is garbage. You're just trying to distract me to make it easier for you to win and impress Sirena."

"Fuck Sirena!"

I blew back, eyes popping. Real vitriol laced the shout.

"She uses Calix when it's convenient, ignores him when it's not." Rue readied her stance. I sensed another strike coming fast. "As for Xander..." She snorted. "He needs someone who challenges him, not another fawning sycophant. You think this dance you're doing will end with his falling for you, but it'll never happen. Xander knows trash when he—"

Rue jabbed. I threw myself out of the way, narrowly missing her vicious strike to the gut.

"—sees it!" She came after me, snapping her staff across my back.

I screamed.

"Calix hasn't touched me since that night you stripped in the mess hall. Xander looks at no one but you."

"Make up your mind," I gritted. "Which one of them do you want? Or are you really mad that neither one of them want you?"

She hit me again, bouncing my skull off the pad. "Back off. Your innocent act doesn't fool me. I wouldn't put it past you if you got Galen killed on purpose—just so the imperial heirs had no choice but to acknowledge your existence."

"You're insane!"

Rue wielded the staff high overhead, fury peeling her lips from her teeth. I would not get up from the next hit.

"Argh!"

Grabbing my staff, I gripped it like a club and swung at her ankles. Rue flew off her feet. Scrambling up, I towered over her, stunned and wheezing, and pressed my staff to her throat.

"Now who is on their back?"

"Adequate, novice."

I snapped up, surprised to see Vasili standing there. How long had he watched Rue treat me like her whipping toy?

"Improper form on the ankle strike, but it served the purpose. You, girl," he said to Rue. "I expected better. You got emotional and left yourself wide open. Sit on the stands. You're out until you re-member why you're here."

"But, sir!" she croaked.

I rode high on her humiliation until Vasili got me a new part-ner. Lysandros did that strange head-rolling, lurching walk up the steps. I took my stance, steeling myself. He would not go down easy.

Two hours later, I shuffled out of the history hall—wincing as I stretched and popped my sore muscles.

Lysandros did not know the meaning of the words: form, struc-ture, or proper method. He swung wild and unpredictably, and at one point he chased me around, then off the platform. Vasili grant-ed him the win for that reason, and I ended up spending the rest of the lesson sitting too close to Rue and her hissed insults about my dick breath and the cum stains on my skirt.

After that, I was forced to sit some more while I rewrote my assignment and then another four scrolls repeating the proper eti-quette in Remis's lecture hall.

My body needed a hot bath. I fully intended to stay in the wa-ter until I pruned beyond recognition.

I passed through the novice hall, getting deeper into my imaginings of the rose bathwater and assortment of oils they set out for anyone to use. The bathrooms were dim, cozy places with candlesticks lining the space. Most people didn't use them, but that night I would.

I was achy, sore, covered in welts, and still had the day's assignments to finish before bed. An hour in my own oasis sounded—

A hand shot out of Hondros's open door and dragged me in.

"Hey!" I stumbled over my feet, hitting the floor on my hurt hip. Hyacinth slammed the door shut. "What the fuck!"

"Shut up," she said, dusting off her hands. "Do you know how long I've been trying to catch you alone? You're always surrounded by those freaks. Tonight was the first time in almost two weeks you weren't attached to that wolf's ass."

I held on to a chair and forced myself up. Thank you, handmaiden, for adding another bruise to my collection. "Why were you so eager to get me alone?" I scoffed. "Don't tell me, you're going to warn me off Alexander? Or is this about Calix?"

Her pretty, freckled face was blank.

"You know, maybe it's me who's clueless. I have zero experience with how men and women court. I'm guessing they all start out despising, hurting, sabotaging, and violating each other. That's the only explanation for why everyone looks at me and the imperial heirs and thinks we must be tumbling!"

Still, she said nothing.

"Look, whichever one you're in love with, you're welcome to them. You're also welcome to convince them to stay away from me."

Hyacinth shrugged slim shoulders. When she wasn't concealed in Sirena's shadow, it was easier to see how lovely she was. Her reddish-crown hair was woven into a multitude of braids that she twisted, styled, and piled on top of her head. She had a tiny mouth under an equally small nose, but the effect with her large, round fawn eyes made her into Cupid and Aphrodite's love child.

"I'm not in love with either of them. Sure, the plan was to seduce Calix, or Ajax, or maybe even your comrade Theron after they're officially named an heir to a seat. But none of that is necessary now," she said. "Sirena made a deal with me. When she claims her seat, I'll be given a noble title with Kuna City to go with it. The Estefania family will be relocated, and their palace, station, and coffers will be mine."

"How wonderful. Why are you telling me?"

A smile appeared on her lips for the first time since we met. "Because to receive that palace, station, and money, all I have to do is... get rid of you."

I shot for the door. Hyacinth threw me back. Whipping her hands up, she trained them on me.

I tried to rise again and my knees buckled. Gasping, my eyes bugged—jaw working as a deep, gnawing pain burned in the pit of my stomach. I crawled toward her, and collapsed.

"Like it?" Hyacinth laughed. "That's all the food, water, and nutrients leaving your body. I'm a daughter of Limos— Oops, sorry. I forget sometimes that you're an ignorant peasant."

"St-st-st—" My stomach caved in beneath my hands.

"Limos is the goddess of starvation and famine. In about two minutes, you'll be nothing but an emaciated corpse. Ugh, it's so ridiculous that I have to take orders from Sirena. I could kill the 'strongest child of Hera in our age' without blinking, but that would get me nothing."

My fingers were wrinkling as I fantasized moments ago, but not in this way. Dry and cracked to the touch, I felt each drop of moisture as it leached from my body.

"Heeelllppp..." I croaked—throat paper dry.

"Too bad it has to be this way, but you should've gotten it by now. The only thing that matters in Olympia is power."

"No..." I shook watching my skin shrink to the bone. "No..."

Talons sprouted from my nail beds.

"Nooo!"

Scales rippled down my arms. Clawed feet tore through leather. Wings shredded the clothes on my back. Faster and deadlier than ever, the beast sprung from the depths of my fear.

"Oh, gods! What— What are you!" Hyacinth raced for the door.

My talons grabbed and tore out her throat, showering the wood in blood as darkness took me.

I BLINKED AWAKE, VISION clearing on a dusty podium and overturned chair. Thunder cracked outside, heralding the torrential downpour that ripped me out of the dark.

Cold seeped into my bones, chilling my tight, aching muscles. Stiffly, I flipped onto my side, and screamed.

Hyacinth's round, fawn eyes stared into me unseeingly.

Shrieking, I scrabbled away from the body—slipping in her pool of blood.

"Oh, no. Gods," I cried. "Oh, gods, what have I done?"

She was mangled from head to toe. The only proof this was the same pretty, twisted girl were the tangled crown of braids... and the eyes.

I crawled as far as the wall let me. Face pressed to the limestone, I sobbed till I couldn't breathe.

Through warped wetness, I saw my hands.

I threw them away from me and ran to the door. I had to get out. *I had to get out now!*

Falling on the doorknob, my stomach heaved at the ichor. Why didn't I leave? Why didn't I try harder to get away from Alexander, Jason, and Castor when there was still a chance? This is my fault—

—*and everyone will know it.*

I stilled.

This isn't like Kristopher who everyone assumed was a casualty of the apple-induced riot. Hyacinth will be found in an empty classroom with no one else around, barring the girl Madame Remis will say stayed late in the lecture wing that night. Drakos would then pick up his report on Aella Galanis and the man she sliced to ribbons in a locked prison cell.

Drakos and the palace guards would round me up by morning. Once they had me, they wouldn't stop at no. They'd *make* me tell them what I am and why I killed the sweet, unassuming Hyacinth. And after I broke the goddess's one and only rule... there would be blood.

I shuddered so violently, I buckled against the wood. "No b-blood. Gods, please... no more."

Weeping and wailing, I gazed at Hyacinth, realizing what I had to do.

I thought the worst night of my life was when the mother I mourned, prayed for, cried over, and missed with all my heart, strapped me to an altar and pierced me with a bloody blade. I thought it was the night she poured scorching potions over my body. I thought it was the night she chanted an ancient spell that invited an evil, sadistic monster to roost in my soul.

I thought my worst night was when I broke free of the restraints and turned the knife on her. Plunging it into her chest before fleeing the temple so far and fast, the sun rose on my bleeding, blistered feet—still running.

I was wrong.

I carried Hyacinth's body out the window and into the raging storm. Rain beat and lashed at me, a thousand tiny hands reprimanding me for what I'd done. It stole my tears to mix reddish drops from Hyacinth. We'd always be linked by what I'd done.

My hand clamped over my mouth, penning in the whimpering cries leaking through my teeth.

I can't do this. I can't do this. I can't do this.

But I was doing it.

Step after step. My torn boots dragged through the mud, carrying my heavy burden the long, dark way around the castle. The stadium loomed before me.

"I'm sorry," I whispered. "I'm so sorry."

Kneeling down, I placed Hyacinth beside one of the many holes we had yet to fill, and pushed her in.

I cried and shook and vomited twice as I shoved dirt over her body. Once done, I tripped in the mud carrying stones to the grave. The storm was out of control. Water pounded my lids, blinding me to the dips and obstacles in my way, but the thunder was clear. It boomed its message through the heavens: *Con-demn! Con-demn! Con-demn!*

I fell dropping the last stone. My face hit the pile of rocks, opening cuts on my forehead, nose, and cheek. Clawing to my feet, I ran.

It's over. It's done, Aella. No more—

A vision of Hondros's lecture room and the scene everyone would walk into the next morning, crashed through my head.

I was not done.

It was every ounce of strength in me to make that trek again. To climb into the window. Witness the horror of what I'd done. And cover it up.

Denied towels or rags, I was forced to peel off my wet tunic and pants. I cleaned as best I could—running back and forth to wring my clothes out in the storm. My shame washed into the mud and grass as I returned to the stadium. My tunic, pants, and boots disappeared down another hole.

I trudged out into the night—scraped raw from the inside out. Rain rushed into my eyes, nose, and mouth unhindered. Let it finish the job. Deliver Zeus's justice.

My chest squeezed around sobs that wouldn't stop coming. They echoed inside the marble hall, calling someone to hear, to check, to find me.

No one came.

Out into the atrium, into the main hall, and through the narrow space of the dorm wing—I was alone.

My hand closed around dorm eleven's knob. I'd go in, change into my cotton nightdress, push the covers at the bottom of the bed where they'd end up anyway... and find Hyacinth waiting for me in my dreams.

I dropped the knob like it burned, flinging myself away. *No! I couldn't sleep. Reliving this night again and again... I'd rather die.*

I bolted far and away from that cursed bed. Falling on the wood, I pounded for him to wake.

"The fuck?" An irritated shout was my response. "Do you have any idea what time—?"

The door flew open. Calix stood there in nothing but unbuttoned pants and a crown of disheveled locks. The rest of his sentence died on his lips, taken over by looking me up and down—dripping on his threshold in nothing but my breast band and underwear.

I threw myself at him, burying my face in his chest. He grunted in surprise—arms up and out like he wasn't sure if he should hold or shove me away.

"Do it," I whispered. "Please, Calix. Take the pain away."

He went stiff in my grip. "What are you asking?"

"You know what I'm asking." I cradled his jaw—both soft and stubbly on my palms. "I don't want to talk. I don't want to dream. And... I don't want to hurt." I bumped my nose on his, our lips glancing off each other. He sucked in a sharp breath. "Do it. Please."

His voice gruffed and strained scraping from his throat. "What's in it for me?"

"I'll give you whatever you want."

"Whatever I want..." Calix tangled in my hair, tipping my head back. He breathed sharply as though the distance finally let him. "Do you know what I want?"

A finger trailed down my skin, stopping along the thin band that linked the front and back of the single strip of cloth that concealed my most private area. One snip, and it'd be private no more.

"Do you know I want to ruin you?" His baritone slipped in my ears. "That I want to make you not so strong and not so sweet because the first time I saw my brother's killer, I wanted her in every single way." Calix's lips caressed my ear.

"Do you know that I hate you because no matter what I tell myself, and how much shit I snort up my nose... I still do."

My throat bobbed, mouth going dry.

"So what say you, Aella?"

The way he drew out my name fluttered my eyes shut. Reaching behind, my foot nudged the door closed.

"I said anything."

The reply was barely out of my mouth before the pink cloud claimed me. Hyacinth, the beast, the goddess, and that hellish night faded to nothing. All that existed was Calix.

I crashed his lips on mine.

"Wait," he said, pulling away. "Get on the bed."

His wish was my mandate. I padded over the strewn clothes, tossed textbooks, and random scrolls for his messy bed. Sinking in the sheets, cedarwood, musk, and hints of orange-scented bathwater enveloped me. I flipped over as Calix took a bottle out of his desk and tipped the contents. I watched him crush the nectar into powder, then disappear it into his body.

"Why, my love?" I asked. "Why do you do—?"

"Shhh." His shoulders loosened, gait slowed, and orbs glazed before my eyes. "Remember, we don't talk."

"Yes, Calix."

"Come to me."

I shot into his arms, moaning as he finally captured my lips. Calix molded me to him—fitting our bodies together as puzzle pieces put in different boxes. We've been waiting so long to find where we belonged.

My hands were everywhere. Stroking his chest. Tangling in his waves. Memorizing every dip and curve. Tugging at his pants.

He nipped my lips, demanding entrance. The sweet perfection of our tongues tangling weakened my knees. I stayed upright only for Calix's grip on my ass—holding me firm to him, wrapping my legs around his waist, moving his hardness between my middle.

Calix broke free and threw me. I shrieked laughing, soaring across the sheets and landing on the pillows. Muscles rippled on his back as he stalked toward me—the predator and his prey.

He kissed the inside of my ankle, making me shiver. My skin was alive like it'd never been before. I was acutely aware of the silk tickling my back. The glow of the flickering lamp, casting our shadows over the fireplace. And Calix, Calix, Calix.

He skated up my thigh, his lips following in his hands' wake. Little whimpers escaped my mouth under his tender, nipping kisses.

"Has another man touched you, my sweet one?" Calix teased the underside of my garments—the thin barrier between him and my maidenhood. I almost ripped it off myself.

"No, Calix. No one. I'm yours to have. Always."

Calix let out a long, sharp hiss. "I almost wish I didn't know that."

My brows furrowed. "Why?"

"Because," he said, rising to his knees. "Now I have to go easy on you. Slowly." He pulled down his pants. "Gently." They flew into the unlit fireplace. "Claim you in every way a man can have a woman."

His length stood proud for all to see—free of its constraints. I fisted the sheets.

Nerves couldn't find me in the place I was in, though I felt it searching. My love was longer, thicker, and *readier* than I was expecting. Eight years in a cave didn't teach me what to expect, and he surprised me anyway. There was nothing rantallion about him.

"No one ever had to be nice about ruining an enemy, but, of course, Aella, nothing can be the same with you."

He was talking so much. Didn't he say we wouldn't do this?

I grasped his shoulders and tugged him down, occupying his mouth in the proper way. He bit my lips, enticing a squeak, then kissed me soft. Continuing down, Calix found my breastband, and the knotted string keeping it together. He had it undone and off quicker than his pants.

"Zeus and Hera, woman." Calix arched my back, displaying my rounded mound and their hardening peaks for his pleasure. "Narcissus would look up from the water to spend the rest of his life staring at you."

I bit my lip, holding back my grin. Okay, he could talk if he was going to say things like that.

If I expected him to do more, he surprised me again. Calix left my breasts bereft and wanton—continuing his exploration down. A new sensation sprouted between my legs as he tugged my underwear off with his teeth. I fell open before him.

"Tell me, sweet one." He teased a circle around my opening. "Do you taste sweet too?"

I blinked, cheeks heating. I think I tried to answer him, but nothing intelligible came out.

Calix buried his face between my legs, finding out for himself. I made a strangled noise as my legs snapped over his ears—back arching off the bed.

This is new.

Calix plundered my entrance—licking, nipping, and sucking on a particular place that sent Zeus's lightning bolts zipping beneath my skin.

"Holy fucking gods," I gasped.

I twisted and writhed on the sheets, doing my best to pull his head off his shoulders. Calix just laughed while he steadied me—sending delicious vibrations through my sex.

My legs were pushed up and out, spreading me wider than the obscene stuffed turkeys they served in the mess hall. Calix's head dipped. A warm, expert tongue licked my puckered hole.

"Oh!" I jumped, bottom scooting away.

Calix trapped me with a hand flat between my breasts. Slowly. Deliberately. He drew me back.

"Easy, sweet one," he said in that unhurried, dreamy thrall of the nectar. "I'm just getting started."

Sweat beaded on my skin at his final wink before ducking down. It was a good thing his arm around my thigh and palm to my heart kept me down, because living bubbles grew and burst within me—threatening to carry me away.

Or at least that's how he felt as he had his way with both holes—teasing one, tasting one, and then switching it up.

Moans peeled from my lips as loud and begging as the women in the erotic novel the lamia accidentally included in the batch of books she stole from who knew where. Wide-eyed and warm-faced, my sisters and I pored over the descriptions too many times to count, collecting all the fantasies and dirty words that survived my escape.

"C-Calix," I cried. Heat built in my lower belly, contracting it almost painfully. If pain now meant a feeling you never wanted to end even if it killed you. "Calix!"

The son of Aphrodite gently bit that spot, and I exploded.

"Heh-uhh!" I moaned, heels pounding the crown of his ass. Again and again pleasure bowled me over, blowing up my mind as one explosion ended and the other began. The chain reaction carried me all the way down, leaving me a flopping, sweaty mess on his sheets. "Oh, gods. Do that again."

He chuckled. "Bit of a selfish lover, aren't you?" A swat landed on my backside, re-sparking the fire in my middle. "What are you going to do for me?"

"Whatever you desire, my love." I palmed his cock, earning a deep, husky groan that curled my toes. "I live to please you."

"If that's so, lie back."

I did so, taking him with me. Calix linked his fingers through mine and locked my wrists above my head.

"Wrap your legs around me," he ordered.

Again, his wish was my mandate. I snaked around his waist, anticipation climbing. Selfish was furthest from the lover I was. Whatever he asked me to do—even the eye-watering, impossible things they did in that novel—I would do. Anything for Calix.

"Now I want you to"—he ensnared my lips, kissing me to thoroughly scramble my head—"relax and try not to tense up," he whispered. "It'll hurt at first, but afterward, all sweetness."

I nipped his nose. "Hurt me."

Emotion flashed in those clouded eyes. "You know... I might just keep you."

There was no *might* about it. Calix was mine until the end of our days and beyond. He and I would hold each other in Elysium, forever taking the pain away—

A sharp stab of pain rocked me, clenching my legs to my teeth.

"Shh," he crooned. "Just relax, sweet one. Let yourself relax." Calix repeated that to me until my muscles unwound and the pain faded.

He pumped slowly at first, letting my body adjust to the new sensations. I was right that my virgin entrance wasn't built to fit a man of his size. I was wrong to believe she wouldn't find a fucking way.

Calix stretched me to bursting, but what was first uncomfortable, quickly became—

"Oooh," I breathed, thighs tightening on him. Calix bent and wrapped his tongue around my nipple. "Oh!"

A variety of sounds, cries, and moans poured from my mouth as he flicked the poor nub in time with his pumps—bobbing between my legs, bouncing me on the sheets, and playing with my breast. His prize had no way to escape him.

"Oh, Cal, I can't—" The fire was blazing out of control. Our sweat slicked our bodies. My fevered pants hazed the air. "Please, I can't... I'm going to..."

His response was to move to the next breast and put it under the same exquisite torture. I spasmed as the first wave crashed through me.

Half a thought crossed my mind to slow things down. Draw out this perfect moment with Calix for as long as possible.

I angled up and Calix struck a spot that rolled my eyes up in my head. *Fuck slowing this down.*

"Yes, Cal, right th-there. Ahh!" The second crash dragged me under, drowning me in the deepest depths where my fantasies couldn't reach. No part of me could've imagined this. Even if I was as experienced as the imperial heirs accused. The pure pool of self-indulgent bliss that overwhelmed my senses was for us and us alone. I could only feel this with him.

My Calix.

He tensed in my hold, grabbing and crushing the silk. He grunted—back bending in half as he spilled warm wetness inside of me. "Fuck," he breathed, collapsing on top of me.

I wrapped around him, peppering his hair, ear, and cheeks with kisses. "How much time do you need?"

"For what?"

"Until we go again."

SUNLIGHT PRESSED ON my eyelids, calling me from darkness. Groaning, I flipped over, cursing the damn sun for waking me from the most perfect sleep—a dreamless one. The movement jarred my sore spots, and with the pain came the memory of last night.

I snapped awake, jerking up in the empty bed. "Cal—" I turned just as he did the last button on his pants. His empty, hard expression vanished for a second when he tugged on his shirt. Then he was back and I knew as our gaze connected, the real Calix was back.

"You can get the potion from Healer Helena," he said, grabbing up an overcoat and making for the door.

"The potion?" I piled all the blankets and pillows within reach over my nakedness. "What potion?"

He cocked a brow—half in and half out the cracked exit. "I assume you're not interested in having my kid?"

Eyes widening, my lips parted, but nothing came out.

"I thought so." With that, he left.

A whole ten minutes passed as I sat in our tangled mess of sheets, gazing blankly at the wall.

I asked for this. I told Calix to take the pain away. To keep my mother, Kristopher, the goddess, and... Hyacinth... out of my nightmares. In exchange, I gave up one of my dreams. A child's wish of gifting her maidenhood to the one she loved during a night she'd hold close to her heart always. I gave it up to a man who needs drugs to touch me. The same man who's sworn to make me hate myself as much as he hates me. I gave up my dream...

...and I felt nothing.

Why should I? There comes a time when every child needs to grow the fuck up and accept dreams don't come true.

Sirena

"I'm telling you, Xander, it's like he knows."

I watched him pummel a training dummy, near licking my lips at his bare, muscled back and the rock-hard ass straining his pants. To think I used to make fun of him for spending every spare minute in the training room. The time had served him very well.

"How is that possible?"

I shook my head. "I've followed Barba every night for a week and a half. He goes from combat training to the bath. Afterward, he grabs food from the mess hall, takes it to his room to eat while he does assignments, and then he's passed out by eleven. I stay and watch him for as long as I can keep my eyes open.

"He's never left his bed. Maybe it was a coincidence that he wasn't there those nights you snuck in."

"I don't believe in coincidence." Xander delivered one last punch to the medusa, then pushed it back in the corner with the rest. Snatching up his towel, he motioned for me to walk with him. Together we headed back to the dorm. "More likely, he finished whatever business that kept him out all night. Now he stays in his bed because he's got nowhere else to be."

"That makes it easier for us, doesn't it? When it's time, I'll trail him to his dorm and make sure he *stays* there," I said. "I'll slip a feather under the door so you'll know it's time to move. Once we've got him trussed up, what does your father want us to do?"

"He said he'll give further instructions once we've got him under control."

"That's why we're getting him in his sleep." We climbed the steps to the Titan wing. "Still, I don't like not knowing his real power."

"Neither do I, but it's clear he's prepared to keep up this shit for the next four years. This should've been done a long time ago. The council isn't waiting any longer."

I scoffed. "Don't these Hades spawn realize that hiding and lying to the council just makes them more suspicious? If they're loyal, they shouldn't have a problem proving it."

"That's..." Xander trailed off.

"Xander?" I climbed up to the top step, following his line of sight. Walking out of Calix's room was Aella Galanis.

She wore his clothes, ratty hair, and marks on her neck that shown from across the hall. We didn't have to ask what she and Calix did in that room.

Glancing up, she spotted us. The traitor looked hard at me, then she gave us her back and left the wing by the second staircase.

I clicked my tongue. "Wow. Calix really will sleep with anyone. But I did tell you, Xander. That girl will give it away for two coppers and a button. She has no—"

Xander blew past me, storming into his room. He slammed the door so hard, he brought half a dozen people out of their rooms, checking what was wrong.

Sebastian

"She turned into what?"

"I... I can't explain it, my lord." Linus was pale as a bone, and for a ghost, that was saying something. "Hyacinth Kokkinos was draining her of life force. I sensed her leaving the mortal realm. Then, in the space of a breath, she transformed into a—a beast!"

"So, she's a shape-shifter."

His knotted braids flew around his head. It was interesting being in the company of a two-thousand-year-old Greek soldier who refused to move on to Hades, because his duty was on the battle-field—even if his sword sliced through monsters without leaving a nick.

Serving gave him purpose to his afterlife, so I long since stopped trying to convince him he didn't need to call me "my lord."

"She's a freak!" Hyacinth screamed. "A monster! A demon! Xander should've slit her throat the moment he laid eyes on her."

Hyacinth tripped rushing me—though her feet didn't touch the ground. She fell through my bedside table and winced—though it could not possibly have hurt.

"Look what she d-did to me." Throwing herself back, she wailed loud, hiccupping cries that curled my lip. If she had her way, I'd be talking to Aella Galanis's ghost right now. Funny how murderers get deeply offended at being murdered.

I fixed on Linus. "A shape-shifter who turns into a monster. She wouldn't be the first. Nothing scandalous in that. Why... hide...?" I trailed off when he roughly shook his head, eyes huge.

"She is not a shape-shifter. Not in any way we've come to know. They transform into beings of this earth. Whatever she is... I've seen nothing like it in this world or the next." His gaze unfocused.

"But it's more than that, my lord. When she changed it was like... Like the sun went out.

"The world drowned in darkness and cold, and I was alone." He shuddered, voice dropping to a whisper. "So alone."

My brows crowded. Linus? Was he... afraid?

"Same," Hyacinth rasped from the floor. "Toward the end, I almost wanted to die. Just so that empty ache would go away."

"What could do that, sire?" Linus asked. "What could have that kind of effect on a ghost?"

"I don't know. Describe what she looked like again."

Linus relayed his description of the black-scaled winged beast that took the place of the beautiful, sun-kissed Aella Galanis. Again, I shook my head. I never heard of such a thing, and I was frequently in the company of ghosts who lived thousands of years. If they came across such a creature, I like to think they would've mentioned it.

"I need to think about what this means," I said, reclining against my headboard. "It's true I sensed something was different about her and the infection in her soul, but I never guessed this. Is she something ancient? A creature the world has forgotten? Or is she something new? A beast man has never seen before? More importantly, can she be controlled?"

"Sire, I am dead and with nothing left to fear, and in *its* presence I was made a coward. My only desire was to flee for the life I don't have." His hand slashed through the air. "Nothing like that can be controlled."

It was safe to say Linus was rattled, but I wasn't so sure. The creature attacked when a soldier made a late-night visit to her cell, and again when Hyacinth tried to kill her. It proved Galanis, at least, had some measure of control over the beast. If that's the case, she can be useful to me.

She can remain alive.

"I have to think," I repeated.

"What's there to think about?" Hyacinth shot up too fast and ended up dangling over my head. It would take time to learn how to navigate a ghostly body in the living realm. In hades, she would have no such problem. She would have corporeal form again. Her feet would touch the ground, and all of her senses would experience whatever realm awaited her for dying while trying to kill someone. But here in the place she no longer belonged, she'd never be whole.

"I was told you do favors for us. In exchange for information, spying, and keeping you three steps ahead of the many people who want to get their hands on you, son of Hades. You take care of our unfinished business." She drifted down, flashing a smirk that sat unpleasantly on her pretty face. "I want Galanis dead. Do that and I'll tell you everything I know about the imperial heirs and their plans for you."

I flapped a hand. "I already know about the imperial heirs and their plans for me. Cirillo's been very clever, turning into a gnat, following me around the castle, and flying under my door at night. Another ghost with a particular hatred of her has been feeding me every word that comes out of her mouth." I tsked. "The council and their spawn sure do pick up a lot of enemies."

"I'd be of better use to you than whoever the fuck that ghost is!" Red would stain her cheeks if she still had blood. "Kill Galanis."

I straightened, draping my arm across my knee. "You'll be of better use spying on the council, but how will you fare with slaughtering them on their thrones?"

"What?" Surprise chased away her rage.

"I will not be controlled. I will live as no one's slave," I gritted, "nor will I die fighting enemies who never had a right to stand against me. My life will be my own. Always. So when the council comes—and they will come—I'll need powerful allies on my side." I raked her up and down. "Not dead ones."

"I... I can still help you." She didn't sound half as sure as before. "I grew up in the palace. I know its secrets. If you want to kill members of the council without getting caught, I can tell you how."

I crossed to the window, gazing out at the vastness of lush and green, and the undead armada claiming every inch of it as far as I could see. They turned their heads at once—watching me. Waiting.

"It's too late for something as simple as assassination." I shook my head and some of them left. Most did not. "King Midas tried that and a new council regained control in less than a generation. If my people are ever to be free, there must be revolution. There must be war." I turned my grin on her, shrinking her back. "There must be a new king on the throne.

"Tell me, Hyacinth Kokkinos, daughter of the council advisor, Solon Kokkinos. How will you help me bring the council and all who support them to their knees?" I swept out my hands. "How will you serve in ascending the reign of King Sebastian?"

Gasping, she flew away—up and out of my room. Far away from me.

I hummed. "Everyone always leaves when I get to that part. Quite rude."

"But, my lord," Linus said. "Surely you don't think this Galanis creature is the key to your throne? She's too dangerous. I've seen it."

"Now I must see it. I'll provoke her into releasing the creature—witness what it can do for myself." I made for the door. "Afterward, she can dispense with the lies and we'll discuss what she'll do for me in exchange for keeping her secret."

"Wait, my lord— Stop." Linus shot in front of me.

I stopped mostly out of disbelief than his ability to truly be in my way. This kind of defiance was beyond him.

"Please, sire." He ground his teeth, struggling with something. "Forgive me my disobedience. I will punish myself under the harshest conditions. If that doesn't please you and you dismiss me from your service, I will understand."

"Out with it."

"I found Aella Galanis's mother, sire. A week ago, as it happens."

My eyes narrowed to slits. "Why did you keep this from me?"

Linus snapped ramrod straight, raising his chin as if preparing to receive and accept a blow. "Because of what she said. Aella Galanis is already being used. She is the tool of a power far greater and far deadlier than we've ever seen. Far deadlier than you, sire.

"This power cannot be controlled. It cannot be bargained with. And it cannot be stopped. If you provoke its wrath, you will die."

I frowned. "Linus, you know nothing can stand against me—"

"Aella Galanis can," he sliced in. "And she will. Underestimating her would be your *last* mistake."

I gave him a long look. "You said she's a tool. Who wields her?"

"I don't know."

"Besides turning into a taloned beast, what ability does she have that bests mine?"

"I don't know."

Impatience crept into my tone. "How did this *power* turn her into what she is in the first place? If she isn't a demigod, what is she?"

"I don't know, sire."

"What do you know?" I barked.

"What I know with absolute certainty now is that you must run," he hissed. "Pick any direction that leads away from Aella Galanis, and run hard and fast, and pray she never finds you. She is *wrong*, my lord. She's a scourge upon this earth and your only hope is to be leagues away when she achieves her true purpose."

"I assume you also don't know what that true purpose is."

Linus drifted to the window. "According to her mother, it's the end of everything."

"Ominous." Despite his efforts, fear did not touch me. Every being must live in compromise, or die on principle. Galanis and this deadly power were not excluded. "Bring her mother to me. I will question her myself."

"You may speak to her at any time, my lord." Linus pointed out into the distance. "She's always been here. Since Galanis stepped foot on these grounds.

"She will never leave her," he said. "Aella is her unfinished business."

Aella

"Watch yourself, Sisyphean."

A hard hit knocked my strap off my shoulder. My bag spilled its contents across the floor, kicking up laughter all around me.

I turned and came face to face with Calix. Rue hung off his arm along with two other fawning girls. Rue cackled over hitting me as she glanced at Calix for approval.

Visions of our tangled bodies and heated moans flooded my mind, but if Calix was thinking of the same, I couldn't guess for all the gold in a noblewoman's coffers. His expression gave nothing away.

For five nights, I've been sleeping in his bed. The one night I went without his power, I dreamt of bodies and shallow graves, then woke cold in a sweat—vomiting over the side of my mattress. The whole night I shivered in the corner, too exhausted to stay awake. Too wretched to sleep.

I accepted my fate after that night, and the price. Calix would drop me in a land of bliss every night I wished, but only if I woke the next morning feeling lower and dirtier than the goddess could ever make me.

She forced this on me. But becoming Calix's obedient love slave—that I chose.

Calix slid off me, continuing on without a word. He brought a dirty boot down on my fallen scroll as he passed by. I bent to grab it as Rue stomped on it too, then another one from his harem. The last one kicked it across the mess hall.

Howling, the girls led Calix off to a table to pamper, feed, and stroke his cock under the table.

"When will they give it a rest?" Theron gruffed. He ran over and got my scroll, cleaning it off as best as he could for me. "They of all people should have bigger things to worry about."

I stiffened, knowing what was coming before he spoke.

"They still haven't found Hyacinth Kokkinos," he said, leading me back to the food line and our friends. "Drakos ordered a search of the castle but it didn't turn up a sign of her."

"Are you talking about Hyacinth?" Nitsa asked, overhearing us. "The whole thing freaks me out. They say there's no way she left the grounds, but they're also saying they can't find her anywhere. I don't want to think about what that means."

"We shouldn't jump to the worst conclusion," Daciana said. "Maybe she found an out-of-the-way spot and holed up for a break. We did the same."

"We holed up for one day," Tycho corrected. "And Hyacinth saw how much shit we got for it. Taking off for six days..." He shook his head. "No. Something's wrong."

"What do you think could've happened?"

"You wouldn't happen to be speaking about Hyacinth, would you?" The light, musical voice slithered up my spine.

Sirena stepped into my view. "What a coincidence. I was just about to ask if you know where she might be."

Ionna pulled a face. "Why would we know where she is? Wasn't she attached to your hip?"

"Well, I'm sure Galanis must know something." She slid to me. "Hyacinth told me she was going to speak to her about something the night she disappeared."

My breath stopped.

"She didn't come back after that, now that I think about it." Sirena fixed on me, studying my face for the slightest sign of *anything*. "What did you two talk about? Must've been important because she was upset when she left."

"What?" Nitsa said. "Aella, what is she talking about?"

Heart yammering, I kept my voice steady. "I have no idea. Hyacinth wanted to speak to me? She must've said a name close to mine and you misheard her, because Hyacinth and I have nothing to talk about. She liked me as much as you do—and trust me the feeling is mutual."

Sirena's eyes narrowed. "Liked?"

Oh no. Stupid, stupid, stupid!

"I said *likes*. See what I mean? You're having trouble hearing. Hyacinth did not say she was going to meet me, and I know that because she didn't." I set down my half-filled plate. "I hope they find her, though. She was no friend to me, but the thought of her just vanishing is terrifying."

Backing away, I said to my friends, "I forgot something in the dorm, so I'll see you..." I walked away, leaving the sentence hanging.

In the end I didn't go back. Time got away from me while I curled up in Theron's favorite armchair, crying into my sleeve.

Blood. Screams. Pounding rain. Rocks cutting my palms. A thud as her body hit the earth. Con-demn. Con-demn.

I never made it to lessons that day.

Alexander

I kept drifting behind me, scanning the door. The stubborn fool thing refused to open. Galanis's friends came in and found their seats. Where was she?

With Calix?

My reed snapped in my fist. Since the first morning I caught her coming out of his room, she'd been with him almost every night since. How did I know? My midnight visits to her dorm resulted in me staring at an empty bed.

"Let's begin." Hondros dragged my attention forward. "Today, you'll work in pairs. Three scenarios in which you're under attack by two monsters. You and your partner were sent out to collect supplies. You thought the area was safe, but while on the road, a freak typhon storm rolls through the sky. You try turning around and find a sphinx between you and your mora. What do you do?"

Hondros went through the other scenarios and set us to work. "You need only turn in one scroll," he said, flicking in my direction. Sirena linked her arm through mine. "Both names on the paper. You'll share the grade."

I got on with it.

The soft, green children around me likely thought all these drills were farfetched and unnecessary. It'd be an easier life if it was. Just that summer while I was traveling with the border guards, an empousa tracked me through the forest, staying wisely out of sight as she herded me into a gorgon nest.

The first and last mistake a soldier makes out there is assuming monsters were stupid. They often joined forces to deadly effect.

Focusing on my battle plan with Sirena took my mind off Galanis fucking my brother in all but blood—mostly.

Calix would not do this to Galen.

But he was doing it.

Calix had no love for Aella Galanis. He's lost himself on nectar every night since Galen died. A too-often habit had become a full-blown addiction—because of her.

Then what does it mean that he also spends every night with her?

This had to be a form of revenge. Like the dance he made her do in the mess hall.

Calix never used his power to make a woman fuck him. He's never had to.

"Arugh!" I punched the desk, snapping another reed.

"Xander?" Sirena cried. "What's wrong?"

I shoved the finished scroll away. "I'm done with this. And this," I said, snatching up my bag.

"Damien, where do you think you're going?" Hondros advanced on me. "You don't walk out that door until I—"

Sirena shot up. "Let's go, Xander." She darted behind me, burying her face in my neck. "I can't stand to be here either."

A vein ticced in his jaw, looking from me, then drifting behind. Hondros unclenched his fists. "You two may go."

Frowning, I glanced between them. Sirena took my hand and left before I completed the thought.

I didn't fare much better in my other lessons. Every block I waited for Galanis to walk through the door or step onto the field. Every block, her space remained empty. Where was my traitor?

And who was she with?

I walked out of combat training early, ignoring Ajax's calls asking where I was going. I only let up on her because he demanded it. She used that free rein to hop in a bed worse than Barba's.

Every night with him she taunted me. Ajax chose forgiveness. Calix chose *her*. I was left stewing in hatred and revenge. I was the one who looked ridiculous for not moving on and letting an accident be an accident.

She plastered herself to Cal to make a fool of me—all the while, her teal pools pled innocence and our hands over her heart begged for mercy.

I turned left, not right, in the Sisyphean hall, walking farther away from my staircase. The doors to the baths rose ahead—the first doors in the t-shaped hall. I caught the strip of her towel and a wisp of blonde strands as Aella slipped inside.

If Aella was done playing games, so was I.

This would end one way—her or me.

Aella

I mixed different bath salts in the water, breathing deep the aromas drifting from the heated pool. It helped some to open my clogged nose. Soothe my puffy eyes.

I'd taken to long baths at night. It was as if part of me believed if I got myself as clean as possible, I wouldn't leave Calix's room the next morning feeling as dirty.

I wouldn't ask myself if it was working. What did work was hiding in here for the privacy I couldn't have in a room full of people and only one door.

The Sisyphean dorm baths were like many public bathhouses in that they were shared. The difference in this grand castle though was there were ten bathing pools in this dim, candlelit, black-marbled space. Each one was circled by three walls and a black curtain, shielding me from passersby and their passing glances. There were four more rooms like this one on the first floor, meaning no single one was ever crowded.

Often, I came in and there were one or two people sloshing in the neighboring pools. They were gone long before I left to see Calix.

Drawing the curtain shut, I let my towel pool at my feet. The steamy water beckoned, inviting me to find all my problems within its depths.

I obliged.

Was there any hope of escaping the academy or making it to the border? I wanted to leave to protect the trainees from me. To flee the goddess's reach and keep my hands clean of bloodshed.

Too fucking late.

The beast killed two people, and thoughtless, ignorant Aella killed the third. What would running accomplish now other than the death of a fourth? Alexander.

At all costs, the goddess could not complete the ritual and trade a mindless killer for an obedient assassin, but what could I really do to stop her? I couldn't ask for help, nor could I tell innocent from foe.

The single face I knew in that temple was my mother's, but the others I hadn't seen before. I didn't know the goddess's allies or if she had more. In eight years, the lamia gave not one sign that she was the mad keeper of the child who'd become a sacrifice.

Border watchers would be on me by the second step I took outside the academy gates, and the next time they captured the traitor and monster who let down her people, they'd be right.

My life was forfeit from the moment the blade pierced my skin and the beast was born. I nearly did the right thing the morning I chose to end my life, until fear and a child's dreams tossed away the knife.

Ever since then I've killed, and killed, and *killed* again while swearing it'd be the last time. I'd find the answer in the next mile to the border, or in the traitor's noose, or another book on enchantments.

How many more people had to die while I tried to save myself?

One more. My enemy. My opposite. My jackass. Alexander.

They would execute him for letting me escape, but didn't he deserve it for all that he'd done? He captured a traitor as he was sworn to do. He granted me life in place of a death sentence. He brought me to a place where I made the closest, truest friends I'd have in this life or the next. He turned on me when I got one of his killed. He was harsh and cruel and had a smirk that made me want to slap it off his face.

But what had he done to me or my friends that was worth a death sentence? And was it worse than what I've done? Why should he die for killing no one? And I live for killing everyone who witnessed the beast?

Didn't I already know the solution to end an eight-year-long misery? Shouldn't I just—?

I slipped under the water, sinking to the bottom of the pool.

Let go.

Lavender-peppermint-and-eucalyptus-scented water rushed my nose, ears, mouth, and pores—filling me up to make me a part of it forever.

It was better this way. No one would die because of me again. Their screams wouldn't echo in my ears as I cowered uselessly at the back of a cave. For the first time, I'd be brave.

"What do you think you're doing?"

Her clanging voice came from farther away. She couldn't touch me where I was going. I was too far out of her reach.

"Rise, child. Do it now," she shouted when I ignored her. *"Death will not bring you release. You are mine, pet. Your fate is woven into the threads of my cloak. We shall never be parted. Not even after our work is done. You will sit at my feet and gaze upon a burning world, mourning what you have done."*

"No," I said, expelling the last breath of air in my lungs. "This time, I get to choose."

Aching grew in my chest. A tremble began in my limbs. I drifted to the bottom of the bath—calm. Soon, my body would accept the inevitable. This was where we had to be. It was time.

"Rise, child."

Black crept into my vision, guiding the way into the dark.

"Rise!"

The candlelit haven bent and shifted through glittering prisms. This was a peaceful place. The kind you hoped for at the end—

"*RISE!*" A horrible, shifting face shot out of the depths. A terror of changing, gnashing teeth; blackened eyes; and divinity my mortal soul was never meant to see, bowled me through.

I screamed and found I couldn't. My burning throat choked on a sea of eucalyptus salt, and my panic and fear flooded in.

Thrashing, my feet scrabbled on the marble basin. I clawed for the surface—twisting, kicking, swallowing water by the mouthful.

My toes caught, then glanced off the bottom, dropping me short of the surface. Harder I flailed, lungs on fire.

Come on. Stand up. Get up!

Black bled in around the edges of my vision, crowding out the candle-drenched mosaic. I found purchase again and launched off, shooting for air and my last chance.

My fingers broke through, reaching for the rim...

...and missed. I slammed to the bottom, punching out the last breath of fight in me.

Darkness took me.

"Aella!"

Hands snatched me out of the dark, hauling me to the surface. I popped up coughing and sputtering—sucking in deep lungfuls. Hauling me around, Calix's boundless amber eyes were filled with something I'd never seen in him nectar-free—concern.

"What the fuck happened?"

I couldn't answer, too busy heaving and clinging to him like the water would take me again.

"Do you not know how to swim? Not that you need to know to take a bath." He was gentle tipping my chin, checking me over. "Are you okay?"

"I—I'm okay," I croaked. "What are you doing here? How... did you know?"

"I didn't know. I've got somewhere to be tonight, so I won't be there when you come knocking. I knew you'd be here, so I'm telling you if we're doing this, we're doing this now." He flicked to the bath. "But I'm guessing we're holding off."

I glanced down, seeing myself at the bottom of the basin—thrashing and kicking for my life... after I lay down to let it go.

My grip tightened on his arm. He couldn't leave. I didn't want to be in this pool alone. "No," I said. "We're doing this now. Will it still work if we don't fall asleep together?"

Calix didn't ask what I meant. "Couldn't say. Never knew my powers had side effects. You tell me how it works."

I didn't need to think about it. Even if he didn't chase my demons away for a night, he'd free me for an hour. He'd take those awful gnashing teeth, black-dipped claws, and changing faces out of my mind.

Straightening, he peeled off his clothes and tossed them in the corner. This was humiliation for him and survival for me, but no matter how quickly we parted when we were done, I could not deny Calix Lambros was sculpted perfection.

He was the personification of male beauty that artists tried and failed for decades to capture. He was the bawdy, impossible descriptions in that erotic novel. I didn't know how skin could glisten, or could ripple, eyes could be swimmable, or a cock could be powerful... until him.

I waited in silence as he crushed nectar on the rim of the basin and snorted it into his body. He released a long, deep sigh as he was transported away, and the tender, dreamy version who shared my body took his place.

"What's that face, sweet one?"

"Will you ever tell me," I whispered, "what you're running from?"

Calix held out his hand for me. Drawing me close, he blew that cloud over my eyes. I forgot all about my question.

"Calix." I melted into him. "I love you."

"Save those declarations, sweet one." Calix lifted me out of the pool, placing me on the rim. Excitement built as he spread my legs. "You'll find better use for it later."

My forehead scrunched in confusion. My love said such strange things sometimes. I did not understand them, but that wasn't my duty. Mine was to please him. It was to chase his gloomy moods away and keep him safe in the shelter of my love. I told him so and received his husky, velvety laugh.

"And what's my duty, sweetness?" He swirled a finger around my pussy, collecting the drops of wetness already coming. "To keep you high on orgasms and your own brand of nectar?"

I giggled, splashing him in the face. "If you insist."

We laughed lighter and freer than I'd ever been. No one could question that we belonged together. Calix and I made each other whole.

His tongue slipped between my folds and my head fell back, welcoming the shooting sparks of living explosions bursting beneath my skin.

"Ahh, yes, Cal." I moaned deep and loud, knowing there was no one around, but not caring even if there was. Calix loved it when I was loud.

"Ooh," I squeaked, jumping a little when a finger joined the party. Calix had introduced me to a lot of new things in the week we'd been together, ridding me of maidenhood in every way. Even so, it all felt new. Every time with Calix was the first time.

He teased that bundle of nerves with his tongue, raising my temperature in our own steamy, private world. Calix pushed another finger inside me and spread them apart—together, apart, together, apart, in, out, in, and fucking out.

"Cal, you're so—"

The curtain flew open.

Jerking up, I saw nothing but a black blur race around my vision before it landed in the bath and spattered half of it in my face. Calix abruptly pulled out of me.

"Not her!" The blur grabbed Calix by the neck, slamming him against the wall. "You can fuck anyone, Cal. Why her?"

I swiped the water out of my eyes, vision clearing on Alexander, choking the love of my life.

"Are you so fucked up on that shit you forgot about Galen!"

Calix's head lolled. "Zeus and Hera, man. Calm down."

Alexander punched him in the face, snapping him around and dropping him beneath the water. I jumped on his back.

"Leave him alone!" I hooked around his neck and squeezed. "I won't let you hurt him. Stay away from my Calix."

Damien reared, flipping me over his head. I hit the water with a smack and took down Calix again when he tried to get up. Blinking in my watery basin, the finest ribbon of blood floated past my face. My Calix was hurt.

Fury boiled the bath a hundred degrees. I burst up, my hands claws to wrap around Alexander's throat and never let go. Calix's laughter made me freeze.

"What are you doing, brother?" Calix asked, howling. "Do you even know? All this hitting and shouting and shit. You're ruining my high."

"Then let me cut this short." Damien shoved him at the bath steps. "Get the fuck out. You don't touch her. You don't look at her. If I see her walk out of your room again, I won't be responsible for what I do. You and Aella are done."

"What? No, we're not." I launched at Calix. "He's mine. We're going to be together forever. No one will stand in our way!"

Damien hauled me back and trapped me between him and the wall. "Go."

Hands up in surrender, my perfect, handsome, caring love grinned lopsidedly and shrugged as if saying *what can you do?*

"No, Cal, please. Don't leave me." I pummeled Alexander—fighting and thrashing to break his iron grip. "I love you. I love—"

Gathering his clothes, he ducked through the curtain. The haze swept out of my mind, abandoning me naked in the bath with Alexander.

I darted under his arm for my towel. Splashing out of the water, my voice reached decibels unheard of by man. "What the fuck are you doing?!"

Eyes hard, Alexander climbed out. "I don't need to repeat myself. You two are done. Stay away from him."

"Excuse— You can't just— Don't walk away from me!"

Alexander strode off without looking back. A glass jar of peppermint bath salts bounced off his head. "Did you just—?" He whirled around as the lavender salts barreled toward his forehead. It cracked him between the eyes. "Fuck!"

"No, fuck you," I screeched. "How dare you crash into my life and tell me who to sleep with. I must've missed a lot about men and women the last eight years, because the last I remember, that's my choice and mine alone."

"Make your fucking choices, Galanis, but *not with him*," he roared, blowing me back. "He touches you again and I—"

"What? You'll what, Damien." I threw out my hands. "Tell me what you'll do, because I will be with him again."

"No, you won't." His voice was a low, dangerous hiss.

"Tonight, and tomorrow night. And the night after that." Hot, angry, and bitter—the words were flying out of my mouth faster than I could stop them. "I'll let him do *whatever* he wants to me, and I mean anything. Stuff I bet you and your innkeepers have never even—"

"Enough!" Storms raged in his darkening eyes, sparking electricity that jumped to his hand as he snapped it on me—readying to burn me where I stood.

"Do it," I rasped. "Go on. Do it!"

His veins popped, as unrestrained as the thousands of emotions that raged across that handsome, chiseled face. "Argh!" he bellowed, flinging away.

"No, not this time." I seized his collar, forcing him around. I slapped him across the face. "Kill me. Go on." Alexander blocked my next hit.

"Stop," he growled, ducking a punch.

"No! Calix and I aren't done, but we are." I hit and slapped and tore at him. His tunic ripped in half. "I won't do this with you anymore. We're ending it right now, so kill me."

I wrestled his hand back up, training it on my face. Images of me at the bottom of the basin flashed before my eyes. "Do it!"

"Get off!" Alexander threw me off, and I came rebounding back—jumping on and locking my legs and arms around him. "Hmm ggh hm agh!" he shouted into my breasts.

Punches rained on him, riding an explosion of fury that burned on a long, slow fuse for eight years, and finally detonated.

"Now's your chance. Avenge Galen. Kill the traitor." Grasping his ears, I slammed his head against the wall.

"Argh!" Alexander wrangled my arms. He shoved, flinging me off, and taking us both down. Limbs tangled, we pitched into the bath.

Our bodies swirled beneath the surface. Up, down, and sideways, we battled for dominance.

Alexander ripped my towel off me. I automatically covered myself and he used the panic to twist the cloth, and bind it around my chest—pinning my arms down. He dragged me gasping to the surface. "That's enough, Aella!"

I kneed him in the groin. His eyes bugged. Grabbing his crotch, Damien released me, doubling over.

"Will you kill me now?"

Damned if he didn't want to. Tartarus itself reflected in his flared nostrils and burning eyes.

"You promised this is how it would end. With my death. What are you waiting for?" I grabbed his arm, straining to get it up and pointed at me. My towel floated between us. "Go ahead. I won't stop you. Take your revenge. End your pain. One of us should!"

I raised a hand to strike him. Damien flashed. It happened so fast, I couldn't relay it even if I saw how. He secured my wrists over my head, locking them in place. Damien knocked my legs apart and plastered himself between them. I kicked back on his thighs, getting nowhere near his crotch.

"I said," he forced through clenched teeth, "that's enough."

I snapped and smashed my skull on his forehead. Dazed, he almost loosened his grip.

"Rhea and Cronus, woman! What the fuck is wrong with you?"

"What do you want from me!" The scream blew his brows up. "You're not happy unless I'm suffering, but that doesn't make you happy either. You h-hate me," I cried, voice cracking. "You want me gone, so why don't you just do it? I don't want to hurt anymore. End it for the both of us."

"Dammit, Aella. I won't kill you."

"Why?"

"Because—"

"Because why!"

"Because then you'd be dead!"

I blinked—surprise chasing my tears away. Damien's chest heaved like a boat in a storm. His wet locks dropped water as rain down his face, clinging to those impossibly long lashes. We gazed at each other, his confession hanging in the air between us.

"What... the fuck does that mean?" Disbelief dripped from my lips. "Because then I'd be dead? What? All of a sudden you don't want to kill me? What's the last two months been about, then?"

"Aella—"

"Is this some kind of game to you?" I cried. "Did you have your fun batting me around in your paws? Going off to torture some other girl to her breaking point now?" I bucked and twisted in his hold, uncaring of the extreme sexualness of the act. "Well, you have your fun with her. I'll be with Calix, letting him play his *games* with me and if you think you're going to stop—"

"For fuck's sake, will you shut up?" His mouth crashed on mine, catching me mid-shout.

Alexander skipped all pretense. He deepened the kiss, curling his tongue around mine and swallowing my cry.

I got a hand free and slapped his cheek. He rocked back, looking too dazed for it to be from the hit.

Panting, I surged forward and claimed his lips for my own. We attacked each other in a flurry of grunts, moans, and growls. Our tongues battled—viciously darting and defending in a fevered swordfight until Damien demanded, then forced my surrender. I moaned in his mouth as he tasted mine, then bit hard on his lip.

"Agh! Fuck." He snapped my head back and bit me in turn.

I only had cloud- and drug-fueled kisses with Calix to compare it to, but this kiss with Alexander was nothing like it was supposed to be. Neither kind, sweet, nor loving. We tangled like two people who thought they discovered a new way to hurt each other.

I fisted his hair, half ripping it from the roots. Alexander slammed me hard enough against the rim to leave a bruise. Scrabbling between us, I ripped his shirt the rest of the way and flung it somewhere with my towel. I raked my nails down his chest.

A pained groan pushed on my ear. So did the growing hardness between my legs. "Gods, I fucking hate your ass."

"The feeling is mutual."

Alexander licked a stripe up my neck to my chin, enticing a groan that he smothered with another kiss. My hands found his waistband, and drew it down and off his cock.

Clang! Clang! Clang! Crash!

"Whoops."

We jerked apart, hearts jumping out of both our chests. Voices filled the room, echoing on the final clanging rings.

"Man, do you know how to walk?"

"I tripped," someone bit back. "You could give me a hand, you know."

Alexander and I connected, and suddenly we were leagues apart.

I clapped my hands over my body—face heating up hotter than the tub. Alexander heaved over the side, one hand snagging his pants up and the other threw aside the curtain. He was gone before it crossed my mind to say something.

I don't know how long I sat there, touching my puffy lip and drowning under Alexander's phantom touches. Eventually, I dragged myself out and trudged past the fallen candlesticks and half a dozen broken bath salt bottles that saved me from potentially doing something even worse in that tub than letting myself sink to the bottom of it.

THAT NIGHT, I GOT A better idea of Calix's power's side effects. Waking up sweaty and jaw aching from clenching through the night, I accepted that his mind-drugging fog lifted when I could no longer see or touch him. If I didn't fall asleep in his arms, I fell asleep with the god of nightmares. There were no other options, except Alexander told me mine. Stay away from Calix or else.

I groaned thinking of Alexander. What the hell happened that night? It was like months of tension exploded into... Hades, I don't know what it became. His kissing me made no sense. My grabbing and kissing him back made no sense. Us hurting each other even while my hands stroked that muscled chest I peeked at much too often in combat training, and him stroking tender circles on my ass that pooled wetness between my legs then and now—made no fucking sense!

My feelings about Alexander Damien hadn't changed a lick from before. He was still a cruel, vicious jackass who dared rip a man from between my legs and say he was never to touch me again, as if he set rules for my body. If anything, I hated him more.

So why did I do it? Why did I pull down his pants? Why was I ready and willing for what came after?

I buried my face in the pillow, smothering air and the light. I didn't let myself breathe until thoughts of him finally floated away.

I couldn't think of Alexander now. From how quickly he abandoned me in that bath, he didn't plan to spare me more thought either. I just had to get through the night, then the morning, then the conversation with Calix telling him that he had to lie to his all-but-brother and continue, so I could sleep.

Peeling off my nightdress, I lay there in the dark, gazing at the gods painted in the stars. Mama told me the names and stories one night as we stretched out on our thatched roof. I'd gasp in wonder as she brought those stories to life, turning those dots in the sky to incredible illusions coming to life before my eyes.

It was the same scene I saw as I floated at the bottom of the basin, black bleeding into my vision. Of all the things to see at the end, fate brought me a good, happy memory with my mother. I didn't mistake this as a gift.

Oh no. It was far from a kindness to remind on the other side of that darkness, she was waiting for me.

I MUST'VE DOZED OFF because sometime later, a *thud* peeled my eyes open. A blurry figure stood beside me, hunched over my desk.

Alexander? My goodness, he did come. He's not pretending we didn't do what we did, but is that a good thing or...?

My vision cleared on a man who was definitely not Alexander Damien. Lysandros riffled around in my desk drawer and pulled out my pregnancy potion. He stilled when he saw I was awake.

"Lysandros," I said, slowly sitting up. "Put that back, please. Put that—"

He bolted—my last dose clutched in his grip.

"Lysandros!"

Tipping out of bed, I chased him into the common room and over a shouting Theron reclining in his armchair. Lysandros ripped out the door, beating it into the hall. I ran out and slammed into a hard body—popping them off their feet. We crashed to the floor in a flail of limbs.

"For the love of Hades," Sebastian groaned. Lysandros's cackling faded around the corner. "What do you think you're—?" Sebastian flicked down to me and surprise blew his irritated mask to shreds. "Never mind. I find myself quite fine with this."

It hit me like a bucket of cold water to the face. My nightdress was in a pile on the floor. I splayed across this man in nothing but a breast band and flimsy underwear. I wouldn't let myself look at how far they both shifted in the fall.

"Don't look!" Panicking, I did the first thing I could think of. I snatched his open long coat and forced it around me, tucking myself in his clothes. "Cover your eyes," I cried, slapping a hand over his face.

"—the situation." His voice floated into the hall. "It wasn't like that, man. I was high, but I'll never be that high."

Calix rounded the corner with Alexander by his side. The son of Zeus was covered in scratches and bruises from our fateful bath.

My lips parted but nothing came out as three pairs of eyes, and one blinking through my fingers, stared at each other.

Alexander's face chipped from stone. "You don't have to explain, brother. I understand the situation perfectly now."

Calix—the real Calix. The hard, broken Calix—slid off me like I wasn't there. "So do I."

The two stepped over us and continued on, leaving me with a thousand explanations dying on my tongue.

"Shit, Aella, are you okay?" Theron rushed out with a coat, covering me so I could untangle from Sebastian. He was another man to just walk away from me without a word.

Helped back into our dorm, I had no choice but to dress quickly and chase after that shit-licking, troublemaking menace born from the pits of Tartarus. I searched for him all over the castle and found Lysandros in the mess hall of all places—eating honey cakes and sausage with my potion lying innocently on the table next to him.

I grabbed it and stormed back, swallowing the dose on the way. Unfortunately, all those dramatics were necessary. Healer Helena explained that demigod seed was persistent seed. The gods wanted us to procreate. They wanted us to grow and spread until the population of worshipers and believers was enough to return them to Mount Olympus.

Preventing pregnancy required potions brewed by the most skilled children of Hecate, and it had to be taken in doses every morning for five days after *contact*.

Lysandros hadn't calmed down a fraction since the stadium. He still very much enjoyed scaring the crap out of us in various unpredictable ways, changing moods in the blink of an eye, and all around making our lives difficult—that morning was proof. Even so, one change was that he was a lot less free with handing out his apples.

Maybe Drakos reached him in the swirling pit of chaos that was his mind, because he had to know life in the academy was much better than a life of hard labor.

For some.

With Lysandros out of my mind, everything else flooded back in. I couldn't miss another day of classes, but that I had to do it with the memories of Alexander burned on my skin, Calix's coldness as he walked away, and another night of Hyacinth condemning me from beyond the lonely, unmarked hole I chose as her final resting place.

My pace slowed the closer I got to Hondros's class. The hall was packed with novices brushing past and knocking into me on their way to lessons.

"When will you die, traitor?" someone called.

"Show us your tits again before you do."

The group of guys laughed like hyenas. Their noise faded in the background as I stood before Hondros's room. I reached for the knob, pants picking up speed as it shrank away from me. It grew smaller. The roaring in my ears boomed louder.

I jerked my head down. My heart shot in my throat at the pool of blood seeping under the frame.

Dropping my hand, I whirled away. I would take whatever punishment for skipping his lecture twice in a row. I couldn't be here. I couldn't do this.

"Ah, Miss Galanis." Drakos entered the hall, bringing the shoving and hooting hyenas to a quick retreat. "Go in ahead. I'll be addressing your lecture group this morning."

"I... I..." What was I supposed to tell him? *No, Headmaster. I'll be skipping classes today.*

Taking a deep breath, I forced myself inside. It was early enough that all the seats weren't taken. I jumped on the opportunity to sit with my friends, relaxing a fraction as I claimed my place next to Daciana. Being in this room was hard enough. Doing it while sitting next to Sebastian after the morning we just had. That was asking too much.

Drakos climbed the dais and fell into soft conversation with Hondros. I had a feeling I knew what brought him out of his dim office. They talked until the room filled up. Silence fell without either one asking for it.

"Morning, novices," Drakos began. "I'm certain you have an inkling of why I'm here. I wish I could say I had good news, but as the matter stands, we've conducted two thorough searches of the academy and its grounds, and were forced to come to a grim conclusion. Hyacinth Kokkinos is missing and we suspect foul play."

I held very still—my only movement the slightly too fast rise and fall of my chest.

"But, sir, how is that possible?" one of the Titans asked. "She can't have left the grounds."

"We don't believe she left the grounds."

Whispers broke out. Everywhere I looked, I saw trainees connecting the dots.

Rue got to her feet. Her voice trembled. "You think she's dead, don't you, sir?"

"I sincerely hope that's not the case, and she turns up this evening with a valid explanation for her whereabouts, but... yes," he replied, inclining his head. "I've been in contact with her parents. They assure me their daughter would not shirk her duties, or hide away worrying everyone around her. After a week, we have to conclude reasons out of her control have kept her away."

"What are you going to do about it?" Sirena asked, voice hard. "Whoever did this to her will not get away with it."

Drakos shifted to her—as ever the controlled, placid headmaster. That morning he wore black as he always did, but there was something about the long overcoat, shiny boots, and iridescent sheen on his tunic that gave the air he was dressed for mourning. It was as though he chose that outfit to condemn her killer—me.

"That's not in question. Which brings me to the reason I'm speaking to you this morning." Stepping off the dais, he weaved through the aisles. "Now that the search aboveground is complete, it's time for the search below ground. As you all are now intimately familiar..." His soft baritone tickled my ear as he passed behind me. "I have the power to summon the dead from their resting places. If Hyacinth's body is somewhere on these grounds, she will come to me when I call."

White blotted out my mind.

"When that happens, imperial bone readers will arrive from the capital to examine the body and learn everything there is to know about her death."

Nothing was going through my head. Not even the signal telling my body to breathe.

"The culprit will be caught and given the punishment fitting of a heinous, cowardly murderer." Drakos passed in front of me. His dark orbs probed my soul. "Instructors are having the same conversation in every lecture hall, but I am here telling you all personally as those that knew Miss Kokkinos and spent every day with her.

"If you have information about her death, or indeed are responsible for her death, now is the time to make it known. There was never a single hope that you'd get away with what you've done, but you can spare me, the bone readers, Miss Kokkinos's family, and the imperial court much time and heartache if you confess now. You also spare yourself and reduce your sentence from execution to life imprisonment. Think carefully about what you do next," he said, voice soft. "This is the only offer of mercy you'll receive, and it's more than you deserve."

Silence spread like spilled ink.

Titans and Sisypheans looked around, flicking from novice to novice. At their feet, a pool of blood spread from Hyacinth's phantom body.

"Sir, I must speak." Sirena stood up, swinging every head in her direction—including mine.

"Yes, Miss Cirillo?"

"Forgive me, sir. I should've said something sooner, but I wasn't sure until now. I know who killed Hyacinth." Sirena leveled a finger. "It was Aella Galanis. She killed her."

The reaction was immediate.

"What?" Daciana shrieked.

"That's a lie!"

"What the fuck is wrong with you?"

My friends shouted over each other at once, piling abuse on Sirena. It all reached me from far away. There was only me and that accusatory finger.

"Enough," Drakos said. "Miss Galanis, stand up and come with me."

Daciana grabbed my shoulder, pushing me down and keeping me right where I was. "Sir, you cannot believe a word that comes out of her mouth. Sirena hates Aella and never made a secret of it. She attacked her the first day of classes and hasn't let up since. Everything out of her mouth is a lie."

Sirena reddened. "Bitch! That's not—"

"I said enough."

The command didn't rise higher than a conversational tone, but Daciana and Sirena closed their mouths. Drakos fixed on me.

"If Miss Galanis is innocent, the truth will bear out. Come with me."

I didn't fight. Rising from my seat, I followed Drakos out the door. Sirena walked right out of Hondros's room and followed us.

"I should come with you, sir, so I can tell you everything Aella's done to Hyacinth. She'll only lie or paint herself as the victim."

An emotion finally cracked my shell: disbelief. Was this woman serious? What *I've* done to Hyacinth? This psychopath offered her gold and a title to kill me, and now—

—she's seeing her plan through to the end. Hyacinth couldn't kill me, so now she'll have me executed for her murder.

At that moment, I finally saw the cold beauty of Sirena's plan. Of course the daughter of Hera was more than capable of killing me herself, but by using Hyacinth, she was prepared for every outcome. If Hyacinth succeeded, everyone won. If I killed her, she'd make sure the tribunal guards hauled me away. And if we both survived, Sirena would deny any involvement, and Hyacinth would ultimately go down for trying to kill me in the first place.

The shining imperial heir flies off to her golden throne without a mar on her perfect life, and the peasants she used and manipulated suffer.

She's smart, I thought, eyes narrowing to slits. *Smarter than I gave her credit. Being a jealous, obsessed monster didn't make her an idiot. If I don't do something, she'll not only get everything she wants, but she'll inadvertently give the goddess her wish. For the beast to go on a rampage and slaughter everyone in the Imperial Palace.*

That's where the tribunal will hold the sentencing for the deserter-turned-assassin who was under the charge of Maximos Damien's son. When they force me to reveal who I am, everyone in the room will have their own sentences passed out. And if I escape, there'll be no stopping me until I run out of bodies.

But what am I going to do about it?

An answer did not come.

I buried Hyacinth in one of the very holes his army of the dead used to emerge. She will burst from the earth, carrying the violent slash marks matching the report he received from Jason. They'll clap me in spelled irons so fast, I won't have a chance to get scared and release the beast.

"You are very quiet, Miss Galanis." Drakos faced ahead as we passed through the atrium and hall of gods. "No passionate remarks in your defense? No denial of the crime?"

I lifted my chin, straining to ignore the hole Sirena bore in my head. "No, sir. Why should I rant and cry? I had nothing to do with Hyacinth's disappearance. Just like you said, the truth will bear out."

"I'll tell you the truth," Sirena snapped. "The truth is Aella Galanis is a sneaky, underhanded traitor without a trace of morals or conscious. After she was dragged to this academy in *chains*, she's done nothing but make trouble for the imperial heirs to get back at Alexander for forcing her to come here.

"She got Galen killed. She had her no doubt lover, Scala, poison our group with his apples. She attacked my bird, Tawny. She provoked a fight that got nearly everyone in the novice wing killed, and she never misses a chance to get in our faces." We passed through the entrance, setting down the grand front stairs. "The night Hyacinth vanished, she told me she was going to confront Aella and tell her to back off. I guess we all know now how that went."

"Hmm," Drakos hummed, giving nothing else away.

"Again, I don't need to say anything," I spoke up. "Everything she just said is nonsense and you can ask anyone who doesn't have their heads up the asses of the imperial heirs. They've made my life hell since that terrible night with Galen. I have no idea what happened with Hyacinth, but I am asking myself why exactly Sirena is trying so hard to frame me?"

"Excuse me? What are you trying to say?"

"You know exactly what I'm saying."

Sirena bared her teeth. Behind Drakos's back, her hands morphed into harpy claws.

"That'll be enough from both of you. Miss Cirillo, put those away."

Jerking back, Sirena quickly regained human form.

"Since I have an accused, an accuser, and no confession, it's time I put an end to the matter." We climbed off the last step, standing small in the shadow of the castle. Drakos turned to us. "If Kokkinos's body is anywhere on this campus, she will join us momentarily. Before you're subjected to that sight, is there something you wish to tell me, Miss Galanis?"

"No, sir."

He slid past me. "Miss Cirillo?"

"Me? Of course not. I had nothing to do with this."

You had everything to do with this, and in the end, you won't be punished.

My eyes fluttered shut as Drakos began. "Rise."

This was for the best. Sirena's part in this could be denied, but it was me who killed her. Me who walked these halls knowing I was a danger to everyone I passed by. Calix refused to kill me. Unbelievably, Alexander refused to kill me. And every time I tried, the goddess stopped me.

It would take a feat I didn't want to think about right then to provoke the soldiers into giving me a quick death on the road, but as long as I never make it into that tribunal chamber, I will get my wish.

The pain will finally end.

I waited for the moment of truth. Any second, Sirena would crow her victory in mock horror, wailing "I knew it" as Hyacinth's body lumbered down the path. Drakos would have me thrown in the reflection room while the bone readers—children of the gods of medicine—used their powers to determine how she died. The goddess would scream and wail in my ear, but I would know no fear as her *glory* ended in failure and defeat.

Her *tsk, tsk, tsk* laugh echoed in my skull. "*Don't be so sure, pet.*"

I waited, and waited, and waited.

Finally, I opened my eyes, looking around for a sight of her. Was it supposed to take this long? When Drakos summoned his army in the stadium, they burst forth to do his bidding in minutes.

"Hmm." Drakos lowered his hands. "It would seem the matter is settled."

"What?" Sirena cried. "What do you mean? Settled how?"

The headmaster was calm straightening his coat and dusting off imaginary lint. "You saw for yourself, Miss Cirillo. Miss Kokkinos's body is not buried anywhere on these grounds. Not only would she have arrived by now, but I would've sensed her coming."

"She could've buried her outside the grounds. The traitor's been trying to escape since she got here."

"Miss Cirillo, are you saying that someone who found a way to get off these grounds undetected with a body in tow, would then turn around and come right back?"

His tone stained her cheeks. "No, but that doesn't mean she's innocent." Sirena swung on me, that accusatory finger returning. "All that proves is that she isn't as stupid as she acts. She knows you can summon the dead. She must've—must've burned the body or found another way to leave no trace."

My brows blew up my forehead. "I did what? Are you even hearing yourself? What part of mundane don't you understand? If anyone can burn a body to ash, I bet it's the girl who turns into a fire-breathing dragon."

"I only take the form of a dragon," she snapped. "I don't have any of its abilities, you inbred fool. Demigods only get one power."

"Don't sell yourself short, Sirena." My voice dropped to a low hiss. "You have many, *many* talents for killing."

Her expression shuttered closed. Too late for me to miss the flash behind her eyes. She knew I knew.

"Please, sir." She spoke to him, but gazed at me. "Don't let her get away with this."

"I'm not letting her get away with anything. There is simply no proof she harmed Miss Kokkinos. This battle of she said, she said does not count as proof either," he said when she opened her mouth. "The search for Miss Kokkinos or what happened to her will continue. For now, I want both of you to return to your lesson."

"Yes, sir."

Sirena just knocked my shoulder shoving past me and storming up the stairs. I followed at a sedate pace, chancing a look behind at Drakos one too many times.

What the hell happened? Where was Hyacinth?

My friends rushed me coming out of Hondros's class. I returned in time for the block to end.

"Aella, are you okay? What happened?"

"I'm okay." I hugged Nitsa back. "Drakos did as he promised and summoned her. She didn't come. She's not on this campus." I said it like a statement, but it was a question. I needed someone—anyone—to tell me how that was possible. Hyacinth was buried on these grounds. Why didn't Drakos's power work?

"But... that's good news," Nitsa said. "If he can't summon her, it means she's not dead. Gods, that's such a relief. I was so freaked out thinking someone in our group or sitting across from us in the mess hall was a cold-blooded killer who made a girl disappear."

I tensed in her grip.

"Now Drakos and the staff can focus on finding out where she really is. I just hope she's not trapped somewhere—alone and scared. It's been a week. She's running out of time."

"Yeah," I said, dropping my gaze. "I'm relieved too. We should head to history."

My friends trailed me, but they didn't let up on their theories about Hyacinth. Theron reminded that more than a few demigods in the academy had the power to end a life without leaving a trace. Tycho said Hyacinth didn't have time to make an enemy with such a power, she was too busy bowing and scraping after Sirena. Ionna said very little—adding that she was seeing a ton of futures, but none of them had Hyacinth in it. Daciana said she picked up Hyacinth's scent in many places around the castle, but it was fading.

I said nothing as I went from leading the group to trailing behind, desperately wishing I could just slip away unnoticed. *The cold-blooded killer you fear is right here, Nitsa. What will you all do when you find out?*

I passed the day in a daze, and was called on it many times. Proficient Catherine dismissed me after knocking me on my ass once. I didn't even move to defend myself against her. "If you don't care, novice, neither do I."

I just walked away, tucked myself against the platform, and thought of another stadium riddled with pits and holes. I didn't fare better in field medicine either. I mixed up two different berries and almost sent myself to the infirmary with hives and a nasty rash. Bad enough until I did it again. Not paying attention, I heard holly berries cure stomach cramps and nausea, instead of causes stomach cramps and nausea. Cassia banished me to Healer Helena.

"Don't worry, dear. It happens all the time." She helped me onto a bed and slid the bucket across with her foot just in time. I emptied my meager lunch. "I have plenty of potions on hand for this very situation. The field medicine instructors send at least two trainees to me a week."

"Thanks." I eased onto the pillow, clutching my stomach. It was frightening how quickly two red berries brought me down.

She returned with the potion and tipped my chin to help me swallow. Rather than direct me to combat training, she tugged on the blankets and drew them over me.

"It takes about an hour to work," she explained. "There's no use sending you to Commander Vasili in your current state. While we wait, you can tell me what's ailing you up here." Helena tapped my forehead.

"What do you mean?"

She raised a brow. "I've been doing this for a long time, dear. I'm a daughter of Circe—another powerful enchantress. But unlike children of Hecate whose powers come from within, mine come from without. I draw on the essence of living things to create my potions.

"This works better with plants, animals, and elements, but humans are not completely foreign to me. I sense when someone's wrong and their essence bears the dark stain of sickness. Sickness of the mind is just as prevalent as sickness of the body."

"My... mind isn't sick," I croaked, shuddering as another cramp seized my body.

"You carry a heavy burden, Aella Galanis. I've known this since I first laid eyes on you."

I said nothing for a long time. "What heals a sick mind?"

"I'm afraid there is no potion or spell that can. Some healing journeys can only begin when you take the first step."

What did that mean? When I took the first step? As if it was my choice to end the nightmares, rid myself of the goddess's curse, or do the impossible and make myself never feel fear. Some healing journeys never begin... because even a sickness of the mind can be incurable.

I flipped over—a cold, plain sign that I had no more to say. After a while, her footfalls softly led to her office. She shut the door and left me in peace.

When the potion did its work, I picked myself up and went straight to the mess hall. I couldn't stand to see Alexander—glistening and savage in the orb light as he made short work of everyone who stood against him. How crazy is it that I couldn't decide which I hated worse—his tormenting me or his pretending I didn't exist.

All day, he didn't so much as look my way. Not even when Sirena accused me of murder and Drakos led me out for what could've been the last time. He didn't look.

He didn't care.

I slammed my wine goblet down too hard. Sighing, I dropped my face in my hands. What was going on with me? Alexander hurt me. He boiled my blood, wrapped me in chains, dragged me to the one place I begged not to go, tortured my friends, tricked instructors into giving me endless assignments and punishing drills, got in between me and Calix, and then to make sure he thoroughly fucked with my head—Alexander said he didn't want me dead and that he hated me all while giving me such a searing kiss, my lips were still burning.

It was criminal all that he'd put me through and madness was the explanation for why after everything, I wanted to spare him having to cross my path before I did what I must do next.

The mess hall began to fill as trainees left their final lessons of the day. Soon, Calix was among them—arms slung around two girls.

I sat up straighter. I didn't care about whatever idea he got into his head when he saw me on the floor, tucked inside Sebastian's coat like the tamales I loved so much. And I *couldn't* care about Alexander and his warnings of what he'd do if he caught us together again. I needed to not dream. Calix's power was my only saving grace.

Chewing my lip, I barely noticed my friends piling inside. *I'll follow him out when he's finished. Catch up to him in the hallway. He won't need an explanation for why we can't stop. He knows what it is to need to escape the hurt.*

Alexander chose that moment to come in with Sirena hanging off his arm. Her eyes found me immediately, and the hatred in them reached inside, stirred nothing, and dissipated. I dismissed her, flicking back to Alexander. Flashes of me wrapped around him like a tree nymph quickened my pulse.

There were many reasons he couldn't see me go after Calix. I wasn't ready to find out what he'd do if he discovered we were still tumbling. He found a new way to hurt me, and I couldn't say which was worse.

It'll be safer to find Calix in the library. He preferred to slip off into nectar dreams there.

A figure blocked my view. "You, novice."

I glanced up at a round, freckled face; long curly hair; spectacles; and an annoyed expression like I forced her to talk to me.

"Do I know you?" I asked.

"Do you think you know me?" Rolling her eyes, she dropped a small, brown parcel beside my goblet. "Someone gave me five gold coins to deliver this to you with a message, like I'm a damn daughter of Hermes," she added under her breath. "They said: *next time be more careful. There won't always be someone around to clean up your messes. Stay strong. It won't be long now. Your destiny approaches.*"

"My destiny approaches?" I unwrapped the parcel, peeling away the waxed paper. "What's that supposed to mean—?"

I removed the final layer, revealing my gift. I screamed and flung it away from me. Lying within the folds was a dried, flattened purple flower.

A hyacinth.

"For the glory of the goddess."

I snapped up, landing on the stranger's back as she swiftly darted away from me. I was up and chasing her in a blink, blowing past Theron and Tycho.

"Aella? Hey, Aella, what's wrong?"

"Come back," I shouted. "Come back here!"

She broke out into a sprint, racing to the exit. A group of proficients chose that time to arrive. Moving fast, she slipped within the crowd.

"Hey! Stop her!" The same crowd jostled, shouted at, and shoved me.

"What do you think you're doing, novice? Get out of our way."

I forced through them and spat out into the hall. Head swinging left to right, I searched the bobbing head for a crown of golden curls. *No one.*

She was gone.

Sirena

"He did nothing. Nothing!" I slashed the bed canopy, turning fine gossamer waves into shredded ribbons. "That fool Drakos just let her skip off without even questioning her."

"Are— Are you sure she killed Hyacinth?" Tessa's blubbering was endless. She'd been red-rimmed and puffy-faced since Drakos confirmed the search for Hyacinth would not end in good news.

"Of course she did it."

Tawny screeched her agreement. The owl rode by shoulder, bumping the side of my cheek to comfort me. I barely noticed.

"But it doesn't make any sense. Why would Hyacinth tell you she was going out to meet Galanis that night? She can't stand her. What would they have to talk about?"

I turned my back on her, moving to my window. It made perfect sense when you knew Hyacinth was biding her time until she could finally get the mundane shit stain alone to kill her. That night, Hyacinth broke off after we left the mess hall, nodding at me to let me know she was off to complete her end of the deal.

I didn't know what to think when I saw Galanis alive and well the next morning, doing the toova morning-after slink-off after Calix spent the night fucking her. I guess I assumed Hyacinth messed it up again, and wasn't able to get her alone. But then she never showed up that day... or the day after... or the day after that.

The idea that a useless Sisyphean who'd been stuck on the same proficient in self-mastery class for over a month, took down a daughter of Limos, was laughable. There was simply no way Galanis bested Hyacinth.

But now... I balled my fists, teeth bared in the window's reflection.

"Galanis did this, Tessa. There's no question. What is in question"—I faced her, eyes hard—"is if we're going to let her get away with it?"

She blinked at first like she didn't understand what I said. Her expression changed in an instant. "Fuck. No."

"Good. Now, here's what I need you to do…"

An hour later, I stood outside his room. Hondros's back was to me when I came in. He was in the process of changing out a tapestry and replacing it with another famous battle that would serve as the backdrop to tomorrow's lesson. I fought a smirk.

How funny it was that a great strategist like Timothy Hondros, who led the charge against a colony of giants and didn't lose a single soldier, was bested by an eighteen-year-old novice.

And it wasn't even that hard.

"Good evening, sir."

He whipped around, taking the tapestry he just hung with him. It fluttered around his shoulders—the Labours of Heracles and the three golden apples no more.

"What do you want?" he forced. Hondros took a step to the side, closer to the short sword lying on his worktable.

"Go ahead," I said. "Pick it up. You'll need it."

He straightened, raising his chin. "You've come to kill me."

I laughed. "Uh, what? Is that how you thought this was going to end? By the Fates, why on earth would I kill you when you're so useful? Mother is delighted to hear I'm passing all of my classes with high marks. Why break in another instructor when I've beaten you just fine."

"Then what do you want!"

"I'd watch that tone if I were you." I bore down on him, amusement leaking out my pores. "I want one thing and one thing only.

"You're going to kill Aella Galanis."

Hondros frowned. "I beg your pardon?"

"You heard me," I hissed. "I want her dead. Tonight. *Now*. Another second that she breathes air, is a second I'm tempted to bring your world crashing down around you. I hope that motivates you to move quickly."

"No."

I stopped with one foot on the dais. "What did you say?"

"I said no. I will not kill a trainee. That you would think I would. That you would even ask." He shook his head, gazing at me in— Was that disappointment? "You've lost your way, girl. That you can't see how far you've fallen is the greatest tragedy."

My muscles went rigid.

"You play with lives and order executions because you can't see the enemy is out there," he said, gesturing to the window. "They are not within these walls. They're not your fellow demigods. Until you see that..." Hondros looked me up and down like he'd never seen such a disgraceful sight. "You'll never be fit to sit upon the seat of Hera."

"Shut up!" I shrieked, bounding up the dais. My ringing slap echoed off the stone walls. "Shut up! What do you know of enemies? You haven't lived a single day in the palace, forever looking over your shoulder for the supposed friend waiting to plunge a knife in it. I fought for what's mine, and I'm not giving it up for the likes of you, or that bitch!"

I backed him against the podium.

"She dies, Hondros. Galanis doesn't live to see another dawn, or it's your head. From Hondros the Giant Slayer, to Hondros the Rapist," I flung, delighting in his wince. "You'll be worse than disgraced. There'll be nothing left for you in this realm or the next. Tell me, is protecting that mundane worth your life?"

"It's worth my honor. Your lies will not make me into an abuser, and your threats won't turn me into a murderer." He pushed away from the podium, facing me down. "Especially because those threats are hollow. You just admitted you won't take the chance of pulling your disgusting, vile manipulations on another instructor. It's too important that no one else finds out that you can't read."

I jerked like he struck me, lurching back.

"Oh, yes. I know the truth. It was the only conclusion after the lengths you went through to get out of writing your own papers. You can't read or write." His words were daggers launched from his lips. "Considering who you and your mother are, that fact is unconscionable. How you reached this age without learning is one matter, but what I suspect is most pressing in your mind is that when the current Hera councilwoman finds out, she'll never name you her successor.

"Even if you learn by the time she steps down, the shame and humiliation of an illiterate imperial heir would follow you throughout your reign. You'll have lost authority before you ever had it. If you're so incompetent that it took you decades to learn letters children are singing in the nursery, where else are you lacking?"

"I lack nothing," I screeched. "I was never incompetent. I wanted to learn but—" I caught hold of my tongue, sense returning. This wasn't a story a lowly piece of dung like him was entitled to. I owed Hondros no explanation. I certainly did not owe him the satisfaction of believing he got under my skin.

I was in charge here. I had him under my thumb, wing, and claw as I would all of Olympia. Nothing would stop me, not even myself. At all costs I would have power... and Alexander.

My mind flashed to that night. Following the request of my love, I flew behind Sebastian Barba, the unsuspecting gnat over his shoulder. Sebastian strode through the dorm wing, and up ahead stood Alexander. Sebastian turned right for his dorm, and my Xander turned left.

I followed Xander of course. What business did he have in the Sisyphean wing? What was he doing going into one of their gross bathrooms?

I flew inside, and saw it all.

Alexander flying into a rage and ripping Calix off Galanis. How many times did he catch me with other men and didn't blink an eye?

Alexander threatening Calix if he ever touched her again. Since when did he care about the toovas Calix stuck his dick in?

Alexander battling with her while she ordered him to do the first sane thing that came out of her mouth—kill her.

And what did he say? What did he do!

I breathed hard, skin rippling as the hold on my power slipped. I could be any flying creature I imagined, and right then, I was imagining two dozen creatures that could rip out Aella's throat before she thought to scream.

When she ripped off his clothes, spreading her legs like a bitch in heat to fuck my Xander, I pounced on the two Sisypheans that walked in. I changed, shoved the guy into the candlesticks, and changed back too fast for them to notice. I ended their illicit tryst as quickly as I decided it was time for the traitor to go—permanently.

I lifted my chin, the smirk riding my lips once again. "You're wrong. Just because I'd prefer not to have another tiny, wrinkled dick rutting between my legs, doesn't mean I won't do the same to the grizzled old man they choose to replace you. Tonight ends one way—either Aella Galanis dies or you're hauled out of here in chains.

"Choose quickly," I sang, climbing off the platform. "The choice will be made for you in about five—no, four minutes."

"You can get off this path, Cirillo."

I snorted, making for the door.

"The blackmail, the lies, the fear. Would you rather live your life like this, or would you rather I teach you?"

"Teach me? Teach me what?"

"To read."

I halted in my tracks, grin fading.

"And write," he continued. "You're quick and clever. I have no doubt you'll learn easily once you have a teacher to set you to the task. Your future is still within your reach. If you can lie and scheme your way to it, imagine how much better it'll feel when you earn it on your own merits? That is the better path," he said softly. "It isn't riddled with insecurity."

I shook, fists balling and unballing at my sides. Insolent, presumptive peasant. What was he implying? That I was insecure? That I'd always feel I didn't earn my seat and my place on my own merit? Nothing could be more laughable. It was me out there training morning and night—learning to fly in every form, from the cumbersome bee to the iron-winged basilisk. I learned to navigate lumbering figures fifty times my size. I never quit. I never stopped.

The seat of Hera was my birthright. I earned it by being the best, and if I wanted to sit around reading dusty tomes, I could do that too.

And I do.

My lips trembled. I bit down on them hard.

I did want to learn. I was tired of pretending I knew what the signs on the roads and shops read. Sick of paying people to read to me or write my assignments. Ashamed of the reason I didn't learn long ago.

All that could change. I turned, lips parting.

Voices floated through the door.

"—think she needs help."

All that would change, but Aella Galanis wouldn't be dead.

My expression hardened. "Time's up, Hondros. What's it going to be?"

"I won't—"

I ran to him, falling on hands and knees before the dais as the door banged open. Healer Helena rushed in.

"Timothy? Timothy, what's going on? I was told a trainee was hurt."

"They will be," I hissed under my breath to Hondros. "If you give the right answer."

"No! Helena, whatever she makes you see is a lie," he bellowed. "It's all lies—"

I whipped to Tessa behind the doorframe. "Do it!"

"Lies? Timothy, what are you...?" Helena swayed—rocking forward and back as one does when Hypnos drags them off their feet into sleep. Shaking herself, she came to and flicked between me and Hondros. Horror leached her color. "Timothy!"

"Helena, you must not believe your memories. They're false—"

I burst into wails, drowning out his desperate pleas.

"Get away from her," she bellowed. "You monster. How could you!" Helena picked up and dragged me away. "You're entrusted with these trainees. To teach them strength as well as honor. You're a disgrace."

"No, listen to me. She is manipulating you!"

Helena's lips twisted. "That is what men like you all say."

"Sirena, stop this," Hondros said, rushing us. "Tell her the truth—"

The healer slashed the air. The fallen tapestry came to life and smothered Hondros. Knocked off his feet, he thrashed and fought, shouting beneath the heavy threads. It wrapped him shoulders to feet. He was going nowhere.

"Oh, Healer Helena." I sniffed and whimpered against her chest. "Please, I want to go."

"Of course, dear. You're safe now. It's over." Her concern vanished looking at him.

"The headmaster will be along shortly for you, Timothy. The imperial guards will follow after." She spat on him. "I hope never to hear your name again."

"Wait."

Helena led me away, murmuring soothing nonsense in my ear.

"Please, wait! I was enchanted. She forced me to do those things to blackmail me. Helena, listen!"

She didn't so much as turn her head. Helena helped me out of the room, preparing to slam—

"All right," Hondros bellowed, spittle flying across three aisles. "All r-right. I'll do it."

I ripped free of Helena. "Tessa."

"Sirena? What…?" Tessa's power washed over her. The healer collapsed in the pile at my feet.

Stepping over her, I swiped away the fake tears. "You really thought that would work, didn't you?" I asked. "Tell her the truth and she'll believe you. Of course she will. You've been friends for years. Aww, too bad."

Hondros started to cry.

"Ugh. Have some respect for yourself." I crouched beside him. "You experienced for yourself what'll happen with that memory in her head. She won't believe you. Drakos won't believe you. And the imperial tribunal that strips you of rank and tosses you in a cell won't believe you either. So what will you do?"

"As y-you ask," he sobbed.

"No, I want to hear you say it."

Starting and stopping, his jaw worked to form the words. "I will kill… Aella Galanis."

"Tonight."

Slowly, he nodded.

"Say. It."

Hondros dropped his head to the stone, the light behind his eyes dimming to nothing. "Tonight."

Aella

"She has curly hair, brown skin, and freckles. You haven't seen her around?"

"No."

"Not anywhere? She looked older. Has to be a competent, or maybe an expert."

Theron just shrugged. "Aella, I'm sorry. I don't know everyone in the castle. What's the deal with her anyway?"

"She... She said..." My friends were staring at me from their seats around the common area. They were waiting for an explanation for why I spent all of dinner questioning them and random people in the mess hall about that woman. "She just said something really disturbing to me. It felt like"—I swallowed hard on the truth—"a threat."

"What?" Ionna kicked off her blankets and crossed to me. "What did she say?"

Didn't matter the words because I got the message. The goddess has worshipers here, and they took care of Hyacinth's body so that I would stay here. There's only one reason that could be.

In five simple sentences, she told me to run.

"Something about what happens to traitors who don't watch their back," I got out. "Freaked me out to hear that from a person I've never seen before." *Freaked me out more than I can say.*

"Gods, of course it did. But whoever she is, she wasn't too smart to announce herself. Now we know to watch out for her." Ionna tugged me to the couch, the blankets, the plate of honey cakes, and the warmth of my friends. "We've got your back."

"Thank you, guys. I hope you know how much you all mean to me. I appreciate everything you've done—"

Lysandros tackled me from behind, sending us both crashing on the couch. He tickled me into submission, bit one of my flapping arms, then laughed when Tycho and Nitsa chased him off. I sat there nursing my chewed-up arm, cursing the name Lysandros Scala. Even more so when he came back and splayed across my lap, making himself comfortable.

Eventually, the cursing stopped. Theron pulled out a deck of cards. Daciana told us of life in her home. Ionna regaled us with some of her wildest visions—including one of Madame Remis and Commander Vasili kissing passionately. I was too kind to say that one was very real.

We laughed, joked, and talked into the night until one by one, we drifted to our beds. I lay there in the dark—thankful for Ionna, Tycho, Daciana, Theron, Nitsa, and maybe Lysandros. I was thankful at the very least... for the chance to say goodbye.

Theron's breaths evened out, signaling he made his descent into Hypnos's arms. I swung my legs to the floor. Fully clothed, I shoved my boots on, dumped the books out of my pack, and filled it with clothes, essentials, and the last of the honey cakes.

I slipped out the door, closing it softly behind me, and ran.

I ran through the dorm hall and out into the atrium, making one stop on the way. My scurry down the grand stairs would've ended with another bone-breaking fall with a single slip on the marble, but I made it all the way down, proving the goddess of good future never doled her hand when it mattered.

Racing to the point where lawn became forest, I disappeared into the tree line.

Branches ripped and tore at me, reminiscent of the night I ran through poisoned rain, fleeing to the gorge—my last hope of freedom. That's how it always is in the end. No one walks to their last hope. They run, crawl, limp, and drag themselves to it, because inevitably there is always someone behind, ready to take it away.

I didn't know how her worshipers got into the castle, or if they were always there, but I did know they would never get their hands on me again. Once the ritual was complete, she'd have complete control over the beast. She'd turn me at will, and her slaughter would begin in Deucalion Academy—with my friends.

Dryads welcomed me on my path, flinging bits and bobs at my head, and racing to keep up with me. I just ran faster—not slowing for ensnaring branches or tangled vines.

The gate appeared through a break in the trees, daring me to challenge its mettle. Slowing, I tripped to a stop before the wrought iron, pants wracking my chest. For a moment, we stared at each other. I saw only one barrier, but I knew another—possibly half a dozen more—awaited me.

All those books and spells, magical theories and the rules that governed each child of Hecate. For weeks I stuffed my head for an answer other than the one I already had. I know what'll get me through a barrier I shouldn't cross.

I withdrew the dagger from my pack.

My life must be in danger.

Moonlight reflected off the blade and broke through the gloom shadowing my pale cheeks. This was the only way. The ritual cannot be completed.

"What are you doing, child?"

The goddess's fated thread of victory snaps here.

Grasping the hilt with both hands, I positioned the blade above my stomach. Pain throbbed my fingertips, but she wouldn't be fast enough.

"Stop!"

I closed my eyes and plunged.

Hands gripped my wrists, snapping them back. "Whoa!" The dagger was wrenched from me, causing me to stumble forward into—

I blinked open. Moonlit-touched lakes blinked back.

—Sebastian's chest.

"What the fuck!" I threw myself away, snagged on a root, and fell flat on my ass. "What are you doing here?"

"Isn't that for me to ask?" Sebastian shook his head at the dagger. "Suicide, Galanis? Because you killed Kokkinos in self-defense? A tad dramatic, don't you think?"

"Wha— Wha— How—?" I couldn't breathe—couldn't speak—scrambling and crawling to get away from him as fast as I can. "How did you know that? How did you get here? You weren't here, then you were in front of me." I whipped back and forth, brain seizing. "You followed me again. How did you follow me? Where did you come from!"

Sebastian closed the distance. "I would be happy to answer your questions if you slow down enough to let me—"

"Stay back!" I snatched up a rock and flung it at his head. Sebastian blurred—going out of focus like the world does when you're underwater.

The rock sailed through his skull.

I screamed.

"Come now, that's an overreaction," he breezed. "You're in an academy full of demigods."

"Stay away from me, stalker!"

He stopped approaching, holding up his hands in surrender. "There. Can the screaming stop now? I'm not a stalker. Well, not by the actual definition. Someone else has been following you around day and night. They just report to me."

I threw another rock at him. His cocked brows shimmied like caterpillars as it once again passed through him. "Really?"

"What do you want with me!" I didn't know my voice could reach such decibels, but if it ever would, now was the time. A desperate midnight run to stab and haul my bleeding body through the barrier spells, was interrupted by a crazed lunatic who admitted to having me followed day and night. My stress was understandable.

"Again, I would be happy to tell you. Let's start with you taking a few deep breaths."

"Let's start with me fucking you up!"

"You'll find that a difficult task," he deadpanned.

I threw everything at him—rocks, twigs, branches, and my pack. It all passed harmlessly threw him.

Lungs burning, I collapsed against a trunk, out of ammunition.

"That's what I like about you, Galanis. You don't give up easily." He waved the dagger. "So, what the hades is this about?"

"None of your business," I wheezed. "Fuck off back where you came from."

"If I may..." Sebastian dropped down beside me. I was too drained to prevent him. "Let me see if I can put this together myself.

"You've been trying to escape the academy since you arrived. At some point, you reasoned that the barrier spells let through demigods who are in mortal danger, and you thought if that loophole would let you in, then it'll let you out."

I said nothing.

"So, tonight you got a dagger from one of the training rooms and planned to stab yourself, bind the wound, haul yourself over, and travel as fast as you're able to the nearest town before you bleed out." Sebastian spoke like we were two comrades sitting down for a chat. "The plan started out well. You're correct the barrier spells will let you through. If the school is ever attacked, it won't do for us all to be trapped in an invisible cage with no way out.

"But where you veer from genius to fatally stupid is the last stage in your plan. The nearest town is a seven days' ride. You'll be on foot with a wound in your stomach and monsters on your trail. You'll be long dead before you get there."

Slowly, I shifted, meeting his gaze. "At least, I won't be here."

He hummed. "This isn't your only option, you know. I can—"

"Why were you having me followed?" I sliced in.

"Because you're different." Sebastian dropped his head against the bark, peering through the leaves at the Cassiopeia constellation. "I sensed it from the moment I saw you. There's an— I don't know another word for it. An infection in your soul, Galanis. It shifts and moves and hides, but it's always there."

I gaped at him. Whether I was surprised by his response, or that for the first time, he gave me a straight one, I couldn't tell. "You *sensed* it?"

He nodded. "I wanted to know what you are, and if you're dangerous. I had a ghostly companion of mine follow you around—discover what you're keeping secret."

Alarms went off in my head, signaling her arrival. "*Kill him.*"

"I assume the eight-foot winged beast you turned into when you killed Hyacinth has something to do with it?"

"*Kill him!*"

Her words were claws through my skull. "Sebastian, stop," I cried, clutching my head. My talons pierced through my skin.

"It's okay, Aella. If you change, you can't hurt me, remember?"

I stilled as the sentence penetrated my fear. *I can't hurt him. My claws will go right through him. Whatever she does... he's safe.*

She screamed at me, pounding her divine voice against my brain. I ached, but I did not fear. *This time, she can't make me kill.* My claws retreated.

"So... you know?" It came out as barely a whisper.

"Not everything. I know what Linus saw." He blew out a breath. "I tried to find out the rest, but I've been dealing with a particularly stubborn lost soul who doesn't trust me worth a damn."

"A lost soul." I was taking this surprisingly well. "You were lying about your powers."

"Through my teeth."

I chuckled. "What can you do?"

"Does that matter?"

"If you want me to fill in what that stubborn soul didn't share, you bet your ass the lies stop now."

"Fair enough. What do you want to know?"

"You can see the dead?"

"I can see souls that haven't moved on to Hades. When we die, we all find ourselves at the gates with Kharon on the other side waiting to ferry us where we belong. Some spirits can't get through the gate—for various reasons."

My brows drew together. "If that's your power, how did you lose form? Demigods only get one."

"My power isn't that... defined," he finished. "Hades was both the god and the realm. His power was his domain. In a way, I was born of hades the place, not Hades the god. Hades doesn't exist in this realm, and when I choose, neither do I."

"And you can see the lost souls because they're not of this realm either."

He dipped his chin. *Yes.*

The pieces came together. "So with this power, you used it to have a soul stalk me and violate my privacy. Have they told you I sneak honey cakes out of the mess hall? Or how about the freckle under my left breast?"

"The screaming is about to start again, isn't it?"

Fury reignited in my chest. "Keep your form so I can slap you, Barba! Do you have any idea how creepy that is?"

Sebastian grinned—an unwise move. "Ghosts are everywhere. No matter where you are, chances are there're at least three floating behind you. Wave, Galanis. We've got about a dozen listening in on this conversation."

I swept the darkness, unease climbing my spine. I could've gone my whole life without knowing that.

"All I did was ask one to find out why you're like no one I've come across—dead or alive. The actions were creepy, but the suspicions—" He pinned me with a look. "Tell me they're not valid, Galanis. Tell me you're not a danger to everyone here."

I tried to hold his gaze. Flicking away, I said, "I can't."

"Then you understand why I had to know."

"That I understand, but this I don't." I pointed to the dagger. "Why did you stop me? What difference does it make to you if I don't make it to the next town?"

"I stopped you for many reasons," he replied. "The first will make you hate me, but the second will make you stay."

Tensing, I shifted away from him. "Why will I hate you, Sebastian?"

He was still grinning. "Remember you said the lies stop now."

"Tell me."

"I stopped you from embarking on a journey of certain death, because as a ghost, you're of no use to me. There is a lethal, unstoppable beast lurking inside you, and I believe she'll serve me well. With the right binding spells, of course."

Sebastian did not shift out of the realm, allowing my palm to smack its print across his cheek. "Goodbye, Sebastian." I darted and grabbed the dagger from his grip. "We won't see each other again."

"She tried to hit me too when she heard my plans for you," he called at my retreating back. "I had to promise I'd protect you above all else just to get a 'fuck you.' But it was me she woke when you came here with that dagger," he said, raising his voice. "Saving your life has earned the privilege of sharing your mother's story."

I stumbled, eyes widening. *My mother's soul? He spoke to her? She gave him answers?*

Does it matter?

"No," I shouted. "I don't care what she has to say. Nothing will make up for what she did to me. Especially not sending you here to stop me. I know the true reason she wants me alive."

"Aella, I'm not talking about that monster in human skin who kidnapped you when you were a baby. I mean your true mother, Elara. The one who named you after a warrior, and turned back at the gates of hades to watch over you all your life."

My feet slowed.

Dagger falling through numb fingers, I turned around.

Sebastian

Aella appeared through the trees, skin paler than moonlight. "What did you say?"

"Tell her." Elara tried to shake me, giving no care that her arms were passing through me. "Tell her the truth."

"I said Maia Galanis was not your mother. She stole you from your real family, and brought you to a faraway port town where no one would track you down."

Aella held still, staring at me through the trees. "You're lying."

"I'm not."

"Maia was my mother."

"She is not!" Elara flew to her daughter, again trying to take her into her arms. "You are mine. My baby. My Aella."

Seeing the two of them side by side, there was no denying they were mother and daughter. Elara gifted her daughter the same crown of spun gold, her full lips, and those haunting eyes. No wonder Maia whisked her far away where no one would notice these otherworldly beauties shared the same face.

I stood up, facing her across the ghostly audience riveted on our every word. Ghosts were nosy little shits, but they didn't have much else going on in their afterlife.

"You were born Aella Vanda, the first child of Xenos and Elara Vanda. They were a noble family that ruled over Crassus—a city in the north. The Vandas had a traitor in their household. A servant who, it turned out, served another master." I flicked to Elara. "Who?"

She glared. "I will tell you no more, son of Hades. That is Aella's story to tell. You are to tell mine."

Aella definitely gets her stubbornness from you.

"She won't tell me who this traitor served," I announced. "The point is when you were born, you proved to be special in some way. She won't tell me what made you special either. But somehow, it made you the perfect host to the creature that's inside you."

I paused for Aella to say something, but still... nothing.

"That servant slaughtered your parents while they slept, then handed you to Maia. Maia raised you until you were old enough for the lamia—"

"Wait. You know about the lamia?"

I motioned to Elara. "Your mother knows. She was with you in the cave, Aella. All those years. Every day."

Aella swayed on her feet. She sat down hard, gripping the tree root to keep her falling the rest of the way down. "This isn't happening. It's not real."

"It's all real, Aella, and you knew it, didn't you?" Kneeling beside her, I tipped her chin, gazing in those teardrop-flecked eyes. "Elara won't tell me exactly what happened, but she did say that Maia Galanis sentenced you to years of misery and isolation. She helped put that creature inside you. No true mother would do that to their child."

Her chin trembled in my hand, tears spilling down her cheek. "But why? Why me?"

"I was hoping you would tell me that."

Aella's expression changed in a blink. "What? Tell you why I'm so *special* so you can use me too?" She batted my hand away. "Goodness, I almost fell for it. There is no Elara Vanda. There was no unassuming servant who turned traitor."

Elara choked on a sob.

"You're one of them, aren't you?" Her eyes narrowed to slits. "One of her worshipers."

"Whose worshipers?"

"Save it," she snapped. "You gave yourself away by admitting you've had me watched. You saw what I did to Hyacinth that night and where I put her. *You* did something to her body. *You* sent me that awful parcel and the messenger to go with it. And then *you* ran out here to stop me before I ruined her plan to complete the ritual again. You're sick, you know that?"

I shrugged. "I do know, but not because of any of the confusing things you just said."

"Get away from me. I'm done with your lies."

"Barba," Elara cried. "Tell her!"

I looked into her daughter's chipped-from-ice orbs. "When you were seven, you found an injured baby siren washed up on the shore. It was too young to have a voice or kill you, but you didn't know that. You just saw a creature that needed help."

Her snarl faded away.

"You brought it to a cave where you bound its broken wing, and fed it food you snuck from home. One morning, you went to see her and she was gone. Her wing was healed and she flew away. But you never told a soul about those weeks you cared for a monster that would one day become a killer of men. You feared you'd be punished for your compassion.

"Aella, Maia never knew what you did. No one knew what you did. So how could I know if I wasn't told by the silent, unseen companion who has always been by your side?"

She tossed her head. "No, I— Someone must've seen then. You can't—"

"Do you want more? Elara's got dozens of stories like that one. Things that only the two of you know. Please, I can do this all night."

"Okay!" she burst out. "Maybe you are talking to someone who claims to be my mother, but that doesn't mean I can trust you."

"Who asked for your trust? I want your service."

"Fuck you, Barba."

"Yeah, that's the general sentiment I've been getting from the Vanda women, but at least my reasons for wanting you as my ally are noble."

"People only need allies in a war," she spat. "And I won't fight yours."

"Then fight yours." My reply was calm. "This can be a mutually beneficial relationship. You want that thing out of your soul, don't you? When you and I have done what we must, I will devote all my resources to curing you. You can have your life back."

"In exchange for...?"

"You can't control what's inside you. It's being controlled by someone else," I said. "There are ways to ensure that someone else doesn't use the creature to betray me and return you to their side. There are ways to ensure that creature serves me instead. Binding spells. Wards. Oaths of fealty.

"Agree to those and I'll give you something you want right now." My gaze drifted to the gate. "I'll free you from the academy."

"What? You can't."

"I can." I took her hands, channeling my power through them. Aella grew fuzzy. Undefined. She disappeared.

She ripped away from me. "What was that? What did you just do?"

"I phased you out of the physical realm," I said, sweeping out a hand. "The gate and the ward spells are a part of this world. I've always been able to walk right through them. I can transfer the power to you, and I've already proved that. It was me that prevented Zervas from turning the novice class into a mass of charred, unidentified bodies."

"That was you?"

"There was never any need for that dagger, Vanda. I will take you anywhere you want to go."

"Don't," she whispered. "Don't call me that. It's too soon."

"All right, if you wish."

Elara knelt beside her daughter, stroking her cheek with a touch she couldn't feel.

I did favors for the dead in exchange for their loyalty, service, and information. But there are some desires not even I can fulfill.

"You can get me out of here tonight?" she asked softly. "You can take me to the border?"

"Forget the border. I can take you directly to the mundane dominion." I dipped my chin as her eyes widened. "Although, I don't recommend it. Strange place. Even stranger people."

She seized my shoulders. "You can really take me to the mundane dominion? Right now? Tonight?"

"I really can *after* you swear by those binding oaths that we discussed, and make clear that you understand one day I will come for you and bring you back, so you can hold up your end of the arrangement."

Aella leaned away, dropping her hands. "You still haven't told me what my end of the arrangement is."

"Nor will I. Not until you're bound to keep my secrets. Don't give me that look," I said. "You've yet to tell me all of yours. I'm very eager to know how that creature was put inside you, and who holds its chains if not you. Care to share?"

She looked away, lips pressed in a thin line. The pretty little hypocrite had nothing to say.

"You're asking me to transfer those chains to you," she finally replied. "Without knowing what you'll make me do. How do I know you're not twice the monster she could ever be?"

"You don't," I whispered—soft and sly as the grin tugging my lips. I had her. I could feel it. "But this monster is willing to take an oath in return. When it's all over, I will free you from myself and the beast. Your life will be completely your own. Did *she* make the same promise?"

Aella didn't shake or nod, but she didn't have to. You don't steal a babe from their crib and stash them away in a mountain prison, just to one day pat them on the head and say "you can go now." Those chains were meant to stay. Whether she liked it or not, she was looking at the only person who could set her free.

Eventually.

"I don't know," she stalled. "I need to think."

"It took you how long to decide to plunge a knife in your stomach, but this you need to think about?"

Her glower peeled the skin off my face. "Don't push me, Barba. Swearing to serve a man who is clearly manipulating me takes a bit of mulling."

My smirk was full blown. I did like this one. She was no meek little thing, which I bet did not please Maia Galanis.

"Tell her this, boy," Elara said. "Darling, you must let him take you away from this place as soon as possible. Once you're free, betray him and his evil plans, but you must get free." She looked down an imperious nose at me—ever the noble. "Say it. Word for word."

Irritation ticced my brow. I could've done without "evil plans" but if I didn't say what she wanted, Elara Vanda wouldn't have another word to say to me for the rest of her afterlife. I needed her. She would keep Aella coming back to me. And in exchange for me looking out for her daughter, Elara would tell me what made her babe so special. That way I could see about creating a few unholy monsters that were loyal to me.

I forced her warning through clenched teeth—word for word.

Aella twisted around like she was looking for her. "Why does she say that?"

"Because you were right to fear that message," I repeated. "A worshiper of the dark one is in the castle. They followed you here, my Aella. The one who killed me. The one who stole you from your crib. They are here, and they're ready."

"Who is it?" Aella and I asked at the same time.

Elara's reply made my vein tic harder.

"She refuses to tell me. She thinks I'll run to them and make a deal to hand you over in exchange for having their power, and the power of the dark one on my side."

Aella gave me a hard look. "Would you?"

"I believe in the right to choose one's own path. Anyone who looks upon an innocent babe and sees a toy to control and enslave..." I flashed back to the first and last time I stood before the council. "They're my enemy as surely as they're yours."

"Hmm." Aella stood up, dusting off her hands. "You've given me a lot to think about, Barba. Tonight was an insane moment of panic. Stumbling through the forest with a bleeding wound isn't a plan, but all I could think was to get out of here and save my friends." She smiled mirthlessly. "Now that you've given me an equally unattractive option, I need time to decide."

She was a few feet away when I spoke. "What about this worshiper of the dark one? You don't fear them anymore?"

"I don't have the words to describe my fear of them, but I've got you now." She tossed a smirk eerily similar to mine over her shoulder. "Your ghostly companions follow me where I go. If that twisted psychopath ever snatches me, you'll pop in and whisk me away. Maybe this will be a mutually beneficial relationship after all."

I watched her and her mother go, no comeback on my tongue.

Oh yes, I liked her very much.

Sirena

I woke early that morning and shed my nightgown on the carpet. Padding to the door, I walked out—naked as the day I was born.

I had beautiful dreams the night before. Xander and I were standing at our wedding feast, toasting the whole of Olympia that came out to celebrate us. Our children ran around our feet—somehow school-aged and mischievous, even though Xander and I were as old as we are now.

It was perfect. The kind of dream I stopped having when I was a child. No, perfect wasn't the word. The dream was an omen. For all my frustration and anger with Xander for not seeing what was right in front of him, deep down I knew we were meant to be together. Soon, he would know it too.

And now there was finally nothing in our way. Xander can focus on me again with that traitor out of the way. He should've fallen into my arms and let me comfort him after Galen was killed. Instead, he channeled all his grief and hatred into Galanis, and flying into that bathroom proved just how mixed up and crazy that made him. He confused both emotions with lust.

But that was over. As his future wife and reigning councilmember, I had to act in his best interests. Save him from himself when he was too blind to see his actions were leading him to disaster. Alexander should've killed the traitor seconds after he captured her.

I stopped before dorm eleven and shrunk to the smallest flying insect there was—the fairyfly. A name much prettier than I actually looked.

Alexander would be thankful when the news rang out through the academy that she was dead. Who was I kidding? There'd be celebrations for weeks. Deserters had no place among us. They had no business touching what was mine.

I flew through the keyhole—the silent, flapping visitor flying into the alcoves to ensure there was an empty bed.

Wonder how Hondros did it? A son of Anteros can't have a useful power, but a soldier knows his way around a sword. I hope he gutted her like a—

I flew into the alcove sharing the biggest window, where Aella Galanis sat up reading a book by candlelight—very much alive.

Fury consumed my tiny form, fighting to wrangle my grip on it. All I had to do was turn into a harpy, or a wyvern, or griffin, or any of the endless beasts whose claws, beaks, and razor-sharp wings were at my disposal, and finish what I asked fools and weaklings to start.

No, I thought, regaining control of myself. *I can't dip my hands in her blood after accusing her of killing Hyacinth. I'll be the first person Drakos suspects.*

I zipped out of there, flying up to my room where I quickly dressed, then slammed back out. I assumed Hondros got the message, but it looked like the giant slayer had all the stubbornness of those oversized, hideous monsters.

I marched into the lecture wing, ready and willing to fly into his quarters next and rouse the stupid fool that slept while Aella relaxed in her bed without a care.

"Hondros?" I shoved on the door. "Hondros! What do...?" I trailed off, rant slipping off my tongue to die in my throat.

It was his blue and bloated face I saw first—as twisted in the anguish I witnessed when he tangled in the tapestry, crying. It was the same as the night before. The tears had yet to dry on his face.

Timothy Hondros hung from the ceiling, swaying gently in the noose wrapped around his throat.

Silently, I backed out the door, and softly closed it shut.

Aella

"Aella, turn left," Lysandros said. "You're about to run, hit, kiss a wall."

Head buried in my book, I pivoted on my heels, and ran smack into a pillar. Lysandros raced off howling.

"Dung hole!"

Nitsa helped me, laying a cool hand on the lump forming under my skull. "What's so interesting between those pages that you fell for that?" She checked the title. "*History of Nobility in Olympia?* Why are you reading that?"

I held the book against my chest, palm stinging from the bound edges digging into it. After leaving Sebastian the other night, I went straight to the library—thankful they never locked the doors. I left with every edition on the noble families in Olympia. The day before, I did nothing but pore over them. I had the day to devote to the books after... they found Hondros.

"I still can't believe yesterday happened," I said. "Poor Hondros. Who knew he was hiding so much pain."

"It is sad for him and his family." Nitsa and I continued on, falling in step behind our friends.

"He had a family?"

She nodded. "A wife and daughter. Must've been hard being away from them. Carrying out your duty can be lonely."

"I wish there was something we could do. What if we asked Drakos to hold another memorial?"

"I'm sure they're already working on it. The staff here live and work together for years. They see more of each other than they do their families," she said. "They won't let his death go by unnoticed."

Nitsa tossed me a look. "But don't think I didn't notice that you dodged my question? What's up with those books, Aella? You've been acting strange since yesterday. Are you still trying to find out who that woman was that threatened you in the mess hall?"

I clenched my teeth thinking of her. If it wasn't for the fact she was too young to have been the traitor in the Vanda household, I'd have wondered if she was the one the spirit warned me about through Sebastian.

Even though she wasn't, that didn't mean she wasn't a worshiper of the goddess. It was just Maia Galanis in that temple—chanting and spilling blood as the entity poured from the chest, and flooded into my eyes, ears, nose, and mouth. There were four acolytes and one chained captive in the temple that night. What if that's how many they needed again to complete the ritual and grant the goddess complete control over the beast?

Four enemies lurking within these walls. And they could be anyone.

"Aella?"

This would be so much easier if I could speak to the spirit myself. Sebastian is as upfront about using me for his own gain as the goddess. How could I know if the messages he's passing on are the truth?

"Aella, are you okay?"

I shook myself. "I'm fine. And no, it's not about the creepy threat I got. It's just that there's so much about Olympia I don't know, even though I've lived here my whole life. I'm tired of standing there blankly when people speak." I tapped the book. "I thought I'd start with the different cities and the nobles that rule them.

"Kind of weird to think about. In Port Delphin, we didn't have nobles or rulers. The town council governed, but all the important decisions were voted on by the town."

"That's how it is in most of the smaller towns and villages. They have no need of nobles telling them what to do," she said. "They get along just fine working and living together in harmony. It's not so simple in the cities. The wealthiest merchants operate out of them and someone has to regulate them, so the competition doesn't get out of hand.

"There are complex trade agreements between other major cities. The imperial tax collection. And monsters attack the cities more often—all those demigods in one place. The governing family will employ moras who station themselves in the city permanently. The noblemen and women handle all of that, and the imperial council has only one representative to deal with from each city. Rather than an entire city council."

I nodded along, absorbing what I read dozens of books to understand, while Nitsa condensed it all in five minutes. I had to remember I had friends who lived these lives.

"Did you ever hear of a town called Crassus?"

She bobbed her head. "Visited a few times too. Every year they hold a winter festival. People eat, drink, and skate on the frozen lake."

"If you've been there, then you must've heard of the Vanda family."

Her face fell, happy memories fleeing. "Such a tragic story. I didn't know them, but my mother did. She went to university with Elara Vanda. Murdered and they never found out who did it."

I chose my words carefully. "Did they have a child? A daughter?"

"They did," she said, tightening my grip. "She was killed too."

"What?"

"All they found of the baby were bloody sheets in the nursery."

My mind spun. If that's all they found, that meant there wasn't a body. Could Sebastian have been telling the truth? Was my true family murdered so that eighteen years later, the goddess could destroy my life?

"Were they?" I hissed.

Her laughter echoed from the depths of my mind.

"Were they what?"

I opened and closed my mouth a few times, forcing words past the lump in my throat. Up ahead, the stadium for self-mastery beckoned us forward. "Were they good people?" I asked. "What was Elara like?"

"I don't think they were close. Although, Mother once told me that Elara is how she knew Father was the one for her." Nitsa smiled. "Elara was the most beautiful woman she'd ever met. When she walked into a room, every eye drifted to her... except Father's. All he saw was Mama."

"That's so sweet."

"It is, isn't it?" she said, rolling her eyes. "They're so sloppily in love, they chase me and my brothers out of the room at least once a day when they start kissing and talking of things a daughter should never hear from her mother's lips."

"Dare I ask?"

"Cock, Aella." Her wretched grimace let me know her pain. "She said *fat cock* and I almost threw myself out the window. There aren't enough mind healers in the world to heal that trauma."

I laughed so hard, I walked into the stadium with a stitch in my side. Of course I'd risk death to save my friends. They were the ones who showed me I could laugh again.

Instructor Kazran waited for us in his usual place atop the platform. "Pick up your feet, novices," he barked. "Five of you are on your last proficient. When those five have defeated them, this portion of training will be at a close. The rest of you will be marked by how many proficients you've defeated by this point. Those who have yet to defeat a single one…" Kazran's attention trailed me to Proficient Catherine. "You will fail."

Of course I would. The woman tossed me around like a pillow for two months. There were other proficients who turned to iron, wielded fire, and spun illusions. While I couldn't beat one who was fast. No one in their right mind would say I was ready to move on to the next stage of training, or even on to the battlefield. If my humiliation with Proficient Catherine proved anything, it's that I would be killed immediately.

"No, my pet. You will be unstoppable. Soon, nothing and no one in this paltry land will harm you. A gift, child. Your goddess accepts your gratitude."

"Don't talk to me!"

"Excuse me?" Catherine's eyes bugged. "Who do you think you're talking to, novice?"

"Not you. I was talking to… someone else."

She didn't look any less pissed. After facing her five days a week for weeks, I knew that wasn't a good sign. I was flying higher than normal today.

"Galanis." Kazran approached as we squared off. Crossing his arms, he planted his feet. He wasn't going anywhere. "This is your last chance."

"Once again, sir. I'd appreciate any and all advice you feel moved to give me."

He chuckled like I was kidding. Why did he keep doing that? "Begin."

Catherine blurred. I spun on my toes, whipping my arms around. I glanced off skin and heard the faintest grunt. Triumph blossomed in my head.

A hard force slammed into me, tossing me off my feet. I crumpled at Kazran's feet.

He raised a brow, making no move to help me up.

"Truly, sir," I wheezed. "Whenever you feel moved."

Amusement tugged on the corner of his mouth. "I won't be there to give you tips when you're facing gorgons, giants, and sirens. You have to win this fight like you'd any other—by using your opponent's weakness against them. Figure out how to do that, or die."

Wincing, I forced myself up and met her across the divide. I was her only novice challenger that day. All the others had moved on, which left Catherine free to toss me around for ninety minutes straight.

No, not today. Not anymore. If Aella Vanda is me, it means that people have fucked with my life since I was no more than a squalling infant. They used, tricked, manipulated, lied, and made me a pet my whole life, and after all I've endured, I walk the halls of this school where everyone looks upon the mundane who isn't worth anything.

My eyes narrowed.

I'm done being everybody's victim.

Catherine vanished from her spot. I dropped down and grabbed a handful of gravel. I flung it in the air.

"Ahh!" Catherine snapped out of the hyper-speed world. Clutching her eyes, her feet tangled and she went flying. I hissed as she hit the ground—sliding over the stone, it took bits of her skin as its prize.

Kazran spared his proficient the barest glance. "Well done, Galanis. You figured out the first lesson by yourself," he said, turning to leave. "Don't hold back."

Nitsa, Tycho, and Daciana rushed me, hugging and congratulating me for finally winning in the hundredth bout.

"He can't fail you now," Tycho said. "Thank Persephone, because you definitely don't want to fail a course here."

"What happens if you fail?"

"Expulsion," Nitsa and Tycho said.

"And hard labor," I finished. "Wow. They really enjoy holding that fate over our heads. Makes for effective control."

"But you don't have to worry about that," Tycho said. "You're going to—"

"Ahhh!"

Screams broke out all over the stadium, snapping our heads around.

"What are they?!"

"Monsters!"

"Kill them!"

I followed the pointing fingers, eyes growing huge.

They flooded the sky, coming in from everywhere. Black wings blocked out the sun, shedding feathers vanished into vapor before touching the earth. They had the bodies of men—naked as nature. Powerful thighs flowed to blackened, feather-covered talons. On the opposite end, riding bare shoulders, were the heads of ravens.

"What are they?" Daciana cried.

Tycho ripped around, not knowing where to look as more, and more, and more blanketed the stadium. "I don't know," he shouted. "I've never seen— Watch out!"

The raven men tucked in their wings, and dived.

Shouts rang out. Powers flew. I ducked swiping wings that skated over the tip of my head, missing me.

"What's happening?" I bellowed. "What do they want?"

"No, get off!" Raven men swarmed Tycho, easily dodging his punches. Catching him under the arms, they lifted him off his feet. "Ahh!"

"Tycho," we screamed.

Daciana howled and her muscles rippled, black fur sprouting from her skin in a blink. She transformed faster than I'd ever seen, filling her space with a six-foot wolf whose girth knocked me and Nitsa aside. Crouching, Daciana leaped higher than the thrown bolts of lightning, fire, water, vines, and every power we had thrown at the raven men carrying dozens of us away.

"Daciana!" Tycho reached for her. Winging by his side was the raven man carrying a thrashing Sebastian.

Daciana's fangs narrowed the distance, closing in on the wings of Tycho's raven man. She snapped—

—on air.

The raven men... their captives... Tycho... all vanished.

"Tycho?" I breathed. "Tycho!"

A voice boomed through the stadium.

"Everyone, calm down!" Kazran stood atop the platform, a silver horn pressed to his throat. "There's no need for alarm." Inexplicably, he turned a grin toward the sky. "The culling has begun."

SELF-MASTERY WAS OVER after that. Nitsa, Ionna, Daciana, and I trailed Kazran out of the stadium. Theron and Lysandros were taken too.

"What were those things?"

"Where did they take them?"

"How is that the culling?" I asked. "Did they take them off to—to—?"

I couldn't finish the question.

Kazran didn't slow his stride. "If you're told too much about the culling, the challenge will—"

"We already know bird men swoop down and snatch us from the sky," Nitsa snapped. "What difference does it make now if we know what they're called?"

He sighed like we were annoyances. "Very well," he said, turning to face us. "Those bird men are called Oneiroi. They're spirits from the land of dreams. That's where you novices will be taken and tested. Whether you rise or fall to the challenge, they will return everyone here at the completion of the culling."

"Whether we rise or fall?" I repeated. "What does it mean to fail the culling?"

The look on his face said it all. Turning his back, he continued on into the castle. None of us tried to stop him.

"Land of dreams," Nitsa whispered. "Once ruled by Hypnos. The Oneiroi are his sons."

"Once ruled because Hypnos scattered," Ionna said. "His sons are in charge now. They must've changed the laws of the land now that he doesn't have the power to stop them."

"Is that bad?" Daciana asked.

Ionna nodded slow. "Think of your dreams, Daciana. Your nightmares. Think of how helpless and scared you are—trapped in a hell where the rules of reality don't apply. Everything and anything can change. You can change. A fearsome werewolf in the waking world. A mundane in your dreams.

"Think about all the terrible things that happened that made you relieved when you woke up, and realized none of it was real. Now imagine your true self thrown into such a hellscape. In the land of the Oneiroi, dreams can kill."

I swallowed hard. "Now it makes sense why they didn't tell us this was coming."

"What do we do?" Nitsa asked. "Spend the night researching the Oneiroi and land of dreams?"

"There isn't any point," Ionna replied. "It's like my visions. I can do everything to prepare for a future, and then it never happens. You don't know what you'll dream about before you dream it, and you can't control anything while it's happening. We go in blind—just like they said."

A thick silence smothered us.

"Well, I'm not doing nothing," Daciana said. "Our instructors knew for two months that those creatures were going to swoop out of the sky, and they didn't bother telling us that when that happened... it could be the last time we see our friends alive." Daciana took my and Ionna's hands. She gestured for Nitsa to add hers. "Tonight, I'll read and research and laugh and be with my friends, before they come."

We all agreed. There was nothing we wanted to do more, but we were not dismissed from classes. Though we were reduced by a fifth of our numbers, we still had to sit through Titan training, field medicine, combat practice, and a mess hall with more empty tables than usual.

The novice class had never been so subdued. No one shouted *traitor* at me, hooted for a mealtime show, or looked my way at all. The instructors claimed they couldn't tell us about the culling because knowing would change what we faced in the land of dreams, but Daciana was right.

That morning could've been the last time I saw my friends alive, and we didn't know to wake up with potential goodbyes and good wishes in Elysium on our lips.

We found our table, making soft, pointless conversation to distract from what we truly wanted to talk about, and what I *couldn't* talk about. The Oneiroi claimed Sebastian. Who knew how long he'd be gone or if he'd return. If the goddess's worshipers came for me that night, no one could stop them.

The arrival of Alexander and Ajax drew my attention, and my shame. My pulse quickened remembering my mad dash the other night, and the consequences it would've had for both of us if Sebastian had not shown up and ripped that dagger out of my hands.

I had never been more confused about a person in my entire life. The lamia I understood. Vasili I understood. I even understood Maia and that fanatical faith in a psychotic goddess warped her into a terrible person. But Alexander Damien, I did not understand a single thing about him, or what happened between us that week. What I did still know to be true was I didn't want him dead.

What are my choices? I stay and her worshipers capture me again. They turn me and I slaughter everyone in the castle—including Alexander Damien. Or I accept Sebastian's deal. I pledge my loyalty to a man I don't trust, he whisks me far away where Olympia will be safe from me, and then Damien is executed for letting a traitor escape.

Were any of these good options? In both situations, I was under someone else's control. Sebastian said he would free me after I helped him achieve his goal, but his plans could be just as bloody as hers. I did not know the man. Why would I assume he wants a monstrous killer on his side for a harmless reason?

But the goddess can't succeed. Her motives have always been clear. She wants every godly parasite-infested host in this land dead. Could I risk the end of Olympia to prevent the death of one man who she'll kill anyway?

My stomach heaved. These questions of life and death weren't mine to ask or decide. Alexander should be free to live his life without being shackled to my fate or the goddess's whims. None of this is right.

He can't die because of me, a voice whispered. *That is right.*
So what do I do?

No voice—not mine or divine—had an answer for me.

"Let's get out of here," Nitsa said. "I can't eat a bite, and I want to hit the library before all the books on the Oneiroi are gone."

"Yes." I was up and out of my seat before her. Being this close to Damien was torture. I needed space to think.

Our eyes met as I walked past his table. His unreadable. Mine plagued by confusion.

He was first to look away.

"How long do you think they'll be gone?" Nitsa mused. "I'd give anything to walk inside the dorm and see them grinning over a plate of honey cakes, asking if we missed them. Even Lysandros." She pulled a face. "Okay, maybe they can keep Lysandros a little longer, but I'd still want him back in a few days."

We chuckled half-heartedly.

"He does have a way of growing on you," I mused. "He's unpredictable, but whenever people shout stuff at me in the halls, he shouts right back at them. I have no idea how he knows all these things, but it's hard to be mad at a guy who sticks up for me."

"He does like you most of all," Ionna said. "I have a feeling he stopped spreading his apples because he's got a reason to stay in this school now—you."

"Lysandros does not have any particular feelings for me."

"No, he doesn't have any particular feelings for us," Daciana corrected. "We're just the people he steals from, scares out of bed in the morning, and bites. At least he defends you on top of doing all those things."

I winced, remembering the morning Daciana woke up yelping. Lysandros buried his teeth in her leg. When Daciana chased him out the door, she had no trouble catching up to him. Son of Eris got a new scar that day.

We veered down the corridor leading away from the dorm wing. The hall was packed with more novices than usual. We were all headed to the library.

"Truth is none of us knows what Lysandros is thinking," I said. "Which makes me wonder... what does he dream about?"

Ionna let out a low whistle. "I can't imagine the dreams of a child of Eris. Why would they put us through a test like this? We're just novices. What is taking us to the land of dreams supposed to prove?"

None of us had an answer for her. We knew nothing called the culling could be good, and still we weren't prepared for it to be this frightening. For months, I battled my nightmares nearly every night, and lost. This time I wouldn't have Calix to make it all go away.

It took a while, and searching high into the archives, but we eventually made it back to our dorm with everything we had on the Oneiroi and Hypnos's abandoned kingdom.

"Okay." Nitsa slammed her tomes on the table. "One thing we know is that the dream land won't let us be prepared. We could think of all our worst dreams and fears, and that's exactly what we won't face when we're in there."

"True, but the instructors knew this was coming even though we didn't," Ionna offered. "That's what all this training is supposed to be—preparing us for the culling."

I nodded along, popping out of my seat just as I sat down. "She's right. Field medicine to teach us how to survive when we can't run to Healer Helena for help. Self-mastery has us going against every kind of power and ability Kazran could think of. Battle strategy to get us thinking with our heads in a fight. They knew we'd be alone in the land of dreams facing beings from our nightmares." I flapped a hand. "We don't need those books. We need to remember everything they were trying to tell us without actually telling us."

"I'll get my scrolls," Daciana said.

Ionna raced off to her alcove. "I'll get my books."

We came back together with new energy. None of this helped Tycho, Theron, or Lysandros, and it may not help us, but having a plan was a million times better than sitting around in silence with all our fears.

The four of us stayed up half the night—going over old assignments and reading ahead in our textbooks. I didn't think about Alexander once.

Or I didn't think about him too much.

Okay, I thought about him every time there was a break in the conversation, or considered what I'd do when Sebastian came back.

Or if he didn't.

Eventually, we broke up and crawled into our beds. My friends would dream of raven men and berry bushes that night. I slipped under my sheets, knowing exactly what awaited me.

My mother gathered the woman's hair on top of her head. Tipping her chin up, she sliced her throat without a moment's pause.

"Nooo! Oh, gods! What have you done!" Blood gushed from her neck, soaking me in warm red liquid. I twisted as far as the restraints would let me and vomited over the side.

Mama threw the body away. "Sisters, silence the vessel as I pray."

Hands clamped over my mouth. Mother began chanting in a harsh, guttural language that didn't exist as far as my limited knowledge knew.

"For the glory of the goddess." Centering the knife over me, my wide eyes reflected in the blood-soaked blade as she brought it down.

I screamed. The metal was hot, liquid fire burning a hole above my navel and spreading through my body. This wasn't normal. What did she do to me?!

"To the goddess, we offer this vessel." The sisters of the sky and sea passed over me holding the chest. "Unworthy and impure, let the vessel be cleansed in the service of you. Make her worthy to carry out your will."

Raising the knife, Mother sprinkled my blood on the chest. It was the first I'd gotten a proper look at it. There was a heaviness about it. As though its age gave it bearing you didn't find in the new and mod-

ern. I sensed it was old. Older than this crumbling temple. As old as the ancient characters etched into the wood.

My breath trapped in my chest as my blood dripped on the writing and it sizzled. Burning like acid, it bore deep groves in the characters, destroying them.

I fought harder, near wrenching my shoulders out of their sockets. The chest burst open.

"Ahhh." Mother and the hooded women threw their heads back, crooning joy and exhalation.

"Rise, divine queen of darkness." Mother's joy echoed off the wall. "Rise and take your rightful place."

A thick, cloying smoke spilled over the chest rim—unnatural in the slow, slithering way it leaked over the side.

"Let me go!" I yanked and yanked, feeling something give away the slightest fraction. "Help!"

The smoke blanketed my legs, climbing higher to the wound on my abdomen, and diving in.

Pain stole my scream. Completely consumed, agony claimed me.

My bones broke. Veins burned. Lungs withered. Eyes melted. Heart turned to ash.

Every part of me was broken and remade, and I felt it all.

"Yes. Yes!" the worshipers cried. "It's working. She's returning to us! Goddess of despair."

I wrenched, snapping a black-dipped taloned hand free of the leather.

"To the goddess, we offer this mind," Maia continued. "Dull and undeserving, let the mind be gifted enlightenment in the service of you." She positioned the blade above my skull. "Our goddess. Queen of the broken and damned, you are—"

"Argghh!" I slashed, prying the knife from her grip.

Wide eyes reflected in the blade as it plunged toward her heart.

I bolted upright, kicking the textbook I fell asleep with to the floor. My pulse raced. Sweat covered my skin. Wetness ran down my chin, proving I'd bitten through my lip again.

None of that mattered.

I usually woke up before getting that far into the nightmare—the memory. I'd blocked it for so long, I forgot what happened before I grabbed the dagger.

I forgot she said a name.

"The goddess of despair," I whispered. "You're the goddess of despair."

"*I am indeed,*" the goddess replied.

"She named you. The last thing she said, Maia called you—"

A shadow shifted outside my alcove, snapping my head up.

"Who's there?"

"Shhh," a voice crooned—deep and masculine.

I froze. "Alexander?" He came to see me. To talk to me after all this time. "Come in."

The shadow moved again.

"I don't know if I wanted you to come or stay away," I confessed. "But now that you're here—"

A figure filled my entrance.

It was not Alexander.

They pounced on me mid-scream. Clamping my mouth and neck, he shoved my head at the wall. Pain exploded in my skull, and then there was nothing. No goddess, no Maia, no Hyacinth.

Nothing.

Ajax

I carried the bitch through the darkened halls, meeting no one else on my way. That time of night, the castle inhabitants were meeting our stolen in the land of dreams.

Slipping through the doors, I began the long journey down the staircase. *Finally,* I thought, hitching her higher up my shoulder. *Finally.*

Nothing but a mundane, and she proved disturbingly difficult to kill. Hiding out of sight and creating a puddle of water at just the right place, at just the right time, and down she tumbled off the grand staircase—hitting every bone on the way down.

Did not kill her.

I tried again while she soaked in the Sisyphean baths. She never knew I was only one bath over—listening, watching, waiting. Galanis ducked under the surface, and I kept her down. It would've been the end if Calix of all people hadn't shown up!

I knew the nectar made a mess of him, but I had no idea it brought him that low. Fucking the traitorous bitch that got my brother killed. I escaped out the back entrance as the moaning started.

Again I had to wait, and by then, I was out of ways to make it look like an accident. And out of the patience to try. I would simply drown her and toss the body in the lake. Then, the culling started.

Huffing, I climbed off the last step—sweat dotting my brow. Galanis stirred.

I ignored her. I didn't need to rush. She had no power, strength, or fighting skill to stop me. That night was her last.

Entering the room, I laid her on the stone and got to work binding her legs and hands. Galanis's eyes fluttered open, blinking through the blood leaking from her forehead.

"Wha... What happened?" Her gaze cleared. "Ajax? What are you doing?"

I grinned, my darkly humorous side returning for the first time since the death of my twin. All it took to bring it back was finally giving Galen peace.

"What does it look like?"

She tried to push me away, striking me with bound hands. "What is this? Let me go." Panic leached into her voice. "Let me go right now!"

"Um, no," I sang. "That'd be rather counterintuitive after all the trouble I've gone through to kill you. We're finally at the end now, Galanis." I wrenched her head around, pointing it at the iron maiden.

"No. No!" She thrashed harder. "What do you think you're going to do to me, Ajax? Why have you brought me here!"

"Because drowning and throwing you down the stairs didn't work," I shouted, blowing her back. "I was getting rather impatient, then the Oneiroi came like an omen, telling me now was the time." I laughed. "It's genius. You'll disappear and everyone will think they took you to the land of dreams. It'll be days before anyone questions why they haven't brought you or your body back. By then..." I trailed off, clicking my tongue. "It'll be too late."

"Too late? You're not..." Understanding dawned. "You made me fall down the stairs. And now you're going to lock me in the maiden and abandon me down here."

"Without Tantalean bread, naturally."

She gaped at me. "Have you lost your mind?"

"What a stupid question." I hauled Galanis to her feet. "Obviously, I have."

"No, get off!" She pummeled my arms with bound hands—kicking and bucking in my hold.

Gritting my teeth, I dragged her step by step to the waiting iron keeper, already open and eager for her prize. "Get in there!" I threw her in, delighting in her inhuman, echoing scream as dozens of spikes pierced her skin.

Galanis slumped, the fight leaving her as quickly as the blood beginning to pool at her feet.

Smiling, I gripped the lid—taking in one last look at the worthless bitch who cost Galen his life. "It took us too long to get here, Galanis, but I have Xander to thank that it's finally over." Her lashes fluttered, brows narrowing. "He played his part perfectly. First, torturing you and your traitor-loving friends. Forcing you to climb through windows and slink through the halls with your head down.

"When he let up, you were so grateful for the peace, you got comfortable. Sloppy," I drew out. "You fell into a routine that let me know where you were every minute of the day. Your long baths in the afternoon. The rare times the worthless class wasn't around to protect you." He shook his head. "No one trusts quicker than a fool who believes they've earned their enemy's forgiveness."

I pushed on the door, grinning wider when her protests kicked up.

"Ajax, p-please. Don't do this. I'm sorry about Galen," she croaked. "Please, don't— Please!"

Her begging made my pants tighten. I'd have blissful, perfect dreams that night, replaying this moment over and over.

"This is for you, Galen." The latch clicked shut. "Rest well, my brother."

Aella

My forehead drooped. The maiden stabbed it, viciously forcing my head back up.

Stay awake, Aella. I licked cracked lips. My parched tongue made not a difference. *You must... not... sleep.*

Thoughts came slow in my sluggish mind. I couldn't tell how long it'd been since Ajax trapped me in this underground hellhole. It was long enough my stomach long since stopped growling for food that wouldn't come.

Strength drained from countless cuts, soaking my bare feet. In my many nightmares, I dreamed of the revenge Ajax, and sometimes Galen, would take against me. Ajax drowned me on dry land. Galen held me frozen in the flow of time while he brought the rock down on my skull.

It's almost fate to have come full circle the same day the Oneiroi arrived. They didn't need to take me to the land of dreams. My nightmares were more than happy to kill me in reality.

"Have you nothing to say... before I go?" My eyes fluttered shut.

The goddess didn't answer.

"At least tell me... my true mother's name." I swayed on my feet, slipping into the darkness.

"*The boy already told you,*" she snapped. "*And he will come. He must come! We were so close. My victory finally draws near. Wake up! Wake up, girl!*"

She clanged the gong in my skull, sounding the pain meant to bring me back. I would've laughed at her if my throat could make the noise. My world was pain. Every inch of me trumpeted agony. There was nothing more she could do or say.

"Finally," I whispered, echoing Ajax. "It's over. You... failed."

Snarling, she shouted obscenities old, new, and foreign. They were my filthy lullaby as my eyes shut for the final time.

"Fuck you too."

"—bread. It'll suspend your need to eat, drink, or make waste." The maiden swung open. "You will— By the gods! Aella? What on earth are you doing in there?"

Swaying, I fell forward. The land of Hypnos stole me before I hit the floor.

I CAN'T SAY WHAT WOKE me. One moment I was lost, the next my vision came into focus on a familiar lantern. Healer Helena should put my name above it. This infirmary bed was quickly becoming mine.

I lay there a while, taking stock of myself. A shift, turn, and probe revealed no cuts or bandages. That was Madame Remis's voice I heard at the end. She used her power to heal me. Bring me back from Hades.

Sitting up, I twisted my head to the window. I didn't know what day it was, but by the soft dawn rays piercing the blanket of night, it was early in the morning. The castle hadn't woken yet. Everyone would still be in bed—except him.

I dropped my feet to the floor and quietly padded out. Ajax took me in my breast band and underclothes. The thin linen nightdress covering had to be a gift from the healer.

The hem softly whispered against my ankles, the only sound in the long, white hallway. Reaching the training room, I cracked the opening, seeking and finding the bare, muscled back of Alexander Damien.

His breaths came in panted *hphoo hphoo hphoos* as he pummeled the training dummy—completely focused. Soundlessly, I entered... and took a weapon down from the wall.

I held it high, closing the distance. The smell of him—sweet and musky—hit my nose, flooding me with useless memories of us kissing furiously in the bath.

I struck.

Alexander spun, glancing the staff's hit off his forearm. "What the— Aella?"

I threw the staff away and launched at him. We crashed into the dummy, the three of us going down in a knot of limbs and stuffing.

"What the fuck?" Alexander cried, protecting his face from my wild smacks and punches. "What is wrong with you?"

"Me?" I yanked on my arm, forcing it down to claw his face. "What is wrong with you! The whole time it was all a trick. You pretend to ease up on me to clear the way for Ajax. Did you just leave him? All done laughing over mugs of ale about me wasting away in the reflection room? Thought you'd get a workout to burn off the stress of being a lying piece of shit!"

Alexander's jaw hung slack. He beheld me, mossy eyes tangled with confusion. Ever the fucking performer.

"How could you do that to me?" I didn't realize I was crying until my tears painted his brow. "I told you to kill me that day in the bath. I *begged* you! But what did you do?" My cheeks warmed even then, recalling how I pawed him—ripping his pants down to accept all of Alexander Damien within me. "You granted me one final humiliation before sentencing me to—"

Alexander flipped, tossing me off. I tumbled across the mat and landed smack five feet away from him. Teeth bared, I pushed up, nails tearing the mat.

"Galanis," he huffed. The scratches on his face shone stark red. "I have no idea what you're talking about."

I got to my feet, taking a step. Then another.

"Whoa, hey."

My hand closed on a dagger.

"Put that down, Galanis. Just tell me what's going on. Don't—Aella!"

I charged him, howling my rage. I agonized over this man. I considered putting all of Olympia in danger to spare his life! The whole time, the kiss was a lie. His saying he could never kill me—all a lie.

Alexander was just keeping me stupid and compliant while Ajax found his opportunities to kill me. I offered him my death and he refused... because he wanted me to die alone and cold in the dark.

"You monster!" I slashed.

Alexander threw himself back, bellowing.

"I believed you. I wanted to protect you." I swung a wide arch, snagging and slicing through his pants. "Congratulations, Damien. You're another person I loved who turned out to be nothing but a deceiving, honorless, sack of—"

"What?" Alexander grabbed my wrist and plucked the knife from me without effort. "Did you just say love?"

I slapped his cheek with my free hand. "No."

We grappled—him fending me off, and me fighting to give him scratches to match the other side of his face.

"Dammit, woman!" Alexander hooked me around the ankle, dropping me flailing to the mat.

"Let go of me!" He straddled me, pinning my arms to the side. I merely kicked up and aimed for his balls. Alexander sat on my thighs. "Let go!"

"For fuck's sake. I swear you're insane! How do you explain the constant baffling shit you do every hour?"

"I'm insane?" My shriek could've cracked the mirrors. "I didn't tumble you, and then try to kill you!"

"What do you call what you're doing right now, you madwoman." He might've torn out his hair if releasing my hands would've not been a huge mistake. "I haven't gone near you in days, and now you're coming after me with a knife?"

"Save the innocent act," I spat. "Ajax told me all about your plan, before he locked me in the maiden!"

"Our plan?"

I barked a loud, humorless laugh. "Oh yes, very good, Damien. Nice clueless face. Now let me hear you say *I had nothing to do with it* in your best befuddled voice." I bucked harder. "You want to kill me? Fine. But you didn't have to kiss me! You shouldn't have made me think—"

"Think what?" His tone was low—strange. "What did you think?"

"Let me up right now."

"Did you say love, Aella?" His grip on my arms tightened. "You love me?"

"I could never love you," I burst out, sobs cracking my voice. "You're a cruel, stubborn, lying hostage to the rules that's made my life difficult at every turn. I'd rather live with the lamia than spend another second in your company."

"Oh yeah? Well, I could never love you either. You're an arrogant, selfish, rule-breaking traitor who crushes the will of men under your boots, then wonders why they don't thank you for the pleasure!"

"Is that why you couldn't face me like a man? You sat back and let Ajax take care of me because you were afraid I'd crush you under my boots?"

"I don't fear you, traitor," he hissed, getting in my face. "I could end you right now, and sleep like a swaddled babe."

My glare stuck him through. "Do it. No maidens. No midnight attacks. No tricks.

"Look into the eyes of the woman you don't love, and kill her."

The veins in his brow and jaw ticced out of control. His lips flattened in a thinning line. "And what if you're the woman I love?"

I froze at the soft question.

"Should I kill you then? Finally end your plague on my mind and body? Will I then be able to wake up and not have your face as the first to enter my thoughts? Can I walk into a room without searching for you? Can I sleep without finding you waiting in my dreams? Will I stop looking at my oldest friend and wishing I could boil him alive for touching you—for *tasting* what you have no reason to give me, but I want anyway?"

My lips parted but nothing came out.

"If I kill you, will it end the battle between love and hatred that's raged ever since you opened that pretty mouth in your jail cell and a string of filth came out?" he tore out. "You are everything I named you and more. But you're also fierce, strong, beautiful, and insane!

"I shouldn't love you, and fuck if there aren't days that I don't," he whispered, voice ragged. "But then I see you again.

"Tell me, Aella. If I kill you, will all of that go away?"

I lifted my hand and he let me. Cupping his cheek, I said, "Yes."

"Then I won't."

We gazed at each other for a long time.

"Did you know Ajax planned to lock me in the reflection room and leave me to die?"

"No."

I studied every inch of him, searching for a trace of deceit. "He said his plan only worked because you let up on me. Allowed me to get comfortable."

"He asked me to let you walk the halls again. He didn't tell me why. Whatever revenge he took wasn't between me and him," Alexander said. "It was between him and his brother."

I nodded, accepting this easily. Or much easier than when I walked through the door.

"What now?" I asked.

Alexander climbed off me. "You go."

I lay there feeling colder and more naked than if I was in nothing but a thin, cotton nightdress.

What did I expect? I picked myself up, giving him my back. *This couldn't have ended any other way. We were born on opposite sides. Destined to end in ruin whether we loved or hated each other. So why should it make a difference if we do both?*

My hand closed over the knob.

The room whirled, pulling a cry from me. Alexander slammed me against the wood. "Fuck, you make everything difficult!"

I opened my mouth to hotly refute that nonsense when his slammed on mine. I promptly forgot what I was going to say.

It was like our first kiss, except better in every way.

Alexander cupped the back of my head, tipping me in his hold. I clung to him—the only thing keeping me up. Anchoring me to everything.

Eyes so cold, but his lips were soft and warm. They banished my hate, anger, fear, and the horrible decision I still had to make. Nothing existed in this room—in this life—except me and Alexander.

He guided me onto the mat, our bodies and mouths still connected. I'd never drunk to excess before, though I had to believe this is what it was like. My head spun. Pulse raced. Breaths quickened. I felt clear and silly at the same time. Like I was about to jump off a cliff without wings, but the joy of falling through the air was worth the end.

His tongue tangled with mine, inviting me to play. I moaned as he caressed me, suddenly sure that this was nothing like being drunk. If wine gave this feeling, no one in the land would set down a bottle.

Fingers tickled my ankle, skating higher along my thigh and slipping under my nightdress. I dropped my knee, making clear what I wanted him to do.

Alexander brushed over my band, and kept going—chuckling at my grunt of irritation. His arm tugged my nightdress along with it. My heart thumped as he slipped it over my head. Why? I did not know.

I was horribly nervous and we'd gone further than this before. Alexander held me naked and wet against him.

But that time we were hurting each other and ourselves. This time is different. We know without it needing to be said.

I pressed my palm to his heart, secretly thrilled it beat as hard as mine. Alexander walked through the hall, not looking left or right because no one else was worth his time. They dare not demand his attention.

But I always had his. He turned to look at me. I broke his hold on his temper. The son of Zeus boiled everyone's blood, but I boiled his.

Maybe those watching did know something I didn't. Despising someone was a step away from loving them.

Alexander popped my breast band, tossing it somewhere over his shoulder. I smothered a laugh when it landed square on a typhon dummy's head. Our scant clothes came off in a flurry of kisses and moans.

I feasted on his body, mentally taking back everything I said out loud and in my head about his manhood. Alexander was not a jackass because he was overcompensating.

Alexander kissed under my ear, rippling goose bumps down my flesh. "I will erase the memory of Calix, Barba, Theron, and all other men from your skin."

Heat bloomed in my chest. He wasn't overcompensating, but he was still a jackass.

"I have not been nearly so busy as rumor and delusion led you to believe," I snapped. "You're the one who—"

He captured my lips, ending my rant full stop. I broke from him gasping. The ceiling spun overhead as his mouth moved lower, leaving nipping, teasing kisses down the valley of my breasts to my tender stomach. Alexander flipped me over, continuing his path one by one, kiss by kiss up the ridges of my spine. I melted like putty on the mat.

His need to erase *all other men* from my skin was quite unnecessary, but who was I to stop him trying?

My excitement built as he turned me back, and dipped his head between my legs. Alexander kissed the hollow between my thigh and entrance, then pecked up to my knee.

"What made you this way, son of Zeus?"

A low, rumbling chuckle tickled me. He enjoyed teasing me just as much as tumbling me. This would be a problem.

Growling, Alexander buried between my legs—tasting me with abandon. I gasped on a cry, back arching off the mat. Okay, he definitely enjoyed this more.

Alexander both took his time and chased me to a high. His tongue probed, and rolled, and flicked my tortured nub, waiting until my cries grew hoarse to stop and start all over again. I was a sweaty, limp mess on the sticky mat in no time at all. Damien could've skipped the threats, attacks, and sabotage. If he wanted me helpless to his mercy, this was all he had to do.

"By the g-gods," I stuttered, feeling the fuse lighting and zipping, burning through my veins. One more and I'd—

Alexander flicked the nub and I exploded—snapping over his head and flipping him over as I spasmed on the mat, coming so hard white spots danced on the wall.

He escaped my trap and draped himself over me, humming as he bit the shell of my ear. "Was that moan fake and exaggerated?"

My breath fogged the mat. "I can't even spell those words right now. Wow."

Alexander tipped my chin. We kissed slow, sweet, and mind-scrambling.

"On your back, Damien."

His brows climbed his forehead. "Am I in trouble?"

"Often, I suspect. But not this time."

I guided him back, marveling at his sculpted, powerful body. It was sinful to be this gorgeous. Alexander had all of Calix's power without the pink-and-silver smoke.

Flicking down, I bit my lip. His cock stood erect and proud between his legs, daring me to take it on. If anyone's cock could be brash and smug, it'd be his.

"You don't have to," Alexander said, threading through my hair. "If you don't want to."

"I do want to. I've... never done this before."

Surprise widened his eyes. "Never?" he asked carefully.

I shook my head. "Never."

Of all the things Calix and I did—and we did many, many things—he never asked me to swallow him while I was under his thrall. Aphrodite knows I would've done whatever he wanted, but in our haze, he focused on my pleasure.

This would be the first I truly gave instead of received. And I would do so of my own mind, body, and will... for Alexander.

Palming him, I pushed down on my nerves as the smug bastard and I came eye to eye. I would have Damien out of control and begging under my mercy on this mat.

Feeling it out, I licked his tip. Alexander hissed a sharp breath, thighs tensing. *Good sign.*

Emboldened, I swallowed his head and copied the things he did with his tongue.

"Rhea and Cronus, Aella," he groaned, saying the words like they pained him.

Very good sign.

My head bobbed between his legs—licking, sucking, and nipping his length to my heart's content. Filthy promises and sweet nothings poured from his lips.

"Gods, woman, you're incredible. Come here."

"Oh." Alexander tugged me up with a pop and a squeak. I flew into his arms as he opened them, wrapping my legs around his waist. We rolled on the mat kissing and laughing—happier than I knew either one of us had been in a long time.

Rolling to a stop, I found myself beneath him—his forehead pressed to mine. Endless, flinty pools beheld me, transporting me to a land of mossy beds, tickling grass, and a blanket of leaves overhead, shielding us in our own private world.

"Ahh," I moaned, lids falling shut as he slid past my folds. Alex kissed them, enticing a giggle out of me.

"I love and loathe you, Aella Galanis."

I kissed my jackass. My enemy. My downfall.

My Alexander.

"I love and loathe you too."

We moved as one, meeting each other rise for dip. I brushed my lips over the scratches, murmuring apologies. He told me he wouldn't change one insane thing about me. We were sweet and sour. Rebellion and duty. Honey porridge and olives. Nothing about us made sense, but then... there's something about an imperfect pairing.

We came together in a fury of moans and promises—bodies shuddering against each other as he spilled inside me.

For hours, days, weeks, an eternity, we made love on the mats, exploring every inch of each other. It was too soon that we collapsed in an exhausted, sated heap.

I laid my head on his chest, drifting off to the steady thrum of his beating heart. All that time I wasted agonizing over staying or leaving. As long as there was Alexander, there was only one decision, and I made it.

Consequences be damned.

ALEXANDER WALKED ME to my dorm and kissed me goodbye.

"I expect to see you tomorrow morning in my training room. You can leave the staff and knife on the wall."

I flicked his nose, then kissed it. "Surely our meetings aren't confined to a smelly old training room."

He caressed my cheek, smile dimming around the edges. "I need time to explain you to Ajax and Calix," he confessed. "And time to decide if you're worth the trouble."

"Asshole." I spun around, grabbing the knob.

Alexander snaked my waist and drew me back to him. "I have to make things right with my brothers so that they can be right for us." His lips pressed to my ear. "Tell me you understand," he whispered.

I melted, softening under his touch. Galen, Calix, and Ajax were his brothers like Iris, Evangeline, and Chloe were my sisters. I knew what it meant to lose them.

"Of course I understand. I don't wish to cause the three of you any more pain. Smelly old training room it is."

He chuckled. "Well, we can definitely do better than that. This castle has many secrets. I'll find one for ours."

"Can't wait." We shared one last lingering kiss.

I watched him go until he disappeared around the corner.

Walking inside, I was nearly knocked off my feet by four pouncing hugs.

"Aella, you're all right," Ionna said. "What happened? We went to see you in the infirmary this morning, and your bed was empty."

"We were terrified whoever put you in the reflection room, got to you again," Nitsa said.

"That someone was Ajax," I said easily. I wouldn't protect my attempted murderer, no matter his valid reasons for hating me. "He was hoping no one would find my corpse for weeks."

"You have to tell Drakos," Daciana said. "He's gone too far, and he's not going to stop. You can't spend every day looking over your shoulder."

"Ajax will not touch me again." I slipped out of their hugs. "How long was I gone?"

"Two days," Daciana replied. "It's Sunday now and..." She stepped out of the way. "You're not the only one who returned to us."

Theron and Tycho sat on Theron's bed, speaking in low tones. They saw me, nodded blankly, but made no move to get up. Turning his back, Theron went back to their conversation.

"They've been like that since the Oneiroi returned them," Nitsa whispered. "They won't talk about what happened there. They won't talk to us at all."

I nodded. "Give them time. It's a hard thing to face your nightmares."

"Just wish there was something I could do," Daciana said, lingering on Tycho.

"Did anyone else come back?" I heard myself ask. "What about Lysandros?"

"Lysandros is still there. Kosma and Sebastian Barba returned this afternoon," Ionna said. "So did Calix Lambros."

"I pray they all come back safe and sound." I backed toward the door. "I'm off to see Drakos. End this once and for all."

"Want us to come with you?"

"No, that's okay. Stay with the guys. Be here when they're ready to talk."

I ducked out, and turned right instead of left. My boots were soundless on the steps, carrying me up to the Titan wing. It was time to end this.

Stopping in front of Sebastian's door, I raised a hand to knock.

"—warning. I don't buy that they couldn't tell us anything before."

Sirena topped the staircase. The person she was speaking to trailed a step behind. Our gazes locked.

Ajax's eyes bugged. I could read nearly every thought as it flashed across his horrified face. *How did I escape? Why wasn't there a scratch on me? Why wouldn't I die?*

Knock. Knock.

Sebastian's door swung open. I flicked off him, stepping inside.

I immediately forgot about Ajax on the click of the knob. I had to do this before I lost my nerve.

Sebastian brushed past me and sunk into a chair by the fire. He stared into the flames—blank, silent, and unmoving. I had a feeling he was in this same position before I disturbed him.

"Sebastian?" I crossed in front of him, crouching at his feet. "Are you okay?"

He didn't speak for a beat. "I'm not certain."

"Is now not a good time?"

Fire danced in his icy blues. "Say what you came to say, Galanis."

"I came to say that I made my decision." I let out a long, slow breath. "I accept your terms. I'll swear an oath to serve you when the time comes, in exchange for taking me far beyond Olympia, then finding a way to free me from this curse when it's all over."

Sebastian shifted from the fire, color returning to his cheeks. "You accept?"

"I do," I said clearly. "Under one condition."

"Only one?"

"It's the only one that matters." My fingers brushed my lips, the taste of him still lingering. "If his own father truly sentences him to death, promise me you'll free and protect Alexander."

He barked a laugh, startling both of us. "What? Protect the son of a councilman? The son of *the* councilman. Are you kidding?"

"I'm not kidding," I said, moving to the chair across from him. "You'll swear it in the oath you make to me, or there's no deal."

"I thought you hated him. And the feeling was mutual."

"I do, and it is. But that doesn't matter. I won't allow Alexander to die because of me," I said. "You can get through the barriers of this realm, which means the imperial gates are nothing to you. Free Alexander and keep him safe. That's all I ask."

"And that's a lot," he said, frowning. "Do you think Damien will thank you or me for this? He'll go from imperial heir to fugitive and traitor. He'll spend his life hiding from the forces his father commands."

"But he'll be alive," I sliced in, fists balled. "If I stay within these walls, I'm putting everyone in danger. I have to go, but not if it means sacrificing Alexander. This is the only way, Sebastian, and he'll see that. After you get me out of here, I want you to give him a letter. It'll explain everything. Alexander will understand why it had to be this way."

He leaned forward, propping on his knees. "Say we do this. I whisk you away, give him this letter, protect him from the noose, and he turns around and betrays us both. His father would give anything to know my power and where I reside when I'm outside of these walls. I'm risking far more than you in this trade, Galanis."

I copied his position, staring hard. "You mean it's risky to swear an oath to exchange your life and freedom to a man you can't trust? Goodness, you're right. What do I know of that?"

Sebastian chuckled darkly. "Touché."

"Do we have a deal or not?"

He lifted his shoulders. "Why pretend we ever didn't? I need what you can do, Galanis, and you need what I can do." Sebastian held out his hand. "We have a deal."

I hesitated, but only for a moment.

We shook.

Sebastian and I stayed up long into the night, going over the plan. The oaths themselves had to be presided over by a child of Hecate who would make it binding. Our first stop after fleeing the academy would be to one who owed him a favor. Afterward, he'd set me up with money and food, and drop me in the mundane dominion.

"And then you'll return for Alexander," I said.

"Yes." Sebastian guided me to the door, his hand on the small of my back.

"Give him my letter first so he'll understand. I know once he reads it... he'll understand."

"I will."

"What time will we meet tonight?"

"Midnight," he replied. "In the same place. It's better you leave your things behind so they'll assume you've been taken for the culling. The more time I have to get you free and clear of Olympia, the less you'll have to worry about the guards picking up Damien while we're gone."

"You're right. That makes sense. Let everyone believe the Oneiroi took me." I shuddered thinking of the last person who had that plan for me. "Midnight."

I glanced back as I passed over the threshold. "See you then."

THAT NIGHT, I LEFT my friends behind carrying nothing but the clothes on my back. Sebastian promised he'd get me everything I needed to begin my new life in the mundane dominion. That was enough for me. Truth is, I did not have things that I cared about leaving behind.

Only people.

"I'm sorry, Daciana. Tycho. Ionna. Nitsa. Theron. And even you, Lysandros. I hope one day, when this is all over, we can meet again and it be as it was."

I softly shut the door, thinking of my parting words for Alexander. I hadn't written his letter yet. In it, I would tell him everything of the goddess, the ritual, the horrors she made me commit, and the horrors that would've come if she'd gotten her way.

The very thought of saying goodbye to him scared me. I was asking a lot of him. Giving up his friends, family, position, and freedom to hold on and trust that one day I'll come back—and fulfill a dark purpose for Sebastian Barba. His anger will be terrible. He'll hate me. He'll want nothing to do with me, but he'll be alive. As long as Alexander lives, there's hope I can find his love within the hatred again.

But I first had to find the right words to keep that spark smoldering. The time to do that wasn't when my fear of running, leaving my friends, and putting Alexander in danger lurked beneath the surface, waiting to break free and give the goddess time to stop me.

"*You will be stopped, girl!*"

I cringed, clutching my head and falling sideways against the marble. She'd been shouting at me since I left Sebastian. Part of me thought she was trying to assault my mind into unconsciousness, and ruin my plans for escape.

"*Run. Run to the ends of the earth and beyond. You will be found wherever you go, Aella Vanda. My will is fate.*"

I ignored her and pushed on. If she was this upset, it was proof I was doing the right thing.

My thoughts drifted to the training room. The sweet, sinful memories were a balm to the pain.

Alexander made me feel things on that mat that made me ache to leave him. How would I survive weeks, possibly months without his touch? His husky voice in my ear as he moved inside me. His hands cupping my breasts while his mouth explored.

Once was not nearly enough for us. I needed more time with him. A chance to get past the point of loving and loathing, and just love.

A thud sounded behind me, tearing me from my daydream. I twisted and saw...

...nothing.

The hallway was empty.

I'm jumpy. Nervous. All this will soon prove to be the right decision. The only decision. First, I have to get past those gates.

I faced the entrance, turning in time to see a large, gnarled hand fly at my face.

My scream muffled in its palm.

"TEEHEE."

An object struck my forehead, tugging me out of sleep. I blinked awake as the second pebble bounced off my nose.

What happened? Where am I?

Pushing myself up, I squinted at the dryads. I was in the forest but I didn't remember—

That hand came at me, jarring the memory loose. I jumped to my feet, whipping around. A heaviness dragged on my back.

All that met my eyes were trees, trees, curious dryads, trees... and a few inches from me, my pack.

What was it doing here? What was *I* doing here? Was it Sebastian? Did he free me from the academy as promised?

If he did, where is he? And why would he have gone back for the pack he told me to leave behind?

"Hello?" I called. "Sebastian? This isn't funny. Where are you?"

"Only me, I'm afraid."

I lurched back and tripped over my feet as a figure emerged from the woods.

"But it's interesting that you should call his name." Drakos scanned our surroundings. "Is he with you?"

"What—? I— What are you doing here?"

His brows chased his hairline. "I do believe that's my question, Aella Galanis. What are you doing here? Outside the grounds."

I opened my mouth. Not a sound came out.

"I couldn't believe it when I received word you escaped." He stalked closer. Morning light streamed through the branches, and somehow my darkly dressed headmaster was cloaked in shadows. "I nearly dismissed the report. Yet, here you are."

His eyes darkened. "You understand what this means."

"I can..." I licked dry lips. "I can explain, sir. I didn't escape. I was brought here. Last night. Someone grabbed me and I woke up here."

"And they kindly packed your bag for you?" he asked, sweeping out a hand.

Dread climbed my spine, shaking my bones even as I said, "Yes."

"I see, and they..." Drakos reached into his pocket. I shot back before I saw it was a note. "Left goodbyes on your friends' pillows?"

"Goodbyes? I didn't write that!"

"Who did? Sebastian?" He crept ever closer. "Is that why after waking up from being abducted and brought here against your will, he is the first name you called?"

I couldn't handle his questions. I didn't understand what happened myself. What was I doing here? Someone grabbed and left me outside the grounds? Who would do that? Why?

Was it Sebastian?

Why would he make such an intricate plan only to go back on it? another voice said.

"Because I was dreaming," I blurted. "Sebastian was in my dream, but he's not here. I shouldn't even be here. Sir, I'm telling you, the last thing I remember is something grabbing me in the hall. Next thing I know I'm waking up here and—"

"Are you going to come without a struggle, Miss Galanis?" he asked softly. "Or shall I call up reinforcements?"

My breath trapped, noting he said *up* not in. If he summoned those rotting corpses, I'd change right in front of him, and the lies I was desperately thinking up would not matter.

"No, sir. I won't struggle."

"Excellent." He stepped to the side. "Lead the way."

"I... don't know the way, sir." My voice was nothing but a strangled rasp.

"It's the same way you came."

I squeezed my eyes shut, fists balling. He didn't believe me. Drakos would not hear a word I said, and I knew what came next.

I picked up my feet, trudging in the direction he pointed.

"What was your plan?" he mused. "Where did you think you'd go?" He paused. Maybe he was waiting for me to say something. "It's no matter, Miss Galanis. The truth will shortly come out."

"Like the truth of who reported I escaped? That's who you should be talking to. They're behind this whole mess, sir. I'm innocent."

"It is not them I found a mile from the academy, calling out to her coconspirator."

"I didn't—!"

"Silence."

"No, I won't be silent," I burst out. "I was taken and brought here, but that doesn't mean that sneaking bastard didn't do us all a favor. I don't belong in the academy! Just let me go, sir. One mundane is no great loss."

"But you are so much more than that." His words whispered through the trees. "I see it. I've always seen it, Aella Galanis. There is death in your soul.

"It calls to me."

And then I was silent. I did not utter a single word as I tramped through the forest—the soundless, enigmatic specter at my back.

The gates swung open as we neared—a pet responding to its master. Drakos drew ahead as they shut, leading the way inside and to his office. The shadows were so thick, I didn't see them until it was too late.

Sirena materialized in the candlelight. Her smirk wide and her grip firm on Alexander. His eyes were dead—unreadable.

"Alex..."

"Don't talk to him," she snapped. "See, sir. She was exactly where I said she was, wasn't she? Just like she and Barba planned. You can call for the imperial guards now." Sirena's grin was a wicked sight to see. "I sent word to my mother while you were hunting the traitor down. I'm sure she's expecting your request."

The night before came into sharp focus. "It was you. You turned into some hideous creature that finally matched what you are on the inside. You dropped me outside the gates, packed my bag, and left those notes!"

She blinked lazily. "Do you hear yourself? How could I have done any of that? I can't get beyond these gates, but apparently Sebastian Barba can."

"This is easily rectified." Drakos swept off his coat and claimed his throne. "Bring Mr. Barba to me."

Sirena stood there for too long till she realized he was talking to her. "Oh. Yes, sir."

She whispered something in Alexander's ear before leaving. He stood there carved from stone. I closed the distance in a bound.

"Alex, it's not what you think. Whatever she told you, she exaggerated or made up, so she could be where she is now. Standing opposite me with her arm around you."

Alexander looked right through me.

"Take a seat, Miss Galanis."

I hesitated, explanations on the tip of my tongue. Alexander walked away from me.

My eyes were on him when the hinges creaked open.

"You asked to see me, Headmaster?"

"I did, Mr. Barba. An accusation has been made that you plotted with Aella Galanis to leave the academy without permission. She was discovered beyond the grounds this morning, and apparently you helped her get there."

"Ridiculous," he said, drawing my attention. "How could I? The barrier spells are even stronger now since the Teresi family had them upgraded. I'm not a child of Hecate. What could I do to get past them?"

Sirena stepped forward. "Lies, sir. All lies. I overheard them speaking last night in his room." She shot me a triumphant smile as my stomach shot to my throat. "They're traitors, Headmaster. Call the guards."

"In my room?" Sebastian could've been talking about porridge for all the inflection in his voice. "Funny, I don't remember inviting you into my bedroom last night."

"You didn't. I've been tasked with watching you, Barba, because you're a rebel and a traitor who's dodged his duty for eighteen years." She jerked a chin at me. "And you help others do the same.

Don't bleat about privacy to me. You turned out to be exactly what we all knew you were."

"Who would that be?" he asked. "Someone who's sick of suspicion and rumor following him around? If I wanted to dodge my duty, what am I doing here? I reported for training. I'm fulfilling my duty to Olympia. What other responsibility do I have? I've taken no oaths."

"Enough." Drakos cut off whatever Sirena was about to reply. "Barba, did you conspire to help Aella Galanis desert her training? Be warned, I have ways of finding out the truth."

"I did not conspire with her."

"Liar!" Sirena jabbed a finger at me. "It wasn't just me who saw her go into his room. Ajax Teresi was with me. He'll tell you the same. Didn't see her last night? You mean you didn't see two witnesses."

Sebastian's expression didn't change. "I didn't say I never spoke to Aella. I said we didn't conspire. Conspire makes it sound like I was a willing participant. What this spy heard was Aella blackmailing me into helping her escape."

"What!"

"She didn't!"

The cries came from Sirena and me. I gaped at Sebastian, finally finding a reason to leave Alexander, and get in his face.

"What are you saying?"

Just like Damien, he looked through me.

"Explain," Drakos demanded.

Sebastian sidestepped me. "Like everyone else has assumed my entire life, Galanis thought I was harboring some kingdom-toppling power that could free her from the academy, and then shield her escape like I've hidden for the last few years. She came into my room last night, made a bunch of threats, and then left. End of tale."

"It's not true," Sirena said, shouting over me. "I heard everything. They had a plan to visit a child of Hecate who'd make their oaths not to betray each other binding. Then, Barba was taking her to the mundane dominion."

He snorted. "Now we're swearing eternal devotion and eloping to the mundane dominion? Do you hear the nonsense coming out of your mouth? I barely know this woman. Why would I risk the traitor's noose for her?"

"Why would Miss Cirillo lie?" Drakos probed. "She's already proven right about Galanis's midnight flight and your meeting. You say now that she lies?"

"Of course she's lying, and she told you why. She admitted to sneaking in my room and listening in on my conversation. That's not an assignment she was given by any instructor here," he said. "Her precious mother and the other councilmembers told her to watch, listen, and wait for the first opportunity to rip me free of the academy's protection and hand me over to them. She got her chance last night when Galanis revealed herself. Two rebels for the betrayal of one.

"How quickly did she demand you call the guards to haul me away, sir?"

Sirena's reddening cheeks couldn't be hidden in the dim light.

"They'll offer me the noose... unless I drop on my knees and swear their oaths."

"All he does is lie, sir. The filthy Hades spa—" Sirena choked, clapping her hand over her mouth.

If there was a right thing to say, that was not it. The air darkened around Drakos.

"I'm lying?" Sebastian asked, wise to keep the triumph out of his voice. "You said you have ways of finding out the truth, Headmaster. Ask her exactly what her and her boyfriend's orders are concerning me. Ask her if they're any different from the orders there once were against you."

Drakos rose from his seat. "Plotting and scheming to remove a trainee from my academy." Something in his voice made Sirena step back. "How is that offense any different from Miss Galanis's? Maybe the imperial guards will be taking more than one away this night."

"But, sir. I'm telling the truth. That's what they said, I swear. He's twisting everything to make himself the victim!"

"He is a victim of your spying and suspicion—both of which you freely admitted. You ask me to believe your motives concerning him are honorable, yet you've broken the first rule of this academy. The enemy is out there, not in here."

"Sir—!"

"If the plan was for both of them to journey to a magic-wielder, why was he not with her?"

The question cut her to the quick. Sirena froze—mouth open, pallor washing out.

He tsked. "Already your story begins to fall apart. I will hear no more from you, Cirillo. Leave my sight."

She wisely didn't argue. With her gone, his gaze turned on me.

"Unless you have something to add. You've been strangely silent, Miss Galanis. Is what Barba says true? Did you attempt to force his hand in helping you escape?"

"I didn't! Everything he said... is..." I trailed off, flicking down.

Sebastian gestured wildly behind his back. His hand signals meant nothing to me, though the meaning was clear. *Stop. Don't!*

In the space of a blink, his plan struck me over the head. We were caught. Sirena heard everything, and we were both destined for the noose in my case, and lifelong servitude in his. With me being found outside the gates, there was no chance of convincing Drakos of my innocence, but there was still a chance for my escape.

Sebastian could get me out of an imperial prison as easily as this one. There was no change in the plan if I was caught, but there was if he's caught too. The council can't know what he can do. Or how much of a threat he truly is.

But this only works if our stories match.

I squeezed my eyes shut, lips trembling. *I'm sorry, Alex.*

"What he says is true," I rasped. "Last night, I tried to blackmail Sebastian into helping me escape the academy."

"And did he?"

"No. Sebastian told me where to stick it and threw me out of his room. I left and turned to my last resort."

"Well," Drakos said when I didn't continue. "Do go on. You have a captive audience."

"I—" The words lodged in my throat. "I felled a tree, sir, and killed a dryad. I figured if danger to my life let the demon through last time, it'd let me through the barriers too. I just had to run in the opposite direction. The dryads chased me. I got over the fence. The rest you know."

No one spoke for an agonizingly slow spell.

"Clever, Galanis. Quite clever," he said. "I partly blame myself for putting the notion in your head, but the fact remains your cunningness is wasted. If put to serving Olympia instead of betraying her, you would've been magnificent."

I barely heard him. "Alex, I know what you're thinking, but everything I said to you yesterday morning was true."

"You signed my death warrant."

"I had a plan to protect you," I cried. "I never would've let them hurt you. I swear. Yesterday was real, Alex." Something flickered in his eyes. "You know it was. Just like you know I'm telling you the truth now. I wouldn't have run if it meant hurting you."

"What say you, Damien?" Drakos asked. "This is her second escape attempt and this one succeeded. The law is clear."

"Of course it is." Alexander looked me in the eyes. "Send for the guards.

"Execute her."

"Alex!"

He stormed past me.

"Alex, please—" He slammed the door hard, jostling bottles off the shelves in a shower of glass.

"Hmm. That settles the matter, Galanis."

I sobbed, holding my fist tight to my chest. It wasn't working. My heart was clawing its way out, aching to chase after Alexander.

"Or it will be in a few moments." I heard his barely audible footfalls cross the room. "Your threatening a student into treason, and killing an innocent dryad changes things. I have no need of the imperial guards. I'm well within my rights to execute you here and now." The *zing* of a sword leaving its sheath snapped me around. "Barba will stand as witness. I execute you in the name and service of Olympia."

"What? No!" Sebastian and I cried.

"Sir, that's not necessary," Sebastian rushed. "Can't really call what she said last night a threat. She doesn't have power over me. I'm fine to let the guards handle her."

"Only a coward passes off a grim task to avoid doing it himself. To wield the authority of sentencing death, is to accept the responsibility." He stalked me through the dark, sword glinting in the candlelight. "She committed unforgiveable acts against those in my charge. I will not shirk my duty.

"On your knees, girl."

"N-no!" I backed away, racing toward the door. "You can't—!"

"Rise!"

Curtains rustled. A wooden door banged open.

Figures burst out of the dark.

I screamed. They came from everywhere—eyeless sockets two black holes swallowing me in unending fear.

My talons ripped from my fingertips.

"Hold her down," Drakos ordered.

"No!"

They pounced on me, hard skeletal grips forcing me to the floor. Drakos raised the sword high.

"Stop," Sebastian bellowed, rushing him. Black bled into his eyes.

"Argh!"

A shout ripped through the chaos, snapping their attention to the door.

That voice. "Alex? Alex, what's wrong?"

His bellows echoed, then abruptly stopped. I struggled under the bodies of demigods past—talons digging deep grooves in the floor. Forcing my head free, I locked on to his eyes.

The raven man screeched, piercing my eardrums. His wing lashed out and knocked my captors flying. Seizing me under the arms, he soared to the rafters, leaving Sebastian, Drakos, and his death guards to grow small beneath me.

They blinked out of sight as we entered the land of dreams.

COLORS SWIRLED. MOVING, shifting, spinning, changing, and whipping past too fast for me to capture one and recognize. A headache pounded my skull.

Get me out. Put me down! The cry no sooner echoed in my skull than it all winked out.

We floated in an infinite pool of starlight. It flowed around me, tickling my skin like flower petals. A world both devoid and full. I cradled in the echo of time, lids growing heavy.

Through my blurring vision, an ivory gate loomed high as it grew small. My eyes drifted shut, giving in to dreams.

"Wake up. Fuck it, Galanis. Wake the hell up."

I jerked, coming to on a bed of soft grass. A familiar, pissed-off face floated above my head.

"Alex?"

"Ander," he finished. "Call me by my name. I never gave you permission to do anything else."

Stung, my face fell. Was it only a day ago that we tangled on the training mat—laughing, kissing, and happy?

Was it only a day ago? It all came back to me. Waking up outside the gates. Drakos. Sirena. Alex walking out on me. The sword. A raven man.

"We're in the land of dreams."

He looked up. "What was your first clue?"

Pushing up on my knees, I fell upon a new world.

We looked to be in a forest of chaos. Trees of every kind, type, and height crowded too close together, and too far away somehow. Some stood bare and stripped of life. Others brimmed with health and happy, playing dryads. The trees dared not match their brothers, making for a woods befell by winter, nourished in summer, thriving under spring, and wilting in autumn all at the same time.

I dropped my gaze, unable to stand the wrongness of it, and noticed we were on a yellow-sand road. Looking both ways, I saw nothing but trees and sand.

"What are we doing here?"

"The culling," he replied. "The more important question is why am I here with you?"

I flinched at his hard-set jaw. He was so angry with me. He thought I lied to him. Played him for a fool, then skipped out the gates and left him to die. What action would make him see what words didn't?

"Alex, please. Nothing happened like I said."

"I won't talk about this."

"Sirena set me up—"

"Enough."

"Tell me how to make it up to you and I will!"

"You can't, Aella. Get it through your head." Giving his back, he walked away—again. "You can't."

Alexander headed down the path. When he was ten paces ahead of me, I picked myself up and followed. He didn't speak.

I did.

"—made a plan to get me out of the academy," I said. "The deal was that Sebastian had to come back and save you."

His shoulders went taut. The only sign he was listening.

"I was going to make him swear an oath, promising he'd put your life above rivalries, councils, and secrets. And if you chose, he'd bring you to me and... we'd be together." I shook my head. "But none of that had a chance to happen. I was grabbed by the winged spy and *she* dropped me outside the gates. She—"

"Quiet."

"Alex, you need to hear this! If you're going to hate me, then hate me for the truth."

"I'm serious," he said, twisting around. "Quiet. Listen."

Stopping, I tipped my ear to the cloudless, sunless, but still bright sky. A faint sound floated to me.

"What is that?"

Damien appeared at my side. "Galloping."

"Someone's coming."

"Or something."

"What do we do?" I asked, grasping his forearm. "Should we hide in the trees?" The question left my mouth as a figure appeared in the distance, moving fast.

He shook me off. "You can do whatever you like, Galanis. We were brought to the land of dreams to face and battle our deepest fears and regrets, not run from them. But you run," Damien said, his curled lips my parting gift as he picked up his feet. "It's what you do."

I bristled. Alex was trying to get under my skin. Provoke me into lashing out so we could return to the relationship that made him comfortable: enemies. "You're the one who's running from me instead of letting me explain. Have the courage to face this conversation."

"I would," he said, "if I cared about what you have to say."

He was spared my reply by the growing party approaching us. It wasn't one person. Three men traveled down the road. One on horseback and the other two on a horse-drawn carriage. They slowed at the sight of us.

"Wait, is that—? Damien," called the man on horseback. "Alexander Damien."

His long hair tied behind his shoulders. The guy was a sturdy fellow with broad shoulders, trim beard, and a dusting of sand covering his pants and tunic. His companions looked to be family. The older man shared his face except his was covered with wrinkles, and the young man had the same long, fine hair.

"What do you want with Alexander Damien?" Alex asked.

"You're the son of Maximos Damien, are you not? Representative of the imperial council."

"I am," he said slowly.

"Who is your companion?"

"A fellow trainee," I answered before Alex could do it himself, and say something less than flattering.

"From the academy? Excellent. You're authorized to handle this matter and stand as witness."

"What matter?"

The three of them gestured behind. Skirting the cart, my eyes grew big on the bound and struggling occupants in the back.

A woman with gray streaks in her hair and tired eyes came alive when she saw me. Muffled shouts bled through her gag. The teenage and adolescent boys with her took up the pleading.

"What do you think you're doing? Let these people go!"

"Can't do that, miss," said the elderly gentleman. "My name's Hesperos. This is my son, Augustin, and his son, Delias. We live and work a farm that backs onto the border. Once every few years, we get traitors who think they can sneak across our property to the gorge."

He spat on the woman's tattered dress. "So we started laying traps. Caught this bunch last night, and we're bringing them into town. With you here, sir and miss, we don't need the magistrate. You can deliver their sentence."

"But why?"

"Excuse me?" Augustin asked. "Why what?"

"Why were they trying to get to the border? Did you ask?"

Father and son shared confused looks. "I don't understand."

"You can't just go around trapping and throwing people in the back of your cart. You—"

"Incredible, Galanis." Alexander hopped on the cart. "The challenge has just begun and you're already failing."

"What are you talking about?"

His eyes were shadowed. "We're in a dream. I, who catches traitors. And you, who is a traitor. Do you truly think our task is to argue about fairness and justice?"

I flicked from him, to the struggling captives, and the men staring at me. "You can't mean we're actually supposed to..."

"Get up here."

It took me a minute. Stiffly, I climbed on the cart, looking anywhere but at the people whose cries were getting more desperate.

Of course the raven men didn't drop us here to have a lover's spat. Their task was to cull the unworthy. It was no coincidence that on a long, sandy road, I'm met by three deserters.

We lumbered into town—a silent party except for our three prisoners. Alexander couldn't look at me, though I gazed at him, wishing I could see inside his mind. Was there any trace of the man who lowered his guard and let himself love me—if only for a morning? Could I get him back?

The noise and chatter of village life soon reached our ears.

"Welcome to Tanif," Augustin called.

Tanif was a modest little village of stone homes, sandy streets, a single inn for weary travelers, and a water fountain in the square that served as the meeting place for playing children and lovers relaxing on the basin's rim.

Hesperos stopped the cart in front of a two-story limestone building of arched windows and a large wooden door. The men lifted and dragged the captives inside, leaving me to trail behind—wishing I could turn around, get in the cart, and abandon this land of dreams.

What did the Oneiroi expect me to do to these people?

Exactly what was done to you every night you closed your eyes on the long trek to the gorge.

Madame Remis warned the culling would not let me be prepared. I expected to bury Hyacinth on another horrid thundering night. I'd struggle on an altar while the woman who raised me lowered the knife. I'd flop in the mud, screaming as Alexander tortured the traitor to death.

I pictured every possible test, except what I'd do if the noose was in my hands.

We entered a courtyard with nothing to say for itself except for four wooden posts staked in the sand. Augustin went into the building and came back with more rope and a man in a long white robe.

"Macarius Mila. He's the head of the town council," Delias said, gesturing to the man in white. "He says he knows this family, and isn't surprised to hear they're traitors. He doesn't object to their sentence."

"No reason he should," Alexander said, overhearing what Delias told me.

"What are you doing with those?" I made for Augustin as he approached the boy, carrying the rope. "Put that down and untie the ropes you put on him. He's only a child."

"He looks thirteen to me." Augustin shoved the boy at the post. "The law is clear. Thirteen is old enough to know the law, therefore he's old enough to obey it. He should've turned these traitors in instead of running by their side."

"Turn in his own family? Of course he wouldn't!"

"Then he spun this thread of his own doing."

"You can't— Stop!" I rushed him when he looped the rope around the crying boy's wrists. Alexander snaked around my waist and snapped me to him, holding me firm. The shock of our closeness rattled me. Even in the land of dreams, he smelled like man, pine needles, and rain.

"I trust you've got everything in hand now," Hesperos said to Alex. "It's a half day's ride back to our farm."

Alex nodded. "You may go. The council thanks you for your service. You've made Olympia proud today."

The men shuffled out—puffed with pride. Shaking free of him, I crossed to the captives and undid their gags.

"What is she doing?" Macarius demanded. "Get her away from there."

"I will hear their supposed crime from their lips, and be quiet," I snapped. "You're an observer and no more."

He sputtered, clutching his chest. I ignored him and focused on the mother. She gasped and licked her lips like she was suffering from thirst. I doubted the farmers fed and gave them water before tying them up for a half day's ride.

"Alex, we need water."

"Stop being ridiculous," he snapped. "Complete the task so we can move on. Hopefully to separate places."

Biting back frustration, I returned to her. "Ma'am, what's your name?"

"I am Ianthe. These are my sons, Jason and Yannis. Please," she murmured through cracked lips. "You must let us go."

"Why did you run?"

"Galanis," Alexander warned.

"I am ill. There is nothing the healers can do, and no money to afford it if they could. I petitioned again, and again, and again for my Yannis to be excused from training." She looked to the curly-haired, pleasant-faced young man no older than me. "Each time I was denied. I will be gone from this world soon. Who will look after my Jason if Yannis must train? Who will care for him if... he doesn't come b-back?"

"Aella!"

"My boys must have each other. This was the only way."

"Please, help us," Jason whispered—his voice smaller than his big, glassy eyes. "Please."

"I will—"

"That's enough." Alexander gripped my collar and drug me back. In his right hand, he held a sword. "Let's be done with this."

"Put that away. Did you hear what she said? She petitioned for her son to be excused from training and they denied her," I said. "You can make it right. As a representative of the council, grant her request and everyone can go home."

"Aella." He grabbed my hand and forced it around the hilt. "Stop wasting time. Execute the traitors."

"Did you hear anything I just said? We don't have to kill them. You can settle this right now."

"Oh, can I?" Alexander tipped his head to the sky. "I grant these traitors pardon. Yannis, son of Ianthe, is excused from academy training and army service. Let them live merrily ever after." He made a show of looking around. "Oneiroi? Where are you? We beat your task. Take us to another one."

Heat built under my collar.

"Oneiroi?" He gave me a look. "Seems that didn't work. Are you ready to stop playing games?"

I swallowed through needles. "This isn't the only way."

"Do you want out of this place or not!" I blinked and he was in my face. "You're a coward, Aella. You've always been one. You'll always *be* one unless you get it through your head. Duty above all. Maybe if you'd figured that out sooner, we—" Cutting off, he flung himself away cursing.

The look on his face chipped off a piece of my heart. "This isn't about us," I said softly. "This is about right and wrong. A mother trying to protect her sons isn't wrong."

"A good mother would've taught them protecting Olympia is the highest honor." He looked down at the sword still clutched in my hand. "There's a reason we're both here. You're here to prove you can make the hard decisions, and for some reason, I'm here to see you do it. Prove to me now that there's more in a traitor's heart than cowardice." He made me face the family. "This time, Aella, don't run."

The family cowered before me. Gazing at my expression, Ianthe and Jason burst into tears.

They faded before my eyes, replaced with a young woman—scared, alone, and searching for kindness, sympathy, and friendship in a world that had none to give.

Me.

I accepted my escape to the border could end in my death. I knew the law and was willing to bend to the consequences. Ianthe set out knowing she may face the same.

The culling was supposed to break me. Take me apart piece by piece, and send back the perfect soldier to Deucalion—ready and willing to die and kill for Olympia. If I couldn't do this in a dream, how could I walk onto a true battlefield?

"There is more in my heart than cowardice." I dropped the sword. "There's compassion. I won't kill someone who risked their life to protect others. A soldier should understand that."

"For the love of— Enough." Alexander tossed me aside. "If you won't, I will."

"What? Alex, no."

He raised his palm to Ianthe.

"No!"

Ianthe seized, body bending in half over the post. Her screams echoed through the village.

"Alex, don't—!"

Ianthe exploded in a shower of blood and bones.

"Mom!"

Eyes bugged and covered in blood, Jason fainted.

"What is wrong with you?" I screamed. "How could you?"

"You had your chance to give them a quick, less painful end." Voice calm, he turned his palm on Jason. "I have no mercy for traitors even if they are figments of a dream."

"No, please!" Yannis strained against his bindings, fighting to throw himself in front of his brother. "What kind of beast are you? He's only twelve. He's twelve!"

Alexander—my love, my enemy—shrugged. "Close enough."

Jason wrenched from unconsciousness, a soundless scream on his lips.

I tackled Alex. Forcing him down, I wrangled his arms by his sides. "Whatever lesson we're supposed to learn, it's not this. This is not the man you are, Alex. No matter how much you want to hurt me!"

He bucked—breaking my hold and tossing me across the sand. "And that's the lesson you've learned? That everything is fucking about you!" Spittle dotted the ground. "I do my duty, Aella. And the one time I didn't... I got you."

I flinched at his naked hatred. He stepped toward me.

"But I see now. My test isn't them," he said, gesturing behind him. "It's you."

"What are you talking—?"

My blood caught fire. Screaming, my body contorted, dropping me face-first in the sand, as I was once face-first in the mud.

Bones melting. Jaw cracking. Skin boiling. This was no dream. The pain was more real than anything I'd ever felt. I would die here in the land of nothing that is or ever was—killed by the first man who made me believe in dreams.

A blurred shape appeared over me, his words clear through my cries.

"I finally understand, Aella. You were my nightmare.

"Uh."

The pain vanished. Gasping, I rolled—scrambling away from him fast. *He almost killed me. I can't believe he tried to do to me what he did to Ianthe.*

"How dare you!" I shrieked. "I am not your test... you mad... man..."

I trailed off, overheated blood freezing cold. Alexander swayed on his feet, staring blindly at the spot I'd been. Sticking out of his chest, was the sword's blade.

Jason—the boy who was only twelve—released the hilt. Staggering back, he tripped over his cut ropes, caught himself, and found me. "Thank you, ma'am."

I couldn't move. Couldn't breathe as he freed his brother and they both ran. Mila watched it all without a word.

"Alex..."

He dropped to his knees.

"Alex!" I ran to him, catching him as he fell. His weight pulled us both down and we collapsed on our sides, my tears falling as fast as his blood. "Alex, I'm sorry. I'm so sorry. This is my fault."

His jaw worked as I held his face. So handsome. Eyes a green never seen in art or nature. Cheekbones sharp against my fingertips. Beautiful in the memory of us lying just like this—safe in our created world of feverish kisses and fun lovemaking.

"I love you."

"This," he rasped, "is what happens when you show mercy to traitors.

"They kill you."

I sobbed. "Oh, Alex, please forgive me— Alex?"

His face changed. Features shifting, black bled across his cheeks, repelling my hands. He tossed his head, and a raven's beak smacked my chin.

"Ahh!"

The Oneiroi soared up. The blade fell from his chest without a mark.

"A trick?" I whipped around as Mila began blurring around the edges. A deep, shaking chill still clung to my bones. "Alexander was never here? You bastards."

I swore the raven man smirked. Diving, he came straight at me. I snatched up the blade and slashed—passing harmlessly through him.

The flying man bowled me over. I fell back and kept falling, sinking into the lake of starlight.

My lids grew heavy.

WETNESS TICKLED MY chin, tugging me out of sleep. My eyes cracked, gifted me a view of a long, pink tongue licking the bits of Ianthe still clinging to me.

Shouting, I shot up and shooed away the dog. It ran off with a furious yelp, scolding me for denying his meal. Sweeping the horizon, I saw why.

I was in Tartarus.

I lay on the cobblestones of a once great city. I knew from the foundations of buildings now brought to rubble, pulverized statues with only their feet remaining, and the bodies.

Dozens upon hundreds of demigods—in nice silks, golden circlets, and the look of health and posterity—littered the ground with frozen expressions of shock on their faces, and slashes down their bodies.

Overhead the sky tinged red, as if the spilled blood evaporated into the air and soaked the clouds. Fire burned unchecked, sending dark billowing wisps that hazed a sun that stopped bothering to shine.

"Hello?" I stood up, gazing around for someone—anyone. "Hello?"

Gods, what happened here?

Shaking, I staggered down the grimly lined street, covered in the blood of Ianthe and the fake Alexander. Why was I still covered in their blood?

"Is anyone out there?" I rasped, voice falling quieter. Deep down in a small, frightening place, I knew I was calling for no one except that dog.

I was alone.

"Nothing can prepare you, can it?"

I spun, coming face to face with a tall, dark-haired man in robes.

"For the boundless depths of cruelty a creature can reach."

"Who are you?" I backed away fast, almost tripping over a bare foot sticking out from a pile of rubble. "Did you— Are you responsible for this?"

He smiled almost kindly— No, kind wasn't the word.

Pitying.

"No, child. I did not do this. You did."

"What are you talking about? I didn't do this," I cried. "I just arrived."

He walked carefully around the obstructions in his path, stepping lightly with bare feet. "No, you didn't do this. Yet. But you will."

I scowled. "You're speaking nonsense and now is not the time. Help me look for survivors. I'll go this way. You go that way," I said, setting off.

"You may walk in whichever direction you wish, Aella Vanda." I stopped dead in my tracks. "You will find nothing but monsters and animals to the east, west, north, and south. The demigods are dead. All of them. In every corner of Olympia. Dead."

Slowly, I faced him, eyes narrowing. "Who are you?"

"I am Pello." He inclined his head. "I am the spirit of prophetic dreams. You have met me many times when you closed your eyes, child. Those strange, familiar nights where you dreamt something that later came to be. You dismissed those dreams as mere coincidence, or your mind's eye manifesting a goal you were already working toward.

"But this is no coincidence, for you know the being who is fighting to bring this very future about. Here in my domain, I can be much more direct, and tell you she does not lie. The Fates spun this weave long ago. The goddess of despair will succeed in wiping the demigod race out of existence.

"Unless you stop her."

"Me? I'm supposed to stop"—I swept the destruction—"this? How?"

"You've already been told how."

"Excuse me? If that were true, I wouldn't be asking you—who I'm sure is just another raven man borrowing a human suit." My volume climbed higher. "Just tell me what awful task I'm supposed to complete here, so I can be on my way! You've already taught me that compassion is a fool's errand that gets those you love killed.

"After shoving a lesson so terrible and twisted into my heart, I'm sure now you'll want to bring it home by showing me what'll happen if I refuse to sacrifice the lives of my friends and my love to stop her. Because that's what every good soldier must know! Damn your friends, family, loves, hopes, and dreams. Nothing comes before Olympia."

Pello weathered my fury without a change in expression. "That is not the lesson to be learned here, Aella."

"Oh no? Then, if you can be direct, be direct. What is it I've already been told? How do I stop her?"

"The goddess has waited thousands of years for her revenge. Why? She had her devotee commit a terrible atrocity and steal a babe—you—from her crib. Why? If she could've brought this fate about sooner, she wouldn't have waited," he said. "The fact is she did... because she needed you."

I frowned. "She needed a mundane. I know this."

"She needed you," he repeated, drawing closer. "She has gambled all of her hopes on you—her last chance. If she loses this vessel now, it is over. This future will never come to be.

"Aella, the answer is simple. To save your people..." He swept his arm out and everything around me changed. The buildings reformed, red leaked from the sky, and the sun shone on a bustling street. Merchants called to each other as children played, flitting across the cobblestones as happy as people who never knew pain or destruction.

"...you must die."

I beheld my Olympia, expressionless. "You're right. I did know that answer. If you know me, then you know I've tried. Every time I was stopped by fate or by her."

"Those beings do not have power in this realm." Pello waved and the scenery changed again. I gazed down at the tickling grass, marveling over the spreading, lush green. The meadow was too beautiful to be anywhere other than the Isles of Paradise. "You can end your journey here, Aella Vanda."

I turned as a marble pedestal rose from the ground, bearing a single curved, silver-hilt dagger.

"But..." he continued, snapping my head up. "If you choose to live. You'll return to your realm and aid in carrying out the end of Olympia. Afterward, the goddess of despair will reward you."

"Reward me?"

Nodding, he stepped to the side, revealing a small beautiful house... made of windows.

My breaths slowed, then stopped as two small children ran out—giggling and attacking each other with tickles. An older woman who could only be me watched from the doorway, smiling and content as she rubbed her heavily pregnant belly. As I watched, a handsome dark-haired man hugged her—me—from behind, making her laugh at something he whispered in her ear.

"She will gift you your dream after you've helped her achieve hers. You will not make a life with Alexander Damien. You cannot, for she won't allow him, your friends, or the demigods to live. But you will meet a kind, loving mundane man who holds you while you sleep under the stars.

"You will be very happy. So happy, one day you stop crying yourself to sleep every night."

I was crying then—whole body trembling as I gazed upon everything I wished, and everything I thought I'd never have.

"The choice is yours," he said as the family faded. "If you die in the land of dreams, you die in every realm. The Oneiroi will return your body to your people, and they'll never know they buried their greatest hero.

"Or you can choose to go on knowing every plan you form against her will fail, until she ultimately brings about Olympia's greatest destruction, and your fondest dream."

My children's giggles vanished off the air.

"What will it be?"

I stared at the dagger for a long, silent spell. "This is a test."

"The hardest one you'll ever face."

"No, it's more than that. You're asking me to *cull* myself," I said. "The point of this place is to break the weak within their own fears. I've struggled with the hope of life and the sad victory of death for months, and now you're here saying just the right words with just the right visions to achieve *your* fondest dream: to see I don't leave this realm alive."

"I am who I claim to be," he said. "Everything I've shown you will come to pass, depending on the decision you make here. Now."

Tossing my head, I backed away. "You're supposed to twist and torment us. Showing me that vision of my children and that home? It was cruelty, not kindness. I can have everything I dreamed of as long as I'm willing to let Alexander, my friends, and Olympia die.

"You want me to see myself as nothing but another monster for daring to choose anything other than my duty to save my home. Why kill me when your manipulations will put the dagger in my hand of my own free will?"

He was patient through my speech. "Let us say all of that is true, Aella Vanda. I am nothing more than an Oneiroi disguised as Pello, using visions and dreams to bring about your end. Your death is another victory under my wing, and a conquer for the land of dreams. Even if all that is true... does it matter?"

I rocked back like he struck me.

"Would your dying here not stop the goddess's plans and achieve the grim end you've sought many times at your lowest moments? My lies or truths are not important. The fact will always remain that the goddess of despair is your realm's greatest threat. Which means you have the potential to be its greatest hero." He closed his fist and the pedestal winked out, reappearing in front of me. "The choice is yours."

He's right. Whether he wants it or not. Whether he schemes or not. My death would end the goddess's threat to Olympia, and mine to Alexander.

My hand closed over the hilt.

I never really had a choice.

"Congratulations," I said, positioning the blade over my heart. "You win."

A grin stretched across his face as I plunged, burying the knife in my chest.

"It is Olympia that would've won," he said as I fell, tumbling into the darkness.

"You truly were their greatest champion."

I BOLTED UPRIGHT, SLAPPING my chest.

Nothing.

Not a scratch or trace of blood.

"What happened? Was it another trick?"

No answer came to me. Standing up, I took in my new surroundings. I knew instantly that I was in a temple.

Grand columns held up a green and gold arched ceiling. They carried throughout a large chamber where, at the end, the statue of a huge and lovely woman surveyed her domain.

Soundlessly I padded through the columns, drawing closer to the depictions on the temple wall. There was a woman. The same woman? I couldn't be certain. There was more life in these drawings than upon a stone face.

It showed a woman—pale, lovely, and born before time. She rose from the primordial pits and...

I continued on, following the birth of the world, the Olympian gods, and the human race. The woman stood apart from it somehow. Like a shadow in a painting—there but not there.

"Beautiful, wasn't she?"

I jumped, twisting around as a woman stepped out from behind the statue. She bore a bucket and rag in her left hand, explaining why the temple was spotless. Closing the distance, I read curiosity in her acorn eyes and kindness in her smile. Wisps of brown hair escaped from her veil.

Oneiroi, I thought, tensing. *Be on your guard.*

"Who was she?" I stepped back when she got too close. The woman got the hint and came no farther.

"I'm not surprised you don't know. Many have forgotten her story." Her gaze roamed the temple. "That's why it's only me, day after day."

"I would like to hear her story," I said, because what else should I say?

"Tell me, do you know of Pandora? The first woman on earth."

I nodded. "She was created to punish man for accepting the gift of fire. Zeus gave her a box and told her never to open it, knowing one day curiosity would overwhelm her. Finally, it did and she opened the box. Out flew greed, hatred, poverty, death, war, and all the ills that plague the human race. Quickly she slammed it closed, leaving only hope behind. It's why through all our pain and struggles, humans can still hold on to hope."

She smiled. "Very good. That is the tale of Pandora... and it is a complete lie."

"What?"

"Lies," she said, motioning high. "Pandora was no lowly human who fell prey to Zeus's trickery. She was a goddess."

"Pandora was a goddess?" I beheld the statue in new light. "How could I not know this?"

"You weren't meant to know. These walls will tell you why." I didn't stop her taking my hand, leading me to the painting of the maiden rising from the primordial pool. "Pandora was one of the first beings to spring from the weaving fabric of the universe. She stood aside as the Titans claimed rule of the world, and when they ultimately fell to the Olympian gods."

We passed the scene, taking in the fall of the Titans, and the rise of Zeus.

"The Olympians had no quarrel with Pandora until the birth of man. You see, the humans' faith and worship made her stronger as it did the Olympians. She became a mother," the woman breathed, tracing a description of Pandora holding a babe. "She birthed many children. Geras, Apate, Moras, Momos, Eris, Nemesis, Oizys, and Keres."

My brows rose with every name. "But— But they— They're the spirits of old age, deceit, doom, blame, strife, revenge, suffering, and carnage."

"They are."

"So, Pandora didn't release these spirits from a box of trickery. She birthed them. They were her children."

"And they were despised by the Olympian gods," she said, moving on. "Her children caused untold harm to their pet humans, but not even they came close to the suffering she brought on them."

"No wonder she wasn't a favorite among the gods."

"Oh?" She faced me, head cocked. "Were the gods any kinder? Was Hera the sweet, benevolent queen—cursing and killing Zeus's mistresses? Was Athena the wise and noble beauty when she punished Medusa for being raped by Poseidon? Was Poseidon the rapist an honorable god?

"Make no mistake, young one. The gods were never a friend to man."

"That's true," I heard myself say. I couldn't say anything else. Demigods only existed because humans couldn't stand the cruelty of the gods for a moment longer.

"When man forced the gods from Mount Olympus," she said, following my thought. "Scattering was their last and final hope. There was only one issue: Pandora."

"Why her?"

"Pandora refused to join them. She existed before the earth and man. She would exist long after them. But for the scatter to work, and for the gods to one day be returned to Mount Olympus, they needed humans to believe in them again. They had to create demigods who'd spread far and wide, repopulating the earth with humans who could not deny their existence, because they were living within them."

"But what did that have to do with Pandora?"

"Demigods couldn't spread far and wide with her and her children preying on them. They didn't trust Pandora to behave while the temple was empty—so to speak. With no one in her way, she'd be free to claim the throne of Mount Olympus and create a world where she and her children ruled unchecked."

We moved on, stopping before a drawing of the Olympians huddled together—plotting.

"There was no war, no battle, no warning. One day, the Olympian gods and every one of their allies attacked her. With the combined strength of their powers, they stripped her of form and bound her within a cage for all eternity."

"Pandora's box," I whispered, coming face to face with the box of legend. "It wasn't hope or evil spirits inside. It was her."

"Oh, yes. That silly story about earth's first woman and false wedding gifts was Zeus's ploy to further humiliate her. The world forgot who she truly is—a goddess. An all-powerful being. Instead, they tell their children about some stupid girl who couldn't heed one rule."

"That's awful."

"It is indeed," she said, patting my hand. "You understand her fury. You see why she bided her time for thousands of years, waiting for the day she'd burst forth from her prison and destroy all the Olympian gods ruined her to protect."

The corner of my lips tugged down. Pulling free, I backed away from her.

"And for years she did wait," the woman cried, holding her hand up to the statue. "With her box safe and protected in the land of dreams, she bled into the sleeping minds of demigods—finding and influencing faithful worshipers who'd hunt till the ends of the earth to find her the perfect vessel."

The hairs rose on the back of my neck. *No. It can't be...*

"One that would survive the process of removing her from the chest and binding her to a human soul. Without legs, without arms, without form—she couldn't carry out her plan." She snapped to me, shooting my heart into my throat. "But now she has you."

"Pandora." The name scraped from my throat. "It's been her the whole time. She did this to me? She's the goddess?!"

"She is so much more than the goddess," she cried, eyes lighting in fervor. "She is the mother of misery. The devourer of hope. The queen of suffering.

"I am Pandora," she shrieked, morphing before my eyes—becoming the shining, burning, terrible, wonderful shifting plague of my madness. "Goddess of despair."

I fell to my knees screaming, crying, clawing my eyes for daring to look upon her. I was worthless before her divinity. A speck before a giant. Mud on the slippers of an empress. Let me die for being in her presence. Let me burn!

"Calm, child." Pandora tipped my chin—once again the sweet, beautiful washerwoman. "You needn't be afraid of me. My gratitude to you knows no bounds. Because of you, I will wash away all the Olympian gods hold dear." She pressed her lips to my forehead. "You will serve your goddess well."

"No!" I swiped, narrowly striking her across the face as she smoothly moved out of reach. "Knowing your name and story makes no difference. I will do whatever it takes to stop you, Pandora. You'll never get out of that box."

Her grin stretched wide. "But I already have, child. When my dear Maia performed the ritual that night, she transferred my body into you." She laughed. "It was never some pet or monster. Whenever despair filled you, I was set free to take over your body." Pandora flapped a hand over herself. "This is simply the form silly, lusty men prefer. I've always thought my finest shape was dipped in scales and crowned by wings."

"You're... inside me?" I promptly heaved, retching on the floor.

"Only part of me," she continued. "You stopped the ritual before she could transfer my consciousness, but enough of my essence is within you that I can find you through realms and speak in your ear.

"Soon, the ritual will be completed and I will control you—mind, body, and soul. Then, my work can begin."

"Never," I hissed, pushing up to my feet. "Now that I know, I'll never let this happen. Sebastian can bind me in all the spells he wants. When I'm free of this hellscape, he'll take me farther than you'll ever reach. You've failed, Pandora."

A smile still hung on her lips. "Oh, my pet, you truly do not understand what is happening here. You're already too late. The Oneiroi found a new master in the absence of their father. They brought you and my faithful followers to me, at this, the prophesied hour."

I snapped around, searching the shadows for black-cloaked women. "Bring them the fuck on! I'll stop them like I did the first time."

"Oh, pet," she cooed, almost pityingly. "You just don't understand. You've been dreaming for a very long time."

"No..." Awful realization sunk to the pit of my soul. "What did you do?"

"What did *we* do, pet." She winked. "Nothing yet."

Moving fast, Pandora shoved me—flinging me into another bottomless abyss.

"—TO THE GODDESS, WE offer this mind. Dull and undeserving, let the mind be gifted enlightenment in the service of you."

I jerked awake, screaming—scattering the cloaked figures standing above me.

I was in the temple again. Dirty, cracked, and crumbling in my reality, it was made new within the realm of dreams. Marble floors gleamed. Stone walls were free of graffiti. Candles burned in polished copper holders, casting flickering light on the stone table, and the woman lashed upon it. At my feet was an ancient, blood-soaked box.

"Let me go!" I screamed. "Let go of me!"

"It's much too late for that, my Aella," said a voice I thought I'd never hear again.

Maia lowered her cloak. "The ritual is almost complete. Our goddess returns to us."

"Mama?" Warmth leaked through my body, giving way to the altar's biting cold. "It can't be... You're another raven man."

"I'm afraid not, dear one. The Oneiroi brought me from the waking realm as they brought you. I didn't die that night you escaped from me," she said, gesturing beside me. "Thanks to the quick action of the Sister of the Sky."

"Thank you, sister." The Sister of the Sky shed her cloak, revealing the smirking face of Madame Remis. "It is my pleasure to serve for the glory of the goddess. As I did so long ago when we first met, sweet Aella."

Roaring smothered my ears. Her speech came from far away.

"I was a bit hurt that you didn't remember me when you arrived at the academy," Remis said, "but then again, you were just a baby when I took you from your mother's arms and slit her throat."

My jaw went slack. "You... You... You monster!" I leaped at her, wrenching my arms viciously in the chains. Yes, chains. No leather bindings this time. "I'll kill you! I'll kill you, you evil, twisted bitch!"

Remis laughed. "One day, yes. But not today.

"Let us continue, sisters," she said over my noise. "Our goddess has waited long enough."

The three women retook their place. At their feet, the fourth sister lay dead. Her spectacles and curly hair burned in my mind as it did when she handed me the hyacinth wrapped in wax paper.

"Don't do this," I cried. "Pandora is insane! She wants to destroy Olympia and rub demigods off the face of the earth. Everyone will die!"

"Yes," Maia crooned, joy etched on her face. "In her glory. Our lives are nothing."

Dark, sludgy smoke leaked over the rim—moving fast up my body.

"We offer this mind," Maia shouted. "Our goddess. Queen of the broken and damned, you are Pandora. Rise and take your rightful place!"

Maia brought down the dagger, piercing my skull.

My scream echoed through the far corners of the realm.

Pandora

I flew high, near purring at the feel of the sun on my wings.

Oh, yes, this body was perfect. My essence bound to it effortlessly. There was nothing I couldn't do.

There was no one who could stop me.

I burst through the paltry barrier surrounding the academy, swooping down atop the highest tower. There were so many places to begin my slaughter of the Olympian parasites. Trono City where the humans who thought themselves gods ruled in another room with twelve thrones. Crassus where the children of Hephaestus built their finest weapons for the army. The Isles of Paradise where the fewest monsters lived, and the people fooled themselves into believing this made them safer.

But no. In the end, I was always meant to start here. Deucalion Academy. The dominion's hope for the future. I will slaughter their best and their brightest—the young men and women who lifted their parents' chins in pride.

With one strike, despair will spread across the land.

I lit on the group heading to the stadium. "Ah, there you are. My pet's little friends."

The cow girl and the wolf half-breed laughed about something, so content in the ignorance of not knowing this was their last day.

"Let's start with you."

I dove off the tower—claws extended and aching for blood. Their screams reached me before I them. I laughed—delighting as I seized the cow and wolf, and ripped them off their feet.

"Bow before me," I boomed. The weakling hosts pelted me with powers that didn't so much as scratch my scales. "I am your goddess. Your ruler. Your better.

"I am Pandora."

Keep In Touch

Join Ruby's mailing list for news, teasers, and more:
https://www.subscribepage.com/rubyvincentpage
Join Ruby's Facebook Reader Group:
https://bit.ly/3bNuCOq

ABOUT THE AUTHOR

Ruby Vincent is a lover of all things romance from contemporary to fantasy to paranormal. She loves saucy heroines, bold alpha males, and weaving a tale where both get their happily ever after.